HARLEQUIN OFFICE ROMANCE COLLECTION

Who says you can't mix business with pleasure?
Definitely not these couples...

Office politics can be messy as it is, but mix in
a handsome boss or irresistible coworker and
work life becomes plain messy. And the stakes
have never been higher for these couples.
Not only are their careers on the line,
but so are their hearts.

These men and women may have started out
with opposing agendas, intending to keep
things professional, but once the spark is lit,
they know that life on the job is going to be
anything but business as usual.

Professional rivalry never felt so good...
or so complicated!

Abby Gaines writes funny, tender romances for Harlequin Superromance and Love Inspired Historical—she's currently at work on her eighteenth novel for Harlequin. Always keen to learn new skills, she's also experimenting with a young adult novel and a women's fiction novel, and learning Chinese. Abby loves reading, skiing, traveling and cooking for friends, as well as spending time with her husband and children.

CONTENTS

THAT NEW YORK MINUTE
Abby Gaines
7

BURNING AMBITION
Amy Knupp
321

THAT NEW YORK MINUTE

Abby Gaines

To the memory of
Sandra Diane Hyde
(1965–2011)

As Sandra Hyatt, a wonderful writer of romance.
As a wife and mother, the heart of her family.
As a friend…irreplaceable.

CHAPTER ONE

HE'S BREAKING UP WITH ME.

Rachel Frye took a swig of champagne. No longer the appropriate drink for the occasion, but she needed something to do with her hands. Something other than clasping them together on the table while she begged Piers not to end it.

Given they were sitting in one of Manhattan's coolest bars, a little dignity was called for.

"Don't get me wrong, you're really attractive and smart. I enjoy spending time with you." Piers leaned forward with the earnestness that Rachel found ninety-nine percent charming and one percent temptation to tell an off-color joke. "But, you know... Oyster?" He pushed the silver plate they were sharing across the highly varnished table for two.

"Thanks," Rachel muttered, as her mind scrambled for compelling arguments as to why they shouldn't break up just yet. She picked up one of the mollusks remaining from the dozen they'd ordered. She'd suggested Crush, a new champagne and oyster bar, for this date because she'd been considering sleeping with Piers tonight.

Also because it was around the corner from her Madison Avenue office, but still. When a woman suggests to her boyfriend of three months that they start their evening at a place serving well-known aphrodisiacs, the last thing she expects is to get dumped.

She'd unbuttoned two buttons of her blouse, for goodness' sake!

"It's just, I get the feeling we're not on the same page," Piers said.

Rachel realized too late that slurping an oyster from its shell wasn't dignified. She swallowed hastily, the salty mass gliding past the lump in her throat.

Was this about sex? Piers had wanted to sleep with her on the first date, something Rachel would never contemplate. Nor the second. Nor the third. Was it unreasonable to want to believe they might have a future together before she jumped into bed?

"Actually, I think we have a lot in common," she said, as she set the empty shell back on its bed of crushed ice. They were both hardworking, capable people. And Piers had the kind of family she'd *like* to have come from: his father was the second-generation owner of an upstate accounting firm, and his mother ruled the local bridge club with an iron, yet friendly, grip.

"You glanced at your watch when I walked in tonight," he said. It sounded like an accusation.

"I…was checking the time," she said uncertainly. She dabbed at a drop of oyster juice on her chin with her napkin.

"Rachel, I was two minutes late. It's not a crime."

"I never said it was. I never even thought it. *That's*

why you're dumping me? Because I looked at my watch?" Ugh, she needed to rein in that shrillness.

She turned away from Piers's concerned gaze to take a deep breath.

And encountered another gaze, this one altogether unsympathetic.

Garrett Calder, her fellow creative director at Key Bowen Crane, New York's largest independent advertising agency, was watching her from his black leather bar stool.

Rachel had noticed him at the bar when she walked in, noticed the bottle of Dom Pérignon champagne—which would set him back at least two hundred bucks in a place like this—in front of him. She'd assumed he was waiting for someone, but he was still alone and she realized there was only one glass on the bar.

She knew the guy was a loner—small wonder, with that scowl on his face—but drinking a bottle of champagne by himself?

"—and it feels like you're *clinging*," Piers said, finishing a sentence she'd failed to hear.

She jerked back to face him. "I don't cling!" She was loyal and committed, sure. But those were good things. "I admit, punctuality is important to me, but I never meant to make you feel, uh, pressured."

What was wrong with him, that a glance at her watch could terrify him into thinking she wanted a pledge of undying love?

Which she didn't. Not yet. She just wanted to be certain the relationship would last more than five minutes.

"We shouldn't rush to break up at the first obstacle," she said, "when there's every chance we can get past it."

Piers was an actuary, a man who calculated risk to the nth degree, and she liked the way his analytical approach spilled over into his personality. There was a lot she liked about him, frankly. His low-key sense of humor, his easy conversation. She was attracted to him physically, and they'd done some serious making out to prove it.

Though now, when she eyed his receding hairline, she saw it for what it was. Imminent baldness, not a sign of dependability.

Nothing wrong with bald. Hair was unarguably a nice-to-have, but it was nowhere near the top of the list.

"When I'm late," Piers said, "I get the feeling that you worry I'm not going to show up. When we're together, I feel like you're always watching me, to make sure I'm still interested. That's a lot of pressure, Rachel."

She forced a laugh. "Piers, I'm a businesswoman with a high-level job and an excellent salary." She felt as if she was interviewing for the role of Steady, Nonclinging Girlfriend. "I hardly think I'm that insecure."

She didn't assume a guy was a no-show after five minutes. It was more that she started to wonder just how reliable he was. She knew it was illogical, so she tried not to let Piers's occasional tardiness color her opinion of him.

She reached across the table for his hand. A nice hand. Neatly squared fingernails. Pale, but that was okay. "I don't think we should be too quick to end a good thing. How about," she continued, lowering her voice to what she hoped was husky, "we go back to my place and...work this out."

Wariness flickered in his eyes. Then his gaze dropped to those two buttons she'd undone—*about time*—and the hint of black bra she knew he'd see there.

Rachel wriggled her shoulders just a little.

He let out a sigh. "You *are* a very special woman, Rachel," he admitted.

That was more like it! He'd simply had cold feet. Rachel pushed her chair back. It scraped loudly on the wooden floorboards. "Let's go," she said.

Piers stood. "Just so you know, I have an early start tomorrow. I won't be able to stay the night."

She paused as she reached for the jacket she'd slung over the back of her chair. "That's okay, I have a meeting first thing, too." The most important meeting of her life, in fact. But was now the time to be discussing work? "We can do dinner tomorrow, instead of breakfast."

If her meeting went the way she anticipated, they'd be celebrating her inevitable promotion come dinnertime. She grinned at the thought, and her worries about her love life eased.

Piers helped her into her jacket, then pulled some bills from his wallet. When he frowned, Rachel knew he was calculating the seventeen-and-a-half percent tip he liked to leave.

Shouldn't he be tossing money onto the table willynilly, in his haste to get out of here and into her bed?

Rachel turned away. And once again met Garrett

Calder's gaze. His scowl had gone. He raised his glass to her in a toast that was intended to be ironic, if the tiny, mocking curve to his lips was anything to go by.

What was that about? She didn't know Garrett well—no one did—but he always managed to unsettle her, even when she was at her most together. Not because of the stupid nickname they gave him in the office: The Shark. That little piece of hyperbole didn't bother her at all. What disturbed her was the blend of intelligence and aloofness in his eyes, the suggestion that he knew everything and he didn't give a damn.

Now he looked as if he knew exactly what had just transpired between her and Piers. Knew they were headed to her bed.

She willed the sudden heat in her cheeks to subside. There was no way Garrett could have overheard their conversation. None.

At last, Piers wedged some neatly folded bills beneath the pepper grinder, and they could leave. The bar's layout and teeming Thursday night crowd meant they had to walk past Garrett. As she drew level with him, she gave him a polite nod.

"Let it go, Rachel," he said.

She stopped, unsure if she'd heard him correctly over the hubbub of reveling office workers. "Excuse me?"

Piers bumped into her, jolting her toward Garrett. Who leaned back against the bar, as if he didn't want her in his space.

"Begging never works," he said, his enunciation careful and unfortunately crystal clear to both her and, she was certain, Piers.

Her heart lurched in her chest. Mortification...
and fear.

"I don't know what you're talking about," she said.
"You're drunk."

An exaggeration, maybe, but he sure wasn't sober.
The bottle next to him was empty.

"Who is this guy?" Piers asked.

"No one. A colleague." She tugged the lapels of her
jacket together, because Garrett's eyes were definitely
straying in that direction. Maybe, when she got her promotion, she could fire him.

The delightful fantasy didn't last more than a moment. Garrett was too good at his job. Which was how
he got away with acting like a jerk.

The bartender removed Garrett's empty Dom Pérignon bottle and began peeling the foil from around the
cork of a second bottle.

"Oh, look, Garrett, your date's arrived," Rachel said.
"Let's go, honey."

Piers looked startled at the endearment, but he took
her elbow.

"Just so you know," Garrett said, "offering a guy sex
so he won't break up with you smacks of desperation."

The bartender paused in his loosening of the wire
cage around the champagne cork and looked Rachel
up and down. Was it her imagination, or did he register the black bra and give her a knowing look? Piers
let go of her.

"Whatever's driving you to drink alone, Garrett—"
her voice shook "—keep it to yourself." That was the

way he usually operated. Could he have picked a worse time to attempt something resembling a conversation?

"Sleep with him, by all means," Garrett said, with a generous, alcohol-fueled sweep of his arm toward Piers. "Though, personally, I think you could get a guy with more hair."

Piers's hand went protectively to his head.

"But whatever you do, do it on *your* terms," Garrett said. "Not his."

"Uh, Rachel, I'm going to take a rain check," Piers said. "My early meeting…" He kissed her cheek—were his lips always that dry?—and was gone.

"Wait!" she called.

Too late.

The champagne cork popped; the barman poured the first gush of frothing liquid into Garrett's glass.

Garrett picked up the glass and raised it, once again, to Rachel. "You'll thank me in the morning."

CHAPTER TWO

GRATITUDE WAS *NOT* RACHEL'S primary sentiment as she waited for the elevator in the Key Bowen Crane building lobby at seven o'clock the next morning.

Exhaustion and frustration, on the other hand, were flourishing.

She'd lost a perfectly good boyfriend—okay, maybe not perfect, but who was?—thanks to Garrett. After the way Piers had almost sprinted out of the bar, she didn't believe for a moment that he was only "taking a rain check." When she'd phoned him later, he hadn't picked up.

She and Piers could have made it work, dammit, if not for Garrett's stupid accusation that she was using sex to stop Piers from dumping her.

Kind of hard to get past that. Unfortunately, it had taken Rachel a few hours of tossing and turning to conclude the relationship was beyond salvage.

As she yawned, a ding signaled the arrival of an elevator. It would take at least another twenty seconds before the doors opened. This building was one of the earliest Manhattan skyscrapers and it still had the original elevator cars. Gorgeous…so long as you weren't in a hurry.

The elevator doors wheezed open, and Rachel stepped into the wood-paneled interior. She pressed for the fifty-sixth floor, hit the door-close button and stepped back to enjoy the rare experience of having the space to herself.

Only to have a laptop bag wedged unceremoniously between the almost-closed doors, forcing them to rumble open again.

To her horror, Garrett Calder followed the bag into the elevator.

"You!" she blurted.

A grunt and a jerk of Garrett's chin acknowledged her as he set his laptop on the floor. He jabbed the button to close the doors.

Charming. Rachel resigned herself to a long ascent. Not that she wanted social chitchat with Garrett, not after last night. She stared straight ahead, focusing vaguely on the safety certificate which, from numerous rides spent avoiding eye contact with other New Yorkers, she knew expired in November.

Garrett leaned against the wall to her left, facing Rachel. *No idea of elevator etiquette.* Mind you, most of her female colleagues would be delighted to have such an excellent view of him. No question he was good-looking, if you liked your men tall, dark and brooding. And with a thick head of hair, damn him.

She'd noticed before that he took up more than his fair share of space. How did he do that? He was tall, but there was no excess bulk to him. Nor could Rachel attribute it to his larger-than-life personality—last night was the chattiest she'd ever seen him. Unfortunately.

The recollection had her shifting in her high heels. She realized he hadn't selected a floor destination, and stretched a hand toward the panel. "Fifty-four?" That was the floor they both worked on.

He winced and pressed his fingers to his right temple. "Could you please stop shouting?"

His deep voice held a faint croak, suggesting he might actually have finished that second bottle of bubbly. There was no sign of mockery in his dark eyes. In which case…maybe he'd forgotten their conversation. Maybe it was lost in the depths of his hopefully agonizing hangover. She was torn between relief at the thought, and annoyance that he could destroy her relationship without remembering a thing about it.

"Which floor?" she asked, louder.

His eyes, dark as coal, narrowed. "Same as you."

Rachel's hand dropped. "You're going to fifty-six?" To the partners' floor?

Garrett ignored her.

She registered that he was wearing a tie—charcoal gray, an elegant contrast with his dark shirt and perfectly cut black suit. Something shifted, as if the elevator had jolted in its slow, straight course.

No way. She knew exactly how this morning was supposed to pan out. She would attend the partners' breakfast along with the other candidate, schmoozing her heart out with the Key Bowen Crane partners. At the end of breakfast, she would be named partner designate, poised to cement her place in Madison Avenue's largest independent ad agency. The other candidate would also be named partner designate, though only one of them could ultimately win the partnership, along with the coveted role of chief creative officer.

Rachel knew it would be her. Just yesterday morning, Jonathan Key, chairman of KBC, had said with a no-need-to-worry wink that he was sure she could guess who her competition was.

It wasn't—*couldn't be*—Garrett Calder. He'd been at KBC for mere months, and was renowned for moving on the minute he got bored. Not partner material.

Surely there weren't *two* other candidates? The walls of the elevator seemed to close in. Rachel sucked in a sharp breath—*better*—and checked the illuminated number above the door. Tenth floor. *Hurry up.*

"So, Garrett, when were you invited to the breakfast?" she asked, trying to sound relaxed.

A glint in his eyes suggested she'd fallen somewhere short of the mark. Landed somewhere right around tense. "A couple of weeks ago. I told Tony I wasn't interested, but last night I decided I might as well come along."

Mention of last night made her pause. But this was too important not to pursue.

"What, uh, changed your mind?"

"You did." That glint turned diabolical. Telling her that, hangover or no, he remembered every word.

"I suspect that second bottle of champagne dulled your memory," Rachel said briskly, trying not to blush. "I did *not* encourage you to attend this meeting."

"'Do it on your own terms,'" he quoted.

She racked her memory for when she would have said something so self-absorbed. "*You* said that."

"Did I? Damn, I'm good."

Rachel gritted her teeth. "The whole idea of partnership is working with others—it's not about your own terms."

He didn't reply, but one dark eyebrow rose lazily.

Garrett *was* lazy. He arrived around nine most mornings, when other people had been there since seven-thirty. Outrageous that he should think he could turn up to the partners' breakfast on a drunken whim, and snap up the job she'd been working toward for so long.

"Has your boyfriend cashed in that rain check yet?" he asked.

She clamped her lips together. Then, unable to resist, muttered, "What made you think we were talking about...what you said?" Not that she was about to tell him he was right.

"Been there, done that," Garrett said. "By which I mean, I've been the offer*ee* before. I've never begged someone to stay, but I recognize the body language." He shook his head, all phony sympathy. "Like I told you, begging doesn't work."

Rachel's eyes smarted. She blinked hard, twice. "Here's some advice right back at you. What happens in the bar stays in the bar." Switching gears, she said crisply, "So, Garrett, you've been at KBC, what, six months?" But she was well aware it was longer than that that she'd been subjected to his suspiciously bland expression whenever others acclaimed her work.

"Eleven," he said wearily, as if he was already bored with the topic. Or maybe a three-syllable word was too much effort this morning.

"That's got to be a record for you. Come on, Garrett, you don't want to be a partner." He was renowned for his refusal to settle in one firm.

Her insistence had a shrill edge, and he winced. "If I agree I don't want to be a partner, will you shut up?"

As if he would be so agreeable. He hadn't earned his nickname—The Shark—by backing down from a fight. No, that moniker was born of his reputed killer instinct for winning pitches. It had become one of those self-fulfilling prophecies—Rachel suspected he had an advantage over rivals intimidated by being up against The Shark.

Not today. She wasn't about to be intimidated.

He probably made the name up himself. Which was good marketing, she'd admit. Perhaps she should start calling herself…The Terrier.

Didn't have quite the same ring to it.

A glance at the numbers above the elevator door revealed they were at the twenty-fourth floor.

"I guess Tony had his reasons for inviting you to attend this morning," she said, "but, Garrett, you won't win. Why put yourself through that?" Perhaps she could convince him to get out on fifty-four.

He didn't say anything. Tension flattened his lips and he obviously had a pounding headache. Drawing his dark eyebrows together in that thunderous way wouldn't help the pain. He must realize, in his heart, that she was right. He was an outsider, and everyone knew that outsiders seldom won. Rachel's shoulders relaxed. She could almost feel sorry for him.

Maybe that's why he was drinking alone last night. Out of a sense of inadequacy.

She ignored the fact that the word didn't gel with anything about him.

"It's not about you," she assured him. "I've been at KBC eight years. Around here that counts for something."

His expression lightened, as if he'd heard her entirely reasonable explanation and discounted it. Rachel shifted uneasily as he scanned her, top to toe, lightning fast.

"You must have joined when you were twelve." His tone was chatty.

Garrett Calder didn't make idle conversation.

"I was eighteen," she said warily. "I started in the mail room."

"She Worked Her Way to the Top," he intoned.

"You bet I did." Her response was clipped—he didn't get to mock her achievement.

"So, it's your eight years versus my eight gold CLIO awards," he mused, sounding a whole lot more cheerful. "Think they might *count for something?*"

Eight gold CLIOs! It was practically obscene, how successful he'd been in the advertising industry's equivalent of the Oscars. *But those awards came while he was working at five different companies. And he's made more enemies than friends.* Making partner was about loyalty and long term. *Rachel* was about loyalty and long term.

She dismissed his awards with a *pff.* "Style over substance."

The Shark bared his teeth. It might have been a smile.

Then again, he might have been anticipating dragging her beneath the surface and chomping on her drowned body.

Rachel folded her arms across her chest, realized she looked defensive and dropped her hands to her sides. *Surely we must be nearly*—nope, only the thirty-sixth floor.

"I have an excellent track record, and that's how I'll get the partnership," she assured him.

"Right," he said encouragingly.

He clearly meant *Wrong*.

"Do you know something?" she demanded.

He closed his eyes. "You're shouting again. And I'm having a bad week. Bad enough that I might take off this stupid tie and gag you with it."

He was a jerk. Jerks didn't make partner at KBC. It was different at some other agencies, but not here.

He's a jerk with eight gold CLIOs.

She shouldn't bother explaining, but the urge to convince him he was wasting his time was overwhelming. "It's not just the eight years. I've put in more hours than anyone, I've won more pitches…"

"You've won a bunch of clients too scared to do anything interesting," he said. "Your work is tame."

Rachel clenched her jaw to hold back her outrage. Tame! She prided herself on her ability to take clients beyond their expectations.

"Do you want to know what your weakness is?" Garrett asked.

"No."

"It's those eight years," he said. "You're relying on

past experience, but everything can change in a heart-beat around here." He folded his arms, and on him it didn't look defensive. "In a New York minute, you could say."

She'd never liked the song "New York Minute," with its suggestion that everything—business, family, life—could be turned on its head any moment.

"Your weakness is that you don't think on your feet," Garrett said. "Reacting to those moments of insight, freeing yourself from reliance on what others have told you, is what drives creative power."

As if she would trust the impulse of a moment over a carefully crafted solution. Her hands fisted at her sides. "You don't get to waltz in here with your Dom Pérignon hangover and your eight CLIOs and your custom-made suits and your fancy cologne—"

"I don't wear cologne." He spread his hands, palm out, as if declaring himself innocent of some heinous crime.

Wow, The Shark sure knew how to zero in on the main issue.

"Uh-huh. So you just happened to sleep on a bed of—" she sniffed "—pine needles and citrus peel."

Ever so slowly, one corner of his mouth kicked up.

The effect was more potent than any full-throated laugh. It was that stupid Shark thing, Rachel thought crossly. It gave him an aura of power.

"Whatever it is you're smelling, Rach, it's all me," he said. "Cologne is for sissies."

No way a man could smell this good without help. "Rach*el*," she corrected. "Strange, I don't remember that sissies line from your award-winning Calvin Klein Fragrance campaign."

"That was last year. I believed in cologne last year."

Typical of his *here today, gone tomorrow* style. "Whereas I prefer to take a long-term, truth-based approach," she said. Which did *not* mean she was tame.

Garrett gave her a pained look through half-closed eyes. "Integrity in advertising," he said. "Interesting concept. But not, I fear, a partnership-winning one."

Floor fifty-one. Nearly there, thank goodness.

"Who else do you think will be here this morning?" Garrett asked abruptly.

No thinking required. "Just Clive."

"That's what I figured."

Clive Barnes was the only other executive creative director, the same level as Rachel and Garrett. His seniority meant he had to be on the partnership shortlist. But...

"Clive's a nice guy," Rachel said.

"You know what they say about nice guys." Garrett's white teeth flashed.

Out of loyalty to Clive, who'd been at KBC almost as long as she had, she sent him a disapproving look. But she didn't consider Clive a threat, either.

The elevator dinged to indicate they'd reached their destination. Finally. She couldn't wait to get out of here and spend a few minutes alone, restoring the calm confidence she would need during breakfast. She stepped toward the doors, but they didn't open.

Garrett pressed the open button. Nothing happened.

"Come on," Rachel muttered.

Garrett was already stabbing at the intercom. It rang three times—prompting more wincing from the hungover Shark—before an operator answered.

"We'll have you out of there in a jiffy, sir," the woman chirped, once she ascertained how many people were in the elevator and that no one needed medical treatment. "Well, when I say a jiffy...hmmm...okay, we have a software glitch, but don't you folks worry about a thing!" She hung up.

Rachel groaned.

"Just go with the flow," Garrett advised her. "Live in the moment."

She turned her nerves on him. "I don't know why you bothered to come in when you're so, *ahem*—" sarcastic, fake throat-clearing "—unwell. Get real, Garrett, and get out of here. You don't have a serious shot at this partnership."

He eyed her for a long, silent moment. "You remind me of someone," he said. "Someone I don't like."

Ow. That definitely qualified as a shark-nip. One she deserved, if she was honest—she shouldn't have let him rile her.

But you should never show weakness to a shark.

"Your opinion won't matter when I get the partnership," she said. "I'll be your boss."

His hands slid into his pockets and he leaned back against the wall. Instead of being scared off by her splashing about, she had the distinct impression The Shark was beginning to circle.

"Protesting too much, methinks," he said.

He couldn't really believe he would beat her, could he?

The intercom buzzed. Rachel lunged for the answer button. Garrett reached it first; her fingers, clammy with sudden anxiety, pressed against his. She whipped her hand away.

"How're you folks doing?" the operator trilled. "Just wanted to let you know we're almost done fixing you up. We'll have you out in that beautiful New York summer day in just a—"

"Jiffy," Rachel muttered. She pressed the off button. "Thanks a lot, Doris freakin' Day."

Garrett said, "My mother used to love Doris Day movies." Something flashed across his face, maybe shock that he'd told her that much about himself.

"So your mom has bad taste," Rachel said. "She probably likes *you,* too…though if she's ever seen you hungover and surly she might think twice about—"

She stopped. His face had shut down so completely, it was as if he was no longer in the elevator.

Uh-oh. "Um, Garrett, when you said your mother *used* to love Doris Day, was that past tense because Doris Day retired, or—" she cringed "—because your mom died?"

He stared at the stuck doors as if he could see right through them. *Now* he rode the elevator like a proper New Yorker. "Both."

Damn. "I'm sorry," Rachel said. It felt inadequate, when she'd been sniping at him the last fifty-six floors. "How did she—how long ago…?"

His gaze cut to her. "Today's my birthday."

She grabbed the non sequitur gratefully. "Happy birthday! So, that champagne last night…"

"It's also the anniversary of my mother's death," he said. "So, yeah, I'm hungover and surly, as you so delicately phrased it, but I have my reasons."

His skin looked suddenly pale in the elevator lighting. Rachel opened her mouth, but couldn't think of a thing to say.

"And, yeah," he continued, "maybe Doris Day is too perky and not to your taste, but when my mom was dying of cancer, those movies were the only thing that kept her smiling through months of chemo. Doris Day was the difference between an unbearable day and an okay one."

Man, she had totally screwed up. "Garrett, I didn't know. I'm sorry." Rachel stretched out a hand, half thinking he might bite her arm off. Half *wanting* him to because she felt like such a jerk.

Before she could get within prey distance, the elevator doors hissed open.

Garrett shot her one last disgusted look, and left.

CHAPTER THREE

RACHEL PULLED THE END OFF her croissant and shredded it into tiny pieces.

She'd far from sparkled throughout breakfast, which should have been an opportunity to impress those partners she didn't work with. She'd been distracted first by Garrett's presence, then by her guilt over dissing his mother. On the anniversary of her death. Which happened to be Garrett's birthday.

She groaned inwardly.

Her one weakness in her work was that she wasn't good in unexpected situations. Give her a creative briefing and a week, and she could come up with a fabulous pitch. Ask her to spout ideas off the cuff and she was hopeless. This morning's breakfast…it wasn't a pitch, but she'd prepared for it in the same way, thinking hard about how she could outshine Clive Barnes, anticipating questions.

She hadn't imagined Garrett would wreck her relationship last night, then show up like a hungover nemesis this morning. Or that she would say something so tactless as to leave him looking utterly bleak. No wonder she had zero spur-of-the-moment techniques for outclassing him in the eyes of the other partners.

At the far end of the Key Bowen Crane boardroom table, Tony Bowen, chief executive officer, pushed himself out of his maroon leather chair. An immediate hush fell.

"I hope you all enjoyed your breakfast," he said.

Rachel murmured her appreciation for the shredded croissant on the plate in front of her. Garrett hadn't eaten, either, probably more from nausea than nerves—he'd drained a couple of cups of black coffee. Only Clive had tucked into his food with gusto.

"It's time to get down to business," Tony said. "We don't call this the partnership shortlist announcement breakfast for nothing."

Rachel laughed politely.

"So I'm delighted to announce that our three candidates are Clive Barnes, Garrett Calder and Rachel Frye."

Why did he say my name last? Please, let it be alphabetical.

A round of applause from the existing partners. Only one of them was female. Definitely time for another woman on the team.

"It's been some years since our last partnership vacancy, but the selection process hasn't changed," Tony said. "All three candidates will be required to prepare a new client pitch, with the help of their team. And I'm delighted to say that this year, we have an opportunity that's worthy of your best efforts." He paused for effect. "Brightwater Group."

Wow. One of the largest private education providers in the country was looking for a new ad agency? The account would run into tens of millions of dollars.

Rachel took quick stock of her rivals. Clive's expression was neutral—he was strongest in sports advertising, so this wasn't his forte. Farther down the table, Garrett's eyes were closed. Was he asleep, or was his shark-brain already devising some incredible campaign that would blow hers out of the water?

Not on my watch, buster. When it came to expensive fragrance or luxury cruises, Garrett might be hard to beat. But for campaigns aimed at the family market— Aunt Betty's pies were a prime example—Rachel was the go-to gal. Brightwater was exactly the kind of account where she excelled. Its facilities might be private, but it was targeted firmly at lower income families.

The confidence Garrett had managed to puncture with his stabs at her creative ability surged back. *I can do this.*

"We want all of you to have every chance to impress us."

Tony was talking about the partnership; Rachel steered her attention away from The Shark.

"That's why we're going to be up-front about the reservations we have about each of you as partner material," Tony said.

Reservations?

"Ladies first." Tony nodded at Rachel.

Oh, yeah, the not-good-at-thinking-on-my-feet thing. She tried to simultaneously sit up straight and look flexible. Garrett smirked.

"Rachel, you've been with us a long time, and your loyalty means a lot to us," Tony said.

She smiled loyally.

"But we wonder if that makes your work a little... what's the word...stale?"

Excuse me?

"No, that's not it," he said. "*Safe.* Your team's work is solid, but safe."

Was that the same as *tame,* as Garrett had called it?

"Well, Tony—" Rachel cleared her throat, her face hot "—my clients place a lot of trust in me, and I honor that trust by not taking unnecessary risks."

A faint snort from Garrett, who no doubt thought that taking risks won CLIOs.

Possibly true.

"The results of my campaigns speak for themselves," she said.

"They do," Tony agreed. "And they're saying *safe.* We'd like to see your work winning some awards out there in the marketplace."

"You've always said KBC is about more than flashy awards," she reminded him. "It's about teamwork, and the whole being greater than the sum of the parts."

Garrett snorted again, louder this time. Obviously a loner like him wouldn't share that view.

Tony chuckled. "Seems our clients are quite attached to those gold statues. Bottom line, Rachel, if you want to make partner, we'll need to see more risk-taking, more brilliance." Why didn't he just come out and say it: more *Garrett.*

Rachel forced a smile. "Then that's exactly what

you'll get, Tony." Dammit, risky brilliance was so not her thing. The partners would likely never have made such a demand, if Garrett hadn't come in and made her look *tame*.

"Moving on to you, Garrett." Tony grinned at Mr. Brilliant Risk-Taker. "From the day you arrived at KBC, you've shaken up our creative work and we're all the better for it."

Garrett nodded an acknowledgment.

"Obviously you've moved around the industry somewhat," Tony continued.

"I've had some excellent jobs," Garrett agreed. Which wasn't what Tony had said. "I appreciate the chance to make partner at KBC."

Why now? Rachel wondered. *Why here?* She knew why *she* wanted—needed—this partnership, but why couldn't Garrett keep on flitting around the industry?

"Good, good." Tony nodded his approval. "But the real issue for us is your team skills."

Garrett stilled. Rachel half expected to hear the *da dum...da dum*...theme from *Jaws*.

Tony looked slightly nervous. "A partner must be capable of motivating a team and forging strong interpersonal connections."

Based on something other than fear of losing a limb, Rachel could have added. Just last week she'd spent half an hour in the women's washroom comforting a junior account exec Garrett had chewed out.

Exactly the kind of behavior that made him unsuited to the one-and-only partnership up for grabs.

"We'd like to see more evidence of your ability to

engage with your colleagues, in particular your team," Tony said. Several other partners nodded.

"I can do that." Garrett's voice was arctic.

Ha! It was all very well to sit there broodingly handsome, *but handsome is as handsome does, buddy.* The old aphorism of her mother's made Rachel smile for the first time since he'd stepped into her elevator.

Mom was right…which meant this wasn't so bad. Garrett might be a genius, but he had never made the slightest effort to engage with others, and he was well-known for his scathing put-downs. A shark didn't change its spots—fins?—that easily.

All I have to do is let Garrett harpoon himself in the foot with his own inability to be part of the team. The partnership's still mine.

"Excellent." Tony rubbed his hands together. "That's it, then. Good luck to all of you." He raised his coffee cup in a toast, then sat down.

"Uh, Tony?" Rachel said. "What about Clive?"

A lip quirk from Garrett…but he looked interested in Tony's answer.

Clive, ever the nice guy, said, "Thanks, Rachel," as if he meant it.

"Sorry, Clive." Tony didn't bother to get up. "What can I say? Your last couple of creatives have really sung, your team's working great together…we're very impressed. Just keep doing what you're doing."

Rachel's gaze swung to Garrett—she saw her own shock mirrored in his eyes. *Clive Barnes* could do nothing to improve? Did that make him the front-runner?

Now that she thought about it, he'd won a CLIO a few years back.

Dammit, how had this meeting gone so wrong? If she'd been more on the ball she wouldn't have allowed Tony to get away with saying she was too "safe," wouldn't have allowed the others to agree. With her lack of a real denial, she'd effectively proved his point. *Idiot*.

"There's something else you all need to know," Tony said.

He launched into a commentary on the tough economic climate. Advertising budgets were down, in line with household expenditure. Old news. Was he softening them up for an announcement that the chief creative officer wouldn't earn as much as they might hope? Disappointing, but money wasn't everything.

Rachel popped a flake of croissant into her mouth.

"I want you to know that this is as difficult for me to say as it is for you to hear," Tony said.

She paused in her chewing.

"HR has been assessing our staffing needs in the current economic climate," he continued. "They've determined that KBC is top-heavy."

"Too many partners?" Garrett suggested.

Rachel fought an inappropriate urge to laugh. *Go ahead, Garrett, that ought to win you a few votes. Not.* She swallowed her croissant.

"Not exactly," Tony said. "Too many executive creative directors."

The croissant stuck in her throat; Rachel coughed.

There were three executive creative directors at KBC, and they were all in this room.

"You want to get rid of one of us," Garrett said. Way too calmly. Didn't he realize this was a disaster?

"*Two* of you." Tony turned disaster into cataclysm. Rachel felt as if her throat was closing up. Her eyes started to water.

"Whoever isn't named chief executive officer will be deemed surplus to requirements and therefore redundant." He might have couched it in HR-speak, but they all knew what he meant. *Fired.*

Rachel gulped down her cold coffee, clearing the stuck croissant. "Tony, you can't mean that. We're all assets to the firm. *Loyal* assets."

Okay, Garrett wasn't loyal, but she didn't need to point that out.

"*Expensive* assets," Tony said. "And I have a hundred and eighty-five loyal staff on the two floors below. If we don't rationalize, the whole company suffers. This will give us a chance to promote a couple of deserving people to creative director."

The firm already had four creative directors, a level lower than executive director and therefore less well compensated.

"This approach seems shortsighted," Clive said. "The firm's reputation is likely to suffer."

"We believe this will be a wonderful opportunity for junior staff to rise to the occasion," Tony said. "Now, it goes without saying that all of this is confidential. It's only fair to give you guys a heads-up, but we don't want staff to feel it's not worth giving every one of your pitches their absolute best."

Rachel glanced at Garrett and for one brief moment,

she could read his thoughts, plain as day. Total contempt for Tony's maneuverings. An intention to quit in disgust.

Do it, she urged him silently. *Move on to your next firm now. Improve my odds.*

To her disappointment, Garrett said nothing. Maybe he would quit later.

Tony stood, signaling the meeting was over. Dazed, Rachel pushed back her chair, headed for the elevator with Garrett and Clive.

Her stomach churned. Fired. *I could be fired.* Eight years, up in smoke, just like that.

We can start over. Another of her mother's sayings. *But I can't. I can't start over again. I won't.*

The elevator spat them out onto the floor where the real work was done. It was barely eight o'clock, but most people were at their desks.

Garrett peeled off to the left, ignoring the few greetings called out to him. Rachel took some hope from that. He really was useless with people.

She headed to her own office, her progress slowing as she stopped to answer Alice's question about the storyboard she was working on, to inquire after Natasha's boyfriend's torn Achilles tendon, to congratulate Talia on her engagement and admire the ring.

At last she was in her office. Rachel stopped still, and surveyed all the things that anchored her here. Her Carolina beech desk, her red leather ergonomic chair, the whiteboard where she and the team spent long evenings brainstorming, the glass wall that allowed her to look out on "her" domain.

"How'd it go?" Haylee, the team admin, walked in behind her, a small sheaf of mail in her hand.

The mailroom, where Rachel had started, was now officially titled the communications center, handling actual letters and packages only a small part of its work.

"Not great." Rachel perched on the edge of her desk and forced a smile. "I failed to fire on all cylinders." For now, she would respect Tony's request for confidentiality about the imminent sacking of two of the executive creative directors.

"That's not like you." Haylee fiddled with the cord of the window-blinds until they were wide-open, exposing the view of Madison Avenue far below.

"I said something to Garrett that put me off balance." Rachel nodded in acknowledgment of Haylee's small sound of surprise—Haylee hadn't expected Garrett to be on the list, either. "A stupid joke about his mom, and it turns out she's dead."

Her distraction might have even worse consequences than she'd feared. How many of the partners would deem her unworthy of even her current job based on today's performance? The sooner Garrett quit, the better.

Haylee grimaced. "Oh, yeah, his mom died in that plane crash."

Rachel frowned. "No, it was cancer."

"Uh-uh," Haylee said with complete certainty. "It was a plane crash. One of those scenic flights...at Thanksgiving, maybe five, six years ago? I asked Garrett about his family back when he joined, and he told me. Poor guy, he's still pretty cut up about it."

Rachel froze.

Garrett's sob story about the chemo and the Doris Day movies and "the difference between a miserable day and an okay one"... *He'd made it up?*

Why?

What kind of person would lie about his mother's death?

She scanned the work area beyond the glass wall, where her colleagues, the hardest-working group of people she knew—people she might soon be forced to leave—bustled around. Then she saw him.

Garrett, chatting to Julie, a junior creative—one of *Rachel's* junior creatives—his face a study in determined friendliness.

Julie looked overwhelmed...then, when Garrett touched her shoulder lightly, she peered up at him through demurely lowered lashes.

What the—? Before she even thought about what she was doing, Rachel had crossed to the glass wall, banged it hard with the palm of her hand.

"Rachel?" Haylee said.

Julie looked up, waved and returned to her work. Garrett swiveled to face Rachel. Their eyes met.

The events of the past twelve hours flashed through her mind. Last night in the bar, this morning's elevator ride, the meeting, her guilty discomfort, her distraction, the way she hadn't fought back when her work was questioned. What had Garrett said in the elevator? *"You don't react in the moment. That's your weakness."*

Last night took on a whole new significance. Garrett had known he would see her in this morning's meeting and he'd set out to humiliate her. Still, she could have recovered from that. But this morning, he'd spun her that garbage about his mother knowing it would set her off-kilter.

That one minute—that New York minute, as he called it—had changed everything.

Rachel didn't have it in her to hide her outrage. Garrett took careful observation of her rigid posture, her hand still slammed against the glass, her doubtless heightened color.

One side of his mouth curled.

What kind of person lies about his mother's death?

Not a person...a Shark. A slimy, ruthless predator. And the blood in the water was hers.

CHAPTER FOUR

GARRETT WATCHED HIS FATHER approaching, plowing through the crowded bar like a frigate through a flotilla of pleasure craft.

Garrett drained his beer glass. The beer here at O'Dooley's was on tap, rather than the bottled beers favored by the other bars in the locale. "Here comes my date," he told Clive Barnes.

Clive took one look at Admiral Dwight Calder's uniform—service khakis, suggesting there'd been no high-powered meetings today—and much-decorated chest, and stood. "I feel like I should salute," he said out of the corner of his mouth, though the admiral would never hear him over the din of the Friday-night drinkers.

"Don't encourage him," Garrett said.

Clive polished off his beer. "Time I went home to Wifey." He nodded to Garrett's father as he left.

"Who was that?" his father asked. He pulled out the chair Clive had vacated and sat.

"A colleague."

Dwight frowned. "He was wearing a pink shirt."

"I have one just like it at home," Garrett lied. He cursed his own childish reaction. When would he learn not to rise to his dad's narrow views? "You want a beer?" he asked.

"Thanks." Dwight glanced around the bar. "So, this is the kind of place you hang out."

Garrett signaled to one of the waiters, distinctive in green polos with a shamrock motif, to bring two beers. "Sometimes."

Not often, actually. He wasn't much of a social drinker, and drinking alone didn't appeal—last night excepted. But when his father had asked to meet tonight, Garrett hadn't wanted to commit to a whole meal. He'd suggested his dad meet him here at seven, giving him plenty of time for the "drink and chat" that Clive had suggested.

Neither he nor his dad was a fan of small talk, so they waited for their beers in silence.

Garrett pondered his conversation with Clive, who'd been keen to understand how genuine Garrett's interest in the partnership was.

The truth? He'd initially refused to let his name go forward because a partnership smacked too much of losing his independence. But his refusal had niggled at him. He wasn't sure if he'd done the right thing. At the last minute, he'd decided he might as well keep his options open.

This morning, his knee-jerk reaction to Tony's announcement had been to quit. He didn't doubt for a second that he could outperform both Rachel and Clive, but that wasn't the point. He hated that kind of manipulation.

But even worse, he hated to display his emotions in

public. He would quit on Monday, right after he told Tony, in private, what he thought of KBC's idiotic plan to save money. Garrett wasn't about to hang around in a firm that thought so little of him it would toss him out on a whim. Always be the first to leave—the philosophy had served him well.

He would walk out of KBC with no regrets. Last night, two bottles of champagne had convinced him the partnership was something he could do on his own terms. This morning had proven him wrong, and that was fine. Like he'd told Rachel yesterday, "Let it go."

Of course, he'd been aware of the irony of those words. Aware he was drinking in a futile attempt to *let go* himself. He'd failed, as he did at this time every year, to stem the rising tide of regret. Of bitterness.

Rachel's situation had seemed blessedly uncomplicated, compared with his own inner turmoil. It was obvious her boyfriend was dumping her; equally obvious she was hanging on for dear life. Begging.

Twice in his life Garrett had begged. *Big mistake.*

The waiter arrived. He set down two beers and a bowl of nuts, picked up the old glasses and started to leave. Dwight cleared his throat significantly, then lowered his gaze a fraction to indicate a ring of liquid on the table. The waiter muttered an apology as he wiped the table, double-quick.

Garrett took a slug of his second drink of the night, which at last took the edge off the headache he'd been squinting through all day. He just wanted to get through this meeting, or whatever it was, and go home to bed.

His father cleared his throat again, but this time it

wasn't in lieu of a spoken command. "Many happy returns of the day."

His dad would never say *Happy Birthday* if he could find a more formal alternative.

"Thanks." Garrett forced himself to respond reasonably, instead of saying something inflammatory like, *What do you care?*

A woman carrying a guitar squeezed past their table, followed a moment later by two guys, one of them also lugging a guitar case. Must be the band, headed for the small stage in the far corner.

"Did you. Do anything special?" Dwight asked. He never said *um* or *uh,* so any hesitation sounded like a full stop. "Thirty is. A milestone." He took a quick drink.

Two hesitations in the space of a minute. What was going on?

"I got shortlisted for partner at KBC today," Garrett said, buying himself time to work out his dad's agenda.

Why had he said that? What was the point of telling his father about a promotion that he didn't intend to stick around to get? It wasn't as if Dad would be impressed.

He braced himself for a lecture about getting a "real job." Namely, one in the armed forces, one that mattered.

His father surprised him by saying, "Good." He took another drink of his beer. Not his usual measured pace.

"If I get the partnership—" *shut up,* Garrett warned himself, *stop right there, you're not doing this* "—I'll be chief creative officer." Dammit, the alcohol he'd consumed over the past twenty-four hours had loosened his mouth.

Dwight's glass thudded onto the table. "Chief *creative* officer?"

This was why Garrett should have stopped.

"What would anyone there know about being an *officer?*" his father asked. "About discipline and structure?"

"Nothing at all," Garrett said with heartfelt relief. His father's rigid adherence to *discipline and structure* were what had driven them apart, and Garrett's choice of career had done nothing to fill the gap. Dwight derided the advertising industry as frivolous, billions of dollars spent giving people choices they didn't need. As far as he was concerned, there was only one way to do anything: his way.

As Dwight leaned forward the four metal stars on his collar denoting his rank, polished to a high gleam, caught the light. "Wouldn't a job like that involve commanding a team?"

"Leadership is part of it, yes." Might as well give his father enough rope to hang him.

"You don't have the right attitude for that," Dwight said. "You need to blend authority with a genuine interest in your men."

"I'm definitely not interested in men," Garrett agreed, using flippancy, guaranteed to drive his father nuts, to mask his annoyance.

Without knowing the first thing about it, Dwight had decided Garrett didn't deserve the promotion. Garrett was tempted to prove him wrong. To stick around, win the partnership. Then quit, which would give Tony and the other partners a lesson in how not to run a partnership selection.

Not worth the hassle, he decided. There were other agencies he could go to right away. Lots of them.

Dwight was inhaling noisily, his face turning slightly purple. If Garrett had been one of his father's "men," he'd have feared imminent court-martial.

"If you want to learn leadership, Garrett, you should get a real job," Dwight said. "You could make something of yourself."

Here we go. Garrett drained his glass, glad he hadn't been naive enough to think they could survive a whole meal. He stood. "See you around, Dad," he said, confident it was highly unlikely. Madison Avenue might not be far from USUN, the United States Mission to the United Nations, where his father was an adviser, but their paths never intersected.

"Sit down," Dwight ordered.

Yeah, right. Garrett wasn't about to start obeying his father's commands at this late stage. He left the role of the "good son" to his brother, Lucas.

"Please," Dwight said.

Garrett stared. *Dad learned a new word.*

When his father pointed at the chair, he sat down again.

Dwight closed his eyes for a moment before he spoke. "I know this is a. Difficult day for you."

"But not for you?" Garrett asked.

Irony was wasted on his father. "That's why I wanted to see you."

His birthday, the anniversary of his mother's death—

not everything he'd told Rachel had been a lie—had been a difficult day every year for the past fifteen years. This was the first time Dwight had acknowledged it. "Are you sick?" Garrett asked.

It would surely be divine retribution for the lies that had Rachel so riled, if his father suddenly confessed to a terminal illness. Not that Garrett felt the least bit guilty about Rachel. He'd done her a favor, telling her a plain truth last night. This morning, she'd got up his nose with her superiority and her dismissal of his abilities. She'd reminded him, in fact, of his father.

Only she'd been far easier to topple than Admiral Dwight Calder. She didn't have the backing of the U.S. Navy to make her feel infallible.

"I'm not sick," Dwight said.

Relief rushed through Garrett. He tilted his chair back. "Then why are you here?"

Over on the far side of the room, the band was running a sound check. In another five minutes, there'd be no possibility of conversation.

"It's time you and I made more of an effort with each other," his father said.

Garrett's chair thumped back on to all four legs. "Are you going to tell me this was your idea?" he asked calmly.

"Stephanie suggested it," Dwight admitted.

"Tell your wife to butt out." Garrett kept his voice even, masking the upsurge of anger. He didn't know why Stephanie should pick now, after all this time, to take an interest in his relationship with his father. He didn't *want* to know.

A whine of feedback came through the amplifier on the tiny stage, hurting his ears.

"She's your stepmother," Dwight said with icy control.

But they both knew that in this area, Dwight had never been able to control his son.

Garrett stood again, and this time, nothing would induce him to sit back down. "Goodbye, Dad."

RACHEL WAS DECIDEDLY on edge early Saturday morning as she mooched around her Washington Heights condo—not a great area, but the best she could afford when she'd bought the place two years ago.

She'd been convinced Garrett would quit rather than give KBC a chance to fire him.

Yet when he left the office last night with Clive—worrying in itself—The Shark didn't appear to have cleared out his desk.

Maybe he didn't want to quit on his birthday, she thought, as she wiped the kitchen counter. If it was truly his birthday, and that wasn't another lie.

She tossed the dishcloth in the washing machine, and set about plumping up the cushions of her giant sofa. She'd never have predicted Garrett would be interested in the partnership in the first place. What if he didn't quit after all?

Their prospective client, Brightwater Group, was tickled pink at the prospect of not one but three fabulous ideas for their campaign, in exchange for giving feedback to the KBC board about the three partners designate. Rachel was beginning to feel like a contestant on *America's Next Top Ad Agency Partner*.

She hated those shows. She wasn't a crier by nature, but she cried when people got thrown out of the house, expelled from the island, kicked off the catwalk.

I could be next. She felt nauseous just thinking about it. If Garrett did stick around, his slimy behavior today had given her a heads-up that he wasn't about to play fair. *If he wants a fight, he'll get it.* She would put the work in, she would leave nothing to chance and she would win.

This would have to be her best campaign ever. She would have to be the best every step of the way. Starting with the meeting she, Garrett and Clive would attend at Brightwater's offices on Monday.

Rachel usually handled briefing meetings with ease. But this time the client would be directly comparing her with Garrett.

What if they *liked* sleazy, lying, tardy but highly creative jerks?

What if the client asked some off-the-wall question, to which she would say her usual, "Hmm, you make an excellent point, Ben/Jerry/Jack. I'd like to think about that and get back to you." While Garrett would produce some amazing spontaneous insight.

It didn't bear thinking about. She needed to be even better prepared than usual, so she could at least *look* unrehearsed and intuitive. Okay, the logic was skewed… but that was what she had to do.

Starting right now.

An hour later, Rachel loaded her overnight bag into

the trunk of a rented Ford Focus, along with a supply of Aunt Betty's Apple Pies, courtesy of her *very appreciative* client—how many bottles of Calvin Klein fragrance had Garrett been given, huh?—and joined the weekend crawl out of Manhattan. Once she was through the Holland Tunnel, she stuck to the toll roads, and the traffic thinned right out.

It was only eleven o'clock when she pulled into The Pines Mobile Home Park in Freehold, New Jersey. She followed the loop road, if you could call the vaguely circular stretch of gravel a road, around to her parents' trailer.

Her mom must have heard the crunch of her tires, because the door of the double-wide opened before Rachel switched off her engine.

"Hi, Mom," Rachel called as she grabbed her bag from the backseat. She loaded up an armful of pies, then closed the door with her butt.

"Honey, did you tell us you were coming—oh, yum!" Nora Frye's eyes lit up at the sight of the red-and-white pie cartons.

Rachel kissed her cheek and handed over the booty. "Kind of a last-minute decision—is that okay?" Cell phone reception wasn't great here, and it was always a hassle to phone the trailer-park office and hope they'd get a message to her parents.

"That's fine, though I guess we'll have to cancel our trip to Paris," her mother said gaily, leading the way inside. As she crossed the threshold, she raised her voice. "Burton, Rachel's here!"

"Did he work last night?" Rachel asked. Her dad's

burly build meant he easily found a job as a security guard whenever her parents' other schemes fell through.

"Got to bed at five," her mom confirmed, "but he can wake up for you."

Rachel followed her mom to the small kitchen area. While Nora filled the kettle Rachel had given her last Christmas and set it on the stove, Rachel dug in her purse to produce a pack of real coffee. Her mom set the jar of instant she'd been opening back on the shelf, and reached high for the French press, covered with a film of dust.

"So, what's new?" Her mom squirted detergent into the press and began to wash it.

"I made the partner short list at work."

Her mom gave a little squawk. "Hon, that's fantastic!"

"I know. Thanks." Just thinking about it had Rachel grinning. She pushed aside the "I might get fired" aspect as she found some scissors in a drawer and snipped the top off the coffee pack. When she was certain her mom wasn't watching, she tucked a folded twenty-dollar bill in the back of the drawer.

By the time they'd carried their cups over to the table by the window, Rachel's dad had emerged from the bedroom. He hugged Rachel before he pulled out one of the nonmatching chairs and sat. "That coffee for me, Nora?"

Her mom slid the third mug toward him. While she fussed with cream and sugar, Rachel took the opportunity to stuff another twenty down the gap between the seat pad and the back of the built-in banquette she occupied. Anything more than twenty and her parents would get suspicious.

Her dad took a sip of the hot coffee and let out a satisfied sigh. "Home is where the coffee is, right, Nora?"

"That's right, hon." Nora blew him a kiss.

Rachel tensed. Comments like that made her want to chime in with something like, "Home is where you put down roots. Where you decide to stick it out, no matter what."

Rachel blew on her coffee so she wouldn't meet his eyes and feel compelled to disagree. Pointing out their fundamental differences in philosophy only led to circular arguments that, despite being right, she never won.

"I'm hoping I can pick your brains," she said, changing the subject. Her family came in very handy when she wanted to run ideas by them or have them try out a new product. It was her mom who'd said, "This is better'n I make, don't you think, Burton?" the first time she'd tried an Aunt Betty's apple pie.

Which had inspired the eventual slogan "As good as Mom makes." Aunt Betty's had seen a nice upturn in sales as a result of that particular piece of creativity.

In the past, Rachel had offered to pay them to be her own private focus group—it would help them financially, and she'd assured them KBC would pick up the tab—but they wouldn't hear of it.

"I'm pitching to a group that's taken over a bunch of private colleges," she said. "They'll be rebranding and relaunching them, along with a finance company offering student loans. But we'll just talk about the academic side today," she added quickly.

She'd learned not to discuss anything financial with her parents, however gently couched. *I don't think this email is actually from the president of Nigeria's largest bank, Dad.* Or, *A hundred percent interest over three months implies a higher investment risk level than you might want to take.*

Instead, she tried to hide enough twenty-dollar bills that they could afford a few small treats. Hoping it was enough to stave off the need to pursue instant riches.

"Sure, we can talk about that," Burton said. "You want to start now?"

"No hurry. I'll stay over, if that's okay."

"Great," her mom said. "When I've finished my coffee I'll wander out to the road—" where the cell phone signal was stronger "—and call LeeAnne. She'll want to see you."

Good thing Rachel had plenty more twenties in her purse. Her younger sister, LeeAnne, was the mother of three-year-old twins. The twins' father had taken off before they were even born, so LeeAnne depended entirely on her parents for backup. She usually tried to live within a few miles of Nora and Burton. Though as Rachel often pointed out, part-time work that paid a decent wage and allowed her time with the kids was hard enough to find without the added complication of moving so often.

LeeAnne always agreed, but she still packed up and moved each time.

"Seen any good ads lately?" Rachel asked her father.

Her dad rumbled on about a Toyota truck commercial—TV with radio and print backup—that Rachel also considered pretty good. "But my favorite is that Lexus ad with the bridge," Burton said.

Rachel stiffened. "Really? You like that?" It was one of Garrett's campaigns, the first one he'd done at KBC. "You don't think it was bit over-the-top?"

"Over-the-top!" her father scoffed. "It's sheer genius."

Rachel grunted. A sound that reminded her of Garrett, as if she needed to think of him.

"It sure would be convenient if you could win a beer company as a client, hon," her mom joked. "Your dad won a gas grill in a raffle at work, so we thought we'd get some friends over to christen it. A few freebies wouldn't go amiss."

Her parents had been here long enough to make friends to invite over. Could they actually be settling down? Rachel treated it with a healthy dose of skepticism, but, still, it was a tantalizing thought.

Rachel's childhood was a blur of different homes— cheap apartments, trailers, the occasional small house. Sooner or later, the Fryes had left them all, most with a cheery toot of the horn to the neighbors, a few in the dead of night in the hope the landlord wouldn't chase after them.

It was amazing none of those landlords had tracked them down and taken them to court…but then, her folks were nice people who always meant well. Their creditors always seemed to end up excusing them.

Rachel excused them, too. They were loving parents, and if she'd had to be particularly tenacious to burrow herself into each new school and earn the grades she wanted…well, that was character building. And it wasn't as if Mom and Dad didn't work hard or try to get ahead.

The problem was their method of doing so.

For as long as Rachel could remember, they'd been suckers for the promise of good times around the corner. Over and again, they'd uprooted themselves so Burton could chase after an exciting new job. Or borrowed more than they could afford to invest in a "sure thing."

Just once, they'd had a great return. They'd lent a thousand bucks to a guy who'd patented a new can opener, and got three thousand back. Other than that, to give it the most charitable interpretation, they were the unluckiest investors in the world.

Rachel had long ago agreed to disagree with her parents. She loved them, but she didn't want their lives, and she couldn't share their excitement about the Next Big Thing. And they'd had enough of what they called her cynicism.

They talked about harmless subjects until LeeAnne and the twins, Kylie and Dannii—named after the Minogue sisters—arrived for lunch. After they'd eaten and cleared away the dishes, the girls stayed at the table with crayons and coloring books, while the adults spread out in the living area, ready to bend their brains to Rachel's latest problem. Her family treated it like a game, and with them it felt like one.

As opposed to feeling as if her life was on the line.

"So let's talk about how people without a college background choose a college for their kids," she said.

"I've been trying to remember the discussions we had when I was in high school."

"You girls could have gone to college," Nora said. "You were both bright enough."

"We looked into the whole student loans thing," her father reminded Rachel. "But you said you didn't want to go."

They'd had no way of funding a college education beyond massive loans. And Rachel had seen firsthand the consequences of excessive borrowing; she'd wanted nothing to do with it.

"I'd love it if Kylie and Dannii went to college," Lee-Anne said wistfully. "Maybe they'll end up in these schools you're advertising and really make something of themselves."

"They already are something," Nora scolded. "They're the two most adorable girls that ever lived. After you and your sister."

"There is that." LeeAnne smiled.

Threads of ideas began to float in Rachel's mind. She knew better than to try pinning them down when they were this ephemeral. If she let them float a while, they might coalesce into something solid.

Solid. That's how Tony had described her work. She needed better than solid.

"Takes four years to get a degree," Burton warned LeeAnne.

"I know."

"I guess we have a few years to come into some money," Burton joked.

Oh, boy. Rachel hoped her sister had more of a plan

than that. Maybe Rachel could start a college fund for her nieces.

They talked for a while longer. Then LeeAnne glanced at her combined watch and pedometer, which sported the name of a well-known cereal company, one of Rachel's clients. "I'd better go, I'm trying to get the girls into more of a daily routine before they start nursery school. It's time for their nap."

Rachel walked her sister out to her rusting Toyota. They each held one of the twins by the hand.

"So this routine thing is new," Rachel said as she buckled Dannii into her car seat.

"Yeah, I sound almost like you." LeeAnne flashed her a grin and clipped Kylie in.

"Don't knock it—it works." Rachel kissed Dannii, then closed the door, stuffing a twenty into the door pocket as she did so. "So they start nursery school in September?"

"Yep." LeeAnne climbed into the driver's seat and lowered the passenger window so they could continue talking. "There's a great school right near us. I hope we're still in the neighborhood."

Had her sister ever expressed a desire to remain in one place before?

Rachel leaned in through the window and said casually, "You could stay. If Mom and Dad move, I mean."

"You know I need to be near them. I couldn't raise the girls without their moral support, not to mention Mom's babysitting." LeeAnne looked in her rearview mirror, back at the trailer.

"Dad's work is steady, right?" Rachel asked. "There's no reason to move."

"Only if something too good to miss comes up somewhere else." LeeAnne let out a breath that was almost a sigh.

"Maybe if you refused to go with them, Mom and Dad would stay put," Rachel suggested. LeeAnne had grumbled a bit when they were kids, but she'd never been upset by their constant moves as Rachel had. Maybe, at last, she was developing an interest in stability.

Her sister looked skeptical. "I'm not sure that's what I want. Moving can be exciting. Though maybe not as often as we do it," she admitted.

"You should think about staying. For the twins' sake." Rachel figured she'd better not push her luck. She stepped back and patted the side of the car. "Off you go, sis."

She watched until the Toyota turned out onto the road. As she headed back inside, a couple of images that might work for Brightwater Group flashed in her mind. Rachel picked up the pace and ran to make notes. If she was going to be number one with the client on Monday, there could be No Idea Left Behind.

CHAPTER FIVE

RACHEL TOOK A TRAIN to Princeton, New Jersey, where Brightwater had its headquarters, presumably so some of the luster associated with Princeton University might reflect on its private colleges. Smart strategy.

She arrived in plenty of time for the meeting. Before her colleagues. If punctuality was a deciding factor for the KBC partnership, she would ace the promotion.

Since the morning was sunny but not too hot, she stood outside to wait. Tony and Clive were next to arrive. They'd caught the same train and shared a cab from the station. Coincidence, or clever planning by Clive? She didn't think of him as a schemer—six foot four, slow-moving and good-natured, he was the epitome of a gentle giant.

There was no sign of Garrett. Dared she hope that he'd thrown in the towel?

"Good weekend?" Rachel asked Clive, trying to gauge how much time he'd spent reading up about private colleges.

"I had my in-laws staying," he said. "They're helping us paint the apartment."

"How nice." Didn't sound like he'd been able to work. She checked her watch...oops, she wasn't supposed to be doing that so often. Three minutes past nine. Garrett couldn't be coming; even he wouldn't dare to be late today. "Shall we go in?" she said cheerfully.

Tony scanned the parking lot. "Any idea how Garrett's getting here?"

He'd barely finished speaking when a black BMW M5 roared into the lot.

"I think," Rachel said, "he's driving."

Garrett parked right in front of them, in a space that wasn't strictly a space. He got out of the car empty-handed. No briefcase. No notepad.

Rachel felt suddenly weighed down by her tools of the trade. Un-nimble. *At least I was here on time.* She waited for him to apologize for keeping them waiting.

"Hi," he said to Tony.

Tony nodded and glanced at his watch.

"Is that peanut butter on your tie?" Garrett asked Clive.

"Probably," Clive said equably.

Garrett's gaze skimmed over Rachel's black silk blouse and dropped to the hem of the *Pick me, I'm the best* cerise skirt that ended just above her knees.

"Love the pink, Rach," he said, his voice deepening. "Your legs aren't bad, either."

Good grief, the guy had a career death wish!

That was fine by Rachel. Tony opened his mouth to object to Garrett's comment, but she held up a hand to tell him she could deal with it.

"Cerise," she corrected Garrett coolly. "And it's Ra-chel. I don't expect my legs to affect the outcome of this meeting."

How pathetic did he think she was, to fall for another attempt to disconcert her?

He peered closer. "Don't underestimate yourself—they're damn good."

"That's enough, Garrett," Tony snapped.

Garrett shrugged. A twinge of envy surprised Rachel. When she'd let herself think about it, KBC's decision to fire two creative directors filled her with fear and anger. Consequently, she was on her best behavior. Garrett's don't-give-a-damn attitude spoke of a courage she didn't have.

In their meeting, Mark Van de Kamp, Brightwater's marketing director, seemed excited about the level of creative talent he was being offered. He gave them a more in-depth briefing about the new colleges—actually a bunch of existing colleges the group had acquired—and their target market. Rachel managed to slip in a couple of what she considered insightful comments.

"Any questions?" Mark asked at the conclusion of his presentation.

Clive jumped in, showing a good grasp of the issues. Some of them, at least.

Rachel stepped up to the plate with one he'd missed. "Mark, there's been a suggestion that companies like Brightwater exploit the low-income families they claim to serve, encouraging them to take out loans they can't afford to pay back. How worried are you that what you're doing will be seen in that light?" With her own nieces in mind, she'd spent half of Sunday researching issues surrounding low-income families and college fees.

Garrett looked surprised—whether at the information or the fact she'd come up with such an unexpected question, she wasn't sure. Tony seemed intrigued. All in all, Rachel felt as if she'd made a strong attempt to step outside the box.

"Good question." Mark smiled at her. "Those other organizations have typically offered punitive loan conditions and poor academic quality. Our loan rates will be competitive, and we're currently lining up endorsements by Action Against Poverty and the NAACP in support of the quality of our programs."

"Sounds good." Rachel made some notes on her legal pad.

Logic dictated it was Garrett's turn to ask the next question.

She set down her pen so she could observe The Shark in action.

For long seconds silence reigned.

"So tell me, Mark," Garrett said, "If Brightwater was a fruit, what fruit would it be?"

What?

Clive glanced down at the peanut-butter stain on his tie, so Rachel couldn't read his expression. Tony froze in his seat. Garrett was straight-faced, totally relaxed.

"Hmm." Mark propped his chin on his hand. "That's very interesting, Garrett, very interesting indeed."

It's a crock! He's kidding!

Both Tony and Clive took their cue from the client, and nodded.

Excuse me? Am I the only rational person in this room?

Garrett's glance flicked toward her, as if he could read her thoughts. She couldn't suppress an eye roll. His eyebrows rose in spurious inquiry.

"I think I'd have to say…a melon," Mark said.

"Cantaloupe or honeydew?" Garrett shot back.

Oh, puh-lease.

"Cantaloupe, definitely."

"I see," Garrett said. "Thanks, Mark, that's useful." He smiled at Van de Kamp, and it was such a rare thing, it was as if the sun had come out from a cloud. Rachel could practically see the man basking in its warmth.

GARRETT OFFERED THEM ALL a ride back to the office. While Tony and Clive were signing out at the reception desk, Rachel caught up with him on his way to the parking lot.

"What was that about?" she demanded.

"What?" He sped up, forcing her to almost jog.

"Melons," she said.

He didn't slow, but his gaze flicked down over her fitted blouse. "No comment, though I'm sure they're very nice. I'm more of a leg man."

She sputtered a laugh…and realized he was paying her legs some considerable attention. "Garrett, be serious. You can't tell me that's how you normally take a brief."

"Oh, dear, have you been doing it wrong all this time?"

She rolled her eyes. "No, I have not. But I don't get what you—" She stopped. "You're quitting. Aren't you?"

He walked faster. "What do you mean?"

"Those comments, way too outrageous even for you. You're leaving KBC." She was unable to contain a triumphant grin as she kept pace.

"No, I'm not," he said, annoyed. Totally unconvincing.

"Hey," she said, "I don't blame you. You could get any job you want. Why would you hang around here?"

They'd reached his BMW. Rachel set her overprepared, overloaded briefcase on the pavement.

He stared down at her, her high heels making no impression against his height. "Maybe you're right."

Before she could encourage him further, Tony and Clive joined them. Garrett pressed the remote unlock on his key chain.

Rachel clambered into the back of the M5, her shorter stature demanding that she cede the more spacious front seat to Clive.

"Nice car," Tony said as he settled in next to her.

"So, Garrett," Rachel said, as he reversed out of his space, "if this car was a fruit, what fruit would it be?"

His gaze met hers in the rearview mirror. "A banana, of course."

"Useful insight," she said. "Thanks."

His dark eyes gleamed.

"You do that fruit thing, too?" Tony asked. "What the hell is that about?"

No one does the fruit thing. It's Garrett's idea of a joke. "I used to do it," she said. "It's a bit passé."

A snort from the driver as he turned out of the parking lot onto Brunswick Pike.

"Guys, I want to give you some feedback on today's meeting," Tony said.

He was certainly taking this reality TV–style evaluation to extremes.

"Rachel, Clive, you were both great."

"Thanks, Tony," she murmured. *I guess that means Garrett goes home.*

"Garrett, you engaged well with the client. I admit, I don't get the fruit thing, but it certainly snagged Van de Kamp's interest. If you can deliver on that stuff, I'm all in favor."

"I'll deliver," Garrett said.

Huh? Shouldn't he be quitting right about now? What happened to *Maybe you're right?* Rachel tried to catch his glance in the mirror, but he wasn't looking.

"But you were late arriving," Tony said, "which made us all late for the meeting. And your comment about Rachel's appearance was out of line."

"It was a joke, Tony," Garrett said. "Rachel knew that."

It wasn't a joke, it was a sabotage attempt mixed up with Garrett's professional suicide.

"Did you take it as a joke, Rachel?" Tony asked.

Industry old-timers like Tony were known to suffer the odd lapse in judgment themselves; Rachel figured he was following up more because he had responsibilities under the New York City Human Rights Law than out of genuine disapproval.

She opened her mouth to say, *Of course, no problem.* Because she was a team player, and this wasn't about her, and anyway, she knew Garrett was playing some game of his own.

But what game was that, exactly? She needed him to quit.

Inspiration struck, inspiration she could only credit to the presence of the man who'd accused her of being unable to seize the moment.

"Actually, Tony, I was uncomfortable," she said. She stifled a twinge of guilt at the lie. Garrett was the guy who'd told Piers she was trading sex for no breakup, who'd lied about his mother's death for competitive advantage. If he needed a push to leave, she was happy to help. Who said she couldn't think on her feet! Feet that happened to be attached to "damn good" legs.

"What the hell?" Garrett's outraged expression showed in the mirror.

Even Tony looked taken aback. It wasn't as if she was a powerless junior; he knew she relished fighting her own battles.

"I'm not saying I feel sexually harassed," Rachel assured her boss. "Not exactly."

"Good, good," Tony sputtered. "Not that I'm trying to discourage you from making a complaint if that's what you want," he added, in a confused but valiant attempt at political correctness.

"For Pete's sake!" Garrett wrenched the steering wheel to the right as he twisted to glare at Rachel. Clive murmured a protest. Garrett cursed and returned his focus to the road.

"Oh, no, definitely not," Rachel assured her boss. "I

think it's just that Garrett has trouble relating to women. Part of his team skills problem."

"I don't have trouble with women," Garrett said ominously.

"Just last week Natasha was in the washroom in tears after Garrett told her off." Rachel didn't mention Natasha had stuck her mascara wand in her eye at the same time as she mentioned her run-in with Garrett. She was pleasantly surprised how easy it was to be devious when you had the right inspiration.

Garrett said, "Natasha left the office to check on her boyfriend's broken foot—"

"Torn Achilles tendon," Rachel interrupted.

"—and completely forgot about the Sheraton pitch," Garrett growled.

"On Friday, after our breakfast, Garrett touched Julie on the shoulder," she reported to Tony. "I could see she was confused about what it meant."

"You're evil," Garrett said conversationally.

Rachel picked up on the underlying anger and felt almost sorry for him. But she'd done that once before, in the elevator, and look how he'd played her. And the catchphrase of his...*Do it on your terms*... No way would he consent to what she was about to suggest. He'd be out the door, voluntarily, before she could say *chicken*.

She smiled beatifically at Tony. "So I'm offering to educate Garrett."

"You what?" Garrett snarled.

"I'm willing to make time to get involved with Garrett's team," she said. "To monitor his interactions, particularly with female staff, and advise him how to handle situations better."

"She's kidding," Garrett said.

Rachel rather liked that edge of desperation. She knew Garrett would hasten his inevitable departure, rather than have her overseeing him. She'd observed his natural abhorrence for authority. *Quit, Garrett, quit.*

"You'll recall I scored a clean-sweep perfect ten in my team's appraisals of my management skills," she reminded Tony.

"So you did," he said. "First time anyone's done that. You're a good girl, Rachel. Uh, I mean, a smart woman. But do you have time to help Garrett?"

"Tony!" Garrett near shouted.

"I'll make time," she said generously. "Not for my sake, but for women everywhere." For a moment, she worried she'd overdone it; in the front seat, Clive's enormous shoulders shook.

But Tony appeared to be in the thrall of an image of multiple harassment suits being filed against KBC.

"Thanks, Rachel," he said. "That'd be great. You should start right away."

"My pleasure," she said, and meant it.

Quit, you ill-mannered, manipulative, *motherless* Shark!

CHAPTER SIX

GARRETT TOOK THE STAIRS to his condo two at a time, powered by frustration and a buzz of adrenaline that caught him by surprise.

Rachel.

The woman he knew to be as predictable as yesterday's weather had picked up on his intention to quit KBC, then gone all out to push him into action because it was what *she* wanted.

He hadn't known she had it in her.

Garrett rounded the second-floor landing and kept going. Sure, it had taken Rachel until they were leaving Brightwater to click that his remarks were the screwyou salute of someone who didn't plan to stick around. Even if they were true...particularly the one about her legs, which he'd never noticed before were sensational. But neither Tony nor Clive had worked out where he was coming from. They'd assumed Garrett was being his usual self, the guy who could never be accused of toeing the party line.

As he passed the black-painted number three on the third-floor landing, he wondered how he'd given himself away to Rachel. Quick thinking on her part, to come up with that sexual harassment stuff in an attempt to force his hand. She was a whole lot more devious than he'd given her credit for. Tony couldn't see she was playing games, it seemed. Eight years of Goody Two-shoes had finally paid off.

Too bad her attempt to manipulate Garrett had triggered his natural resistance. Instead of resigning when they got back to the city, he'd sat in his office mulling over what he wanted to do. To his annoyance, he'd failed to reach a decision.

It was this time of year, that was all. Made it hard for him to *Let it go.* Tomorrow. He'd quit tomorrow.

Garrett fished his keys from his pocket as he pulled open the door to the fourth floor.

Right away, he saw the woman.

At least, he figured it was a woman, going by the ponytail of brown hair.

She sat huddled on the floor next to his door, a small backpack beside her, her head buried in her arms on jeans-clad knees. A light-colored trench coat pooled around her. There were only two condos per floor; she must be a friend of his neighbor's, must have turned the wrong way out of the elevator.

"Miss?" he said.

No reply. He hoped she wasn't drunk, or ill. Or if she was, he hoped his neighbor was home.

He touched her shoulder. "Excuse me, miss?"

She jolted awake with a cry of alarm and lifted her face.

Not a miss. A Mrs.

Mrs. Stephanie Calder.

"What are you doing here?" Garrett asked. Shouldn't she be whipping up a pot roast in New London?

"Garrett—damn, I fell asleep." She rubbed her eyes, then blinked up at him. "What time is it?"

"Why don't you check your watch?" Yeah, it was churlish, but he'd decided years ago never to give his father's wife anything.

She consulted the slim white-gold Piaget on her wrist. "Nine," she muttered. "Do you always work so late?"

"Is Dad all right?" He didn't think he'd ever seen Stephanie in jeans outside the house before. And the ponytail was positively sloppy compared with her usual elegant grooming.

"Your father's your father," she said, her voice clipped. "I gather your birthday celebration didn't go too well last week?"

Celebration wasn't the word he'd have chosen. Garrett shrugged.

She tsked. "Did your father tell you…anything?"

Crap, his dad *was* sick. "He mentioned something about me getting a real job." Garrett feigned casualness.

She groaned under her breath and rubbed her eyes again. Her makeup was smudged; she looked haggard. She stuck out a hand. "Help me up?" Then, before he could refuse, she dropped her hand again. "Don't worry, I'll manage."

Standing proved a strangely awkward process. She rolled onto all fours then pushed herself off the thick carpet designed to cushion the tread of noisy neighbors.

When she was finally upright, the floor seemed

to shift beneath Garrett, forcing him to put a hand to the wall.

"You've been overdoing the pizza," he said, eyeing Stephanie's enormous, round belly.

"The baby's due in June." She planted her fists on her hips, as if defying him to disapprove. The movement thrust her belly out even farther. "I'm seven months along. We would have told you sooner, except we haven't seen you since Christmas—" he'd spent the holiday with them only because his brother had been home on leave from his naval posting "—and we didn't know I was pregnant then."

"And Dad was meant to tell me about this last week."

"Among other things." She bent at the knees to scoop up her little backpack. "Do we have to do this in the hallway?"

"Where's Dad?" Garrett glanced around.

Stephanie slung the pack over one shoulder. "I left him."

Once again, Garrett's world tipped on its axis. "You mean, left him out in the car, right?" But he hadn't seen a Hummer parked in the street.

"I mean, left our marriage." She plucked the key from his suddenly nerveless fingers. "Let's go inside."

In the condo, Garrett used the time spent disarming the burglar alarm and turning on lights to try to get his head around this bizarre new development. Nope, he couldn't do it. "Does Lucas know about the baby?"

"Of course." Stephanie set her pack down next to the sofa and sat. "I wrote to him a few months back."

Garrett wondered what his brother had made of the

news. He'd tried to convince Lucas that Stephanie was the enemy, back when their dad had married her, but Lucas had been twelve years old and he'd wanted a mother. He hadn't seen the wrongness of their dad marrying again so quickly after Mom died, without consulting them, without listening to Garrett's protests. The wrongness of Dwight expecting them to welcome Stephanie and her clumsy attempts at stepmotherhood.

"Aren't you too old to be doing this?" He waved at her stomach without looking. "Is it IVF?" He couldn't imagine his dad submitting to the invasive process.

"I just turned forty-five—it's within the bounds of possibility." She cupped her hands over her stomach protectively. "Though it was certainly unexpected. Your father and I tried for a long time to have a baby. When this happened…the symptoms…I thought I was menopausal."

Too much information.

Garrett headed to the kitchen area. "Coffee?" he said over his shoulder.

"Do you have decaf?"

"No."

She sighed. "Okay, but make it a weak one. You're supposed to cut back on caffeine in pregnancy—though since it took me four months to figure out I was pregnant that didn't quite happen."

Away from that telltale stomach, Garrett pulled his thoughts into order. Okay, Stephanie was pregnant, a little fact that everyone except Garrett had known. Due in June. At which point he would have a half brother or sister.

"Is it a boy or a girl?" he called.

"I don't know." Stephanie spoke from the other side of the island, making him jump. "I want it to be a surprise—your father wanted to know but it turns out the mother's wishes prevail in this sort of thing."

She sounded almost amused. Probably hadn't been too many times her wishes had prevailed since she'd married Admiral Dwight Calder. Wait a minute...

"Did you say you *left* my father?" How he could have lost sight of that detail?

"That's right." She eyed the amount of coffee he was scooping into the press with misgiving.

"Is he upset about the baby? I would have thought he'd be delighted to have another chance at a son he could mold in his own image."

"Dwight would never expect this baby to replace you," she said. "Or Lucas."

Mention of his brother was an obvious afterthought, presumably to make Garrett feel less left out of his father's affections.

"I don't care if it does, if it takes the pressure off me."

The kettle began to whistle. Garrett poured water into the press.

"I asked Dwight to come see you because I don't want him making the same mistakes with this baby that he made with you," Stephanie said.

Garrett's head jerked up; boiling water sloshed over the side of the press and onto his thumb.

He cursed and turned on the faucet. He stuck his thumb beneath the running water. Stephanie moved into the kitchen and took over the job of putting the lid on the press. She was so big with that—that thing in her stomach, Garrett felt as if he couldn't get away from her.

"So now you're concerned about me and Dad?" he asked. "Shouldn't you have thought of that, say, fifteen years ago, and not married him two minutes after my mom died?"

She ignored his dig. "Dwight's been supportive of this baby in the obvious ways...."

"But not emotionally," Garrett said.

She nodded. "I told him if he can't prove to me he can be a loving father, I don't want him in our child's life."

"He's a loving father to Lucas." Garrett still couldn't figure out what the heck was going on, why Stephanie was really here.

"We both know that's because Lucas is in the navy and hasn't yet needed to butt heads with your dad. Dwight needs to open his heart to this baby no matter what choices it makes." She pushed the plunger down on the press. "Cups?"

With his unscalded hand, Garrett indicated a cupboard to her left.

Stephanie poured coffee into one mug. She glanced from the press to the other mug, bemused.

"Fill yours halfway, then top it up with water," Garrett instructed.

She shook her head, as if to clear it, and laughed. "Sorry, I struggle with the most basic decisions these days. Blame the hormones."

"Yet you decided to leave Dad." Garrett couldn't keep satisfaction out of his voice. It seemed like poetic justice. Dwight had abandoned the memory of Garrett's mom for Stephanie, and now Stephanie had abandoned him. He shut off the faucet. "Was he furious?"

She handed him his coffee. "I don't know. I left him a note this morning, and I haven't turned on my cell phone."

Garrett couldn't imagine how mad his dad must be. Served the old goat right to have someone else rebel against his coldhearted rigidity. He found himself grinning. "Well, I appreciate you coming to tell me what's going on. Where are you staying?"

She blew on her coffee, then took a slow sip, closing her eyes as if even a watered-down jolt of caffeine was heaven.

"I thought," she said, "I might stay with you."

Garrett slopped coffee over the side of his mug, burning himself again. "Dammit, Stephanie!" He stuck his thumb back under the faucet. "Why the hell would you think that? Not even the kookiest hormones could make you believe I'd want you here."

Her mouth slipped slightly. "I didn't say you'd want me. I said I'd like to stay."

"You can't." When she eyed him steadily, he said, "I'm not set up for guests."

"And you don't want me."

"That's right."

"I don't have anywhere else to go, Garrett. You may remember my parents died some time ago."

"There are hotels around here. Cozy bed-and-breakfasts. I'll phone one for you."

"I want to be with family."

The fact that his father had chosen her didn't give

her the right to put that label on him. "You must have other family."

"There's no one," she said flatly. "You're it, Garrett. You and Lucas, and since Lucas is on an aircraft carrier in the Persian Gulf…"

"What about friends?" he said. "I'm sure lots of people like you."

"They do," she said. "But at this stage I don't want to humiliate Dwight by telling our friends I've left him, and when they do find out, I don't want to make them take sides."

"I bet they'd side with you," he muttered.

"Probably. I just need a couple of weeks—a week," she amended hastily, seeing him recoil, "to sort myself out. Then I'll go."

"Look, Stephanie—" he paced to the refrigerator "—you and I have never had any kind of relationship. I'm happy for you about the baby, and I hope you and Dad work something out. But don't push your luck by claiming some stepmother bond with me now."

Her eyes filled with tears.

"Crap," she said, beating him to it. "These hormones." She dug a tissue out of the pocket of her trench coat, and blew her nose.

Garrett was reminded, uncomfortably, of Rachel accusing him of making that account exec cry. Of her comments about him being insensitive toward women.

She'd had an agenda, he told himself. And the more he thought about it, the more he was damned if he was going to give her the satisfaction of him quitting.

The thought took him by surprise…because the alternative to not quitting was to actively pursue the partnership. Which he wasn't even sure he wanted.

But if he quit, he'd be hanging around home until he found a new job. Stephanie would doubtless let the fact that he was out of work slip to Dwight. Who'd made it plain he didn't think Garrett was up to the job of chief creative officer. Garrett hated to prove his father right.

So, maybe he should stick around a bit longer. Win the partnership and then decide what to do. Brightwater was an interesting account; he already had a few ideas in his head. He'd be coming from behind, after those wisecracks he'd made today, but that didn't faze him. And beating Rachel after that stunt she'd pulled... There was nothing more satisfying than beating a worthy adversary.

Stephanie had cupped one hand beneath her stomach; she was rubbing it gently, as if to soothe the occupant. *I don't want her here.* Dealing with his family invariably left him feeling isolated and resentful. He was over that, and he wanted to stay that way.

But Stephanie had nowhere else to go. Casting a pregnant woman out on the street would be low, even for Garrett. Especially when the baby was his half sibling. He didn't like the idea of it hearing that story one day. And, much as he hated talking about personal stuff at work, he could drop the fact that she was staying into a conversation with Tony...that ought to help negate Rachel's suggestions he had trouble dealing with women. Plus, it would tick his dad off to know his wife had sought refuge with Garrett. That thought brought a smile, admittedly a grim one, to his face.

"Fine," he said. "You can stay. One week."

She took a step toward him. For an alarming moment, he thought she was going to hug him—something she'd given up trying after the first year of her marriage to Dwight.

"You must have more stuff than that," Garrett said quickly, gesturing to her backpack.

"My case is in a locker at Grand Central," she said. "I didn't want to lug it here if you were going to throw me out."

At least she'd been realistic. But now she was looking at him expectantly.

Garrett picked up the car keys he'd tossed on the island. "Let's go."

As he stepped aside to let her past, her stomach brushed against him. There would be no avoiding her.

He turned his mind to a more enjoyable image: the sexy-legged Rachel Frye, and her horrified expression when she learned he was sticking around.

CHAPTER SEVEN

RACHEL SLIPPED INTO the meeting room where Garrett's team had set up Pitch Central. Ignoring the boardroom-style table, where his team of account execs, artists, copywriters and media specialists sat, she slid into a chair against the wall at the back of the room. She ignored the curious looks that came her way, and didn't make eye contact with anyone, not even those she considered her friends. Her aim was invisibility.

"What are you doing here?" Garrett demanded.

So much for invisibility.

"I'm here for…you know. That coaching we discussed with Tony."

She struggled to say it without cringing. It was never supposed to come to this. Garrett should have taken umbrage and left for a high-paying job with one of their competitors by now.

He was still here.

Unfortunately, Tony had shared details of Rachel's "generous offer" to coach Garrett with the other partners. She'd received a flood of emails commending her on her team spirit, which admittedly helped make up for the substandard impression she'd left at breakfast the other day. She'd been thrilled…until she realized she would actually have to deliver on her offer, and the people who would make the decision on the promotion would be watching.

Garrett had rounded the table while she spoke. Now he was close to her...but not too close. She was reminded of that night at the oyster bar—not one of her most cherished memories, but one she had difficulty shaking—when she'd stumbled into his space and he'd drawn away.

Garrett had numerous ways of putting distance between himself and other people, she realized. Not just physical withdrawal, but the aloofness in his dark eyes, the carefully bland expression he adopted in meetings. The smart-ass remarks.

"We both know you never meant things to go this far," he said, quiet enough that his team wouldn't hear. "How about you walk out now and we forget all about it."

Oh, she was tempted. "Tony's asked me to report back to him, so I'll need to stay."

She figured the best way to handle this was to give Garrett some so-generic-as-to-be-useless feedback on his leadership abilities, since it would be stupid for her to actually help him. No point rolling up her pants to give The Shark a better bite.

He scowled. "In that case, you sit up there." He jerked his thumb in the direction of the head of the table. "Next to me, where I can keep an eye on you. If I hear so much as a peep out of you, you're out. Bring your chair."

No surprise that he didn't offer to carry it for her. Rachel squeezed down the side of the room, her chair alternately clanking against someone else's or banging into the wall. Adam, one of the account execs, offered to help. She gave Garrett a pointed look intended to compare his own manners unfavorably with his junior's, but refused Adam's assistance.

Halfway down the table, Natasha murmured, "Hi, Rachel."

"Hey." Rachel set the chair down and took a breather. "How's Kevin doing?" She sensed Garrett's impatience, and deliberately relaxed her stance.

"Great. His physical therapist says he'll be back playing basketball next month."

"Make sure he rubs liniment on that ankle before and after," Rachel said. She knew how important basketball was to Natasha's boyfriend.

"Will do, Rachel. Thanks."

"Any chance we might resume our meeting soon?" Garrett asked.

Rachel hefted her chair with an exaggerated grunt of exertion and clanked her way forward.

"Okay," Garrett said when she was in her designated position, "I'm going to brief you guys about Brightwater, then I'll take questions. We won't be discussing any creative ideas while Rachel's here as an observer."

Ready agreement from the team, though there were some apologetic glances toward her. The idea of three teams pitching for the same account had generated a buzz of excitement around the office.

Rachel had run the same kind of briefing for her own team yesterday, basically reporting what they'd learned at the client meeting. She didn't expect any surprises from Garrett.

But she got one. Yes, Garrett did say much the same as she had…but his disinterested manner fell away and he delivered a briefing that made Brightwater sound like the most exciting opportunity since…well, since that Lexus campaign the world loved so much.

Was he genuinely that excited about Brightwater? Because although she'd given her own team a comprehensive briefing, she wasn't sure if she'd left them with the kind of fervor she saw on his people's faces.

"Questions?" Garrett asked when he'd finished. "Anyone got any research areas they'd particularly like to cover? I want something from each of you."

He folded his arms and waited. Having said his piece, that wall of impatient aloofness was back in place.

It was as though he'd switched off a light.

The discussion limped along. A team member would present a decent suggestion for a research area, clearly wanting the approval of the man who'd just inspired them all, and Garrett would barely nod his head before moving on. Other, less-smart ideas, he simply shot down.

Rachel had never seen such a glaring lack of engagement. How could he have got so far in his career without paying the least attention to the emotional needs of others?

Rachel believed people gave more when they were encouraged, rather than intimidated. Paul Crane, the partner responsible for HR at KBC, had mentioned in an email supporting her plan to mentor Garret that Gar-

rett's team had the highest staff turnover. And yet...
Garrett was the one with the reputation for pulling together brilliant pitches, while she was stuck on "tame."

How did he ever get a girlfriend? Maybe getting the girl wouldn't be a problem, Rachel conceded—he probably charmed them with the kind of meaningless garbage he'd spouted with their client at the Brightwater meeting. *If you were a fruit, what fruit would you be, Cindy/Tammy/Jodie?* But *keeping* the girl might be more— She pulled her thoughts up smartly. What did she care about Garrett's seduction techniques?

"Any thoughts, Alice?" Garrett asked one of the artists, midway through a discussion of field trips to various Brightwater colleges. Rachel was a step ahead of him there—two of her team members were out at Brightwater campuses today. By lunchtime they would be emailing photos.

Alice made an inarticulate sound, then managed a faint, "No." She was a bright young thing—and Jonathan Key's goddaughter, which had got her the job here—but painfully shy.

"You can't keep doing this," Garrett told her. "The rest of the team can't be expected to carry you. You have two minutes to come up with an idea."

Rachel could practically see Alice's mind going blank. Poor girl.

"Garrett," she warned.

"Not a peep," he reminded her.

As if she would sit by and let Alice get shredded. She leaned in to him so the staff wouldn't hear, garnering a whiff of that pine-and-citrus scent of his. "If you start displaying some people skills, I promise I'll shut up."

He made an exasperated sound. "Alice," he said in a playing-nice voice, "you need to contribute more if you want to keep working at KBC."

Oh, boy. *This* was his idea of people skills? Threatening Alice with the boot? Rachel should be delighted—his incompetence was her best chance at winning the partnership—but Alice had turned white and looked as if she might faint or burst into tears. Or both. She would probably be the next casualty on Garrett's staff turnover list. A fate she didn't deserve, since she was a nice person and a talented artist.

Garrett wasn't done yet. "I'd like to hear your ideas as to what you can offer this firm," he added.

"Is that part of the two minutes?" Alice squeaked.

"No," he said with exaggerated patience that was every bit as intimidating as his ultimatum. "Forget the two minutes. Right now I want some halfway decent suggestions about other research areas." He glanced around the table. "Anyone? Anything?"

The entire team busied themselves flicking through Brightwater brochures, scribbling notes, or staring at their fingernails. If it hadn't been so tragic, Rachel would have laughed.

The silence stretched to biblical proportions as people hesitated to offer up ideas that would be either damned with faint praise, or dismissed. Garrett's face betrayed a mix of irritation and confusion, as if he couldn't figure out why this bunch of bright people didn't have two ideas to rub together.

At last Adam, the account exec who'd offered to carry Rachel's chair, spoke up. "It's going to be hard to promote the Brightwater brand—people care more about individual colleges' track records than they do about the company that owns them."

Rachel's team was already grappling with that issue.

"Maybe we should talk to parents of precollege kids to see if there's something that would make them care about the corporate brand," Adam said.

Garrett nodded. "Or to the kids themselves."

Since that was as close as Garrett came to wild enthusiasm, Adam carried on. "I think this is the kind of thing where kids really value their parents' input." Unfortunately, confidence turned him earnestly self-important, which Rachel could have told him Garrett would hate. "I know *I* did, when I was looking at colleges. It was, like, the first time in years I cared what my mom thought." Sensing he'd lost Garrett's interest—maybe because Garrett was folding a piece of paper into an airplane—Adam said, "You know what I mean? Didn't you pay attention to your mom's views on college?"

Garrett launched the paper plane. "My mom's dead."

Sympathy rippled around the table.

The plane crash-landed into the water jug.

Adam reddened. "Uh, sorry, Garrett. How did she, uh—"

"She picked up malaria on a missionary trip to Africa," Garrett said. "A particularly virulent strain that the doctors here couldn't treat. So, no, I don't know what you mean about parents and college decisions. But I take your point—figure out who you're going to question and how, and run it by me before the end of the day."

He pushed back in his chair. "Let's move on, people. Rachel, your mouth is hanging open."

Rachel snapped her jaw shut. *Another* story about his mother's death. Was this one true? Were any of them true?

Apparently sick of waiting, Garrett moved around the table, assigning research tasks to people who couldn't think up their own.

"Okay, you all know where you need to be," he concluded. "I'm visiting Brightwater's Porchester campus tomorrow—" Rachel and Clive would be on that trip, too "—then I'll be in the library on Friday. Call me on my cell if you need me."

"The library" was the glorified name for KBC's archive of former pitches and campaigns, on the fifty-fifth floor. Rachel wondered what he hoped to find there—it seemed an unlikely source of inspiration for a man who prided himself on his originality.

The meeting over, the team filed out, tension dropping by measurable degrees.

"Join us for a drink at O'Dooley's tonight?" Adam asked Rachel as he left.

"Love to." She noticed he didn't invite Garrett.

"Alice, don't forget," Garrett said, "I want to talk to you soon about your contribution."

Alice muttered something incoherent and fled, leaving Rachel and Garrett alone.

Rachel opened her mouth, but before she could speak, Garrett held up both hands, palms out. "Stop giving me those accusing looks. I don't care whose goddaughter she is, she's not pulling her weight. She doesn't fit here."

"So you threatened to fire her? Nice going." Rachel turned over an unused water glass and reached for the jug. Ugh, it still had that paper plane in it, but she wasn't about to indulge his bad behavior by fishing it out. With the soggy plane blocking the spout, the water came out in a trickle. She gave up when her glass was only half-full.

"I didn't threaten to fire her," he said.

"You told her that if she wanted to work at KBC, she had to contribute more."

"That's the truth, and Alice needs to think about it." He picked up Rachel's glass and took a swig. "This stuff tastes like paper."

"Are you saying you don't think Alice should move on?"

"How would I know?" He picked up his cold coffee, but the milky film on top deterred him from drinking it. "I guess, if this place isn't working for her, she might like somewhere else better."

Just the kind of grass-is-greener attitude that drove Rachel nuts. She turned her glass so she wouldn't drink from the same spot Garrett's mouth had just touched. "Alice is part of the KBC family. You don't tell family to go find somewhere else. You help them find a way to stay."

Garrett blinked. "KBC is an advertising agency, Rachel. Not a family."

"That's not quite true. We're an independent agency,

one of the few large firms that's not part of a global conglomerate."

"It's still an advertising agency," he said.

"Our partnership structure gives us more of a personal, family feel," she persisted.

He snorted. "Doesn't feel anything like my family."

It was hard to imagine him in the bosom of a nurturing family. Easier to picture Garrett Calder arriving in the world fully grown, complete with cool, dark eyes, hard-planed cheeks and toned physique. People-repelling shields firmly in place. Rachel took a swig from her glass, finding the room suddenly stifling.

"If this is family, it must really bug you that Papa Tony is willing to fire you," Garrett observed.

She sputtered on her paper-flavored water. "That's not personal."

"My point exactly."

She felt as if she'd swum out of her depth.

"You should have been nicer to Adam, too." She found firmer ground and dug her toes in. "You didn't need to make him feel bad about your mother's death."

Garrett glared. "I don't see the need to pander to his curiosity."

"People ask because they care," she said.

He groaned. "Not more of this family crap. My mother's death is no one's business but mine."

"Are any of the versions I've heard true?" she asked. "The cancer, the plane crash, the malaria?"

"What part of *none of your business* don't you understand?" Garrett growled. What was wrong with her, that she ignored the don't-go-there signs that worked with everyone else? He'd never met a woman who needled him so much. And so effectively. She was like a terrier with a bone, and the bone was his innermost thoughts. Which like all good bones should stay buried.

"Oh, no." Rachel had frozen in place, eyes wide, fingers pressed to her lips.

Somehow, irritatingly, Garrett knew what she was thinking. He was tempted to let her jump to wild conclusions, to make her feel bad, but doubtless it would backfire on him, as things tended, weirdly, to do with her. "Rein in that imagination, Rachel," he ordered. "There was nothing sinister about my mom's death." No violence, no suicide.

She let out a breath. "Really? You're not just being nice?"

Surely she knew him better than that. He said solemnly, "I swear. On your amazing legs."

"Stupid question," she scolded herself. "Garrett, the thing about juniors like Alice and Adam…" She leaned forward to make her own point, and the movement shifted her chair on its castors, causing her knee to brush momentarily against his.

Garrett edged his chair back a little.

"Will you stop doing that?" she snapped. "Do you really think getting within two feet of another person will kill you?"

"What are you talking about?" he demanded. She was well within two feet, near enough for him to see individual lashes above brown eyes that sparked with annoyance. Lips that, close up, were fuller than he'd realized.

"Every time I get within your privacy shield, you retreat," she said.

"Do I?" He thought about it, and decided she was exaggerating. "No, I don't."

To his shock, she grabbed his hand where it rested on the table.

"What the hell?" he said.

"It's not so bad, connecting with other people, is it?" She curled her fingers into his palm; automatically, he splayed his fingers rigid in resistance. "It doesn't hurt a bit."

"Are you nuts?" He pulled back, but she hung on with sudden, she-devil strength. "You realize this is sexual harassment." He tried her own tactic on her.

"Let's call it therapy," she said.

His hand in hers felt so strange, he wondered if maybe she hadn't been exaggerating after all. His muscles tensed—all of them, it seemed—and the urge to get away, to get out of here, bordered on a physical ache. What was wrong with him?

"Let go," he bit out, struggling to stay calm. Then he realized... "But you can't do that, can you? You don't know how to let go of a dud boyfriend, or a firm that doesn't give a damn about you."

She hissed. "Better than not knowing how to hold on to something good. Like one of your many *excellent* jobs, or the people on your team. Is there anything you hold on to, Garrett? I'd bet money you don't have any kind of relationship with your family."

Dammit, she did *not* get to do this. He chose who

got to talk to him about personal stuff and she wasn't on the list.

No one was.

CHAPTER EIGHT

IF GARRETT WASN'T CAREFUL, he'd end up yelling. He didn't want Rachel to know she had that much power over him.

Deliberately, he reerected the barrier she'd somehow broken through when she'd grabbed his hand.

"This is childish," he said calmly. "I suggest you end this game now."

"Certainly." She matched him for calm. "Just as soon as you promise to apologize to Alice and Adam and to try harder with them from now on."

He snorted.

"Why wouldn't you?" she said. "You need to, if you want to win the partnership."

"Only one thing will win the partnership—" an experimental tug of his hand failed to dislodge her grip "—no matter what Tony's saying right now. And that's brilliant creative."

"That's not true." But she licked her lips. Those full lips.

"Worried you're not brilliant enough?" he taunted.

Her fingers twitched around his hand. "Nope. What's more, I know creative isn't the only consideration.

This firm values its people…and therefore my team-management skills."

"If you're right," he said, "apologizing to Alice and Adam would score me points with the partners. And that would hurt your chances."

"The thought of you out empathizing me is the least of my worries," she said. "What matters is, those guys are your team. Some of them have been my team in the past. We're all a part of this firm."

"Until we're not," he said. "Those kids are replaceable, just like everyone else. And in a few weeks' time, two of us will get fired. I hate to say it, Rach, but your loyalty is misguided."

"Rach*el*," she corrected. "And I don't agree that people are replaceable— What are you doing?"

He'd flipped his hand within her grip, his fingers now curled around hers. Her fingers were slender, fine-boned…but surprisingly strong. The nails were painted a pale pink, a misleading suggestion of demureness.

"I'm showing you I can hold on," Garrett said. "Now you need to show me you can let go."

She pffed. "As soon as you promise to take a gentler approach with Alice. And be nice to Adam. He's trying his hardest."

He scraped his index finger across her palm. She gasped. And tightened her grip.

"Careful, Rach. Are you sure you're brave enough to play chicken with me?" he asked.

She squared her shoulders. "I am if you are."

"That's generally how chicken works," he said drily.

Who would have thought he'd be having such a bizarre battle of wits with Rachel Frye? And enjoying it so much?

They stood like that, holding hands, for maybe another half minute.

"You have sexy fingers," he said in an attempt to creep her out.

"You have a sexy butt," she returned.

He was pretty sure she hadn't been looking. "Thanks," he said. "Good to know."

Clive stuck his head around the door. "Hey, Garrett—" He registered their clasped hands and stopped.

Rachel groaned inwardly. Why hadn't she pulled away when she had the chance? Somehow, it had felt important to rise to Garrett's challenge. Now it just felt stupid.

Garrett squeezed her hand hard enough to not quite hurt. She gritted her teeth and stayed put.

Clive chuckled. "Three's a crowd, right?"

"Sorry," Garrett said with no regret.

"I'll catch you later." Clive waved in farewell as he left.

"Why does he want to talk to you?" Rachel asked.

"No idea." Garrett's thumb traced a circle on the back of her hand. Something clenched deep inside Rachel. Her hand must have tensed, because his gaze sharpened on hers. Slowly, holding her gaze, he traced the circle again. She put every ounce of willpower into not blinking, into suppressing that response.

I am not attracted to Garrett Calder.

"Very good," Garrett said admiringly, sending a flutter of warmth through her.

She kept her face immobile. "I have no idea what you mean."

"I wonder who'll be the next person through that door," he mused. "Probably Papa Tony."

"No!" Rachel said, dismayed. Tony would hardly trust her ability to coach Garrett if he came in and found them holding hands.

To her surprise, his face softened a fraction. "Will you let go if I agree to at least pay lip service to the idea of being nice to the junior staff?"

"You mean...you'll *pretend* to care?" she asked.

"You say *pretend,* I say *fake it,*" he said lightly.

It was a silly offer, a nonoffer. But something about holding Garrett's hand gave the words *lip service* a whole new meaning. Rachel found her eyes drawn to his mouth, her brain following swiftly behind. Making it impossible for her to explain that lip service was not an acceptable alternative to genuine respect for his team.

Though it was a thousand percent better than what he was doing now.

Garrett caught the direction of her gaze...and for the first time since he'd started work at KBC, she felt the full effect of his smile, the real thing.

There was a sudden absence of air.

Rachel concentrated on not gasping. *This is The Shark. Don't show weakness.* "I suppose...what you said...would be a start," she said.

Garrett released her hand. The sudden lack of contact left her chilled, her fingers tingling. Rachel rubbed them against her skirt as he strode out of the room without looking back. As if he'd already forgotten they'd held hands for ten minutes.

Doesn't matter. Garrett had agreed to try harder with his team. Or to pretend to try harder.

I won, Rachel told herself. She ignored the little voice that asked, *Are you sure about that?* Ignored the prickling in her fingers that wouldn't let *her* forget she'd been holding hands with The Shark.

THE SHORT, ASSERTIVE BUZZ of the doorbell at six o'clock on Wednesday evening told Stephanie the identity of her visitor. Her pulse jumped. She hadn't expected him so soon—was this a good sign?

She pressed the button that would let her guest into Garrett's building, then waited for the firm rap on the door of the condo. *Please,* she prayed, as she went to open it.

"Did you even look through the peephole?" Dwight demanded.

He knew she hadn't; he would have been watching. Stephanie didn't answer, just stepped aside to let him in. His service khakis, his daily office attire, suggested he'd come straight from work.

"*And* you buzzed me up without asking who I was." He was rigid with anger, far too much anger over such a trivial thing. "I could have been a serial killer."

"I knew it was you. I recognized your touch on the buzzer."

He stared at her as if she was crazy. Then he turned his head away, focusing on a blank stretch of wall. Garrett really needed to decorate.

"I can't believe you came *here*," he said.

Stephanie had texted him her whereabouts on Monday night so he wouldn't worry. And so he would know where to find her. She hadn't expected him to pursue her so soon. He was more the type to let her cool her heels.

"I wasn't sure Garrett would let me stay," she admitted.

Dwight snorted. "He'd do anything to annoy me."

She didn't doubt that was part of Garrett's rationale, but she believed there was also something less bitter, some buried seam of tenderness inside her stepson. She was counting on uncovering it. "It was kind of him. I'd have been forced to find a hotel otherwise."

"You have a perfectly good home in New London," Dwight said. "You have. Me."

The hesitation jolted her. For half a second, he'd sounded vulnerable.

"I can't come back until things change, Dwight," she said.

"I still don't understand why you left. Your note made no sense."

If he hadn't understood what she'd been trying to tell him the past few months, it was unlikely he'd suddenly get it now. Maybe if she'd said it a few years ago…but it wasn't until she'd had some bleeding in her first trimester, and the doctor had told them to abstain from intercourse for a couple of months, that she'd realized their excellent sex life had been masking other problems. That every other aspect of their marriage was unsatisfactory.

She'd always known Dwight could be too *command-*

ing; it was a by-product of his job. But his desire for her had always balanced the power between them. With sex off the table, she'd discovered how uncompromising he could be, how little he was prepared to give emotionally. The warrior in him, without the moderating influence of the lover, demanded total surrender.

"I don't want this baby to feel as if doing things your way is the only way to be good enough for you. To never know your unconditional love." She perched on an armchair. "I don't want our child to leave us and never speak to us, like Garrett. Though I'm not blaming you for all of that," she said quickly. She did blame Dwight for most of it. But Garrett was far from perfect—too stubborn, like his father—and Stephanie herself had made some mistakes in those early years.

"I've told you I'm willing to. Do things differently," he said. "I meant that."

"But I don't believe you can," she said. "Unless you want to change with your own heart, not just because I want you to, it won't happen."

"This mumbo jumbo psychobabble is meaningless," he said. "Stephanie, you're pregnant and it's playing havoc with your brain. The car's downstairs—collect your things, I'm taking you home."

It was an order from the Admiral.

Funny how she'd got used to obeying him without realizing that was what she was doing. He was sixteen years older than she was, and when they'd married, she'd assumed he knew best about most things. They'd become entrenched in this pattern, where he gave orders and she followed them. Stephanie swallowed. "No."

Dwight reddened. "If you expect me to wait while you get over this tantrum, you'll be waiting a long time."

He'd always described Garrett's behavior as a "tantrum," too. Who knew Stephanie would share this bond with her difficult stepson?

"Did you ever love me?" she asked, then clapped a hand over her mouth. She shouldn't have asked. Because if the answer was no, he wouldn't lie.

He turned almost purple. "Of course I did. I do. And I'll love our baby."

She let out a breath of relief. He meant it...as far as he *could* mean it. Which was better than nothing. But he didn't know the love she meant. The kind of consuming love that would make you go against all good sense and do anything to be with that person. As she had, marrying a man so much older than her, a man fresh from the loss of his first wife. His character had been stamped on his rugged face. She'd known he would be faithful. He would protect her with his life. Powerful factors in themselves. But even more than that, she'd been giddy with the excitement of having this strong, honorable man wanting her so much he'd trembled in her arms.

Yet when he'd proposed, she'd hesitated. And he'd said, "I won't ask you again." She'd loved him too much to let him get away.

"I love you, too," she said. "More than you know. But having this baby has made me realize I can't live with you. Not the way we've always been." She paused. "Dwight, I need to be able to do things my way without being afraid of losing your love."

"This is ridiculous," he muttered. "You have medical appointments...did you think about that?"

"I can get to my doctor more easily from here than from home." She'd chosen an obstetrician on the Upper East Side in order to be close to Dwight's office, if he wanted to attend appointments with her. But he was too old-school for that—his halfhearted agreement to attend was nearly always superseded by some important meeting.

"We have the admiralty dinner in Annapolis this weekend," he reminded her. "I expect my wife to accompany me."

She'd forgotten about the event that was the highlight of Dwight's year. Momentarily, she wavered. "You can go without me."

"And what do I tell people?" he demanded.

So this was why he'd come running so fast. Not because he missed her desperately. Although she knew Dwight was too self-contained, too disciplined for desperation, it stung.

"Tell them...tell them Garrett needed me so I stayed in New York with him," she said.

"But that's not true." He was the most honest man she knew. If their marriage wasn't working, it wasn't because Dwight had pretended to be anything other than he was. It was because she'd refused to face their differences.

She thought about Garrett and the walls he'd built around himself. "Maybe it *is* true."

Dwight snorted, suddenly sounding very much like his son. "He's been spinning stories to turn you against me. He was always much closer to his mother. Too close, it seems."

Stephanie couldn't help smiling. She couldn't think of anyone less of a mommy's boy than Garrett.

"Don't take his side against me," Dwight roared.

Her smile vanished. "You need to leave. That yelling isn't good for the baby."

As if to bear her out, the baby kicked hard. The sensation still felt entirely miraculous to Stephanie. She broke off, to caress her stomach.

"Is it kicking?" Dwight's hand twitched at his side; one thing he was good at was sharing the joy of a kicking baby. In that scrupulously fair way of his, he never assigned the baby a gender. Stephanie alternated between being certain it was another adorable boy, and thinking of an angelic little girl.

"Just go, Dwight," she said. She didn't want to soften toward him, and if she let him feel the baby move…

"I won't ask you again," he said, and she shivered at the echo of the day he'd proposed to her. *I should have turned him down.*

"Come home with me now," he said.

Like all those years ago, she wasn't able to say no. But she did manage to shake her head in refusal.

Dwight's still-flushed face paled. His hand lifted in a jerky movement, as if he might salute her. He let it drop.

Then he left.

CHAPTER NINE

STEPHANIE HAD BEEN occupying his spare room for three nights and Garrett was ready for her to go. He could tolerate her forced cheerfulness and the clutter of herbal tea bags and vitamin pills on his kitchen counter. But she used the bathroom every ten minutes during the night, and while he'd never considered himself a particularly light sleeper, he was used to living alone. He hadn't had a decent night's sleep since she arrived.

When he got up at six on Thursday, she was already in the kitchen, making herself a pastrami sandwich. A strange choice for breakfast. Must be a pregnancy thing.

Garrett poured milk over some granola and ate standing at the counter, wishing he'd had more sleep. Last night had been even worse than the ones before. Not only had he had Stephanie's disturbances to contend with, he'd been oddly alert, thinking about holding hands with Rachel. More than alert...turned on.

Too much going on. My brain is melting.

"You have that college visit today, right?" Stephanie asked.

He grunted. He didn't like talking early in the morning.

"It's a beautiful day. It'll be nice to get out of the city," she said wistfully.

"You could always go home," he suggested.

She didn't say a word, but the knife she was using to slice a tomato clattered against the board.

"Forget it," he muttered. It wasn't like he needed to sleep or anything. On the other hand… "How are you going on finding somewhere else to stay?"

"I'm working on it," she said evasively.

That didn't sound good.

"I'll bet Dad's missing you," Garrett tried. But he couldn't make it sound convincing and her eye roll said it wasn't worth trying.

"He told me you're hoping to make partner in your firm," she said.

"Did he tell you he doesn't think I'm up to the job?"

"*I* think you are," she said.

Garrett neither needed nor wanted the consolation prize of Stephanie's approval. And he certainly didn't want her thinking it was any kind of motivation for him.

"Is there anything I can do to help with the pitch you're working on?" she asked. "Maybe typing documents or searching the internet?"

"Nope."

Stephanie stopped slicing, knife poised in midair, in one of those frozen moments he was getting used to. "Baby's kicking," she said.

"Uh-huh," he said.

"Would you like to feel?" she asked.

He started. "You mean, touch your stomach?"

She beamed, and he remembered her smiling like that when he'd first met her. "You won't get germs," she promised.

"I'm good." He dumped his bowl in the sink and rinsed it with a blast of cold water. "Time I left."

After brushing his teeth, he grabbed his laptop bag. He called a goodbye to Stephanie in the split second before the door closed behind him.

BY THE TIME THEY NEARED the end of their tour of Brightwater's Porchester College campus in Connecticut, Garrett was aggravated beyond measure.

He blamed Rachel. Something about holding her hand yesterday had made it impossible for him to ignore her, even when she was jabbering on at Clive about subjects of zero interest to Garrett. Yeah, she had quite a nice voice, but it was possible to have too much of a good thing.

She'd taken his agreement to *pretend* to be pleasant to his staff—a concession made purely because it disturbed him to witness her blind loyalty to the firm, loyalty that would bite her on her cute butt very soon—as an invitation to involve him in all kinds of conversations in which he had no interest.

So far, she'd asked his opinion of the new corporate values KBC had defined, whether he agreed it would be wonderful for working moms if the firm established a day-care center in that empty space on the fifty-fifth floor, and what would be the best retirement gift for Joseph King, one of the founding partners and the outgoing chief creative officer.

She was wanting him to *care.*

She was out of luck.

His lack of response had discouraged her—eventually—and she'd turned her attention to Clive. The two of them had vocally admired the campus facilities, and now, as they headed to the cafeteria for lunch, Clive was sharing some laid-back anecdote from his days as a student at Columbia.

"Did you go to college, Rachel?" Clive asked, when he'd finished his story. "I seem to recall you were pretty young when I joined KBC."

She shook her head. "My folks were perpetually broke and I didn't want to go into debt to get an education."

Maybe that explained why she'd been looking so longingly around this place, Garrett thought. "Everyone has student loans," he said, in case she was feeling sorry for herself. He'd had loans himself, despite his family's comfortable finances. Dwight had believed Garrett should make his own way in the world, and since he hadn't been "sensible enough" to have the military pay for his studies...

"I didn't want to risk not being able to pay them back," Rachel said.

"You cut off the whole possibility of an education and went to work in a mail room because you were scared?" Everything about her was irritating him today, most of all the fact that his gaze was constantly drawn to her against his will. Drawn to specific parts of her that he was suddenly weirdly aware of: legs, butt, hands, lips. Eyes. "That's dumb."

"It worked out perfectly," she said. "I joined a wonderful firm that gave me the opportunity to move into account exec training within a year, and met some lovely people."

"Oh, yeah, your surrogate family." She sounded almost like an orphan, but she'd said her family couldn't afford college. "What's wrong with your real family?" he asked. "Are your parents in jail? No, let me guess…a psychiatric institution?" he said with relish. That would make sense of Rachel's bizarre hand-holding proclivities.

"Of course not," she said coldly.

That's better, Rach. Back off.

Clive chuckled. "What would you have studied if you'd gone to college, Rachel?" he asked.

She didn't hesitate. "Optometry."

Garrett would have pegged her for English lit or psychology, but he wasn't about to ask. Clive, however, did.

"For some reason optometry just really appealed," she said. "I loved biology."

"Can't have loved it that much, if you weren't prepared to take out a loan to study it." Garrett followed Rachel through the door to the cafeteria, which Clive held open.

"What did you study, Garrett?" she asked.

"Marketing, at Stanford."

"So that's when you fell in love with advertising," she said as they lined up for their food.

There she went again, wanting him to care. "It's a job," he said.

Clive stacked so many cartons of French fries on his tray, you'd think they'd announced an imminent global shortage.

"That's so unfair." Rachel ladled minestrone into a bowl. "I love French fries, but if I eat them more than twice a week I blow up like a puffer fish."

"I can imagine," Garrett said, giving up the battle not to eye those long, slim legs again. He set his laptop bag on his tray while he fished inside for his wallet. His hand encountered a Saran-wrapped bundle. He pulled it out.

"What the hell?" he muttered. A pastrami sandwich. He turned it over, just to be sure.

Stephanie had made him a packed lunch. What was she trying to achieve?

"Garrett's got a girlfriend," Rachel chanted under her breath. Was it his imagination, or did she sound annoyed? He imagined she'd be pretty uptight to think he'd held her hand while he had a girlfriend.

"She isn't my girlfriend," he said. Not to reassure Rachel, he just didn't want to assign Stephanie any role in his life. Whatever his father's wife was playing at, she could quit right now. He wasn't looking for a mommy to pack him a lunch. Even if she'd made a lucky guess that pastrami was his favorite.

His handling had opened a gap in the Saran, and the tantalizing smell of pastrami and tomato and onion wafted out. Dammit, Stephanie was doing exactly the same thing as Rachel. More subtly, perhaps, but she was latching on to him and trying to make him care.

Never going to happen.

He sealed the sandwich firmly up again, cutting off that aroma, then dropped it into the nearest trash can.

"Wow," Rachel said, "she's really not your girl-friend."

"I would have eaten that," Clive protested.

"You're welcome to it," Garrett said.

Clive glanced back at the trash can with a disturbing degree of interest. Then he shrugged. "It's okay. They have burgers up ahead."

Garrett quashed the thought that he'd rather have eaten the pastrami sandwich.

They found a table near the exit. As they ate, Garrett was unreasonably aware of Rachel, sipping at her soup, occasionally dabbing those lips with a napkin.

Clive went to refill his bottomless soda, and since those two had been doing all the talking, silence fell.

"Have you got what you need out of this visit, Garrett?" Rachel asked.

"Yep," he lied. Because it was none of her business if the initial ideas he'd had for Brightwater's creative no longer excited him, and nothing else had popped up in their place. Something would come to him. It always did.

"I've found it quite inspiring," she said. "This is going to be my best pitch ever."

He knew bravado when he heard it. She was worried. Some of his own anxiety, which he hadn't quite acknowledged, lifted.

"Do you think your Brightwater campaign will be better than the Lexus one?" she asked.

"The best is yet to come," he assured her.

She looked a little sick. "So, you're taking it seriously?"

"Of course." They both knew there was no *of course* about it.

She broke a piece off the roll that had come with her soup and spread butter on it. "Why did you leave all those other agencies, Garrett?"

He ran a hand around the back of his neck. "Different reasons at different times."

"So, what are you generally looking for when you join a new firm?" A few crumbs had flaked off her roll and she pressed her finger into them to pick them up.

He wondered if she was considering applying for new jobs now. Smart idea. Or maybe she was just trying to work out his plans. "As far as possible, to be my own boss," he said.

"Wouldn't you be better off starting your own agency?" she asked. "You wouldn't have to answer to anyone at all."

"Tempting as that sounds, big firms have more resources," he said. "I'm not interested in running on a shoestring."

"So your ideal agency is big, but gives you plenty of autonomy," she mused.

"I guess," he said impatiently. He realized she was frowning. "What's wrong now?"

"Do you realize KBC is your ideal firm?" she asked.

"No, it's not."

"Lots of autonomous units, the partnership structure, no head office driving us mad. No wonder you haven't quit in disgust," she said. "You love that place."

"I don't."

But her words struck a chord. He did like it at KBC. More than anywhere else he'd been.

He didn't want to leave yet.

Which meant the partnership was no longer just about proving something to his father, or beating Rachel or telling KBC where it could put its promotion.

All these years he'd stayed detached from anything he couldn't control, always able to walk away, and now Rachel Frye had come along with her constant questions and her insistence on making things matter... And dammit, suddenly he *cared*.

Hell. What a mess.

On Friday, Rachel retreated to a place that offered guaranteed peace of mind: the New York Public Library. For a century, the Beaux Arts building had dominated 42nd Street at 5th Avenue. Its marble halls were as solid and permanent as you could wish a building to be.

She needed solid. The past few days she'd felt horribly unsettled. Worried by Garrett's insistence that whoever had the best creative would win, that team skills would count for nothing. Alarmed at the realization that KBC wasn't just another advertising agency to him. Wasn't as replaceable as he claimed everything was.

Walking down the marble hallway with its carved wooden ceiling didn't produce the usual sense of calm. Maybe the Periodicals Room would do it, she thought, as she stepped through the deep doorway.

More than any other, this room inspired her, with its dark paneled walls, historic murals and brass lamps. Some of her best ideas had come while she was immersed in the sense of something so much more time-less than an advertising campaign.

And right now, she needed to go back to what she knew worked, rather than letting Garrett spook her. She'd exaggerated slightly when she'd told him her cre-ative was her best ever. It was a good start, but it needed more…something.

Research was the antidote to an ideas shortage, and the Periodicals Room, empty at nine o'clock on a Fri-day morning, was the repository of every kind of maga-zine and journal. At the service window, Rachel asked the librarian for copies of *Higher Education Monthly,* along with student reviews from various colleges. She set up her laptop computer on one of the long, polished tables and settled in to read and make notes.

She was so immersed in her reading, she wasn't aware of Garrett's arrival until she heard his voice right behind her. "Are you following me?"

She jumped, knocking a couple of sheets of paper to the floor. "How could I be following you, when I got here first?" She bent to retrieve her pages. "Go away." It was bad enough having to deal with him in the office.

"You heard me mention in the meeting the other day that I planned to come here," he said.

"I thought you meant the library at KBC."

"Why would I waste my time with past campaigns that have already come and gone?" He loomed over her. "I've had enough, Rachel. This is my space. Give it up."

"You can't call dibs on the New York Public Li-brary," she said, outraged. "This is my favorite place in all of New York." He jolted. What was that about?

"Go on, ask that librarian—" She pointed to the woman pushing a cart piled with magazines. "She's seen me here before."

As Rachel spoke, the woman noticed them, and obviously realized they were talking about her. She smiled widely and left her cart to come say hello.

Which was way more recognition than Rachel had expected. "Uh, hi," she said, flattered. "How are you?"

Only to discover the smile wasn't for her.

"Garrett, my dear." The librarian grabbed his hand—the same one Rachel had recently become acquainted with. "How nice to see you."

"Hi, Mrs. G." Garrett kissed her cheek. "I came in a couple of weeks ago, but you weren't around."

"Vacation," she said with a grimace Rachel recognized. That of a person who feels cut adrift when forced to take a vacation.

"I think you know Rachel Frye," Garrett said.

Mrs. G. lifted her spectacles and scrutinized her. "I do believe I've seen you in here."

"Often," Rachel said firmly.

Garrett gave her a pitying look.

"What can I bring you to look at, Garrett?" Mrs. G. asked.

Good grief, he was getting table service.

"The usual, thanks." He propped himself against the table, facing Rachel, legs stretched in front of him. Rachel suspected anyone else would have been told to use a chair. "And do you have any Spiderman comics?"

She figured that was the same kind of question as, *What kind of fruit are you?* A joke.

"No Spiderman." The librarian's smile was indulgent. "I'll be right back with your *MAD* magazines."

"You come here to read *MAD?*" Rachel asked as the woman returned to her trolley.

"Pithy satire on all the essential issues. Much more useful than—" Garrett flipped the cover of Rachel's periodical *"—Higher Education Monthly."*

Surely *MAD* magazine was a joke, too. But it couldn't be, because the librarian had known what magazine he wanted. It would never have occurred to Rachel to read *MAD*. Was that the secret to Garrett's creative genius?

Garrett unzipped his laptop bag. "I know why you're here, Rachel. But you won't achieve anything with this."

He knew she was panicking about her creative?

"I'm the first to admit I'm not a great team player," he said, "but you keep overstepping the boundary."

What was he talking about?

He set a notepad and pencil on the table. "No matter what you'd like to believe, nothing at KBC matters to me as much as you think it should, so don't drag me into your little attachment disorder."

"Excuse me?" she said.

"You're latching on," he said, "and you need to stop."

"Latching on to what?"

"To me," he said, as if she was stupid. "You think that because I don't feel the way you do about KBC, I'm the one with the problem. So you want to fix me...turn me into a codependent person like yourself."

"Garrett," she said, "you've been watching too much *Dr. Phil.* Drop the therapy-speak and try to interact like a normal human being."

"That's exactly what I mean," he said. "You think you get to define *normal*. I have a perfectly healthy interaction system—it just doesn't happen to involve bonding with every person on the planet. So leave me out of your game of office Happy Families."

She leaned back in her chair. "Let me get this straight. You think I came to the library to *bond* with you." She couldn't decide whether to be insulted or to laugh.

"You can't help yourself," he said. "I've seen you giving gum to the janitor. But you're wasting your time with me."

Once she'd given gum to the janitor, for his kids. Probably everyone did things like that, except Garrett. Rachel glanced around the room. Still deserted—if she slapped him now no one would see.

Other than Mrs. G., returning with a small bundle of *MAD* magazines.

"I can't find the latest issue." The librarian set them on the table next to Garrett's butt. Still no admonition to sit down. "I'll keep looking."

"Thanks, Mrs. G." He picked up a magazine and flicked through it, ignoring Rachel.

The librarian regarded him with something like fondness. As if she'd like to go up on tiptoe and ruffle his hair. "Your mother would laugh to see you still reading *MAD* magazine in here," she said.

His mother? Rachel stiffened.

"Yeah," he muttered reluctantly to Mrs. G.

The librarian moved away. Rachel kept staring at Garrett.

He ignored her for a full ten seconds. Then, without looking up, he said belligerently, "I'm not going to talk about it, so don't even try."

"Every time I think you're a jerk, I come back to this thing with your mother," she said, "and it seems there must be more to you."

"You are out of line on so many counts," he said. "First up, you don't know anything about me or my mother, and you have no right to even think about us. Second, there's nothing more to me, and third, if there was, it would be none of your damned business."

She ignored that rant. "And then there's the interesting fact that you couldn't bring yourself to be rude to a sweet old librarian, even when she mentioned your mom."

"I could have been rude if I wanted," he growled.

"Don't worry, I won't tell anyone." She made a zipping motion across her mouth. "So, Mrs. G. knew your mom?"

He scowled. "Didn't you just zip that up?"

"Broken zipper." Rachel pushed *Higher Education Monthly* away. "Is she a friend of your family? Or did your mom work here? Or—"

"I told you, I'm not talking to you."

"Or is she a relative? Godmother? Fourth cousin twice removed?"

"Let it go, Rachel." His favorite line, this time spoken without his usual bored intonation. This time, he was angry.

Oddly, she enjoyed seeing him angry. She wondered what Dr. Phil would say about that.

"Is she your neighbor?" Rachel asked.

"She's a librarian, dammit," he snapped. "This library was my mom's favorite place in all of New York," he said. "And she loved this room the most."

Rachel crumpled a piece of paper and threw it at him. For once, he wasn't prepared and it bounced off his forehead.

"What was that for?" he demanded.

"That's what I just told you about me. You think I don't recognize my own story? Must try harder, Garrett."

"I don't have to try anything at all," he retorted. "But for the record, it's true. Mom did love this place. This room."

She had believed him before and been fooled. But at that stage she'd had no reason to suspect a lie, and hadn't looked for any signs of it. Now she studied his face. Didn't help. Garrett Calder gave nothing away unless he chose to.

He picked up his pencil. "Now go," he said. "I have work to do."

"Was your mom really a missionary?" she asked.

He groaned. "No."

Rachel didn't bother asking if she'd had malaria. Or died in a plane crash or of cancer.

"Did she like Doris Day movies?"

His gaze wandered the room as if he was picturing his mom in this space. His face softened. "She loved them."

Rachel swallowed over a lump in her throat. "Did she—"

"No more questions," he said, snapping back into that irritating aloofness.

"Do you tell so many different stories about your mom just to make other people feel bad?" she asked.

"You heard me say, 'No more questions,' right?"

"Because that's what it seems like," she persisted.

"Do you think the reason your ad campaigns are so boring is because you read dull magazines?" he flashed back.

Ouch! Rachel put a protective hand on her stack of *Higher Education Monthly*. "Did your mom really die on your birthday?"

"Yes," he said tightly. "Did I ever tell you that campaign you did for Finegold Butter totally sucked?"

She gasped. The Finegold campaign hadn't *sucked,* but nor had it been her finest piece of work. "How old were you when your mom died?"

"Remind me how many CLIOs you've been nominated for?" he countered.

"I'm hopeful that Aunt Betty will swing it for me this year," she said. And wished she'd just admitted "none." She truly was hoping the Aunt Betty campaign would garner her first nomination, but now she'd left herself vulnerable. The announcement was only a week away. No way would Garrett forget this conversation before then. "I think your mom died recently," she suggested.

They were playing chicken again, only this felt like far higher stakes than holding his hand. Right now, that hand was curled into a fist around his pencil.

"She didn't," Garrett said, clearly torn between reluctance to tell her anything more and a desire to prove her wrong. "Hey, I have an idea. Since you're so uncreative, have you ever considered sleeping your way to the top? I've seen Tony watching your legs."

She raised her eyebrows to acknowledge a good shot. "What would your mom think of the stories you fabricate about her death?" She felt a bizarre exhilaration that she was still standing, metaphorically speaking. Still in the battle.

Tension pulsed between them. When Garrett spoke, his calm was almost scary. "She doesn't think about them. She's dead."

An evasion, if ever she'd heard one. "Do you even remember her?"

CHAPTER TEN

Too far.

In the silence, the pencil in Garrett's hand snapped.

He leaned right into her, letting her see the fury he knew would be in his eyes.

"I remember her," he snarled. "My father took all of five minutes to get over her death and find himself a new wife. And my brother is so cozy with his stepmother, I doubt he even remembers he had another mom. But I remember everything."

Garrett was so livid, he was literally seeing red spots before his eyes. His long-simmering resentment of his father, Stephanie and his brother had erupted into fresh, hot anger fueled by Rachel.

Who was the most provoking woman he'd ever met. He couldn't believe he'd let her goad him into saying this much.

He was about to tear a strip off her, library quiet be damned, when she started blinking, and her mouth went all soft and—and quivery.

He groaned, knowing exactly why she was reacting this way. Her thing about families. About holding on.

Garrett cursed. "Stop it, Rachel."

"Stop what?" She blinked harder, faster.

He tossed the pieces of broken pencil onto the table. To his annoyance, the softness of her mouth was doing a number on his anger, taking the edge off. "Wipe that pitiful, pitying look off your face." He *liked* that she'd shown a marked lack of sympathy for him until now.

"It's not pity." She sniffed. "I'm just...honored that you told me all that."

"I didn't tell you. You badgered it out of me."

Her smile was watery. "It can't have been easy for you."

"Rachel," he warned. "Back off. So I told you a few things about my mother. That doesn't make us friends."

"We're not strangers," she said, blinking again.

"We're colleagues." But they both knew that he hadn't told any other colleague what he'd just told her. Garrett had only himself to blame if she got the wrong idea. He'd come to the library to get away from other people—Rachel in particular. He should have walked out the moment he saw her here.

At least her mouth was no longer quivering; he wasn't sure how much more he could take of that. Unfortunately, in their natural state, her lips were full and nicely shaped and more tempting than he could believe.

"We're more than colleagues," she said. "Whether you like it or not. And that's not me *latching on*. That's the way it is."

"Or," he said, "you're an attractive woman and I just spun you my best pickup sob story."

She gave him a contemptuous look. "Not even you are that much of a jerk."

"That's what you think. I'm strongly considering kissing you," he said.

Her eyes widened. "Don't you dare."

That was more like it. Now he had her on the back foot. Kissing Rachel might be a very bad idea, but if it put her off-balance and trivialized what he'd just told her, that was good.

"Makes a lot of sense to me," he said. Her bristle of alarm made him feel a lot more cheerful. "You told me the other day you like my butt—"

"I didn't mean that, I never even looked at your butt!"

"And I definitely like your legs." It wasn't her legs he was eyeing right now... He found the vee of her rose-pink wrap-style dress. "Maybe I'd like the whole—"

"Don't you dare say *hog*," she warned.

"Shebang," he said, grinning.

"I apologize," she said quickly. "I shouldn't have pestered you about your mom."

Now she would concede she'd overstepped the mark. Now that she was worried he might do the same, and kiss her.

Why the hell shouldn't he?

She pulled a fresh copy of *Higher Education Monthly* from her stack, flipped open the cover and bent over the magazine.

He gave her half a minute, to lull her fears. "I've always envied people who can read upside down," he said.

Wordlessly, she turned the magazine right way up.

Her focus on the page meant he couldn't see her eyes. Just the sweep of her lashes over cheeks that were pinker than normal. And those lips.

"The more I think about it," he said, "the less I can think of one good reason why I shouldn't kiss you."

"We're in a library," she murmured without looking up. As if he'd commented on the weather. "A *public* library. A library is meant to be a safe place."

"A *tame* place," he agreed.

Her head came up, her blue eyes sparked...and a wave of fierce—and given the circumstance, insane—desire swept over him. She said, "If you think for one moment you can taunt me into—"

He shut her up with a kiss, swift and hard, on her mouth. Eyes stayed open, his and hers, throughout, and he smiled at the thought they were still playing chicken.

Rachel's lips moved beneath his smile, parted just a little, and he realized that if he didn't stop now, he'd be taking this to a whole new level. That he'd leaned right into her, and already his hand was molding possessively to the curve of her waist. Already he was thinking about how she would taste. How she would fit against him...

Hell. He pulled back, ending the kiss as abruptly as he'd begun it.

A copy of *MAD* magazine suddenly appeared two inches from his face, blocking his view of Rachel.

"I found the latest issue," Mrs. G. said.

Garrett took it from her.

"I don't need to remind you about rule number two, do I?" she asked.

"Ah, no," he said. "Sorry, Mrs. G."

The librarian left. She glanced over her shoulder after a few steps, just to make sure no one was locking lips.

"Rule number two?" Rachel's words were muffled—Garrett wondered if she knew she had her fingers pressed to her lips. Pressed to the trace of his kiss.

"'Engaging in sexual conduct or lewd behavior is not allowed.'" He quoted from the library's rules.

Rachel's eyes widened. "She's had to call you on that before?"

"All the time," he said, though in fact it was once, ten years ago. He eyed her broodingly.

"What now?" she said.

"I have to say, that kiss was better than I expected."

"There was a certain chemistry thing happening," she agreed. Then she frowned. "I'm not proud of it, Garrett, so there's no need to look so pleased with yourself."

He realized he was indeed smiling. Rather more widely than a mere kiss warranted.

"We won't do that again," she decided.

He'd been about to say the same thing. "Not in the library," he agreed. "Next time, we'll be somewhere it can last longer."

He expected instant disagreement...but instead, she sat there, staring at his mouth.

"Rach?"

The contraction was enough to pull her out of her trance. "Not anywhere," she said. Her gaze flickered back to his mouth before she resolutely dragged it north. "And it's Rach*el*."

He'd had women find him attractive before, plenty of them. But never with such reluctance. He thought of the way her eyes had stayed open during that kiss, her brain fighting it, her body yielding. Intriguing. Al-

most worth the aggravation of sharing an office building with Rachel.

But not quite.

DWIGHT CALDER STARED through the window of the
shop that sold high-end TVs, at the colorful, flicker-
free screens. Some incompetent store assistant had left
one TV on a different channel from the others, so pass-
ersby saw six identical images of a daytime soap, with
a cooking show in the middle. Stephanie loved those
food shows that seemed to be on every second minute.
Though he had no idea if she ever watched TV in the
middle of the day.

Dwight pulled his coat around him. It was far too
warm—he looked like a damn pervert—but an important meeting this morning had required him to wear
service blues, and the jacket with its gold braiding on
the sleeves was even more conspicuous. The decision
to drive down to the West Village had been spur-of-
the-moment; Dwight hadn't had a change of clothes
at the office.

It was usually a mistake to act on the spur of the moment, any military strategist knew that.

On that solitary cooking-show screen, the chef plated
a serving of pork belly with crisp, golden crackle and
gratin potatoes. Dwight's stomach growled; he frowned
downward, and it subsided. He hadn't had a decent meal
in days. With the exception of the admiralty dinner
in Annapolis, where he'd been too stressed trying to
explain Stephanie's absence without actually lying to
enjoy the food.

I shouldn't have come. He'd told Stephanie he wouldn't give her another chance. She knew he meant it. Even so, he was slightly shocked that she hadn't called. Not even to see how he was. Did she even think about him? He thought about her and the baby. Which was why he was here. Just to see if she was all right. He wouldn't beg her to come back, but that didn't mean she wasn't still his responsibility.

The simplest way to check on her was to phone, but she wasn't taking his calls. He was damned if he was going to ask Garrett, and give his oldest son a chance to gloat.

The next simplest was to knock on the door of the apartment.

But he didn't want Stephanie to think he was giving in. Or needy. Weak. He hadn't got where he was today without commanding absolute respect.

So he'd parked the Hummer four blocks away. To the south, not the north, which seemed the more obvious choice if anyone was looking out for him. Then he'd walked up here with the idea of…what?

He wasn't sure, even though he despised uncertainty. He just wanted to make sure the environment was safe for his wife and baby—some flaky people lived in this part of town. His own son was one of them, changing jobs like other people changed their underpants, and never having a steady girlfriend.

Dwight would make sure Stephanie was all right, then he would leave her alone. What the military called a strategic retreat, a decision not to squander further resources—in this case, his time and energy.

Where was she, anyway? When he'd visited the other
day, he'd seen a Pilates schedule stuck to the fridge,
which he assumed was hers. Assumed his son wasn't
doing some sissy yogalike exercise. She'd circled a
Friday-afternoon class. If she'd attended, she should be
returning about now.

Dwight turned away from the window and scanned
the street for hazards. The cobbled surface was enough
to give him hives. Stephanie had grown clumsier as the
pregnancy progressed. She could slip or stumble on
those cobbles and break her ankle, just like that. And
what about that blind corner? In just the past fifteen
minutes, Dwight had seen three cabs come around it
at reckless speed. Anyone crossing the narrow street
would have been bowled over.

Dwight had almost given up waiting when he saw
her. Stephanie. About a hundred and fifty yards away,
he estimated, but headed straight for him. He recognized the rolling gait she'd adopted in pregnancy, which
reminded him a little of walking on board ship. He
didn't recognize the sweater, a bright red number that
accentuated her swollen stomach. She didn't usually
wear such vivid colors. She didn't look as if she'd been
to a gym class—did she have other places to go, that he
didn't know about? If anything happened to her, would
anyone know to contact him?

He stared back at the store window, the TV sets, his
vision fogged with alarm. He should confront her, demand to know if she was taking care of herself. But he
didn't want her to see him. To think he missed her. Better to let her make the first move. Which would have

to include an apology and an assurance that something like this wasn't going to happen again. If she could offer that, then maybe, just maybe, he would consider taking her back.

He realized that if she looked this way now, she would see him. He needed to move fast if he wanted to remain undetected. Dwight rammed his hands in his coat pockets and headed into the TV store, aware his pulse was racing. The prospect of getting caught had adrenaline surging through his veins.

"Good afternoon, sir." A clerk approached. "Can I help you?"

"Not just now." Dwight moved as deep into the store as he could while still keeping a view of the street.

"We have a great deal on forty-inch TVs this week," the clerk said. "They're optimized for Facebook, for YouTube…" He trailed off, perhaps recognizing Dwight wasn't a big user of what Garrett called social media and Dwight called time-wasters.

Outside, Stephanie walked past the window, chin high, scanning the street in front of her with a smile that seemed altogether too relaxed for a woman who was facing life as a single parent, without a husband to look after her. Dwight was pleased to see that at least her sandals had low heels that shouldn't be too risky on those cobbles. She looked good in her slim-fitting pants; her long legs were the second thing that had attracted him to her when he'd met her at the memorial service at Woodlawn for servicemen lost in Vietnam. Dwight had been a new recruit in that war; Stephanie's father had been a captain who'd died in battle and was buried at Woodlawn.

The first thing that had attracted him had been her wide, bright eyes. Eyes that lately had been filled with disappointment.

"Are you sure there's nothing I can help you with, sir?" The clerk stood beside Dwight, trying to figure out the direction of his gaze, which TV set he might be eyeing.

"You can get me the recipe for the pork belly on that cooking show." Dwight pointed toward the rogue TV.

"Uh…" The man faltered. "We don't have recipes…."

"Then find it," Dwight snapped. Such was the strength of his force of command that the young man hurried to the counter, leaving Dwight to watch his wife. She'd passed the window now, so he moved to the front of the store, where he could watch her all the way to Garrett's building.

Dwight stiffened as a homeless man accosted Stephanie. She dipped into her purse, gave the guy something from the stash of coins she kept for that very purpose and walked on.

"Sir, I have that recipe for you. I found it on the TV station's website." The clerk was beaming with pride at his achievement. Anyone would think he'd single-handedly fought off the Vietcong.

Dwight took the printout the young man offered. "Thank you." Grudgingly, he added, "Good work." Because an officer should give his men credit when it was due. It occurred to him that maybe he hadn't given Stephanie enough credit for her role in their family. Maybe he should say something encouraging. If they talked again. And when they did, he would also make sure she was taking proper care of her health. He couldn't rely on Garrett to do that—his oldest son had never shown any concern for her.

But would Stephanie tell him what he needed to know? She hadn't bothered to contact him since she'd left.

The best way to know she was safe was to observe her himself. He trusted his own judgment. So what if she didn't want to spend time with him? Admiral Dwight Calder wouldn't let a little thing like that get in his way. He would keep tabs on his wife, even if he had to do it discreetly enough that she didn't know about it.

Making that decision made Dwight feel much better. He would take action to protect his own.

Neatly, he folded the recipe the clerk had given him and slipped it into the inside pocket of his jacket. The clerk's eyes widened when he saw the gold bands of rank on his sleeve, protruding from his cuff. Dwight saw respect in his face.

He gave the boy a brief smile. Nice to know his service to his country still commanded the respect of someone. Even if it wasn't his son. Or his wife.

CHAPTER ELEVEN

TONY HAD JUST CLOSED the weekly planning meeting when he said, "Rachel, Garrett, could you two stay a minute?"

They'd been seen kissing in the New York Public Library! The panicked thought raced through Rachel's head.

"Sure, Tony." She smoothed her skirt over her knees and tried to look unconcerned. KBC was relaxed about fraternization between same-level colleagues, and, kissing Garrett wasn't a crime—*criminally good, maybe,* a little voice suggested, but she squelched that. Tony's request was positive, she told herself. She'd planned to stay behind after the meeting anyway; she had some ideas that might remind the partners of her value to the firm.

She'd had a couple more "coaching" sessions with Garrett, and Tony seemed quite impressed with her reports.

But she didn't know if she was doing enough to cover all the bases. And she still wasn't happy with her creative ideas.

Meanwhile, word among the account executives was

that Garrett's team was putting in long hours. She had to figure they had inspiring ideas.

She wasn't so sure how Clive's team was doing. Clive had disappeared to a couple of unexplained meetings out of the office, according to Haylee, reporting from the rumor mill.

Rachel was worried. She needed to bolster her standing in other areas.

She didn't look at Garrett as Clive and the other creative directors, who weren't quite as senior as the three partners designate, filed out. She'd been avoiding him ever since their encounter in the library, other than in their coaching sessions, where she now made sure to keep a proper distance between them.

That kiss… She never should have kissed him back. She had discovered in the small hours of the night that to think of that kiss was to relive it constantly. And to want more.

Not going to happen. Garrett was the exact opposite of what she was looking for. She wanted someone reliable, committed, family focused. Not a guy who lived by the motto "Let it go."

The fact that they were going after the same job was a minor complication compared with all their other differences.

When they were alone, Tony leaned back in his chair, beaming. "I need to give the two of you some kudos," he said.

That sounded positive. Rachel relaxed her grip on her hem. "Great! What for?"

Garrett shook his head. Maybe she had sounded a

bit too puppy-dog eager, but Tony liked suck-ups and she needed every advantage she could get. Garrett was the last person whose advice she should take on how to relate to senior management.

"I've been doing a bit of MBWA," Tony said. Management By Wandering Around.

Garrett's eyes glazed over. He hated corporate-speak, of course.

"I noticed," Rachel said. "My team did, too. They're enjoying the attention our work is getting at the top levels of the organization."

"Good, good," Tony said. "The staff need to know we genuinely care."

"You can't fake that," Rachel agreed. "Who would even want to?"

Her unsubtle dig had Garrett pressing his fingertips to his temples in a pained fashion.

"I mean, I think of KBC as a family." Rachel might as well stake her claim to the people-skills high ground. "And family *cares* about each other." She emphasized the word just to annoy Garrett.

"Does that make you my sister?" Garrett asked. "Because if so, it's kind of creepy that we—"

"Why the kudos, Tony?" Rachel asked brightly.

"Ah, yes." Tony pressed his palms into his desk and leaned forward. "I've had great feedback from your team, Garrett. Alice told me you spent time with her looking at professional development opportunities. She was very impressed with your patience and commitment to her role in the firm."

Rachel stared at Garrett. He'd sat down with Alice

and planned her training? That sounded like more than *lip service*.

Garrett grunted to Tony, somehow managing to convey that he was ignoring Rachel.

"And I know Adam has appreciated your recent encouragement," Tony said. "He sees you as quite the role model."

What? Garrett had taken Rachel's advice seriously enough to work with Adam, as well?

"I'd love to take all the credit for the improvement," Garrett said, "but Rachel's the miracle worker. Thanks to her, I'm a changed man."

"Thanks," she said reluctantly, sensing a trap.

That gleam in his eyes said he knew what she was thinking, and she was right to be wary. "Tony, would you say I've now addressed the partners' concerns about my team skills?" he asked.

"I think I would."

"In that case," Garrett said, "Rachel and I can safely end our mentoring arrangement now. I'm sure Rachel would appreciate more time to spend on her pitch."

"I'm not that busy," Rachel said. "And there are some basic things about women Garrett still needs to learn."

"I already know them," he promised.

"Did you know that the areas of the brain linked to gut feelings are larger in women and more discerning?"

"Fascinating." He yawned.

This was actually part of the material she'd planned to discuss with Tony.

"Which means female intuition is a tool no creative director should ignore," Rachel said.

Tony looked interested.

"Plus, women are four times more likely to cry than men."

"I got that one," Garrett said.

"It's because a man's brain isn't as good at picking up emotional cues. These are things we all need to learn to harness in our work. Actually, Tony, Garrett isn't the only one who could benefit from this kind of knowledge. I'd be happy to run some agency-wide tutorials."

"Sounds interesting," Tony admitted. "But we might park that for now. Garrett, you're done with your coaching sessions."

Rats. Rachel was now out of ideas for how to impress the partners.

"Thanks, Tony." Garrett gave their boss one of his rare smiles.

There was some merit in rationing them, Rachel thought. Tony looked almost honored.

"Keep up the good work, you two," he said, as he left.

"It sounds like you've done a great job with Alice and Adam," Rachel said to Garrett.

He shrugged. "I'm faking it."

"To me, faking people skills is more about smiling when you don't mean it and uttering insincere compliments," she said. "Helping Alice choose a course of professional development and inspiring Adam to consider you a role model sounds quite…real."

"They're not," he said gruffly.

"Maybe," she suggested, "you're enjoying the connection."

"Nope."

"Maybe the rewards go both ways," she said.

He shot her an annoyed look. "The only reason I'm *engaging* with those two is because it benefits me. On my own terms."

"Sorry, Garrett, there's no such thing as on your own terms when there's someone else involved," she said. "Every communication, every action, has consequences. You can't just do your part and not care what anyone else does."

"Can't I?"

His cell phone rang, and he pressed to answer. As he listened, a frown gathered between his eyes.

"I'll be right out." He ended the call.

"Bad news?" Rachel asked.

"Unwanted visitor at reception. I'd better go deal with it." He strode out of the room.

Rachel glanced at her watch. Lunchtime. She returned to her office for her purse, then headed to the elevator.

Garrett was still in the reception area, talking to a heavily pregnant woman.

He didn't look happy; he was speaking in a low voice that nonetheless carried heat. His visitor looked a little older than he was. Pretty, if tired-looking.

Perhaps sensing Rachel's gaze, the woman's eyes flicked briefly to her.

Rachel took that as an invitation. She marched over to them. "Hi, I'm Rachel."

Garrett spun around, irritation etched in the angles of his face. "Go away."

Which interestingly had the same effect on the pregnant woman as it did on Rachel. They stuck out their hands simultaneously.

"Stephanie," the woman introduced herself.

"Congratulations on your baby," Rachel said. She turned to Garrett. "Is it yours, Garrett?" she asked oh-so-sweetly. "It's been a while since we had an office baby shower, but I'm sure—"

"It's not my baby!" he said, revolted.

Stephanie let out a peal of laughter. "I'm Garrett's stepmother. I'm staying at his place for a while. A little while," she amended.

Another piece of the puzzle that was Garrett Calder completely failed to fall into place. A future sibling hadn't featured in any of his mentions of family.

"I guess it was you who made that pastrami sandwich for him," Rachel said.

"That was me." Stephanie shot him a fond look that he didn't return. "Pastrami's his favorite. I think. Did he like it, do you know? He doesn't say much."

Rachel would bet he didn't. "Actually, Stephanie, he threw it in the trash."

CHAPTER TWELVE

GARRETT CURSED.

Stephanie's mouth fell open and stayed that way.

"I'm really sorry to tell you that," Rachel said, "but I've been trying to explain to Garrett that he can't act without regard for anyone else. That being part of the human race has consequences."

"I...see." Stephanie sounded hurt, but also curious. "If you're wondering, Garrett, the consequence of this is that I'm offended."

Garrett glared at Rachel.

"So, you're going to be a brother again," she said brightly. "Congratulations."

"Thanks," he said, so briefly she knew he was far from delighted, and not just because he was mad about the pastrami sandwich.

"I came to invite Garrett along to my sonogram," Stephanie said.

"Did you really think he'd say yes?" Rachel asked.

Stephanie puffed out a breath that sounded like lingering frustration. "No, but I thought I'd try anyway. I realize a sonogram isn't the kind of thing he would go to."

"Who says?" Garrett demanded.

Rachel rolled her eyes. "Garrett, it's a warm, fuzzy, *relationship* experience. You don't do relationships, let alone warm and fuzzy." She shot Stephanie a sympathetic smile.

Stephanie was looking, if anything, even more taken aback by Rachel's explanation.

"We have a very direct communication style around here," Rachel explained.

"Clearly." A small smile accompanied the word.

"I hope your scan goes well. Is your husband going along?"

"No, but it's not a problem, I did the last one on my own. I just wanted to include Garrett...." Her eyes met Rachel's, acknowledging that Rachel had summed him up accurately.

Rachel wrinkled her nose to say *Sorry you ended up with the stepson from hell.*

"Would you two stop communicating telepathically about me," Garrett demanded. "I'm right here!"

"That's why it has to be telepathic," Rachel said. "It would be rude to say it out loud."

"You don't know the first thing about what I will and won't do," Garrett said. "That goes for both of you. As it happens, I have every intention of taking Stephanie to her sonogram."

Stephanie opened her mouth, then clamped it shut again.

"Shall we go?" Garrett said dangerously.

Only concern for a pregnant woman who needed someone to accompany her stopped Rachel from doing a little jig of triumph. She wouldn't want to provoke

Garrett into changing his mind. But she was dancing on the inside. If only she could see Garrett try to *fake* watching an ultrasound.

Stephanie bolted for the elevator as if she was afraid Garrett might change his mind.

"Have a nice time," Rachel said. For Stephanie's sake, she waited in reception until they were both in the elevator and the doors had closed safely behind Garrett.

The last thing she saw was The Shark's murderous glare, fixed on her.

GARRETT TURNED AWAY while the female technician spread some kind of gloop on Stephanie's giant stomach. Hell, what if she had twins in there? Triplets? He darted a glance at her. Quads?

The technician wiped her hands on a paper towel, then picked up a device that looked like a joystick. She switched on a screen next to the bed.

"Will this hurt?" Garrett asked.

Stephanie shook her head. "It's not even uncomfortable."

"So I don't need to be here."

"Yes, you do." She grabbed his wrist.

"Don't you get it?" he asked her. "It's too late for you and me to build a relationship. I didn't need you when I was a kid, Stephanie, and I sure as hell don't need you now."

The technician drew in a sharp, disapproving breath. "We'll wait for the doctor before we get started," she said.

"You're not here for you," Stephanie said, "and you're not here for me, so stop whining."

He blinked. She'd never spoken to him so bluntly. "Then why am I here?" he asked.

"You're here for the baby. This child has two brothers and both of them are going to be in its life. Everything I'm doing—leaving your father, staying with you, dragging you here—is for my baby," she said. "I didn't fight hard enough for you, all those years ago, and I didn't fight hard enough for myself, to make your father love me the way he should. But I'm damned if I'm going to let this baby down. I'm not giving up on a single fight. Do you hear me, Garrett?"

She looked as if she might pop.

"I think the whole clinic heard you," he said.

Behind Garrett, the door opened and someone came in.

"Hi, Dr. Palmer." Stephanie lifted a hand in a wave, apparently more relaxed now that she'd said her piece. "This is my stepson, Garrett Calder."

Garrett shook hands with the physician.

"So, you want to meet your new sibling, do you?" Fortunately, Dr. Palmer didn't seem to require an answer to that question. As he washed his hands, he indicated to the technician to get started.

The woman pressed the joystick gadget to Stephanie's stomach. The screen filled with what looked like static.

Garrett trained his gaze on the screen, rather than that gigantic belly. The static fuzz slithered around the screen, as if the joystick was chasing it, then co-alesced into—

"A baby!" Garrett said.

Stephanie chuckled. "What did you think I had in there?"

A football team. "Is there just one?" Garrett asked the doc, his eyes riveted on the image. Incredible. He could see legs, arms, and now, when the technician zoomed in, or whatever you called it, actual fingers.

"Just one," Dr. Palmer confirmed. The image zoomed out again.

"Looks like it's got a big brain," Garrett said.

"The head is disproportionately large at this stage," the doctor said. "Mrs. Calder, are you still sure you don't want to know the sex?"

Garrett couldn't believe how much he was suddenly compelled to know what it was—a half sister, or half brother. But if Stephanie didn't want to, he wasn't about to beg. Instead, he focused on the baby's nether re-gions...and saw something—not very distinct, but defi-nitely something—between the legs.

A brother. In that half second, he realized he'd been hoping for a girl...but that it didn't matter. And now he really wanted it to be a boy.

Crazy. What was it to him if—

"You're not planning to move away or anything, are you?" he asked Stephanie. "I mean, if you and Dad don't get back together."

She looked perplexed at the change of subject. "No, I grew up in this part of the country—it's home to me. And your father will want to spend time with his child."

Garrett nodded, though he wasn't sure about that last part.

The technician took some measurements on the screen, then turned off the device.

"That's it, Mrs. Calder," Dr. Palmer said. "Baby's a good size, and I don't see anything to worry about, despite your age."

"I'm an elderly mother in medical terms," Stephanie confided to Garrett.

He shrugged. "If the shoe fits…"

She gave a peal of laughter that struck a chord in Garrett's memory. She and Lucas had often laughed like that.

Back outside the clinic, Garrett hailed a cab. He checked to make sure Stephanie was buckled in properly before he gave the driver his address. The taxi pulled out into the Upper East Side traffic.

"Best to go by your office on the way," Stephanie said. "I interrupted your day—I'm sure you still have work to do."

Garrett glanced at his watch. Four o'clock. Yeah, he should probably put in a few more hours on his pitch, which wasn't going well.

"You feeling okay?" he asked Stephanie after giving the cabbie their new destination.

"I feel great," she said.

He nodded. "Thanks—" he cleared his throat "—for inviting me along today." He should say something about that damned pastrami sandwich, but he had no idea what.

Her smile was warm and genuine. "Thanks for coming."

They sat in silence for a couple of minutes. Then she said, "I know you said I could only stay a week..."

Garrett tensed. "Is that why you asked me along? To get my buy-in to this kid before you invited yourself to stay longer?" He might have known. That was probably what the pastrami sandwich had been about, too. At least he hadn't fallen for it. And now he didn't have to feel bad about tossing the sandwich.

Stephanie touched his arm; Garrett pulled away. Rachel would doubtless have something to say about that.

"I know it looks like that," she said. "If I was scheming for an extended invitation, believe me, I'd be more subtle than ambushing you on the way back from the clinic. But I have to admit, your, uh, reaction to the scan did make me think maybe now's a good time to ask for a reprieve."

Garrett didn't believe her, no matter how convincing she sounded. But it came back to that pesky question of whether he could throw a pregnant woman into the street.

"You can stay a little longer," he said. "So long as you keep that bathroom tidier. You're going to slip and break your neck on one of those potions you drip everywhere. And besides, it's a damn mess."

"I'll keep it tidy."

Too easy. "Maybe," he said coldly, "you can help me with something else."

"I'm good with a vacuum cleaner," she said.

"Not that. You asked if there was any way you could help with my pitch."

"Name it," she said promptly.

Garrett smiled thinly. "You might regret that."

MAY 3. A DAY RINGED IN RED on the calendar of every ad agency in New York. That is, if anyone besides Rachel still used paper calendars. She liked the solidness of paper, of being able to see at a glance what lay ahead. Even though she wasn't wild about being able to see May 3 looming.

Because today was the day the short list for this year's CLIOs would be announced. Every year, Rachel tried hard not to dread it. Back in the early days of her creative career, she'd practically salivated, hoping—no, expecting—to see her name on the list. The expectation had lasted a couple of years, then faded to regular old hope. Optimistic, but without that edge of certainty. Because as everyone said—those who weren't short-listed said it to console themselves, while those were said it to make the losers feel better—it was totally subjective. Not necessarily reflective of public opinion, nor of actual effectiveness in the market, which was surely the most important measure of all.

Yeah, right.

With each passing year, Rachel wanted to win a CLIO more and more. At first she'd mentally insisted it be a gold award, but these days she'd settle for bronze. And if ever there was a year to win any award, in any color, this was it.

Tony had suggested she enter the Aunt Betty's campaign. It wasn't flashy or übercool. But it had resonated with the client, and with middle America, and the results had been spectacular. If the strong, silent type of campaign had a shot at a CLIO, then Aunt Betty's would walk it. If, on the other hand, the judges liked fast cars doing mechanically improbable things on high bridges...

Rachel shuddered at the thought of Garrett winning a ninth gold CLIO. *Maybe we'll both get nominated. And Clive, too.* His campaign for the Special Olympics had attracted record viewers and record ticket sales.

Tradition dictated that the short-listed firms would be notified before midday. The call, if KBC was on the list, would come in to Tony. Which was why every year on short list day, the creative directors found excuses to hang around outside his office late morning.

Rachel strolled out of the elevator on the executive floor at eleven-thirty.

While Tony waited for the call, Rachel chatted nonchalantly to Helen, his assistant, who was equally casually hitting the refresh button on her internet browser while she chatted back. The list of nominees would be posted on the CLIO website as soon as the calls were made. One way or another, they'd know the truth in the next half hour.

Clive showed up a couple of minutes later. He didn't feel the need to pretend he was here just to shoot the breeze—he glanced through the glass wall of Tony's office and said, "Any news?"

Helen sighed at what she obviously considered excessive pragmatism. "Not yet."

They all stared at Tony, who was pretending to read something on his screen, hand poised importantly over his mouse. This had to be the least productive hour in the ad agency year, Rachel thought.

"You must have a good chance," she told Clive.

He grimaced. "That's what I've been telling myself. Same goes for you."

"We'll see," she said.

They made desultory conversation about the delays on the subway this morning, about Clive's in-laws and about the interior decoration of his apartment, all the while exercising their peripheral vision, watching to see if Tony's phone rang. His calls were set to go straight through—Tony wasn't up to playing it cool and channeling calls via his assistant today.

Twice, his phone rang. Twice, the party outside his office stiffened, only to exchange frustrated glances when Tony rushed the callers off the phone and slammed it back onto its cradle.

At eleven-forty-five, Garrett arrived. He looked irritatingly relaxed, but when he saw Rachel his expression tightened. He'd been distant—even more distant than usual—since she'd pushed him into going to the sonogram with Stephanie.

"I'm guessing there's no news," he said.

Tony's assistant shook her head.

"Ah, well, you know what they say about no news."

"Which has no logical application in this situation whatsoever," Rachel pointed out. "No news is simply no news."

"Maybe they're running late," Helen said.

Jonathan Key's assistant hollered across the room. "Just got a call from a friend at JWT. They got four noms."

Someone groaned. There'd been no delay in the announcement process that might explain Tony's silent phone. It also meant there were four fewer nominations available for KBC.

"Six at Saatchi," Jonathan's assistant called—she'd had another phone call.

Clive grimaced. His Special Olympics campaign was up against a particularly strong Saatchi campaign.

Marnie Bream, the firm's only female partner, stuck her head around the door of her office, next to Tony's. "Publicity Partners got one for the Kool Water billboards."

Publicity Partners was a tiny agency. It was normal for a few barely-knowns to make the list.

"That's nice for them," Rachel said. Then she realized.

"Tony's on the phone," she said.

CHAPTER THIRTEEN

THEY'D ALL BEEN SO CAUGHT up in the news from other agencies, they hadn't noticed Tony had picked up his handset. Now they turned in unison to stare through the glass.

Tony was grinning into the phone. This was The Call. Sensing their scrutiny, he glanced up, scanned his audience. His smile widened; he flashed a thumbs-up.

At who?

Rachel couldn't tell who was the clever creative director who'd been short-listed. All the facts and figures she'd memorized about the CLIO—especially the one about fewer than ten percent of the submitted campaigns qualifying for the short list—flew out of her head, to be replaced by rampant longing. *It's my turn. Let it be me.*

At last, Tony hung up the phone. He leaned back in his chair, hands clasped behind his head, beaming.

Clive took a long stride to the door and pushed it open. "Get out here, Tony, and tell us who got it."

Tony's grin widened as he made a show of a very leisurely walk to join them. "Congratulations…" he drew out the suspense "…Clive."

Garrett thumped Clive on the shoulder with what looked like genuine pleasure; Rachel stretched her arms around his massive frame and hugged him. "You deserve it, Clive," she said, and almost meant it. Later, she *would* mean it, but right now there was the sting of disappointment that Tony hadn't said her name. Mingled with an uncharitable relief that he also hadn't said—

"But wait, there's more," Tony said, in his best imitation of a home shopping network salesperson. "Congratulations to you, too..." again the pause "...Garrett!"

The bottom fell out of Rachel's stomach.

"Woohoo!" Clive shared the love, shaking Garrett's hand and clapping him on the back.

Rachel had to hug him. To hug Clive and not Garrett would look like sour grapes. Besides, if she didn't hide her face from him, he would see her disappointment. It would only take one mocking Garrett-quip for her to dissolve into humiliating tears.

"Go, Garrett," she said brightly. Too brightly—Tony's assistant winced. Then, before Rachel could make her move, Garrett hauled her into his arms.

Several thoughts struck her, swimming in her dazed, disappointed mind. One, Garrett smelled fantastic—he *so* was wearing cologne. Two, although she'd kissed him, he'd never held her in his arms before and it turned out his arms were strong and sculpted...he must work out. Three, he was saying something against her hair, something no one else could hear. It sounded like, "Sorry, Rach."

He'd broken his vow of silence because he felt *sorry* for her?

Nothing could have worked more effectively to dry her eyes and snap her out of her funk. She stiffened her backbone and pulled away. "Great job, Garrett. Good luck at the awards ceremony."

It occurred to her that maybe Tony would now announce that she, too, had finaled.

But he didn't break off his animated chat with Clive, and then Helen said, "The list is up on the website."

They crowded around her monitor to see who else was up for a prestigious gong. Mostly familiar names, the best of the best. Rachel strove for the right blend of surprise and interest in the other short-listed campaigns, to hide her devastation. She was aware of Garrett standing close behind her, the prickling of the hairs on her nape.

Garrett's cell phone rang. Surely he would remove his disturbing presence to take the call?

He did. She sensed his departure. Then she heard him say, "Mark, hi, how are you?"

Mark? As in Mark Van de Kamp, their client at Brightwater Group? Tony and Clive assumed the same, going by the way they turned to watch Garrett.

"Thanks, yes, I was thrilled." Garrett was obviously accepting congratulations. "Yeah, that would make nine in total, but obviously there's a good chance I won't win gold."

Rachel rolled her eyes.

A minute later: "I'm pretty sure someone else out there must have won nine," Garrett said modestly.

For crying out loud!

After he ended the call, almost before he'd stashed his phone in his pocket, Clive's cell rang. Clive glanced at the display, nodded at Tony to confirm it was his turn to hear from Mark. He moved away to take the call.

The significance of what had just happened wasn't lost on Rachel. One, the client had been watching for the CLIO announcement with as much anticipation as any ad agency. Tony was right—clients cared about awards. Two, although Garrett's campaign was listed beneath Clive's on the website, in alphabetical order by client name, Mark had chosen to congratulate Garrett first. Any analyst of consumer behavior knew that kind of choice was neither random nor meaningless. Even if Mark didn't know it himself.

More than ever, Rachel felt her lack of a CLIO; she felt as if everyone was staring at her, pitying her. When her own cell phone rang, she snatched it from her pocket. Even though there was no chance it could be a forgotten CLIO call...was there?

The display read *Mom*.

Rachel assured herself it was unlikely her mother had been monitoring the CLIO list and was calling to commiserate. Her parents used the internet at the local library once a week.

"I need to take this," she said to no one in particular, pleased to have an excuse to break away from the chattering crowd. Tony had retrieved a bottle of champagne from his office. Helen lined up flutes on her desk. Over by the elevator, Rachel pressed the button to answer her phone. "Hi, Mom."

She wanted to talk to her mother, she realized. Wanted to hear loving words from someone who knew there were more important things in life than CLIOs.

"Hi, sweetheart. What's new?" It was her parents' stock greeting, a subconscious acknowledgment of how they thrived on change.

"Nothing much." Rachel was never more aware of how true her standard answer was. *I'm a CLIO finalist* would sound so much better. "How about with you guys?"

"Funny you should ask," her mom said. And Rachel knew instantly she wouldn't find it funny. Nora took a deep, audible breath. "Your dad and I are thinking about moving to Dayton."

"Dayton, New Jersey?" Rachel asked, ninety-nine percent sure there was no town of that name in the state.

Her mom chuckled. "Dayton, Ohio. There's a new stadium going up there. Your dad has an idea for a fast-food concession—Burt's Brats. This could be a great opportunity."

Inside Rachel, something snapped.

"A great opportunity for what?" she demanded. "To spend money you don't have, setting up a hot-dog stand in the wrong place at the wrong time?"

"Rachel!" Her mom stopped. It had been so long since Rachel had called them on their constant moving, it seemed she didn't know what to say.

Rachel pushed her guilt aside. "Come on, Mom, you know that's what'll happen—or something like it. Why can't you stay where you are? Why should LeeAnne have to move again? The girls are starting preschool in September—ask her, she'll tell you she wants to stay." Her sister might not quite have reached that stage in her thoughts.... Then again, maybe she had.

"I know this is a sore spot for you," her mom said. "But your father and I are adults who can make our own decisions."

Not *good* decisions, they couldn't. "Can't you just commit to one thing?" Rachel asked. "One place?"

She wanted to run out the door, rent a car and drive to Freehold. To beg her sister to be strong, to shake some sense into her parents. But she couldn't afford a day away from the office at this stage of the Brightwater pitch. Couldn't afford to blow any chance to keep her job.

"Your father and I have been happily married for thirty-two years—how's that for commitment?" A short sigh. "Let's talk about this when you're feeling calmer. Now, dear, how's your work going? How are you getting along with that private-college pitch?"

Tears spurted to Rachel's eyes—anger at her folks, mingled with disappointment over the CLIOs and the very real fear she was about to lose her job.

"Oh, Mom, I—" To her horror, just as those tears spilled over, Garrett materialized in front of her, carrying two glasses of champagne.

"Here, Rach, you may not feel like this, but there's a lot to be said for the numbing effect—" He stopped, his expression horrified as he realized he'd just gotten embroiled in an emotional meltdown. That right now, Rachel was *needy*.

Would he run for the hills, or stick around to mock her? Either way, she couldn't bear for him to see her so defeated.

"Rachel?" her mom asked down the phone. "Are you okay? You sound upset."

"I'm upset," she improvised madly, "because you guys refuse to come in here for a focus group, no matter how often I ask you. This is the biggest pitch of my life, Mom." Not a bad effort for someone who wasn't good at spur-of-the-moment. She sounded a little wild, but not pathetic. Not a total loser.

"Honey, of course we'd love to come in." Her mom's rapid response was the only hint of any sense of guilt about their plans to uproot the family once again. "Just name the day."

"Uh…" Rachel didn't actually have a focus group planned. And the main reason she kept inviting her parents to attend—because the payment might help keep them from looking for new opportunities to make money—now seemed like a thumb-in-the-dike attempt at stopping them from making yet another move. Still, according to legend, a thumb in the dike had once succeeded in holding back an inevitable flood. If Mom and Dad came into the city for a focus group, she would have a chance to talk them out of this dumb idea. "Next Thursday," she said.

Yes, that could work. She took a glass from Garrett and gave him a brilliant smile. "Mom, I have to go. There's a bit of a party going on here. I'll call you later with the details."

"Phew," she said, as she slipped her phone back into her pocket. "The lengths I have to go to to convince my parents to come into the city. Luckily, they fall for the fake tears every time."

She saw blatant disbelief in Garrett's eyes. To her surprise, he didn't call her on it. "Parents," he agreed. "Who'd have 'em?"

Which must mean—ugh—he felt sorry for her.

Garrett glanced at Tony and Clive, still clinking glasses and assuring each other they were the best.

"So, you're doing a focus group?" he asked. Was that a clumsy attempt to distract her from her woes? "Aren't they a bit old-fashioned?"

Just the kind of idiotic comment she'd love to tackle.

"A well-run focus group is one of the most effective research tools around," she said, reviving the ghost of her fighting spirit. "I have the stats to prove it. Personally, I find they spark my creativity."

Garrett grinned. "Sure they do."

Tony's assistant had started taking photos of Clive and Tony. Clearly Garrett would be next, and there was every chance Rachel would get dragged into a shot, required to look thrilled for him. This morning had drained her limited acting talent.

"I'd better get back to work." Rachel raised her glass and her voice. "Cheers, everyone."

As she headed for her office, she told herself she was walking away on her own terms, as Garrett would say. For the first time, she could see why that mattered.

IT WAS PAST NOON, and most people had gone to lunch, which meant Rachel didn't need to fend off inquiries about the CLIOs. When she reached her office, she set down her champagne glass without bothering to walk around her desk and, still standing, picked up the phone.

She dialed her sister's cell. LeeAnne answered on the second ring.

"LeeAnne, how are you? The girls okay?"

Her sister began a description of some new game the twins had invented.

"Sounds adorable," Rachel interrupted. "Did you know Mom and Dad want to move to Dayton?"

"No. When? Why?" There was a huff, as if LeeAnne might have sat down suddenly.

Rachel repeated the gist of what her mom had said.

"So, it's not definite yet?" LeeAnne asked, with a lack of enthusiasm that gave Rachel hope.

"It wasn't fifteen minutes ago," she said drily.

"I'd better start collecting boxes from the grocery store," LeeAnne said.

"Or," Rachel said, "you could tell Mom and Dad you don't want to go."

A short silence. "I don't think they'd stay, not if they've got their hearts set on this hot-dog stand."

"You could stay anyway," Rachel said. "Send the girls to that nursery school you like so much." It would be wonderful to have family nearby on a permanent basis.

"I don't know…. I want to be close to Mom and Dad."

LeeAnne's hesitation spurred Rachel on. "Lee, maybe it's time for you to settle in one place, even if our parents can't. Now that the girls are heading toward school, wouldn't it be great for them to have some stability?"

"I know you always think that," LeeAnne said. "And

I can see some benefit to what you're saying." That alone was quite an admission, Rachel thought excitedly. "But the twins adore Mom and Dad."

"Mom and Dad could come back for visits," Rachel said. "And you could visit them. I'd be happy to help out with airfares. I can give you tickets for birthdays and Christmas." Her family would refuse any outright offer of cash.

"It's a lovely nursery school," LeeAnne admitted.

"So, stay. Please?"

"But there might be one just as lovely in Dayton."

"And there might not. Isn't it hard to get into those places—aren't there waiting lists?"

"For the good ones. I've had the girls down at the place near here almost since we moved to Freehold."

"Then stay," Rachel said again. "Please, LeeAnne."

Silence said her sister was considering the idea. *Yes!* There had to be something Rachel could say to swing this her way. She scanned her desk in search of inspiration. Her calendar, with today's date circled in red. The frosted glass paperweight her colleagues had given her for her birthday last year. Her stack of Brightwater files...

"Lee, you'd like the girls to go to college one day, right?" Rachel heard a noise behind her and turned.

Garrett stood in the doorway. How long had he been listening?

She made a shooing motion with her free hand. He didn't budge.

"Yeah, I would," LeeAnne said. "I know it's a long

way off, but I've been thinking about it since your last visit, when we were talking about those colleges."

"I'd like to do something for the girls." Rachel frowned at Garrett and jerked her head to indicate he should leave now.

He came right into the office. "Don't do it, Rach."

What was he talking about?

"Go away," she whispered. Naturally, he ignored her.

"Rachel?" LeeAnne said. "What did you say?"

Rachel forced her mind back to her phone call. This was her big chance. She couldn't afford to blow it.

"I'd like to start a college fund for Kylie and Dannii."

Garrett looked confused at the mention of the Minogue sisters.

"I know you don't like to take money from me," Rachel hurried on, staring down at the carpet in an attempt to ignore Garrett's presence. "But this is an investment in the girls' future, which is important. There are enough years for the savings to be painless at my end, and it could make a big difference."

"It would make *all* the difference," LeeAnne said softly.

She was going to pull this off! "I'll go to the bank this afternoon and open the account," Rachel said.

"Typical Rachel." Her sister was laughing, but maybe crying a little, too. "You say you'll do it, and next minute, it's done."

It's called being reliable. It's not that difficult. "That's me," Rachel said lightly. "But, LeeAnne, there's one thing…."

"Rachel," Garrett warned.

Go away, she mouthed. To her sister, she said, "The college-fund offer only stands if you stay in Freehold. Or somewhere nearby."

Garrett groaned.

"What do you mean?" LeeAnne asked.

"I mean—" Rachel squirmed. This wasn't going to come out right, but she couldn't think of another way to say it. "You and the girls need to stick around. If you move with Mom and Dad..." She couldn't bring herself to say the words *There'll be no college fund.*

She didn't need to.

"You're blackmailing me not to move?" LeeAnne demanded.

More like bribing you to stay. "I'm thinking of the girls' best interest," Rachel said. "They need stability."

"Liar," Garrett said.

Rachel stifled a gasp.

No comment from her sister.

"LeeAnne?" she prompted. "Surely you can see where I'm coming from."

Silence.

"Lee?"

"She hung up," Garrett said.

Rachel shook the phone. "Lee?" He was right. How did he know? She pressed Redial, but there was no answer.

Not good.

Anger surged through her. "Dammit, Garrett, if you hadn't been here distracting me, I wouldn't have—"

"Offered whoever that was the equivalent of sex to keep the relationship going?"

She sputtered.

"Didn't I tell you not to beg?" he asked. "That goes for family, too, you know."

"I was trying to *help* my sister," she said.

"You were trying to make her do what you want." Coming closer, he took the phone from her hand and set it back in its cradle. "It never works, Rach."

"Rach*el*." She needed to stop rising to that bait. But right now it was better than confronting the ring of truth in his words. Suddenly weak, still teary from the CLIO debacle, she leaned against her desk. She'd screwed up.

To her surprise, Garrett leaned beside her, so they were shoulder to shoulder—actual contact, he didn't pull away—facing out into her office. "What exactly were you trying to blackmail your sister into?"

"Bribe," she corrected.

When he laughed, she realized how crazy that sounded. As if bribery was a whole lot more ethical than blackmail. "I don't want her to move away." Briefly, she told him about her parents' transient lifestyle.

"That's tough," he said, "I guess. I mean, if you like your family enough to want to keep them around."

"I do." She sighed.

"On the bright side, you still have your legs." He eyed her legs in her short black skirt with a connoisseur's appraisal.

Rachel couldn't hold back a laugh. "Gee, that makes me feel a lot better." Actually, his blatant appreciation did help, just a tiny bit. "I don't think what I did was so bad," she said, rallying. "You're the one who said I should run my relationships on my terms."

"I'm starting to realize that mostly applies to people you don't like," he said cryptically.

"Now you tell me." She pinched the bridge of her nose. "Maybe LeeAnne will think about what I said and see that I'm right."

Garrett didn't comment.

Then she remembered the hurt in her sister's voice, and her mood slumped. "I'd better call her back. Explain that I'm only trying to help."

Garrett winced. "Not now. You're both feeling emotional—you're bound to mess up. Besides, she's not going to answer."

He was right. Again.

"I suppose you don't have problems like this," Rachel said. "You never try to hold on to anyone." She observed his profile, his straight nose and strong chin.

"Makes life a lot less complicated," he said.

"Are you happy like that?" she asked. "Never taking a risk with your emotions?"

He moved away, breaking the connection of their shoulders, but then he twisted to face her, so he was looking directly into her eyes. "You're not trying to tell me you know anything about risk, are you?"

He had a point. Garrett might not take the risk of connecting, but she didn't risk letting go of a relationship, even one that wasn't working.

She registered that he'd inched closer. It was difficult to process his question when he was so close. When his scent pervaded her senses, when that gleam in his dark eyes seemed so warm, when his mouth was curved in a tantalizing smile that, if she read it right, said he was about to kiss her—and that he was looking forward to it as much as she was.

CHAPTER FOURTEEN

GARRETT DREW BACK SHARPLY, and Rachel felt a rush of rejection…until she saw Clive through the glass wall of her office, one hand in his pocket, the other holding his phone to his ear. Though Rachel couldn't hear him, she guessed from his hunched shoulders that he was talking in an undertone. There was a frown on his usually placid face.

"What's that about?" she asked Garrett. Just as well they hadn't locked lips five seconds earlier.

Garrett leaned forward to watch where Clive went. "Yep, he's gone to the elevator. He's up to something. I haven't figured out what yet."

"You think it's about Brightwater?" It had to be.

"I don't know, but I'll find out. I've asked Stephanie to follow him."

"What?" Rachel squawked.

"She doesn't have anything else to do, so why not?" He pulled out his cell. "I've noticed Clive's been heading out of the office for a late lunch most days. I asked Stephanie to wait in the lobby at one. I just need to call her and let her know he's on his way down."

He was outrageous.

He made the call. Stephanie would have no trouble

indentifying Clive, since he was so tall and big-built. And wearing a pink shirt.

As Garrett ended the call, one of Clive's account execs walked past the window. Catching sight of Garrett, she waggled her fingers at him.

Garrett waggled his right back.

"What, you're BFFs with *all* the junior staff now?" Rachel said, disbelieving.

"Whatever that means," he said. "You're the one who taught me to take an interest in people's lives. It's amazing how much information they share when you do that."

"So she's feeding you with info about Clive?"

"Not yet," he admitted. "Mostly we just wave at each other."

She tried to disapprove, but it was too funny. "I hope none of my team are that friendly with you."

"I've been trying to pump them for information," he said. "But they're disgustingly loyal."

Clive's account exec came by again, carrying a coffee. Once again, she did that finger-waggle to Garrett.

"Why is she giving you that secretive smile?" Rachel demanded. "Are you sleeping with her?" She was shocked how much she hated the thought.

"Of course not," he said, so incredulous she believed him. His gaze narrowed on her, as if he could read how much she would dislike him to be sleeping with, well, anyone.

Oh, hell. Rachel blushed. "It's just, her behavior seems intimate."

"Uh, yeah, I guess it does." He ran a hand around the back of his neck. As if he felt guilty.

"What did you do?" Rachel asked. "Why does that girl think she has some connection to you?"

"She was asking about my family yesterday," he admitted.

Rachel groaned. "So you made up some story about your mom and now her little heart is bleeding for you. What was it this time? Slow death by lead poisoning from old paintwork?"

"No, but that's a good one," he said admiringly. "All I came up with was a fall while hiking the Appalachian Trail."

"And you claim to be a creative genius," she said.

"I'll use yours next time."

"How about not making up a story at all?" she suggested.

Almost imperceptibly, he shifted away from her. "Since you still have your mom, you probably don't notice how often people's mothers come up in conversation."

She wrinkled her forehead. "They don't."

"Exactly. If you asked people, they'd say they never talk about their parents," Garrett said. "But fact is, mothers come into the conversation at every turn. And people ask questions, like that woman on Clive's team did yesterday."

"Can't you just say your mom passed away, without making up some elaborate tale?"

"As soon as I say she's dead, people feel bad about mentioning their own mothers. They can't just drop the subject. Their next question is always how my mother died."

"You can't expect them to ignore that you just mentioned her death," Rachel said.

He frowned. "Sure I can."

"They need to express some sympathy and take some interest. It's good manners."

He looked as if he had no idea what she was talking about.

"Human decency," she elaborated. Nope, still a blank. "Connection?" she suggested.

He straightened and took a step away from the desk. "They can find some other way to connect. My mom is private. Besides, *you* don't express sympathy, give or take the odd lapse. You just badger the hell out of me." But he didn't sound that bothered.

"I learned the error of my ways in that elevator," she said.

He looked down at her, the corners of his mouth tipping up a tiny fraction. Rachel had an urge to run her thumb across those lips, to force them to soften. She wedged both thumbs beneath her butt on the desk to prevent any uncontrollable caresses.

"How old were you *exactly* when your mother died?" She waited for a flip reply.

"Fifteen," he said. "My fifteenth birthday." He looked as if he wished he hadn't shared even that crumb. Why had he?

"Right," she said, forcing down her compassion for a teenager who'd lost his mom at a difficult age, on his birthday.

Garrett looked relieved.

"And how did she die again?" she asked casually.

He chuckled. "Nice try."

"Do you talk about your mom with your family?" she asked.

"None of your—"

"Damn business," she finished. "But, for the record, if you don't, maybe you should. Because you'll probably find the rest of the family would love to even just say her name."

He made violin-playing motions, and she shook her head in amused frustration.

"While I'm badgering you, why don't you like your stepmother?" she asked.

He flinched. "What makes you think I don't like her?"

"Maybe it's the way you flinch at the word *stepmother*."

He flinched again, and his lips pressed together.

"She seemed great," Rachel said. "Really nice."

"Are you *trying* to annoy me?" he asked.

"Is it working?"

A reluctant grin pulled at his mouth. "You definitely have the knack."

"How did the sonogram go?" she asked.

His whole face lit up, robbing her of breath. "It was amazing. I could see everything, ten tiny fingers and toes...." He broke off, clearly appalled at his own gushing.

"I hope you mean ten of each, rather than ten total," Rachel said. "Because that would be weird."

He laughed, obviously grateful not to be called on the emotion.

"Families, huh?" she said. "How does the thing that matters most end up going so wrong? I don't know if LeeAnne will ever speak to me again." Her voice hitched on the last word.

Garrett pushed off the desk and paced to the wall, to the framed photographs of her nieces. His back to her, he stared at it.

"The thing is, Rachel," he said, "I know something about begging."

"*You* do?" she asked. "You told me you'd never..."

"I've never begged a date not to break up with me— only a total loser would do that." He turned, flashed her a grin. Then his smile faded, and he thrust his hands into his pockets.

"I begged my father not to marry Stephanie," Garrett said. He shook his head at the memory, in self-recrimination. "I was in tears."

"Oh, Garrett." Rachel knew without a doubt that was the last time he'd cried. She wanted to cry herself.

"I begged," he said again, quietly.

"And begging never works."

His head jerked in acknowledgment of the advice he'd given her. Advice he'd learned the hard way. "I even tried blackmail," he said. "Told my father if he married her, I wouldn't ever do what he wanted again."

"I'm...surprised he went ahead with the wedding so fast, knowing how strongly you felt." Rachel struggled to keep her voice calm. The thought of Garrett crying, pleading, broke her heart.

That he was willing to admit that part of his past to her did something else altogether—it filled her heart with tenderness. Probably a bad idea.

"He said it was for our sake, mine and Lucas's," Garrett said. "We needed the stability."

More or less the same words she'd used with Lee-Anne. Rachel cringed.

"I'm sorry," she said. Apologizing to him for his father's insensitivity, to LeeAnne for her own.

She held out her hand to him; he took it. In the space between them, something flared. Something powerful.

Rachel saw the moment Garrett started to panic. His eyes widened, he dropped her hand and took a rapid step back, as if she'd just admitted to having Spanish flu and promptly coughed all over him.

Three seconds later, he was gone.

STEPHANIE GRABBED a take-out herbal tea from the tea shop below the studio where she'd just completed her antenatal Pilates class. She added a small handmade chocolate to her order—the caffeine fix she could take without feeling guilty or without facing the overt disapproval of young servers who had no idea of the stress involved in being a forty-five-year-old, single, first-time mom with the only person in the world who truly loved her—Lucas, her younger stepson—engaged in active duty in the Persian Gulf.

Not that she was entirely alone. She had a couple of old school friends in Manhattan, girls she'd lost contact with. Now, she'd picked up those old threads and was enjoying catching up for the odd coffee—or tea—or shopping for the baby with one of them. And she had Garrett, sort of. Though she was hoping and praying for much more where he was concerned.

Balancing her tea and chocolate, Stephanie waited for the walk sign—fifteen years of marriage to Dwight had instilled a safety consciousness deep enough into her that she couldn't adopt the Manhattanite habit of standing out in the road ready to move the moment the light changed. The other side of the road was one of her favorite stops on her route: the Play Time toy store.

Garrett and Lucas had been teenagers when she'd married Dwight, so she'd never bought a toy in her adult life—in fact, not since her own childhood when she'd saved with her allowance for a Barbie doll. She knew her baby wouldn't need toys for a while, but she liked to window-shop.

People streamed across the road, and as soon as the walk sign lit, Stephanie joined them.

When she reached the other side, she almost walked right into her husband, coming the other way.

"Dwight!" she exclaimed. "What are you doing here?"

"Hello, Stephanie." He grasped her elbow to pull her from the crush of pedestrians into the alcove of the toy-store window. "How are you?"

"I'm fine. Thank you." She hoped her hair wasn't frizzing at the ends in the increased humidity. She was more sensitive to frizz when pregnant, it seemed. "And you?"

He nodded, but didn't really answer.

"What are you doing in this part of town?" she asked again.

He hesitated. "I had a meeting. With a reporter."

Stephanie stared. He was lying. Dwight, who never lied, was telling an untruth. And not very well, either. His face was red, his eyes flickering downward. Could he be here to see her?

Her heart thudded. Could Dwight be missing her enough to back down?

"How's the baby?" he asked.

"Everything's fine. I had a scan the other day."

"You didn't tell me." He sounded almost hurt, but she knew she didn't have that capacity. He was as impervious as one of those frigates he loved.

"I know it's not really your thing," she said. He'd accompanied her to her first scan, but out of duty rather than enthusiasm. He'd told her he hadn't done "any of that" with Michelle, his first wife, but he understood times had changed and this was what fathers did today. This was his duty.

"But you don't like to go alone," he said, frowning.

"Garrett came with me." She'd said it to reassure him, but he stiffened. Which was exactly why she was here, because he was incapable of seeing any good in his older son. Incapable of accepting that a refusal to do things Dwight's way didn't make Garrett the enemy.

She knew Dwight would see her as the enemy now. The thought pained her because she loved him so much. Because in his heart, he was such a good man. If only he could choose to define himself by something other than his ability to command.

"It's nice to see you," she said. "But I need to keep moving. I have an appointment."

"A doctor's appointment?" he asked.

"With a photographer," she said. "The husband of a friend of mine. He offered to take some photos that would, um, celebrate my pregnant body."

"Naked photos?" Dwight said, horrified.

She was tempted to say yes. But he might have a stroke and, besides, at forty-five she wasn't keen to flaunt her naked, swollen body. "Some pictures that emphasize this." She touched her tummy. "I might have a few more buttons undone than you would like."

Dwight's mouth worked. He would turn sixty-one soon after the birth of their baby. Far from ideal as a father. He was an old man. In his attitude, anyway.

She realized he was eyeing her stomach, where she'd touched it, almost hungrily. "Dwight?"

"It's my child," he said.

"Of course it is." In that moment she realized why he was there. Not because he'd suddenly discovered he couldn't live without her. He wanted to check up on her and his baby. His responsibilities.

The blare of a taxi horn almost drowned out her words. "If you really want to come to the next doctor's appointment, I'll let you know when it is."

"Don't you dare just schedule me into your life," he ordered.

"You're the one who likes to draw a line, to say this far and no further."

To her shock, he grabbed her arm and tugged her. Into the toy store.

"Dwight, what are you doing?" she asked. But the heat faded from her voice as she gazed around the store.

Dollhouses, tricycles, stuffed animals... She took them all in. Her rapturous smile was in anticipation of sharing such delights with their baby, Dwight guessed.

He felt much better now that he had her inside, off that crowded sidewalk...no matter that he'd derived an idiotic amount of pleasure from watching her cross the street. He loved the way she waited, bouncing gently on the balls of her feet until the walk sign lit up. He found her caution, mingled with her obvious desire to keep moving, deeply sexy.

She'd looked happier, out there in the street. As she had on the other days he'd trailed her around, usually at lunchtime, some days when he had a spare hour or two between appointments. She possessed a quiet, confident enjoyment that worried him. An independent enjoyment that didn't involve him. Not that he wanted a clinging wife, not at all. But he wanted their life together to be the source of her strength, her happiness.

As it was for him, he realized with a shock. He loved the navy, but that inner peace that created a sense of rightness...that came from knowing Stephanie was at home, his wife.

He suspected that wasn't the line to win her back. Which he accepted that maybe he did want to do.

"I'd like to buy something," he said. "For the baby."

"We already chose the crib," she said. "And the changing table. And you built that toy chest."

All of those things were at home in New London, and

the flicker of chagrin across her face acknowledged her uncertainty as to where they would end up.

Not in Garrett's apartment, that was for sure.

"Not that sort of thing," Dwight said. "A toy. The child will need to play. Won't it?" Among the many accusations she'd leveled at him was that he was too rigid. That he needed to lighten up.

Her forehead creased. "Of course. When he or she is a little older."

He bit back his annoyance that she hadn't agreed to find out the baby's sex. It was so much more practical. But there were plenty of—what were they called?— *gender-neutral* toys.

He led her toward a display of teddy bears. They had all kinds, from the old-fashioned Edward Bear he remembered from his own childhood to bright pink and yellow specimens that appeared to be made from bath towels. Stephanie liked bright pink, he knew, but obviously he couldn't buy that one when the baby might be a boy.

"Do you have a teddy bear yet?" he asked, the sweep of his hand indicating she could take her pick.

"No…" Her brown eyes were troubled. "Dwight, of all the things we need to talk about, this isn't the most important."

"What would you like to talk about?" He realized his scowl had scared off the approaching clerk. He didn't want to do the same to Stephanie, so he softened his expression. "I want you to come home, Stephanie. You belong with me, you and our child."

"I don't belong to you," she said.

"I said *with* me." His hands curled at his sides in frustration. "Just like I belong with you. We're married. That's a forever commitment for me, and I know it is for you, too."

"There's more to marriage than a piece of paper," she said. "There's love."

"I do love you," he said. "I know I can be a little set in my ways—" he didn't know why that was so bad, but evidently it was "—but I'll change. Be more...accepting."

"So, you wouldn't mind if our child took after Garrett?"

He winced.

"Garrett is a wonderful boy," she said, apparently ignoring the fact Garrett wasn't that much younger than she was.

"He deliberately sets out to antagonize me," Dwight objected.

"He has a senior job in an excellent firm, he owns his own home, he doesn't do drugs or run wild." She checked off points on her fingers. "But he's a disappointment to you."

"That's not true." But it sounded feeble. Garrett *was* a disappointment. He had so much potential and he wasted it on car advertisements. For fifteen years, he'd refused to consider any suggestion Dwight had made. Let alone obey an instruction.

But talking about his oldest son wasn't going to help him win this battle. Dwight scanned the ranks of teddy bears and found just what he wanted, right at the back. A four-foot teddy bear in an inoffensive pale yellow. He waded in, and wrestled it out from its position between a polar bear and a grizzly.

"This one," he said.

Stephanie stared. "What?"

"I want to buy this for our baby." He held it aloft. She would recognize that buying such a monstrosity wasn't his normal style. He was thinking about the baby, thinking about the things that other fathers—more indulgent fathers—might do.

"But…it's tasteless."

He beamed. Exactly the point he was trying to make. "He'll love it. Or *she* will." That blasted don't-know-the-sex thing again. "Wait right here." With difficulty, he tucked the bear under his arm and headed to the cash register.

When he returned, with a Sold sticker taped across the bear's left ear—it was too big to go into a bag—he presented it to Stephanie with a flourish.

"Dwight, I told you I don't like it." She sounded annoyed.

"It's not about what you or I like," he said. "You said I need to be prepared to accept and love our child no matter what, even if it doesn't agree with my opinions. This is to show you that I don't need to have it all my way."

She stared at the bear for a very long time. It really was tacky, he thought, with a qualm of misgiving.

"Okay," she said at last. "I believe you're making an effort."

"Good," he said, trying not to sound surprised. "Good." He wanted to say, *Now will you come home?*

"But this is just a token, and you're doing it for the wrong reasons," she said. "You're aiming to please me, but that's not why I want you to change."

He had no idea what she meant. "Isn't it a good place to start?"

"Dwight, if you don't believe, deep down, that you need to change in a big way, it's never going to work," she said.

He opened his mouth, then closed it again. He didn't believe he was so horrible a father that he needed a sea change in his personality. Hell, the United States Navy trusted him to represent it in the United Nations. He was one of the good guys!

Stephanie put a hand on his arm, and every particle of him wanted her in his bed, in his embrace, in his heart. In their home.

"I love you, Dwight," she said, and his heart leaped. "But I can't live with a man who doesn't love me, and our children, unconditionally."

This was crazy. She loved him, he loved her, she was having his baby...but they couldn't live together?

"Don't do this," he told her, hating the note of pleading in his voice. "Don't destroy our marriage."

She shook her head. Then she picked up that monstrous yellow teddy bear and walked out.

CHAPTER FIFTEEN

RACHEL LOVED FOCUS GROUPS. They were low-cost, low-tech and, as Garrett had said, not exactly the cutting edge of market research. But she loved putting a bunch of people in a room and subtly guiding the discussion so they gave her all kinds of insights they didn't know they had in them. Insights that would improve her ad campaign, and from there, improve the client's bottom line.

While some creative directors got more out of mind mapping or brainstorming, for her this was the most real part of advertising. The most solid.

The tamest?

Not necessarily. She'd once had a focus group dissolve into a fistfight over ice-cream flavors. They had the potential to be as emotional and instinctive—and creative—as anything else.

She checked the recording equipment in the KBC focus group room one last time. Her "groupies" would arrive any moment. A couple of today's attendees were selected from her focus group regulars, people who matched the demographic of Brightwater Group's target market. But most of them were newbies, sent by a firm that specialized in education research. A couple of them were her parents.

She hoped.

She'd called Mom a couple of days ago to remind her, and her mother had sounded...cool. Maybe because Rachel had criticized her parents' decision process on the phone last week. But maybe because LeeAnne had told them about Rachel's highly conditional college-fund offer.

She was afraid they might not turn up today. Which would ruin her plan to have coffee with them after the focus group. Over coffee, in a nice, neutral environment, she would ask them to consider staying put. The Dayton move wasn't definite...they could reconsider in the light of their granddaughters' needs. How could they refuse?

"All set?" Garrett spoke behind her, startling her so that she knocked the sound equipment cart out of alignment.

Rachel straightened the cart before she turned. "Yep. Catch you later."

He raised one eyebrow at her tone. But the fact was, things were awkward between them. After he'd bolted from her office after telling her about his father and Stephanie, she'd expected he would go right back to ignoring her. Pretending he'd never opened up, or that it was somehow her fault for pestering him.

But he hadn't. He spoke to her most days, about work or the weather or whatever. Trivial topics, the kind he usually disdained to talk about. As if the best way to deal with this attraction between them was to smother it in blandness.

She missed their banter. Their arguments. Even his hostile dismissal was better than this neutrality.

"I thought you·might want to hear what Stephanie had to say about tailing Clive," Garrett said. "He's been visiting an internet café on 64th."

"What's he up to that he can't do in the office?" Rachel asked. "Or on his iPhone?" Of course, office computer and iPhone use were all able to be monitored by the IT department.

"Good question."

"Did he see Stephanie?" Rachel asked. "She's not exactly inconspicuous."

"She's damn enormous," Garrett agreed. "But she doesn't think he noticed her."

"Maybe Clive is getting tips from an inside contact at Brightwater," Rachel suggest. "Or maybe he's…bribing Mark Van de Kamp."

"Seems more like the kind of thing you or I would do," Garrett observed.

She had to agree.

"I do know he wants this partnership more than I guessed," Garrett said. "He's desperate to start a family, but Wifey—" they shared a grin at the atrocious endearment "—says they need to buy a house first. She won't have kids living in an apartment."

"I don't believe Stephanie got that close to him, and there's no way you made enough small talk to get that out of him," Rachel said skeptically.

"I was in the bathroom when he took a call from Wifey," Garrett admitted. "That's my interpretation of a one-sided conversation."

"Ugh." Rachel knew people used cell phones in the bathroom, but she found it vaguely unhygienic.

Garrett picked up the sound system remote and jabbed the on button. The console lit up. "So, you haven't heard anything from any of his team?"

"No one around him is as open as usual, but this competitive pitch is an odd situation." She glanced at her watch. "Can we talk about this later?"

"I thought I'd stick around and meet your parents," he said. "They're coming today, right?"

"No!" She schooled panic out of her voice. "I mean, yes, they're coming, but why would you want to meet them? It's not like you're into the whole family thing." Though now that she knew more about his own family, she didn't hold that against him.

"Maybe I'm interested to meet the people who turned you into the amazing woman you are."

She humphed. "I don't believe you."

His grin was disturbingly angelic.

Before she could say more the door opened and her mom catapulted into the room, as people tended to do after that mind-numbingly long elevator ride.

"Rachel, sweetie," Nora said.

No sign of coolness, Rachel noted, with a rush of relief.

"How's my girl?" her father boomed.

One side of Garrett's mouth lifted.

Her dad swung her off her feet as he hugged her.

"Dad," she protested, muffled against his coat.

Garrett said, "Aw, shucks."

When she turned around, he was shaking hands with her mom.

"You must be Mrs. Frye," Garrett said as Rachel took her mother's coat and hung it on the rack behind the door. "I'm Garrett Calder."

"Nora Frye. It's so nice to meet one of Rachel's friends," Nora said.

"He's not a friend," Rachel said. Hadn't Garrett told her that himself?

"Are you folks local?" Garrett asked.

"New Jersey," her dad said. "Though we're thinking about a move to Ohio. There's a new stadium being built in Dayton. We'll be in on the ground floor with one of the concessions—going in with a pal of mine."

Rachel couldn't hold back a little groan of frustration.

"Family disagreement," Nora explained, unaware that Garrett knew the background. "We get a few of those with a daughter as feisty as Rachel. She takes after me," she added with a pride that made Rachel smile despite her aggravation.

"I can certainly see where she gets her great legs," Garrett said.

"Ew!" Rachel stuck her fingers in her ears. "Did you just tell my mom she has good legs?"

"Is that against focus-group ethics?" he asked.

"No, it's just gross. No offence, Mom," she added.

Her mom's gaze was darting between her and Garrett like an inquisitive bird. "None taken, sweetie. Do you work for Rachel, Garrett?"

"Not yet," Garrett said meekly.

"It's more, he works *against* me," Rachel said.

He chuckled. "I'm an executive creative director, like Rachel."

"Would we have seen anything you've done?" her father, the ad connoisseur, asked.

Don't tell him, she thought in sudden alarm.

"There's a Lexus campaign…" Garrett said.

"Not the bridge one?" Her father actually whooped. "I love that ad."

She expected Garrett, Mr. I'm the World's Best Creative Director, to say something bored and obnoxious, like "Most people do." Instead, he said, "Thanks, that one seemed to come out of nowhere. I lucked out."

"The only thing more objectionable than arrogance is false humility," Rachel told him.

He laughed. "Thanks for the tip." He turned to her parents. "Rachel gives me lots of advice."

"She's good at that." Her mom's tone was heartfelt, but not altogether positive. Rachel felt her cheeks warm. "She's very smart," her mom added, as if she was trying to make it better.

Which was one very short step from *she's a know-it-all*.

"Mom, Dad—" Rachel didn't feel this conversation was going anywhere constructive "—we have coffee and snacks set up over there." She pointed to the sideboard against the wall. Her parents were sufficiently aware of their financial limitations never to turn down free eats.

Sure enough, her dad's face brightened. "Lead the way, Nora. We might as well build up our stamina."

Before he followed his wife, he shook Garrett's hand again. "That Lexus campaign," he said. "Sheer genius."

To her annoyance, Garrett meandered over to the food with them, chatting to her dad. Since when was Garrett a chatterer?

Rachel took the opportunity to pull a folded twenty-dollar bill from her jacket pocket and slip it into the pocket of her mom's coat. A furtive glance over her shoulder collided with Garrett's narrowed gaze.

She stepped away from the coatrack, just as four more guests arrived. While Rachel greeted them, Garrett poured coffee for her mom—since when was Garrett a coffee-pourer?

Rachel steered her newest guests over to the refreshments. She arrived in time to hear Garrett say, "You must be very proud of her."

"Oh, we are," Nora said. "She's done amazingly well, through sheer hard work. No privilege, no fancy connections, just determination."

"Mom," Rachel said. "You're making me sound like a saint."

"She's not a saint," Nora told Garrett.

"I noticed." He gave Rachel a look of exasperation. "Rach, could I have a word?" He didn't give her a choice; he grabbed her elbow and led her over by the coatrack.

"I don't have time for this," she said, suddenly nervous. Because his dark eyes were a little too knowing for her comfort. "I need to get this group under way."

"Why did you put money in your mother's coat pocket?" he asked, his voice silky smooth.

"None of your damn business," she said.

"Sorry, Rach, that doesn't work on me." He hooked his fingers over the pocket in question. "Will you tell me, or should I show this to your mother?"

"No!" She batted his hand away. "My parents don't have much cash, but they don't like to accept money from me. I slip the occasional twenty their way, just to help out. I do the same for LeeAnne."

"And you don't think they notice?"

"I'm sure they don't."

"Rachel..." He rubbed his chin. "People who don't have much money know exactly how much they don't have. There's no way your mom and dad haven't figured it out."

"They would have said something," she insisted.

"What, like *thank you?*"

She colored. "I don't expect that. I can afford it, and it helps them out."

"Rachel, Rachel, Rachel." He shook his head sadly.

"What?" she demanded.

"You're talking to someone who knows manipulation in all its forms. Admit it, the money's for your benefit, not theirs."

"That's not true!"

"It's like that college fund you offered your sister. You're paying your parents to stay put."

"That ridiculous," she said. "As if a twenty-dollar bill would do that."

"Enough twenty-dollar bills might take the edge off their hunger for a new opportunity."

Something must have shown in her face, because he

added roughly, "You need to stop. Or you'll end up with no relationship at all with your parents. For me, that's not a problem. But for you…"

"I have an excellent relationship with my family," she said. Not counting LeeAnne, who still hadn't returned her calls.

"Great," he said. "If you love something, set it free, yada, yada, yada."

"That's a stupid sentiment." Her core froze at the very thought. "My parents are not free. They have responsibilities." She craned to see around him. Her guests were still enjoying their coffees. "That's a foreign concept to you, of course. I'm comfortable that giving Mom and Dad twenty dollars won't be the end of our family."

He rolled his eyes. "Yeah, but, if I know you—"

"You don't," she said. It was spooky how she found herself giving him the same objections he'd thrown at her over the past few weeks.

"Yeah, I do." He didn't look happy at the realization. "There's more to your plan than this. What else are you offering your parents?"

"Exactly the same focus group fee as everyone else."

"There must be more," he said suspiciously.

Rachel pushed past him before he read the guilt in her face. "Ladies and gentlemen, we're ready to get started. If you need another coffee, grab it now, then please take your seats."

She ignored Garrett while she waited for everyone to settle.

One of her regulars stopped in front of Rachel.

"What time do we finish this afternoon? I have a doctor's appointment at five."

"We'll be done by three-thirty," Rachel assured her.

Her mother heard. "I thought you said we should plan on taking the six o'clock train home."

Blast. "That's because—" she turned away from Garrett "—I wanted to have some time with you and Dad, afterward. I thought we might get a drink or a bite to eat."

Nora hesitated. "I guess we could do that."

"Of course you could," Rachel said, rather shrilly. *You're my parents.* Had they guessed why she wanted this time with them?

"Excuse me, Nora," Garrett said.

Rachel wheeled around. "You need to leave. Now."

"I couldn't help overhearing," Garrett said to her mom. "If you're staying around for a little while, would you and your husband like to visit the set where we made the Lexus commercial?"

Rachel let out a hiss.

"We'd love to," her father boomed.

"Mom, I really need—"

"Thank you, Garrett, we'd be delighted," Nora said, far too quickly for Rachel's liking.

She clamped her mouth shut. Her mom wanted to avoid the looming conversation, and Garrett had just made it possible. She should have know better than to expect The Shark to take her side.

But it still hurt.

CHAPTER SIXTEEN

NOTHING WAS GOING as it should. Garrett had monopolized her parents after the focus group on Thursday, and Rachel hadn't had a chance to do more than ascertain that they hadn't yet made up their minds about Dayton. When she'd confronted Garrett about his interfering, he'd said, "You'll thank me tomorrow."

Which she hadn't, just as she hadn't thanked him for her breakup with Piers. The man had a very strange notion of how to earn gratitude.

Things weren't going well on the LeeAnne front, either. Her sister still wasn't returning her calls.

Work wasn't much better. Rachel had emailed Tony some suggestions for improving the team spirit around KBC, but hadn't heard back from him. Her team was doing good work…but not exceptional work. She didn't know how to inspire them to do better. Clive continued to slip out on mysterious errands, and the more she thought about it, the more Rachel worried he presented a threat she didn't fully understand.

As for Garrett… Garrett was focused on his pitch to the exclusion of all else, it seemed. Now that he'd figured out he really wanted to make partner, he was going for it. Rachel had tried pumping Alice for information about how things were going. The breathless answer, "Garrett's a genius."

Apparently, his team had the most brilliant creative since...well, since Garrett's world-famous Lexus campaign.

Rachel prowled the fifty-fourth floor on Monday morning, too keyed up to concentrate on her work, but knowing she couldn't afford to take time out.

She walked past Clive's office and found him in close confabulation with two members of his team. He glanced up, caught Rachel's eye and smiled. There was too much self-satisfaction in that smile for her comfort. Rachel walked on by, as if she knew exactly where she was going. She walked all the way to the end of the floor.

"Hi, Rachel." Jenny, the accounts payable clerk who occupied the southwest corner, quickly put down the nail file she was using. "Sorry, torn nail. I've done all my work for the morning."

"I won't tattle." Rachel hovered next to her desk.

An idea struck her. Jenny had once confided that she hadn't been to college and had been excited to learn that Rachel hadn't, either. It gave her hope she might be able to progress from her current job at the bottom of the ladder. She seemed bright. College material.

"Jenny, what was the reason you never went to college?" Rachel asked.

Jenny eyed her torn nail with irritation. "My folks couldn't afford it, and they drilled some old-fashioned ideas about debt into me."

Rachel sighed, remembering her own parents' eagerness for her to take on massive loans. She pulled up a chair from the adjacent empty cubicle. "Did Garrett or Clive talk to you about this yet?"

Jenny shook her head, puzzled.

"Okay, I need to pick your brain." Rachel wheeled her chair farther into the girl's cubicle so no one would see her and get the same idea. Of course, Garrett probably didn't know Jenny existed. "Let's talk."

It was a useful half hour, backing up the conclusions of her focus group, but adding a younger perspective.

"Thanks, Jenny, that was great," Rachel said, as she stood to leave.

"You're welcome." Jenny picked up her nail file. "You're a real inspiration to me, Rachel, the way you rose up through the ranks even without an education."

"Thanks," Rachel said. "I'm sure you'll start progressing soon."

The girl grimaced. "It can't come soon enough for me. The accounts payable work is so easy I'm left filing my nails, but so far the only promotion I've had is to health and safety officer." She indicated a cupboard on her wall with a red cross on it. "Which wasn't quite what I was hoping for."

Rachel laughed. "Don't knock it—I did a stint as health and safety gal. Though it's a bit more laborious these days—you should probably be recording that torn fingernail."

Assuming nothing else had changed, the cupboard would contain a logbook for accidents and hazards. Along with a first aid kit, a folder full of safety pro-

cedures...and hanging on a rows of hooks, spare keys
for all the offices.

Clive's key was in that cupboard. And Garrett's.

Rachel's palms dampened as an idea hit her, shameful in its deviousness. *These are desperate times.*

Office procedure said the cupboard should be locked at night, but during the day it was left unlocked, so people could get to the first aid equipment in a hurry.

"You've been so helpful, Jenny, answering all my questions. I'd like to do something for you," Rachel said. "Why don't you go have a manicure, fix that nail properly? My treat."

"Really?"

"It's nearly lunchtime. If you leave now, you'll beat the rush to the nail bar across the street. I'll call them and leave my credit card number."

"That would be amazing." Jenny was already gathering up her purse, tossing in the nail file. "Thanks, Rachel."

The moment she'd gone, Rachel opened the cupboard door. Yep, the hooks, just as she remembered, with keys on them. Above each hook was a sticker with the name of the office occupant. Two keys on each hook.

Rachel took a key off Clive's hook and slipped it into her pocket. If he didn't want people snooping around, he shouldn't act so suspicious. She closed the cupboard, then went to phone the nail bar.

STEPHANIE WAS BEING FOLLOWED.

Again.

By her husband.

She didn't look behind her as she crossed 4th Avenue, but she knew Dwight was there. This was the third time he'd tailed her.

Why? He wasn't the kind of possessive man who needed to know his wife's whereabouts. When they'd been together, he'd had little interest in her activities, and she wasn't worried that he'd suddenly developed stalker tendencies. The most likely explanation was that he was concerned for her well-being. But he would see admitting that outright as a sign of weakness.

She'd noticed him for the first time on Thursday, the day after they'd met in the toy store. Which was ironic, because at the time she'd been tailing Clive, Garrett's colleague. The activity made her feel guilty…but this was the first time Garrett had asked her to do something for him. *Ever.* Clive hadn't seemed to realize she was there, which said more about his lack of suspicion than her surveillance abilities. Yet somehow that day, and on other days since, *she* had known that Dwight, a trained naval intelligence officer, was following her. Must be a husband-wife thing.

Last Friday, as usual, she'd gone for a walk in Central Park. Her stroll had taken her to the Chess & Checkers House, her favorite place in the park—she loved to watch the players, mostly older men at this time of day, intent on their games.

She didn't play chess herself, though Dwight was a keen player. When they were first married, she'd asked him to teach her, but he'd said it would be too frustrating for both of them. She hadn't asked again, but she'd gotten into the habit of stopping by this area of the park whenever she was in the city. She would pick a game, and watch it through—it was an oddly compelling sport to watch. Which probably meant she'd grown old before her time.

On Friday, she'd settled on a bench near the pair she'd chosen to watch. Over the years, she'd picked up the moves of the game, so she was soon engrossed. She wouldn't have seen Dwight at all, if a player at another table—a man whose demeanor shrieked retired military, hadn't called out, "Calder! Over here."

Stephanie had looked up at the sound of her own name. And seen Dwight—*her* Dwight—hurrying away. She hadn't seen his face, but she knew his coat and his brisk, controlled walk.

It confirmed her suspicion that their encounter outside the toy store hadn't been accidental.

On Sunday, she'd seen him again, seen his face reflected in a store window. When she looked around, he was gone.

Now, two days later, she'd seen Dwight on the other side of the Bergdorf maternity wear department. She wondered where his assistant thought he was. Or if with his usual rigorous honesty he put *Spy on Stephanie* into his diary.

He wasn't calling her, he certainly wasn't begging her to go back to him…but he was following her. The knowledge filled her with hope.

RACHEL NEEDED TO USE Clive's spare office key soon, and to put it back. Just her luck if Clive lost his key,

asked Jenny for a spare, then noticed someone had pur-
loined—*borrowed*—the other spare.

The easiest thing would be to come back into the
office tonight, she decided. Waiting around for others
to leave wasn't a good idea, when people often worked
until nine o'clock. Better to go innocently home, then
return later.

She waited until midnight. Since her neighborhood
wasn't the best, she called a cab to take her back down-
town, rather than walk the shadowed stretch to the subway.

She considered dressing in black jeans and T-shirt,
as any self-respecting spy would, but that would look
suspicious. So she stuck with her regular jeans and a
copper-colored tee. Totally innocent.

The cab traveled fast in the light traffic, reaching the
KBC building by twelve-fifteen.

The elevator ride seemed every bit as slow as the one
she'd taken with Garrett that day. The day everything
had changed in what seemed like a heartbeat.

On the fifty-fourth floor, she swiped her ID card
for after-hours access beyond the reception area. The
security records would show she'd been here, but that
was easily explained by a sudden burst of creativity.
She'd never been questioned about late-night office visits before.

She'd also never felt anxious about being in the office late before. But tonight, probably because her purpose was nefarious, she had a bad case of the jitters.

Get in, get the info, get out, she told herself, forcing
herself to slow her footsteps to a near-normal pace as

she walked a darkened row of cubicles toward Clive's office.

The key worked without a problem. Rachel had turned on the overhead lights in the common area, but she left them off in Clive's office, just in case someone else had a midnight stroke of genius and showed up to work. One lit office would stand out instantly in the row of dark ones. She pulled out a flashlight and shone it on the file drawer behind the desk where she'd expect to find Clive's Brightwater work. She pulled open the drawer. Ah, there it was, under *B*. Good old Clive.

She lifted the file out and set it on the desk. A twinge of guilt made her pause...but this wasn't just a job, this was her security, her *life*. Besides, she remembered Clive had once been handed a file by a friendly bartender that had been forgotten by a Saatchi staffer. Naturally, he'd read it, as had half of KBC.

Rachel opened the folder. She was more looking for signs of what Clive might be up to with his secret meetings than for the details of his creative, but it was the creative that came to hand. Clive had taken a different tack from her, focusing on the sense of community and friendships that students would develop at a Brightwater college. That was the weird thing about creative work. A hook that was obvious to one person wouldn't be rated by another.

Rachel sifted through to another document, a schedule of meetings. Damn, she should have checked her flashlight before she came; the bulb was showing definite signs of dimming. She moved it closer to the page, casting a yellow spotlight on the paper.

"Find anything interesting?" a voice said from the doorway.

Rachel squawked and dropped her flashlight. It rolled onto the floor and went out.

"Garrett, what the hell are you doing here?"

He turned on his own flashlight, more powerful than hers, and trained the beam on her face. Rachel shielded her eyes with her arm.

"I'm guessing the same as you," he said.

"Could you lower that thing, please?"

When he was no longer dazzling her, she said, "For a guy who doesn't get involved, you have a bad habit of interfering in everything I do."

"I'm not here because of you," he said. "I wanted to see what Clive's been up to." He dangled a key in front of her. "That health and safety girl—"

"Jenny," she inserted.

"—actually left her desk for more than five minutes yesterday, went shopping or something. I took the opportunity to borrow a key."

"So now there's no spare on Clive's hook?" she said, aghast. "Garrett, if anyone had opened that cupboard today it would have been immediately obvious someone was spying on Clive."

"Lucky no one checked, then." He tossed the key in the air and caught it. "To be honest, Rach, I'm kind of weirded out that you and I had the same idea at the same time."

"You're a bad influence," she muttered. "And by the way, I'm still mad at you for butting in with my mom and dad after the focus group."

"I did you a favor," he said dismissively. "You're so damn determined to hang on, I knew you wouldn't take my advice unless I forced you."

"What happened to *On my own terms?*" she demanded.

"That's for the advanced jerk," he said. "You're a beginner." He scanned her figure. "I always thought pink was your color, but that bronzey thing is good, too."

"You seriously sit around thinking about what my color is?" she said.

He grinned. "Okay, I was trying to distract you from whining."

She bit down on a smile. It was hard to stay mad at Garrett.

"Tell me what Clive's up to," he said. "What did you find?"

"No details of any secret meetings or emails," she said. "But if you want to take a look at his pitch..."

"Since we're here..." Garrett began skimming the material.

"He's banging the community and friends drum— his graphics look a bit like Facebook." Though not so similar that they'd have a lawsuit on their hands.

She leaned in to show him what she meant and found herself so close she could see the shadow of imminent beard on his jaw. So close she could smell that damn pineneedle and orange-peel scent.

Rachel shifted from one foot to the other.

"Huh," Garrett said. "His words aren't that compelling, but the graphics are great."

"I agree."

Together, they flipped through the rest of the materials.

"I'm happy to report my pitch is better than this." Garrett gave the last page a dismissive flick with thumb and forefinger.

"You mean your *team's* pitch?"

"Absolutely." He grinned.

Rachel closed the file. "So is my team's." Then she ruined it by adding, "Assuming the client has any taste."

"You worry too much," Garrett said. "You can beat Clive any time."

"Clive might win a CLIO," she muttered as Garrett returned the file to the drawer.

"The CLIOs don't matter."

She snorted.

"They're nice to have," he admitted. "And they convey a certain level of credibility. But if your creative is the best for Brightwater, the client will see that."

He sounded sincere.

Rachel knew better.

"But you don't believe my creative will be the best," she said.

"Afraid not." He shrugged. "If I thought yours would be better than mine, Rach, I'd give up now."

"I don't know what to say about that stunning tribute to my ability. And," she added halfheartedly, "it's Rach*el*."

He grabbed her hand, twined his fingers through hers. "Seriously, Rach, I plan to win this partnership. You need to start thinking about where you'll go when KBC fires you. If you're smart, you'll start making inquiries at other firms now. You're more marketable when you haven't just lost a pitch."

"Quit trying to intimidate me." But in fact, it was the calm practicality of his words, the total *lack* of menace, that struck fear into Rachel's heart. She hated being uncertain about the future. But it was hard not to be when he sounded so confident.

She staged a yawn. "I think I've had enough espionage for one night. Time for bed."

"I guess we could, if you want," Garrett deadpanned.

She shook her head. "That *so* wasn't an invitation."

"Shame," he said. Then he looked her over the way he had a few minutes ago, only more intently, with those dark eyes sexily hooded. "That's a real shame."

The heat in his gaze dried her mouth. She swallowed, but it didn't help.

Garrett ran a finger down her bare arm. "Kiss me, Rachel," he said. "That last one, in the library, wasn't enough."

She knew *that*. "Not a good idea," she began.

"Kiss me," he ordered again. He'd moved closer, and the words seemed to spark from his mouth to hers, leaving her lips tingling.

"Thanks, but I'm fine," she said.

He sighed. "Very fine."

In the next moment, his arms were around her, one hand splayed across her back, the other cupping her derriere. She had no recollection of how it happened.

"That's quite a skill," she said, breathless.

"Actually," he said, "I'm out of practice. You wait till I get going."

She *couldn't* wait. She went up on tiptoe, gliding her body along his, creating a delicious friction that had both of them freezing in position.

A hiss of air escaped between his bared teeth. "Living dangerously, Rach?"

She didn't know what she was doing; she didn't need to know. All that mattered was the sensation of the lean, hard length of his body imprinting on her softness. She shuddered with need and saw the glimmer of a smile before his mouth touched hers.

Fire, was her first thought. Because the heat that sprang up between them was too intense to be anything else.

This was nothing like that swift, hard kiss in the New York Public Library. Garrett's mouth was just as strong, just as firm, as it had been then. But now it possessed a tantalizing softness that made Rachel want to sign up for days of exploration. *Oh, no,* she thought, a mix of delight and despair.

The sweep of his tongue parted her lips, and she moaned as he entered, tightening her grip on his shoulders convulsively.

She might have guessed that when he applied himself, Garrett Calder would kiss with utter ruthlessness.

She never would have guessed that a no-holds-barred, catch-it-while-you-can, limited-time-only offer—because, surely, that's what this was—would create an urgency she'd never experienced, turning her weak-kneed with desire. She pressed against him, palmed the back of his neck, his shoulders, anything to maximize the contact between his body and hers.

"Dammit, Rachel," he growled as he lifted his mouth from hers long enough to move down to her neck. "You weren't supposed to—" His complaint was lost in a muffled groan as her fingers kneaded his scalp. He nipped the side of her neck as he tugged her T-shirt from her jeans.

The first caress of his fingers against the bare skin of her back had Rachel arching into him.

Her hands roamed the contours of his torso, then dived beneath his T-shirt for a more up-close-and-personal inspection. Mmm, he had the perfect chest.

Dimly, a short, high-pitched sound penetrated Rachel's consciousness.

"What was—" she began, but then Garrett's tongue found her shoulder, and she gave up thinking.

"Your skin tastes incredible," he murmured, and he nipped again, sending a shaft of sensation all the way down to her toes.

"I have never," she panted, "felt anything like this."

He stiffened. Then Rachel heard a creak, followed by a thud.

The door from reception closing! Which meant the previous noise had been the elevator. Which meant they were no longer alone.

CHAPTER SEVENTEEN

"SOMEONE'S HERE," Rachel hissed, leaping away from Garrett.

"Crap." He snatched up his flashlight and switched it off. Grabbing Rachel's hand, he dragged her out of Clive's office into the first cubicle in the row outside.

The plush carpet deadened any footsteps. Garrett motioned to Rachel to stay down, then slowly raised his head until he could just see over the partition.

He dropped back down again. *Clive,* he mouthed.

Rachel's stomach lurched. If Clive had arrived five minutes earlier... Had they left everything as they found it?

Garrett leaned into her. "Where's your flashlight?" he murmured.

Oh, hell. Rachel's consternation must have been written all over her face. Garrett grimaced.

"Okay," he murmured. "I'll distract Clive. You go get the flashlight."

She would have liked more of a plan, but before she could object, Garrett stood. "Evening, Clive," he called, as he sauntered down the row of cubicles.

"Hey, Garrett," she heard Clive say. "I wondered who turned the lights on. You working late?"

Garrett's voice moved farther away. "I had a few things to tie up. I'm just finishing."

"Me, too."

"While you're here, I'd like to get your view on an email that came in from Tony." Garrett's voice seemed to be moving toward his own office.

Rachel peeked over the cubicle and saw Clive following. Still ducked low, she ran for Clive's office. There was her flashlight, just sticking out from under the desk. She grabbed it and dashed into the nearest alley of cubicles.

"Sorry about that. I can't think where I put it." Garrett, explaining the absence of the email he'd invented. "Guess I'll head home."

She tucked herself under a desk until she heard Clive go into his office, then crept along the row. When she reached the end nearest the main door, she saw Garrett waiting, holding the door to reception slightly open so she wouldn't have to make a noise getting out.

It wasn't until he'd closed the door and Rachel let out a breath that she realized she'd been holding it. She pressed for the elevator, which opened immediately, still there from Clive's ascent. Garrett followed her in, and the doors closed behind them.

Rachel sagged against the wall. "I think I'm having a heart attack."

Garrett eyed her breasts in the tight-fitting, copper T-shirt. She half expected an offer to perform chest compressions, but he didn't say anything.

"Do you think Clive suspected?" she asked.

Garrett shook his head. "He seemed nervous, rather

than suspicious. Like he's up to something, but he didn't realize I was, too."

Rachel shivered. "Tonight was a total waste of time—we didn't find out anything." She grinned. "Other than, that you and I still have that certain chemistry thing going."

"Yeah," he said. "If Clive has any secrets, he keeps them at home."

"So, what happens next?" she asked.

"I guess I can have Stephanie follow him again," he said, "but with only a week until the pitches…"

She'd meant what happens next between her and him. Was he being deliberately evasive? It wouldn't surprise her. Garrett would never be an easy man to…like. Which didn't mean a relationship wasn't worth trying. Not if kisses like the one they'd just shared came with it.

He checked his cell phone. "Good, there's a signal. I need to call Stephanie."

"Isn't it a bit late?" Rachel asked.

"She brought me here," Garrett said. "I couldn't sleep, so I got up to have a glass of wine and read a book. After a couple of glasses, breaking into Clive's office started to seem like a good idea." He scrolled through the numbers on his phone. "Stephanie came out just as I was about to leave. She doesn't sleep well with the baby kicking and…other things." He pressed a button to dial. "She insisted on driving me. She's parked nearby. I'm supposed to call when I'm ready. Stephanie?" He spoke into the phone.

By the time they reached the bottom, Garrett's BMW

was outside. It had started to drizzle, so they ran for the car, Rachel taking the backseat.

Picking up on their tension—a mix of adrenaline from their near miss with Clive and a hangover from that kiss, Rachel concluded—Stephanie floored the gas through the quiet streets.

It wasn't until she flicked the turn signal and swung into a parking garage that Rachel remembered she should have stopped the car a while ago.

"I'll hop out here," she said, one hand on the door, "and grab a cab."

Stephanie braked. "Sorry, Rachel, I wasn't thinking. We'll drive you home."

"I'm way up in Washington Heights. A cab's fine. You need your sleep."

"*I'll* drive you," Garrett said.

"No," she said quickly. He might want to pick up where they'd left off, with that kiss.... Right now she was doubting the wisdom of that.

"Then at least come inside to wait," Stephanie said. "I don't want you standing out on the street alone at this time."

They took the elevator from the garage to the fourth floor. When they stepped out, both Garrett and Stephanie stopped still. Rachel barreled into Stephanie's back.

"Sorry," she said into the silence.

The man waiting for them was tall, nearly as tall as Garrett, with features that could only be described as imposing. Hawkish nose, strong chin, squared shoulders that looked as if they didn't know how to relax.

"Dwight," Stephanie said.

"Where have you been?" His voice was deep and rough with worry.

"For a drive," she said, apologetic.

But where Stephanie had softened at the sight of their visitor, Garrett had tensed. He stepped quickly between Dwight and Stephanie. Dwight—presumably Garrett's father and Stephanie's husband—clearly didn't appreciate that. His jaw set like concrete.

"What are you doing here so late?" Stephanie asked.

"I saw you drive out, I thought maybe the baby. There was. Something wrong."

"I would have called you if there was," Stephanie said gently. "You should have called my cell if you were worried."

"I left my phone at the office." Dwight reddened slightly.

Rachel guessed such a lapse in attention wasn't a regular occurrence for him.

"Why were you here in the first place?" Garrett asked.

"The Indonesian defense attaché to the UN was hosting a dinner at a restaurant on Christopher Street," he said. "I drove past on my way home and saw you leaving. By the time I turned around, I'd lost you. I decided to wait here."

"Dwight, I'm fine," Stephanie said. "The outing was a—a social thing."

Garrett said, "Rachel, this is my father, Admiral Dwight Calder."

Rachel felt as if she should salute, but instead she shook his hand. "Nice to meet you, Admiral Calder."

He eyed her with deep distrust. As if it had been Rachel's idea that his wife should gallivant around the streets of Manhattan in the middle of the night.

"Let's go inside." Stephanie stifled a yawn. "Dwight, you can stay for a cup of tea."

The admiral looked as if he was unused to being told what he could and couldn't do, and Garrett looked as if he'd like to countermand Stephanie and send his father home...but both men followed her inside, keeping their distance from each other, letting Rachel go first.

As Rachel could have predicted, Garrett's loft-style condo was supercool, rather than comfortable. High ceilings with art deco moldings and fancy track lighting, white walls, dark stained wood floors. His furniture was masculine, but classy. Leather sofas, large armchairs, a wide flat-panel TV on the wall. Entirely out of place was a hideous giant yellow teddy bear in the corner by the window.

Stephanie headed into the striking kitchen area— red, glass-fronted cabinets and top-of-the-line stainless steel appliances. She filled a kettle with water and set it on the stove.

"This place is amazing," Rachel told Garrett from a window that overlooked St. Christopher Square. "Is it rent-controlled?"

"I own it," he said.

Rachel did a double take. The condo had to be worth somewhere near two-million dollars. She had taken a conservative approach to her own mortgage, committing to a loan of twice her salary, on top of her down payment.

"You must be more leveraged than a Ponzi scheme," she joked.

Too late, she realized Dwight was listening. At the mention of speculative financing, a frown settled between his eyes, the same coal-dark hue as his son's.

"I'm sure it was good value," she said quickly.

"Not particularly," Garrett said. "I just liked it."

Dwight's frown deepened. Great, she was about to be responsible for expanding the rift between father and son. She'd wondered if a fifteen-year-old boy could have the strength to live by the threat he'd made to his father, that he would never do what his dad wanted again, but the tension between the two men now made it clear they didn't get along.

"Lucky you're so successful in your job," Rachel said with forced cheer, "that you can afford a place like this." Though she couldn't quite see how the numbers added up.

"Rachel, I'm having chamomile tea," Stephanie said, "but would you like something stronger?"

She felt the need of something *much* stronger. "Coffee, please. The real thing."

Stephanie handed Garrett the French press and the coffee beans, then pulled cups from a cupboard.

Garrett ground the beans in a grinder, effectively preventing conversation for half a minute.

Dwight sat stiffly in an armchair. Rachel tried not to think about a teenage Garrett begging his dad not to remarry so soon. She didn't want to hate the man right off the bat, not when she liked his wife.

"Garrett." Dwight cleared his throat when the coffee

grinder stopped. "How are you going with that partnership at your firm?"

Stephanie sent her husband an encouraging smile which, unfortunately, Garrett noticed.

He scowled. "I'll know in about a week if I got it."

"I. Hope you do." What an odd manner Dwight had.

"Rachel's up for the job, too," Garrett said.

His father inspected her. "Are you as good at your job as you say Garrett is?"

"We have different strengths," she said.

"Rachel's not so strong on the creative side," Garrett said.

Hey! She stared at him, aware of Stephanie turning in surprise, too.

"In fact, she's likely to be leaving KBC soon," he continued.

This was what she got for trying to support him in front of his dad? She was tempted to tell him exactly what she thought of his attitude...but he must be reverting to bad old Shark Garrett for a reason. Probably because that kiss had spooked him. She would give him some space and head for neutral territory.

"I love the red kitchen," she said. "Are you thinking of adding more color to the rest of the apartment?" The walls were very white.

"It works for me the way it is," Garrett said. "I don't care what anyone else thinks of it."

Was that meant for Stephanie—a reminder her occupancy was temporary? Or for Rachel, a warning that no matter how hot their kisses, she shouldn't expect to be a part of his life?

"Good idea not to spend too much," Dwight said. "You wouldn't want to overcapitalize."

Garrett looked wary of hearing words that might constitute approval from his father.

His eyes on Rachel, he said deliberately, "I'm not too worried about the financial side. My bonus should take my income to three hundred thousand this year."

Rachel's jaw sagged. "*How* much?"

Dwight looked torn between shock and disapproval of such indiscreet talk about money.

"Are you telling me you earn fifty percent more than I do?" Rachel demanded.

Silence fell.

From the kitchen, Stephanie called, "Cream and sugar?"

No one answered.

Rachel almost wished she hadn't asked. This looked set to be a major humiliation. But she needed to know.

Garret lifted his shoulder in a shrug. "I wouldn't know."

"I bring as much money as you do into the firm," she said. When he lifted one eyebrow she qualified that with "Almost." Of course, Garrett also brought eight golden statues. Possibly soon to be nine. Not to mention a certain cool factor.

Stephanie poured boiling water into two tea mugs, then handed Garrett the kettle for the coffee. She pulled a plastic container from the pantry. "I made oatmeal cookies."

Dwight's face lit up. "My favorite." Then he appeared to recall she hadn't made them for him, and he subsided.

"I have a few more years' experience, and I've been headhunted for my last few jobs, including this one," Garrett reminded Rachel. "I get paid a premium to switch agencies. Maybe you should put a few feelers out."

Once again, he was telling her she would need a new job soon.

"I'm sure I could make a lateral move to another firm, but I wouldn't get offered a partnership," she said. Partnerships were few and far between. "I want that long-term stability. Besides, I love KBC. It's like home."

Ogilvy & Mather had tried to poach Rachel last year. She'd turned them down from the get-go, hadn't even heard their offer. As far as she was concerned, a bird in the hand was worth a dozen in the bush.

"You love it even though they're not treating you right?" Stephanie asked as she set the coffee mugs on the low table.

"They've been very good to me." *When it suited them.* The sneaking thought surprised her. "I—I'm happy there," she said. Aware she was now starting to sound a little pathetic.

"Maybe you should expect more," Stephanie said. "Sometimes we assume we're still happy, when in reality we haven't taken a good, hard look at our situation in years."

When Dwight twitched in his chair, Rachel realized her insights weren't entirely about KBC.

Then Garrett said, "You need to know, Rach, loyalty doesn't pay."

And she knew damn well he wasn't talking about work. Ever since they'd left the office tonight, ever since that kiss, he'd been demonstrating his lack of willingness to engage. Warning her not to expect anything.

CHAPTER EIGHTEEN

GARRETT WATCHED RACHEL sipping her coffee, her hands wrapped around the mug, her face somber. Try as he might, he couldn't stop thinking about the feel of her fingers against his scalp, when he'd kissed her tonight.

Couldn't stop thinking about the taste of her, the sound of her little cries of pleasure. Her words *I've never felt anything like this.*

That, more than anything, more even than the alarming sensation of being thrust out of his depth by a kiss, had decided him.

He didn't want to be the man who made Rachel feel…however she'd felt tonight. Next, she'd be relying on him, expecting all kinds of things—emotions, commitments—from him that he didn't want to give.

He'd felt like a jerk just now, but at least he'd made his position clear. As soon as she finished that coffee, she'd be out of here.

The silence stretched until Garrett could see Rachel and Stephanie were uncomfortable with it. It didn't bother him; nor, it seemed, his father.

"Are you from New York, Admiral Calder?" Rachel asked Dwight after another moment.

"Boston," Dwight said. "The navy provides a studio

apartment near the UN for my use midweek, but home is Connecticut—New London. We moved there before Garrett was born."

"He means he and Michelle, his first wife," Stephanie inserted easily.

She'd never shied away from mentioning his mom, Garrett realized. Never acted possessive or resentful.

No need to resent a woman who's not around to compete.

"We didn't want to leave, even though the navy sent me on long-term assignments every so often," Dwight said. "Michelle used to say New London was the safest place in the world." He rubbed his forehead. "Which is ironic."

It was obvious he was referring to her death. Damn, just when Garrett had made it plain Rachel wasn't getting anything more out of him. He waited for her to pounce on the opportunity to learn the truth.

"Indeed," Rachel murmured, and took another sip of her coffee. "So, what's been your most enjoyable assignment?"

She wasn't asking about his mother?

His dad launched into a description of the three months he'd spent at Coronado. Rachel gave every impression of interest, while Garrett sat there wondering why she hadn't asked how his mother died.

One possible reason was that she'd lost interest in him. That would be good. Yep, he told himself, that would be excellent. Just dandy.

"Stephanie, you need some sleep." Dwight reached

out, touched Stephanie's arm. "I'll go now. Rachel, can I offer you a ride?"

"I live way up in Washington Heights," she said.

"That's no problem," Dwight said. "Though I should warn you, I drive a Hummer. You'll have to set aside any greenie scruples." It was the kind of heavy-handed humor his father specialized in. It was also a dig at Garrett, who'd called the Hummer a gas-guzzler on more than one occasion.

"Maybe not the most ecofriendly car," Rachel agreed. "But lovely and safe."

Which of course had Dwight beaming.

Rachel stood. "I need to wash my hands before we go."

"Use the ensuite in my room at the end of the hall," Garrett said. "Stephanie's bathroom is a war zone."

Dwight looked startled at the news his wife was a slob. Stephanie lifted her chin and stared him down.

On her way to the bathroom, Rachel gave Garrett's bedroom a once-over. His room was neater than she would have expected. Very neat. A king-size bed with a dark blue duvet. Both nightstands were stacked with books.

She switched on the light in the bathroom and saw a narrow marble vanity unit that looked like it was an original fitting. The shower, though, was übermodern with glass walls and glazed rectangular tiles.

As Rachel washed her hands, she noticed the liquid soap was the same brand as the one in the shower.

She sniffed her fingers. A faint smell of ginger. Not the scent she'd come to think of as Garrett's trademark.

The vanity unit held a mug with a toothbrush and paste. No cologne.

She glanced around the bathroom. The mirror above the washbasin concealed another cupboard, she realized. She looked over her shoulder, then opened the cupboard.

More soap, a razor, aspirin. No cologne.

Where was it? She snapped off the light and returned to the bedroom. No cologne on the nightstands, or the beech dresser. The logical place for it would be Garrett's top dresser drawer. But of course, she couldn't look there.

If Garrett was shutting her out of everything else, he certainly wasn't inviting her into his dresser.

She sank down onto the end of the bed and contemplated her disastrous night. Snooping on Clive had achieved a big fat nothing. The kiss that she'd considered earth-shattering had led Garrett to behave obnoxiously…and to the discovery that the firm she loved valued the fickle Garrett much more highly than it did her.

Rachel badly needed to win at something. Even if it was just by proving that Garrett did indeed wear cologne.

One drawer, she told herself. One look. Though technically she should check out the nightstand drawers, too.

One drawer on each item of furniture.

Quickly, before she could chicken out, she opened the top drawer of the nightstand nearest the bathroom. No cologne.

The top drawer of the dresser was similarly lacking. But it did contain a paper shopping bag bearing the brand of an expensive baby store. Rachel peeked into the bag. A merino sleep-sack, soft gray printed with white sheep. She cursed the wave of tenderness that washed over her. Big deal if Garrett bought a snuggly gift for his new sibling.

She was after cologne, not baby gifts. Last chance, the other nightstand.

Rather than walk all the way around the enormous bed, she threw herself across it and tugged the drawer open. Nothing.

At least, no cologne. Just a heap of shiny stones scrunched up in a corner of the drawer, which, when she lifted them, transformed into a necklace of gems, many of which she didn't recognize, set in gold filigree. It was breathtakingly beautiful.

"Looking for something?" Garrett asked from the doorway.

She shrieked. "That's the second time tonight you've sneaked up on me."

"It's not called sneaking up when you're going through my drawers." He advanced into the room.

She slid off the bed. "If you must know, I was looking for your cologne."

"I told you, I don't wear the stuff." Garrett closed the dresser drawer she'd left slightly ajar.

She held up the necklace. "What's this?"

He groaned. "For Pete's sake, Rachel, what does it take to knock you back? It's none of your damn business."

"It takes a lot more to knock me back than you'd

think possible," she said. "Just because you're running scared, Garrett, that doesn't mean I am." She waved the necklace at him. "Ex-girlfriend? Tramp who broke your heart and stole your wallet but left this souvenir?"

A smile tugged at his mouth. "My mother made it. She was studying at the Jewelry Arts Institute here in Manhattan. She was working on her first collection."

When she died.

Rachel examined the necklace. "She was really talented. I've never seen anything like this."

"She was amazing," he said. "When she chose to do something, she put her all into it. She wanted us—me and Lucas—to be the same. She never tried to force choices on us—we always knew she would love us whether she approved of our decisions or not. But she was adamant that we should choose something that would make us happy, and pursue it until we got it."

"What does Lucas do? Is he in New York, too?"

"He's in the navy, flying choppers on an aircraft carrier in the Persian Gulf."

"Cool," she said. "When did you last see him?"

"Christmas." He straightened the duvet where she'd rumpled it. "Dad would never exert his influence to get Lucas home for the holiday, but obviously the powers that be did it for him anyway."

"Is Lucas like you?" she asked.

"He's a good guy," Garrett said. "He has a lot of integrity, and he flourishes in the discipline of the navy. He's got what it takes to be a leader."

"Polar opposites, then," Rachel said.

He smiled, and to Rachel it seemed bittersweet. "My father's very proud of him."

Rachel swallowed. "Were your mom and dad happy together?" She handed him the necklace, and he pocketed it.

"Yeah. I have no idea how. If Mom had known how quickly he'd forget her, maybe she would've felt differently."

Rachel longed to comfort him, but she knew it was the last thing he wanted. His relationship with his dad was a mess—thank goodness he'd had such a wise, loving mother for most of his youth.

Michelle Calder's advice—figure out what will make you happy, then pursue it—had a lot going for it. Rachel wondered if Garrett's brother had achieved that goal. Unlike Garrett, who was still flitting around the advertising industry, from one job to another. He was—

Realization dawned. "Oh," she said.

"If you're done snooping through my things, you'd better leave," Garrett said. "Dad's waiting...." He paused as he noticed she wasn't moving. "What's up?"

"I just figured out something really ironic."

"You may not be a good judge of irony at one-thirty in the morning," he warned.

"It's all about your mother," she said.

His sigh was exasperated. "What is?"

"You and the way you live. I always thought you had so many different jobs because you can't commit. Because you're a flake."

"No, please," he murmured, "say what you really think."

She grinned. "But really, you're just doing what your mom told you to do."

"Okay, it's late." He headed for the door.

"You discovered that advertising is what you love, what makes you happy," she said, "and you've spent the last few years working your way up. Giving it everything you've got."

"Interesting theory." He left the room, forcing her to follow.

"You don't lack loyalty or commitment at all," she said behind him.

"Yes, I do," he said.

"Nope. You want to be the best damn creative director in New York, and you're going for it. You're committed to your career and loyal to your mom's philosophy."

"Whatever helps you sleep at night," he said. They'd reached the living room. "Rachel's ready to leave, Dad."

Stephanie had already gone to bed, so there were no prolonged goodbyes.

"You know what this means, Garrett," Rachel said as he was about to close the door on them.

"I have a horrible feeling you're about to tell me."

"The bad news, for me at least, is you're going to be almost impossible to beat in the Brightwater pitch."

He grinned. "Now that's the smartest thing you've said all night."

"The reason is that this is way more important to you than you've admitted even to yourself," she said.

He made a winding motion with his hand. "And the good news?"

"You're a decent guy who's quite capable of forming lasting relationships. Your problem is, you're also a big coward."

The door slammed in her face.

CHAPTER NINETEEN

GARRETT WAS IN THE MIDDLE of reviewing the Brightwater creative that he'd be showing Tony tomorrow, when his cell phone rang.

"Hi, Stephanie," he said, aware that a month ago he wouldn't have addressed her by name.

Since then, he'd seen her at all hours of the day and night, learned she was the messiest bathroom user in the history of modern plumbing, had her tail Clive for him and let her drive him to a midnight raid at the office. He'd laced up her sneakers for her when she couldn't reach her feet anymore. Kind of hard to hate her after all that.

"Garrett, I need you to come right away." Her voice was tense.

He straightened in his chair. "What's the matter? Is it the baby?"

"Please, Garrett, just get here as soon as you can— 2300 Southern Boulevard, in the Bronx."

"What are you doing way up there?"

But she'd hung up.

Garrett tried to call her back as he raced out of his office. Her phone was switched off. What the hell was going on?

He kept calling her from the taxi, through the interminable twenty-minute drive. Why wouldn't she answer? What if she was hurt? What if the baby was... gone?

He called Rachel. Who might be the most annoying person in the world, but was also the most likely to understand how he felt at any given moment. Not that he'd tell her that.

"I'm in a cab, heading for the Bronx. Stephanie called. I think something's wrong." He told her the details, heard her sharp cry of distress.

"Do you want me to meet you there?" she asked. The concern in her voice, for him as well as Stephanie, warmed him through his anxiety. Almost enough for him to overlook her kooky theories about what made him tick.

Out the window, Garrett saw I-95 signs.

"Looks like you'll be somewhere near the zoo," the driver said.

"I'm nearly there," Garrett told Rachel. "I'll see what's going on and call you if I need you."

"Let me know either way," she said. "And that's an order, Garrett."

"Yes, ma'am." For once, he didn't mind her bossiness.

"You said 2300 Southern?" the driver asked.

"Yeah." Garrett shoved his phone in his pocket, and pulled out his wallet.

"That's actually the zoo," the cabbie said.

Huh? Garrett stared out the window as they pulled up

near the gate between two tour buses. There was Stephanie, scanning the street. She waved when she saw him.

She was upright, at least. Some of the panic left Garrett as he paid the driver. Maybe her car had broken down and her pregnancy hormones stopped her doing something logical like calling AAA. Though why she was at the zoo...

"What's up?" he asked as he approached her.

"Okay, don't get mad," she said. "The baby's fine and so am I."

Nothing like saying *Don't get mad* to raise someone's hackles. "What's this about, Stephanie?"

A school group, maybe ten-year-olds, passed them, chatting at a hundred decibels about tigers and camels. Automatically, Garrett tugged Stephanie out of the jostle zone, over by a chain-link fence.

"It's about you," she said.

He glared at the teacher, who wasn't telling those kids to keep the noise down. "What?"

"Your childhood ended too early, when your mom died," Stephanie said.

Garrett stiffened. She didn't get to talk about his mom, the woman whose place she usurped. "I wasn't a child," he said coldly.

"Sure, your voice had broken," she said. "Though don't think I didn't realize you were making it deeper than it really was."

Something suspiciously like a blush warmed Garrett's face.

"You were fifteen," she said, laughing. "Of course you deepened your voice."

"Just tell me why you dragged me out of my preparation for the most important pitch of my life," he said. But he had a horrible feeling he knew the answer.

"You're the one who said yesterday that you think better when you take some time out of the office to clear your head," she said. "So we're going to the zoo."

Garrett turned on his heel, only to have her lock her hands around his arm with a determined strength.

"Oh, no, you don't," she said. "You resisted every attempt I made at getting close to you when your dad and I married. I don't blame you for that, but I blame myself for not pushing harder. For letting you get away with it because it was easier."

"You did me a favor—I didn't want your excursions and your home-baked muffins," he said. "I didn't want them then, and I don't want them now."

"You *needed* them," she said. "It wasn't about me replacing your mother—we both know I couldn't do that, nor should I have ever tried. It was about you not having to grow up overnight and be this young man you weren't quite ready to be. No matter what you thought."

Garrett swallowed over something scratchy in his throat. "This is crap."

"No, this is my way of apologizing for giving up too easily," she said. "Please, Garrett, let me take you to the zoo."

"I'm busy, I have a pitch—"

Whoa. Before he could figure what she was doing, Stephanie had grabbed his hand and pressed it against her stomach.

He felt it.

A definite kick, as if—as if there was something *alive* in there.

There is, dummy.

"How does that feel to you?" he said wonderingly.

Her face broke into the most beatific smile. "Amazing. How does it feel to you?"

"Amazing." He realized he still had his hand on her stomach and she was no longer holding him there. He let his hand drop.

"Come on." Stephanie gestured to the zoo entrance, and Garrett found himself following her meekly to the ticket booth.

"Damn, if we'd come here fifteen years ago, maybe we could have passed you off as a child," she joked as she handed him his ticket.

Garrett shook his head, still not quite sure what this was all about. "I'd better call Rachel. She's worried you're in premature labor."

"I'm sorry." Stephanie touched his arm. "I didn't think you'd come if I invited you to the zoo."

Well, duh.

Rachel laughed when he told her what was happening.

"Have fun," she said. "Don't stick your fingers through any bars." She paused. "On second thought, do. A little mauling might distract you from your pitch."

Garrett was smiling as he ended the call.

Stephanie showed him her map of the zoo. "I thought we'd start with the snow leopard, if you don't have a preference."

"I seriously don't have a preference," he said. "Dad would start with the aardvarks, of course."

"Everything in order," she agreed. But her smile was sad, and Garrett wished he hadn't mentioned his dad. Then she punched his arm lightly. "I saw on the website that the snow leopard's pregnant. You can tell me which of us you think is bigger."

She had a definite waddle these days, Garrett noticed. The snow leopard was a crowd-puller, its enclosure a magnet for school trips, as well as mothers of preschoolers, pushing buggies, often in groups.

"Did you ever come here with Lucas?" Garrett asked as he watched the animal stretch in the sun.

"A couple of times. Once on a class trip, once just him and me." She slid him a glance. "I did invite you."

"I'm sure you did." He didn't remember, but he knew he would have refused the invitation.

"I'm glad we're here now," she said. "I wonder what Lucas is doing right this minute."

Garrett glanced at his watch. "Playing the third round of an after-dinner poker game would be my guess."

She sighed. "You're so literal, just like your father."

When he halted, she tsked. "That's a compliment when I say it."

"And yet you left him," Garrett reminded her.

She sighed, and he wished he'd kept his mouth shut.

"Are you serious about Rachel?" she asked.

"We're not even dating," he said.

"She seems to understand you, and I can tell you think she's hot."

"Did you and Lucas used to have conversations like

this?" Garrett asked. "No wonder he took off for the Gulf."

"Sometimes we did," she said. "Not that I knew what to say to him, any more than I do to you."

"Silence can be the best policy," he said.

"Not that." She squeezed his hand. "I did too much of that." She let go of his hand and pointed. "This way to the gorillas. They really do peel bananas, you know."

"Amazing," he said. But he was grinning. He remembered coming to the zoo with his mom, but it had been a very long time ago.

Maybe one day he'd bring his little brother or sister here.

"I think," he said, after Stephanie handed a complete stranger her camera and asked the guy to take a photo of her and Garrett in front of the gorilla, "you'll make a pretty good mom."

Her eyes filled with tears as she flung her arms around him.

"I didn't mean for me," he said, horrified.

She smacked his shoulder as she chortled wetly. "I know you didn't. Thanks, Garrett, it means a lot to hear you say that."

Garrett cleared his throat.

"Now we just need your dad to fulfill his potential to be a great father," Stephanie said.

Nothing like a mention of the old man to strip the fun out of a conversation.

"Isn't there a rhino somewhere around here?" he asked.

"Mom's not the one who was always nagging us to go into the forces," Garrett said, confused.

"*I* wanted to join the navy," Lucas said. "But as for the promotions and medals…you know how Mom always said, 'Whatever makes you happy, pursue it with everything you've got.'"

Garrett took a couple of seconds. "Yeah, I know."

"I always figured that's been behind your meteoric rise up the ad agency ranks," Lucas said.

Which was exactly what Rachel had said.

"No," Garrett said. "It hasn't."

"Oh." Lucas sounded nonplussed. "Guess I was wrong."

They wrapped up the call soon after. Leaving Garrett time to make a couple of calls of his own.

He'd had an idea of something he could do for Rachel. Something that didn't involve committing his emotions or baring his heart.

The first call was to the CEO at JWT. Garrett was unsurprised that he still had the clout to get straight through. He'd won a lot of business for that firm. Not to mention three CLIOs.

"Garrett, good to hear from you." Hardy Campese boomed down the line. "Tell me you're calling because you want your job back. You'll kill me on the salary, I know, but you're almost worth it."

"I'm definitely worth it," Garrett said. "But that's not what I'm after." He proceeded to tell Campese exactly what he *did* want.

CHAPTER TWENTY

"WANNA GRAB A SANDWICH?" Garrett was leaning on the doorjamb of Rachel's office, looking tall, dark and very sexy.

Rachel glanced over her shoulder to the wall behind her.

"Yes, Rach, I'm talking to you." He rolled his eyes and hid a smile.

"Really? Because you haven't done in several days." Not since he'd called to tell her he was playing hooky at the zoo with Stephanie. She would have liked to have heard more about that excursion. But she suspected he'd been avoiding her. Not out of hostility—at least, she didn't think so, despite those unwelcome insights she'd shared with him. Several times she'd caught him looking at her, and his perplexed expression had suggested he simply didn't know what to do about her.

"I've been busy. So have you. But there's something I want to ask you. Are you coming or not?"

Way to get a girl's attention. She capped her pen. "I guess I could eat, if you're buying."

"It's only fair," he said, "since I do earn a lot more than you."

She wanted to talk to Tony about their pay discrepancy, but now obviously wasn't the best time. She glowered at Garrett. "This lunch better be expensive."

"Yeah, yeah." He was already striding ahead of her toward the elevators.

They walked two blocks to an Italian basement restaurant Rachel had never seen before. Once they descended the narrow stairs, a vaulted ceiling, starched white tablecloths and sparkling crystalware told her Garrett had taken her request for a decent lunch seriously. She ordered prawns cooked in vermouth and served on fat pappardelle pasta. Garrett went for the T-bone with hand-cut fries.

She decided to live a little and have a glass of wine with lunch. The Soave was the perfect balance of crispness and fruit.

She lifted her glass to Garrett in a toast. "Here's to the partnership."

He clinked. "You realize you're toasting the fact that in a couple of days one of us will be out of a job."

"Or both of us." She took a serious slug of her wine. "Clive seems quietly confident."

"Can you imagine Clive being noisily confident?"

She laughed.

"Have you thought any more about what you'll do if you don't get the partnership?" Garrett asked.

She drew in a sharp breath. It was the one thing she couldn't allow herself to think about. "I'm planning to win." It didn't sound quite as convincing since she'd told him the other night that he'd be almost impossible to beat. He must be in an unusually mellow mood, because he refrained from commenting. "Have *you* made contingency plans?" she asked.

"No," he admitted.

"I wonder if Clive has," they said simultaneously.

"I don't even have a résumé," Rachel said. "I've only ever worked here, and to get the mail room job I just filled out an application form."

Garrett rubbed his chin. "Wow, Rachel. That's weird. You need any help putting one together?"

"No," she said, annoyed.

"That wasn't a dig—I was genuinely offering to help," he said.

"I genuinely don't plan on needing it," she said. "But in the same spirit, I'll offer to help you clear your desk the day you leave."

His teeth snapped together. Then he relaxed. "No need. When I leave, I don't take anything with me. Not even a paper clip."

A reminder, as if she needed it, that he wouldn't be taking any thoughts of her with him. He'd obviously managed to shut her out of his mind quite successfully the past few days. Unfortunately she hadn't been as successful.

Garrett snapped his fingers in front of her face. "Hey, even if no other ad agency in the world wants to hire you, at least you still have your legs."

"Thanks," she said drily. "And you still have a new sibling to look forward to. Are you excited?"

"Guys don't think about that stuff," he said.

"Oh, really?" She sat back while the pretty young waitress set down her prawn dish. It smelled heavenly.

"In your dresser drawer, I saw a carrier bag from Maybe Baby."

"That's where I keep my gym gear," he said.

"I looked inside."

He sighed. "Because you thought I might be keeping cologne in there?" He didn't sound annoyed.

"Because I wanted to see what you bought, dummy."

Underneath the table, his foot brushed her ankle, and she jumped. But not so far as to break the contact.

"An adorable little baby sleep-sack," she said with relish.

"I know what I bought, Rachel." He picked up a French fry and popped it in his mouth.

"All I'm saying is, don't tell me you don't think about that baby."

"I'm not saying anything to you," he said.

Too late. He'd already betrayed his soft spot for his future sibling, and she found herself liking it. A lot.

"Did you hear Bob Harvey in accounting is running a betting book on which of us will end up partner?" Garrett asked.

"That's disturbing," she said. "A senior accountant who runs a gambling ring."

"I'm fairly certain it's a onetime thing." He sat back, arms clasped behind his head, waiting for her to ask the obvious question.

Who's the favorite?

She wasn't about to ask. Instead, she let herself appreciate the breadth of his shoulders, the masculine planes of his face.

She saw when he read the direction of her thoughts.

Saw how his gaze sharpened as he returned the scrutiny. She was wearing a light pink dress that worked nicely with her caramel-colored hair. He'd once said pink was "her color."

They eyed each other for a little while, food forgotten. Rachel saw the moment Garrett's thoughts turned more explicit than hers. His eyes heated, grew less focused.

"Hey!" She put a protective hand to where the wrap front of her dress showed a hint of cleavage. "Stop thinking whatever you're thinking."

He grinned. "You don't get to police my thoughts, Rachel. And it's not sexual harassment for me to think lewd thoughts about you."

Heat shot to her core. "A major oversight in the legislation," she said.

He laughed out loud. "Which brings me to what I want to ask you."

"Fire away."

"First, I owe you an apology," he said. "I acted like a jerk when you came to my place after we raided Clive's office."

"Yeah, you did."

"I blame you for that," he said.

"Of course you do."

He held up a hand. "Hear me out. That kiss in Clive's office… Rachel, that was something else."

"You mean it wasn't you kissing me?" she asked, confused.

"Something else as in something special," he said.

"Oh." She heard the softening in her own voice. "That."

"You said you'd never felt like that before," he reminded her. "Don't try to back out now."

"Back out of what?"

"Dating me." He returned to his hand-cut fries, as if there was nothing left to say.

"Are you serious?"

The warmth in his gaze, combined with a mild dizziness induced by the wine left her light-headed. Which she could not afford to be when Garrett was talking like this.

"I know we're not the most logical pairing," he said. "But if we go into this with the right expectations, we can both have a great time."

"Why did a dozen alarm bells just go off in my head?" she asked.

"Because you're like that." He sipped her wine, having finished his water. "But if you think about it, you'll see there's some good middle ground for us to explore, somewhere between my natural ethos—Let it go—and yours."

"Mine being?"

"The never-leave-me thing."

"So what, exactly, are you suggesting?"

"That we see each other for a couple of months," he said. "A fixed term, longer than I would normally date someone."

"But shorter than I might want," she said.

"Exactly." He raised her glass to her in a one-sided toast.

"And this relationship would involve sex?"

"Of course!" he said, shocked. Then he grinned. "You know you want it."

She did. Oh, she did. Just thinking about it turned her limbs heavy.

Handing her glass back to her, he added, "But it's more than sex, Rach. I like you a lot."

She'd never expected him to admit so much. And yet he was offering so little.

"What about love?" she asked. "Do you see any prospect of that?"

He was already shaking his head before she finished. "I'm not looking for the long haul here, Rach. You know as well as I do that we're not suited."

She twirled her wineglass by the stem. "So your suggestion is for both of us to compromise everything."

"You're using bad words," he said. "How about, meeting in the middle. Exploring our common passions."

"You sound like an ad for a commune." She didn't manage to pull off the light tone she'd hoped for.

He sighed. "I knew you'd be difficult, but for some reason I like that about you."

"Because I'm worth the effort," she said. "And so are you."

He sat back while the waitress cleared their plates. "You lost me."

"I can't say yes," she said. "I don't want to give any relationship anything less than my best shot, and to start with a time limit…to say everything is going to be a compromise…"

"How else could we do it?" he demanded.

"We'd have to both go into it wanting to play it our own way. On our own terms. And then we see who wins." Could he see what a giant step it was for her to even attempt a relationship with a man like him?

"That's nuts," he said. "Someone's going to get hurt if we do that, and it's going to be you."

"Maybe," she said, "but I won't settle for less."

He tossed his napkin on the table. "Then I guess we're done." He signaled for the check.

"Thanks for lunch," she said formally.

As they walked up the stairs to street level, Rachel sensed Garrett's gaze. She glanced over her shoulder to find him eyeing her butt.

"Highlight of my day," he said when he realized she'd caught him in the act. "I think your butt actually gives your legs a run for their money." He patted her bottom. "Hope that's not too demeaning for you, being seen as a sexual object. I figure you must be used to it."

"There is that," she agreed, matching his flippancy with her own.

She'd thought the effort cost her more than it did him. But the smile he gave her was bittersweet. Neither of them seemed to feel like bantering after that. They had pitches in a couple of days' time. A day or two after that, one or both of them would be fired. If they weren't dating, they'd likely never see each other again.

The sharp pang in her chest surprised Rachel. She would miss him. A lot.

But she couldn't take him up on his offer. It wasn't enough.

On the way back to the office, all Rachel could think was "last." Last lunch together. Last time he would compliment her legs. Last ride with him in the world's slowest elevator. Odd to think that a little while ago all those "lasts" would have had her jumping for joy. Somehow, over the past month, things had changed.

THE BABY'S KICKING WOKE Stephanie from her prelunch nap—a habit she'd gotten into over the past week, since she seemed to have grown even bigger and heavier, and consequently more tired.

She patted her stomach. "You're right, little one. We need to get up." She rolled out of Garrett's spare bed in the maneuver she'd perfected to avoid strain on her back. Presumably younger mothers didn't feel as if their bodies were falling apart through pregnancy.

She pressed her palm to the small of her back as she waddled to the bathroom Garrett described as a "damn mess." Which it was. Stephanie, who'd been tidy all her life, was deeply ashamed that she'd let this personal space become a cluttered shambles. But she couldn't seem to muster the energy to tidy it.

She felt even more guilty because Garrett had been so tolerant with her. Stephanie credited that woman from his office, Rachel, for the improvement. Garrett might say there was nothing going on, but his face came to life when he looked at her.

Odd, because Rachel was the sort of serious, set-in-her-ways woman Stephanie would have sworn he would detest. But there was a definite spark between them. It would be wonderful if Garrett found someone he loved, who loved him back.

Stephanie turned on the shower. As she stood under the hot spray, her mind drifted to Dwight. She hadn't seen him tailing her in the past few days. Had he given up?

Or had she overestimated his interest in the first place? Not just this week, but back when they got married.

She'd always been careful not to feel jealous of Michelle, even when she'd believed it was his heartbreak over her death that stopped Dwight from giving all his love to Stephanie.

She'd naively assumed he'd put up barriers *after* Michelle died and that time and her love would break those barriers down. She'd naively assumed he'd married her because deep down he wanted to recover the kind of intimacy he'd known with Michelle. It was a few years before it dawned on her that she had no idea how much Dwight loved Michelle.

She did know that he'd married again because he'd wanted a wife and a mother for his sons, because that was what a man ought to have.

Stephanie soaped her stomach and wondered if this baby was another son whose head Dwight would mess with. Or would it be a girl, who would be hurt when her daddy didn't treat her like his little princess?

I'm being unfair. Dwight had said he wanted to change.

But that was last week. He hadn't spoken to her since, and he'd stopped following her.

Stephanie squeezed shampoo into her palm and began lathering her hair.

She missed knowing he was near. Maybe it was her turn to make the next move.

STEPHANIE TOOK A CAB to the headquarters of the United States Mission to the United Nations, across the street from the United Nations itself, overlooking the East River. She'd only been here once before—another impromptu visit. On that occasion, Dwight had sent word that he was in a meeting and couldn't come out.

The security was even tighter than last time—her purse was searched while she stepped through a metal detector. They ran a wand over her, too, in case the baby bulge was really a bomb, she supposed.

At last she was cleared and could approach the reception desk.

"I'm here to see Admiral Dwight Calder," she told the receptionist. "I'm his wife."

A flicker of surprise crossed the young man's face as he registered her age and size. "Certainly, ma'am." He pressed a button she couldn't see, and a moment later was talking through his headset to Dwight's assistant.

This was a dumb idea. Why had she thought he would see her? He was probably far too—

"Twenty-first floor, ma'am." The receptionist handed her a visitor card. "Admiral Calder will meet you there."

"Oh." She clipped the card to her purse strap. "Thank you."

When the elevator opened at twenty-one, Dwight was already waiting.

"Stephanie, are you all right?" He grabbed her hands as she stepped out.

Was that why he'd agreed to see her, because he was worried about a medical complication? And yet, he was holding her hands, squeezing them, with something more than anxiety. Something that made her stomach flutter.

"I'm fine," she said. "I just wanted to talk—" She broke off, registering a bustle of activity that seemed frenetic behind him. "You're busy. I'll come back later."

He shook his head. "I have a meeting at two that I can't push back by much. But if you're happy to do it in my office, I'd. Like to talk."

In her most wildly optimistic moment, she'd imagined them going for lunch. Now she was just relieved he hadn't sent her away.

Outside his office, she smiled at Barbara, his secretary, whom she'd met over the years at staff functions.

"Barbara, hold my two o'clock to quarter past, would you?" Dwight said.

Barbara pursed her lips. "But, Admiral—"

"Quarter past," Dwight said in that voice that didn't allow contradiction.

Barbara nodded. Stephanie felt marginally better, since it was out of character for him to reschedule a meeting by so much as a minute. A whole fifteen minutes was a major sacrifice.

He closed the door behind them. Unlike Garrett's ad agency, Dwight's office didn't have glass walls. Too much top secret stuff going on, she supposed.

"Can I get you something?" Dwight asked. "Tea?"

She settled into the visitor chair he indicated. "Just some answers."

He looked wary, but said, "Fire away."

"Why did you marry me?"

CHAPTER TWENTY-ONE

STEPHANIE HADN'T MEANT to start with that question, but it burst out, fueled by resentment and fear.

Dwight got a hunted look in his eyes. But to his credit, he nodded, indicating he wasn't about to dismiss it as nonsense. He perched on the edge of his desk, in much the same way Garrett leaned on his kitchen counter. The two men were so similar, though they'd both hate to be told it.

"I married you because I loved you," he said evenly. "I still do."

"But you weren't swept off your feet," she said. "You wanted a mother for the boys. A wife."

"I did want those things," he agreed, and a knife twisted under her ribs. "But I didn't have to choose you."

"You chose me because I was young and malleable," she said. "Because I was besotted with you and would do whatever it took to make our marriage work. Because I didn't have family who would demand a share of my attention."

"That's a bitter way of looking at it," he said, shocked.

"I'm right, aren't I?"

"On one level, perhaps," he said.

She closed her eyes.

"Dammit, Stephanie, marrying you wasn't the easy way out you seem to think," he snapped.

Her eyes opened. "What do you mean?"

"Do you think I didn't know you were too young for me? That I wasn't worried you would wake up one day and realize you were trapped with an old man and a couple of kids who weren't yours, and decide you want out?"

As you've done now, his tone implied.

"That's not why I left, and you know it."

"I wanted *you,*" he said. "You were so beautiful and calm, but with a passion beneath the surface that I could see in your eyes. Not taking you to bed before we married was the hardest thing I've ever done. I was desperate for you."

Stephanie gaped. "I wish you'd said that."

He made a dismissive motion with his hand. He would never show such weakness.

"Okay, so you wanted me," she said. Their sex life had always been excellent. "But...Dwight, the fact is, I love you more than you love me."

"You're wrong," he said calmly.

"Real love is about priorities, about sacrifice," she said. All Dwight's sacrifice had been for the navy, for his country. "I've always put you first. I gave up work because it was best for your children—and don't get me wrong, I wanted to do it for the boys. Then I stayed out of work because your schedule was so busy it was the only way to make sure we had time together and your life ran smoothly."

"I've appreciated that," he said. "And I've told you so."

"But what have you ever done for me, beyond keep me safe?" she demanded. "You've never supported anything that doesn't fit with your idea of what I should be doing, or what serves the family's needs. You've never supported anything that might inconvenience you."

"Give me one example," he demanded.

"You talked me out of taking accounting classes." She'd thought it might help her return to the workforce when the time was right.

"You hate that kind of thing," he said. "I didn't want you to be bored."

"When I wanted to move into Manhattan." An apartment on the Upper East Side was her ultimate dream.

"Our friends are all in New London."

"And you refused to teach me to play chess—you thought I was too stupid."

"When?" he demanded.

She told him of that early conversation, how he'd said teaching her would take too much time and effort, and could see he was baffled.

"I don't remember that at all," he said. "But I'm sorry. I don't think you're stupid. On the contrary, I've always admired your intelligence."

"I—well, you never said," she said, somewhat lamely. "Dwight, the fact is, until recently I was content to do things your way because I wanted you to be happy. But

I've realized *I'm* not happy. And of course, neither is Garrett."

"Lucas—"

"Lucas is happy because what he wants happens to coincide with what you want," Stephanie said. "If he told you he was quitting the navy tomorrow to write poetry—"

Dwight's recoil made her point for her.

"I want you to love me no matter what," she said. "To put me first. Not all the time, but sometimes. And to love your children—all three of them—regardless of the choices they make."

"You *are* first for me, Stephanie," he said. "I'm starting to realize how important you are."

She caught her breath. She hadn't expected such an unguarded admission. "Is that," she said slowly, "why you've been following me?"

He turned brick red. "I—what do you mean?"

He was a terrible liar, she thought fondly. "I've seen you—in the park, on 4th Avenue."

"I—I—"

It was a heady sensation, discovering she could fluster him like this—it reminded her of that giddy power she'd had to tempt him, back when they first married. "I hope our country doesn't recall you to intelligence work," she said, struggling to keep the laughter from her voice. "It could mean the end of our national security."

"How many times did you see me?" he demanded.

"Three, plus at the toy store."

"I *let* you see me at the store," he reminded her. "And I'll have you know I've followed you at least eight times in the past two weeks, so I'm not as rusty as you think, Mrs. Calder."

"Oh." Now her smile broke out. "When I didn't see you, I thought maybe…you'd lost interest."

"Never," he vowed.

The light in his eyes was one she'd hadn't seen before. Tentatively, she reached out, cupped his cheek in her hand.

He turned and pressed a desperate kiss to her palm. "Have dinner with me," he said. "Please, Stephanie, I'd like to take you out."

Dinner. A date. "We could do that," she said.

"Tomorrow," he said. Then, "Tomorrow?"

His impatience thrilled her. But she said calmly, "That would be lovely." She glanced at her watch. "My time's up, I'd better go."

On her way out, she said goodbye to Barbara, the secretary.

"Oh, good, you're done." Barbara picked up her phone, with a frankly curious glance at Stephanie. Stephanie wondered if Dwight had told her about the separation. "I'll have reception tell the Veep's security detail that the Admiral's on his way."

The words took several long seconds to make sense in Stephanie's head. "The Veep? You mean, the Vice President?"

Engaged in her phone conversation, Barbara nodded.

"The Vice President *of the United States?*" Stephanie asked.

Barbara gave her a frown of confusion as she nodded again. "He'll be right along," she said into the phone.

Stephanie walked slowly to the elevator. Dwight had made the Vice President of the United States wait fifteen minutes so he could talk with her?

Maybe, just maybe, her husband was changing.

GARRETT FOLLOWED ONE of Rachel's neighbors into her building. He'd cadged the address from the KBC Social Club directory, a volume he'd never opened before now. Tailgating the neighbor meant he didn't have to wait for her to buzz him up. He wasn't sure she would want to see him tonight…but he had to say this before tomorrow.

He hoped he hadn't left it too late. Acid burned in his stomach—Stephanie had gone out to dinner with his dad tonight, so she hadn't cooked. Garrett hadn't realized how soft he'd become, until he stood spooning heartburn-inducing chili into his mouth straight from the can because no one had cooked for him.

On the second floor, he knocked on Rachel's door. Footsteps, then she opened it. She wore pajamas, though it was only eight-thirty—orange-and-white-check cotton pants and a white camisole that emphasized the curve of each breast.

"No way," she said. She combed her fingers through her mussed hair.

"For a woman who's famous for never letting go, you sure are unwelcoming," Garrett said. Her feet were bare, toenails unpainted. He wondered if she liked foot massages…and realized he'd never done such a thing before.

"I'm pitching against you tomorrow," she said. "How can it be in my interest to welcome you tonight?"

"Because I'm willing to do this on your terms," he said.

"Do what?"

"A relationship," he said. "Official, no preplanned end in sight."

He'd shocked her enough that she stepped back to let him in. The apartment was smaller than his, but with large windows and decent ceilings. The color scheme—reds, golds, blues—was predictably cozy, but he liked it nonetheless.

The living area was dominated by a huge, squashy sofa.

"What have you been feeding this thing?" Garrett asked.

Still apparently dumbstruck, she plopped down on one end, which he took as an invitation to join her.

"I know the timing's bad, but I need to ask you before tomorrow," he said. "I don't want whatever happens at the pitch to derail us."

He planted a quick kiss on her lips. Which turned into a longer kiss. "You taste good," he murmured.

"That'll be the champagne and oysters." She'd found her voice at last. It didn't sound as happy as he'd hoped.

Champagne and oysters? "You didn't get back with that loser boyfriend, did you?" he demanded. A sudden bleakness—a sense of *too late*—paralyzed his thoughts, his limbs.

"The team wanted to celebrate the hard work they've put in on the Brightwater pitch," she explained, and sensation returned, leaving him giddy. "We hit Crush at four o'clock and didn't leave until six."

"So there's a good chance your judgment is impaired by alcohol," he said hopefully.

"I'll admit to a slim chance," she said. "That's my best offer."

"Deal." He pulled her into his lap and began a thorough exploration of her mouth. His hands did some exploring, too. At long last he had those gorgeous legs right where he wanted them.

At some stage, they ended up lying down on that behemoth of a sofa. Sinking right in.

"If you ever don't show up for work, I'll send a search party to dig into this couch," Garrett murmured against Rachel's earlobe. "It's lethal."

Her hum of pleasure vibrated against his cheek.

"I chose it specifically for its ability to swallow me up." She arched into the work his hands were doing on her curves. "When you live alone, you take your nurturing where you can find it."

He had the urge to utter a crazy promise to nurture her himself, but stopped just in time. Instead, he slipped his hands into the waistband of her pj pants.

"I hope you're not about to do something unprofessional with a colleague," she said sternly.

"I guarantee it won't be amateur," Garrett said.

Rachel believed him. He'd shown phenomenal ability to turn her every nerve ending into a Garrett-seeking missile.

"This is insane," she murmured against his mouth. "Tell me what I'm signing up for again?"

"You and me, making it work for as long as we can," he said. "Both of us being our difficult selves. Maybe someone will compromise on something…maybe they won't."

"There will be sex," she said.

"Very soon," he promised.

"Not tonight," she said. "Not when I have to pitch against you in the morning."

"Not tonight," he agreed.

"There'll be obstacles, too," she said. "Including at least one of us losing our job, my parents having another financial disaster, you getting a new sibling, your dad and Stephanie possibly divorcing…"

Garrett clamped a hand over her mouth. "Enough with the litany of doom."

"Just thought I should warn you," she said against his fingers. "Since your preference is to run at the first obstacle."

"I consider myself warned." He removed his hand.

"What about love?" she said.

He tensed. "I guess…it could happen."

She laughed softly, against his neck.

"What's so funny?" he asked.

"I have a lot more faith in you than you do," she said.

"You're scaring me," he said. She could tell he was only half joking.

Somewhere beneath them, her cell phone rang.

"I'd better get this. It could be about the pitch."

But when she dug into the sofa cushions for her phone, she didn't recognize the number.

"Rachel," a male voice said when she answered. "This is Hardy Campese. You don't know me—"

"I know who you are," she interrupted. CEO of JWT,

one of the world's top ad agencies. She pushed herself off the couch.

"Well, that's mutual, I'm pleased to say. I've heard good things about you," Hardy said. "Sorry to interrupt your evening, but it's always easier to do this after hours. We're looking for a new creative director. You interested in jumping ship?"

JWT wanted to poach her?

"I, uh—" She pressed the phone tight to her ear so Garrett wouldn't hear Hardy's booming voice. "Actually, I'm with a colleague right now."

"Ah, bad timing." Campese chuckled. "Let me tell you a bit about the job, and if you're interested, we can meet later this week."

Later this week. After the Brightwater pitch.

She didn't want to do this now. Didn't want to show a lack of confidence in the work she'd done for Brightwater. She arranged to phone Hardy on Thursday.

She half expected Garrett to ask her who was on the phone and was busy trying to think up a suitable lie when she realized he hadn't asked. For once, his lack of engagement was a good thing.

Rachel tossed the phone back onto the sofa. Right away, it beeped with an incoming message.

Garrett's beeped, too, on the dining table next to his keys. He got up to check it.

"A text from Tony," he said.

"I got it, too." Rachel stared at the screen.

"Meeting, my office, ASAP," Garrett read.

They exchanged glances.

"No idea," Rachel said in answer to his unspoken question. "I guess I'd better get dressed."

CHAPTER TWENTY-TWO

"THERE'S BEEN A NEW development," Tony announced when Rachel and Garrett had barely crossed the threshold. He paused a second to register the coincidence of their simultaneous arrival, then apparently decided whatever he had to say trumped any connection between the two of them.

Clive was already there. He grinned at them.

Rachel slid into a seat. Garrett took the chair two down from her, when she would have preferred him right next to her.

"Thanks for coming in at such short notice," Tony began. "I appreciate that the evening is your own time, and you don't want to—"

"Spit it out, Tony," Garrett said impatiently.

Rachel bit back a smile. He might have learned something about relating to people under her tuition, but he'd never be a diplomat.

She liked that about him. Liked the strength that let him chart his own course.

"I'll let Clive tell you," Tony said, enjoying himself.

Rachel's heart sank. Could Clive have secretly pitched to Brightwater already, and impressed them so much he—

"I quit," Clive said.

"You what?" Rachel squawked.

"Why?" Garrett asked.

"I'm going to start my own agency in Harrisburg."

"Pennsylvania isn't exactly the hub of the advertising world," Garrett said.

"My in-laws are there," Clive said. "Wifey and I want to have at least four kids—we need a decent house with a yard."

Garrett shuddered.

"So I'm leaving," Clive said, as if it was that simple.

Rachel felt a twinge of envy. Not that she wanted four kids...but to choose a whole new path and to feel so excited and happy about it...

"My new firm won't be competing with KBC, so Tony suggested I stay on to do a proper handover," Clive continued. "I'll finish at the end of the month."

"Congratulations." Garrett stood to shake Clive's hand.

Rachel followed suit. "I hope it goes brilliantly for you."

"We need to talk about the implications of this on the Brightwater pitch," Tony said.

"I won't be pitching tomorrow," Clive said. He grinned. "Tony tells me both your pitches are better than mine, anyway."

Now he tells us, Rachel thought.

"The implication seems pretty straightforward," Garrett said. "Rachel and I are head-to-head. It's a fight to the death between the two of us."

"That's a tad dramatic," Tony said comfortably. Rachel could tell he rather liked the gladiatorial metaphor.

She met Garrett's gaze...and couldn't read his expression. *Don't go distant on me,* she telegraphed with her eyes. To no visible effect. Maybe *go distant* was what they both needed to do, until tomorrow was over.

By removing himself from the equation, Clive had changed the dynamic drastically. She and Garrett had talked about Clive, speculated about his pitch—they'd even raided his office together! A third person's involvement had provided an outside focus for the intense competition and the hostility that went along with that.

Now, it was Rachel v. Garrett.

Now, they were two.

Now, her only enemy was the man she'd just agreed to a relationship with.

GARRETT STARED AT HIS bedroom ceiling, washed a ghostly gray by the full moon outside his window.

He felt the relief of a man who'd been spared the noose, courtesy of an eleventh-hour pardon. He felt none of the joy.

Whatever happened, this was going to turn out badly. The only positive thing was that Garrett had figured that out now, rather than later, and could take immediate action.

He would end things with Rachel.

Clive's resignation had made a murky situation crystal clear.

With Clive in the running, the fact that two of the three of them would be fired had never been personal.

But now, it was either Garrett or Rachel. All their energies tomorrow would be focused on defeating each other. The Brightwater pitch was a license to betray. How would they ever get past that?

They wouldn't. Some obstacles were too insurmountable even for someone like Rachel. And *way* too insurmountable for Garrett.

In the past couple of hours, Garrett had had to face the fact that he didn't care enough about Rachel. He liked her a lot—a hell of a lot, and he wanted her, too—but she wasn't as important to him as other things. Like the KBC partnership, which over the past few weeks had come to feel like the culmination of all he'd worked for.

If he really cared about Rachel, he would be contemplating giving up the Brightwater pitch, so she could keep her job. He might not actually *do* it, but he'd think about it before he convinced himself it wasn't necessary.

It hadn't even crossed his mind.

And it wasn't about to.

So. He would tell Rachel the relationship was a nonstarter. Right after their pitches, not before, so he didn't put her off her stride. She'd be upset, because she had that holding-on thing going, but she'd get over it. She might not be a big fan of that unsettled childhood she'd had, but it had made her resilient.

It had also given her a thirst for adventure. She hadn't figured that out yet, but it had been obvious to Garrett in her battles with him. In her unpredictable responses.

A new job might be the adventure she needed. She just had to get over her fear, Garrett thought, her belief that adventure had to equal disaster, when really it was all about risk management.

It was a shame she'd never made it to college. If she had a degree she'd have had more choices, then and now. She wouldn't have been so scared of losing her job at KBC. She'd sure as hell have the confidence to demand a higher salary.

At least he'd guaranteed her a new job to walk into, and a good one. That call she'd taken tonight had been from one of the people he'd contacted on her behalf—Garrett had been on the receiving end of enough poaching phone calls to recognize the signs. Of course, he was way better at handling those calls discreetly than Rachel; she had broadcasted her guilt in the hunch of her shoulders and the pitch of her voice. But what mattered was that another firm had offered her a job. She would be fine.

Garrett turned his thoughts to his pitch. His team had done an excellent job. It was just unfortunate that the creative they'd developed didn't resonate in his gut the way, say, the Lexus campaign had.

Imagine if Rachel won the Brightwater pitch, rather than him. He'd resent the hell out of her, and that was no basis for a relationship, either. As he knew from his own father.

He thought about Rachel's family, wondered if her parents had decided on that move yet. His gut told him they were going to go. She'd be upset. He wondered if, in a close family like hers, her getting a college education might have had a positive effect on the rest of the family, too. That was the kind of thing she should be talking about in her pitch to Brightwater, with its focus on lower-income families. But he knew instinctively she wouldn't. It was too close, too personal.

Shame, because it was a great angle. He wished he'd thought of it himself.

Hang on a minute…he *had* thought of it himself! And now that he had, it was sitting in his consciousness pulsing like a giant neon light, saying "Me first!" Complete with all those gut instincts that had been missing from the pitch he'd showed Tony yesterday.

The meeting at Brightwater was less than twelve hours away. Too late to change pitches now.

It's never too late.

Hell. Garrett ran a hand through his hair. Did he really want to do this? Scrap the pitch his team had crafted in favor of a half idea?

His gut said yes.

He wouldn't be scrapping everything—the media strategy would say the same. But with more emphasis on digital—he could call up one of those nerdy programmer guys they used, get some kind of mock-up underway right now. Those kids stayed up all night.

And while twelve hours would ordinarily be nowhere near enough to come up with brilliant creative, he wasn't starting from scratch. He had a real live example to work from.

Rachel. And her family.

It occurred to him that she would hate to be used as a case study in his pitch.

He wouldn't use her name, of course. Still, she would see it as a betrayal, being so big on loyalty herself. *If*

I do this, I'll kill any chance of a future relationship with her.

Hadn't he already said the Brightwater pitch was a license to betray? Might as well go the whole hog.

Garrett snapped on his bedside lamp and went to find a pen and paper.

CHAPTER TWENTY-THREE

RACHEL HAD BEEN UP since four-thirty, running through the pitch she already knew by heart. No mistakes allowed today. So she wouldn't make them. She could rely on herself for that.

She knew this was the best pitch of her life. She'd pushed herself beyond her own limits in terms of creativity. Thanks in no small measure to Garrett, who had alternately embarrassed, provoked and inspired her into raising her game.

At seven, the limo Tony had ordered turned up. Her boss was inside. Garrett was, of course, driving himself. Rachel swallowed at the thought of them going head-to-head today.

She'd built him up in her mind to be this unstoppable creative force. But today, she needed to stop him.

With the added complication that last night, before Clive had removed himself from the equation, she'd agreed to a no-holds-barred relationship with Garrett.

Except, somehow, she didn't think that was going to be a problem today. Not if she knew Garrett.

"Am I presenting first or second?" she asked Tony, who was watching the breakfast news on the backseat TV.

"We'll toss a coin when we get there," he said.

"Okay." She resisted the urge to pull out her notes and go through them again. She knew this stuff cold.

She also resisted the urge to ask Tony if he thought Garrett's pitch was better than hers. She knew he was impressed by hers—he'd been effusive in his praise, which was rare. That would have to be enough for now.

When they pulled up outside Brightwater's office, Garrett was already waiting. Tony walked in ahead to notify the receptionist of their arrival.

"Hi," she said to Garrett. She was close enough for her to smell his distinctive noncologne, and she couldn't help smiling. Even though he looked exhausted, as if he hadn't slept, and even though she could see what was on his mind.

"Hi, Rachel," he said soberly.

"Just tell me," she said, "did we stumble at our first obstacle?"

His dark eyes burned into her. "You didn't," he said. "I did."

She'd expected it. Garrett was such a complex, wounded man; she'd known this would never be easy. Still, she ducked her head while she blinked away tears.

"I'm sorry, Rach," he said, and she realized the contraction of her name had grown on her.

"Mark has asked us to go on up." Tony returned from the reception desk.

They took the elevator just one floor. Mark and several other Brightwater folk were waiting in the boardroom. Introductions and handshakes all around.

Tony explained why Clive hadn't come, then got

down to business. "In the interest of fair competition," he said, "we'll settle the question of who goes first with a coin toss." With a flourish, he produced a quarter from his pocket. "Loser pitches first. Heads or tails?" he asked Rachel.

"Garrett can choose." Rachel gave him a small smile. "On your terms."

"Heads," he said. He didn't smile back.

Tony tossed the quarter, caught it, turned it over on the back of his wrist. "Heads it is. You're up, Rachel."

She told herself that was a good thing. If she had to wait while Garrett pitched first, she would be second-guessing her own pitch. By the time she walked into that room, she'd be riddled with self-doubt. The client wouldn't believe in her if she didn't believe in herself.

"I'll leave it up to you two to decide if you should sit in on each other's pitches," Tony said.

Rachel glanced at Garrett.

"I don't mind," he said with a strange doggedness. "Your call."

She was desperate to see his pitch. But she didn't want to do hers in front of him. In case he thought it was terrible, and she read that on his face. "No," she said. "No sitting in."

Garrett's shoulders eased a fraction. After he left the room, she unzipped her portfolio and set up her story-boards—she still preferred paper boards to the digital presentations many of her colleagues favored.

"Mark, Bill, Kenton and Margaret—" the clients were impressed she'd remembered their names, she could tell "—it gives me great pleasure to share with you the ideas that my team at KBC has come up with. We believe Brightwater's colleges can dominate the low-income private college sector…"

Her introduction listed the reasons why Brightwater had potential to do just that and the obstacles that might prevent such a thing happening. Nods around the table told her she'd brought her audience along with her. This was the bit she was good at.

"And now," she said, "may I present the campaign that will achieve your goals."

This was the part she wasn't so good at. Or at least, she wasn't the best. Garrett was the best.

But she'd outdone herself this time, and the murmur of pleased surprise from two of the clients told her they agreed.

As she gave her presentation, her confidence grew. And there was no mistaking the approval on the clients' faces. With the exception of Bill Caspar, the CEO, who sat silent, his face inscrutable, flipping a pen between his fingers.

When Rachel sat down, she actually got a round of applause. That didn't happen every day. At least, not to her.

"That was excellent, Rachel," Mark Van de Kamp said.

Tony confined himself to a nod.

She shook hands all around, and then it was time to give over to her rival. Tony escorted her out of the room.

Garrett, sitting with his elbows on his knees, hands lightly clasped, stood. "How'd it go?"

"She was brilliant," Tony said. "You'll have to be damn good to beat her."

Really? Some of her worry eased.

"Well done." The dark cloud hanging over Garrett lifted, and he grinned at her. Rachel saw something proprietorial, like pride, in his face.

"Let's go, Garrett," Tony said.

"Good luck," she said.

She had to assume Garrett had taken a completely different approach from her. Whatever he'd come up with would be amazing; that was a given. But was it more amazing than her work?

As Rachel waited, her mind drifted over the past few weeks, over the time she'd spent with Garrett. She realized she'd loved every minute of it, even the times when she'd been so angry she could have slapped him.

She'd laughed more in those weeks than she had in a year. She'd woken each morning with a sense of excitement, of anticipation for what the day might bring. His kisses had driven her to intensely pleasurable distraction. And when everything had gone wrong—the CLIO nominations, her screwup with LeeAnne—Garrett Calder, the least reliable man in the world, had been there for her. Had made it better.

Oh, help. I love him.

Rachel realized her mouth had sagged open in that way Garrett liked to draw attention to. She snapped it shut. How could she have fallen in love with him? Easily, it seemed. And now, he'd given up at the first hurdle.

"I expected that," she said aloud. Her voice echoed in the empty hallway. She knew he wasn't good at relationships and that he was wounded. That he'd rather let go than be hurt. But she also knew him to be capable of great loyalty, great passion. Garrett just needed to trust that he was capable of giving those things to her. And to trust that she would give them to him.

I'll fight for him. No begging, no manipulation, no clinging…she would just do her utmost to show Garrett she wasn't about to give up on him. When he trusted that, he might trust enough to love her back.

It wouldn't be easy, but it would be worth it.

IT FELT LIKE HOURS before Rachel heard the sound of clapping from the boardroom, though her watch told her it had been a mere thirty-three minutes. It was another five minutes before the door opened and Tony and Garrett emerged. Tony looked slightly dazed.

Rachel swallowed. "How'd you do?" She echoed Garrett's earlier question.

"Good, I think." Did she imagine it, or was he not meeting her eyes?

"Better than good," Tony said, without the smug smile Rachel would have expected.

"Is there a problem?" she asked.

Tony threw Garrett a pointed look.

"I changed my pitch," he muttered.

Rachel tensed, mainly because everyone else seemed so tense. "What do you mean?"

"I mean," he said with an impatience that used to bug her, which she recognized as defensiveness, "I came up with a better idea after Clive quit, and I worked through the night to turn it into a pitch for this morning."

Obviously without telling Tony, who'd approved both their pitches in private showings last week.

What could Garrett have thought of, that was so good it justified throwing out weeks of his team's work?

"When will we know the client's decision?" Rachel asked Tony, trying to sound unruffled.

"Mark said the pitches will receive immediate consideration. I'd say we'll hear in the next day or so. Maybe even this afternoon."

And then, either she or Garrett would be out of a job. She turned to him. "What made you—?"

His cell phone rang. "I need to take this," he said, without even looking at the display.

Whoever it was, he wasn't pleased to hear from them.

"What do *you* want?" he said impatiently into the phone. Charming as ever. Then he cursed. "I'm on my way." He pressed the off button. "I've got to go," he told Rachel and Tony.

"Is it Stephanie?" she asked, alarmed.

But he was striding away, ignoring the elevator in favor of taking the stairs two at a time. It was a safe bet that by the time Rachel and Tony reached the parking lot, Garrett's BMW would be long gone.

"What the hell?" Tony said impatiently.

Rachel said, "I guess we're taking the train."

They had half a carriage to themselves on the train, so Rachel took the opportunity to talk to Tony about the pitches.

"Was Garrett brilliant?" she asked.

He nodded. Rachel forced a smile. "That's great. Another CLIO coming up, huh?"

"Maybe." Tony scrolled through the messages on his mobile phone without reading them. "Rachel, did Garrett tell you anything about his new pitch?"

"Not a thing," she said. "Why?"

Tony grimaced. "Sometimes that guy is more trouble than he's worth."

Tony wouldn't be saying that come CLIO night next week, she suspected.

"That's the price of brilliance," she said. "I know Garrett's not easy, but creatively he seems to leapfrog over everyone else."

"He does."

Rachel cleared her throat. "Tony, now that Clive has gone, I'd like to ask KBC to reconsider the plan to fire an executive account director. Both Garrett and I have made a significant contribution. You're sending a very negative message to the rest of the staff when you show you're willing to ignore that."

He nodded. "I agree, it doesn't look good, but financially…" He sighed. "Rachel, I'll ask the partners to look at the numbers again, okay?"

"Great," she said. "Thanks, Tony."

GARRETT TOOK THE STAIRS to his condo two at a time. His key was halfway into the lock when Stephanie opened the door.

"Oh, Garrett." She took him into her arms, hugged him.

Instinctively, he hugged her back. "Any news?"

"Not yet." His father spoke from the living area. Hell, Dwight had aged ten years. His face was gray, his

Stephanie's, and she realized how much the woman was suffering. She clearly adored Lucas.

Rachel felt like an intruder. "I'm so sorry for barging in." She hitched her purse higher on her shoulder. "I'll leave you in peace."

"That's probably best," Dwight said.

"Stay, Rachel," Garrett said. "Please."

It sounded as if he really wanted her, rather than simply scoring points against his dad. Stephanie nodded, adding her invitation to his.

"I'll make some lunch," Rachel offered.

Three voices started to say they weren't hungry.

"It'll be a long day," Rachel said. "And you, at least—" she nodded to Stephanie "—definitely need to eat."

In the kitchen, she took stock of the supplies. She wasn't a great cook, but she could make a frittata and slice the sourdough loaf she found in the pantry. It was the kind of meal she often made for herself when she came in after a late night at the office.

Despite their avowed lack of interest, half an hour later everyone dug into the meal. The lack of small talk meant it disappeared fast. Every so often, Stephanie would pull out her cell phone, check that it was still working and she hadn't missed anything. Dwight gave her an envious look each time, as if he'd like to do the same, but couldn't show weakness.

After he pushed his plate away, Dwight held Stephanie's hand on the tabletop, his thumb caressing her knuckles.

The silence seemed to grow heavier with the passage of time.

"Isn't there someone you could call?" Garrett asked his dad.

"They'll call me as soon as there's news."

"Is this about looking stoic?" Garrett demanded. "Because now isn't the time, Dad, to prove how cool you are under fire."

"It's always the time to stay cool under fire," Dwight shot back.

"Typical," Garrett said, disgusted. "Heaven forbid that you should actually *feel*..."

"So tell me, Garrett," Rachel said quickly. "If your brother was a fruit, what fruit would he be?"

Stephanie made a little sound of surprise.

"My son is not a fruit," Dwight said, fury turning his face almost purple.

Garrett laughed out loud. He held Rachel's gaze as he said, "Lucas is an apple. Smooth on the outside, the kind of fruit you see every day, but you don't know what you'll get until you bite into it."

"That's him," Stephanie said, a little smile playing around her mouth.

"What the hell..." Dwight growled.

Stephanie squeezed his hand. Incredibly, it silenced him.

"I figured out what fruit you'd be," Rachel said conversationally to Garrett. "Would you like me to tell you?"

His father sputtered.

Garrett held her gaze. "Yes, please, Rachel."

"You'd be a durian," she said. "They look really interesting, but they stink."

He grinned, and a peculiar warmth spread through him. "I thought I smelled of, what was it, pine needles and citrus peel?"

She smiled, and there was a secretive quality to it that made him want to kiss her senseless. But he'd lost his chance to do that ever again.

Or had he? Garrett had made a bad judgment call, but it was Rachel's nature to say they could get past that. He knew how tightly she liked to hang on. Maybe she would forgive him and this would all work out. He thanked God she wasn't like him, quick to let go, slow to forgive.

"I was being polite about the pine needles," she said.

"Of course," he murmured, glad beyond measure that she was here. He wished they were alone so he could… Ugh, what kind of jerk did that make him, when his brother was missing?

He wished he'd said more to Lucas on the phone the other day. Told him he loved him, or something. He squelched a grin at the thought of Lucas's likely reaction. They were both Dwight Calder's sons.

They were both Michelle Calder's sons, too. Maybe Garrett had been a bit harsh in his judgment of Lucas for attaching himself to Stephanie. He'd been twelve years old, for Pete's sake. Fact was, when Garrett thought about what Lucas said on the phone the other day, about taking Mom's advice to heart in his navy career…well, Lucas had done a great job of honoring Mom's memory.

Unlike Garrett, who—

Garrett stopped, stunned. Rachel was right.

This whole partnership thing *was* all about his mother. All about proving he was the best he could be, because that was what Mom had dreamed of for her boys. No wonder the pressure had been so much more intense for this pitch than it ever had been before.

Garrett owed Rachel an apology.

He hoped that maybe, when he admitted that he'd been in major denial, it would help her understand what he'd done with his pitch. And why.

It would help her forgive him.

His father's cell phone rang. Dwight dropped it in his haste to take the call, which was probably the nearest Garrett would ever come to seeing his dad flustered.

"Calder," Dwight barked into the phone.

His countenance was totally neutral. Garrett imagined him hearing news of missile launches, of battles lost, with this same lack of expression.

How could his father be so unfeeling?

"Thank you for letting me know," Dwight said tonelessly and ended the call.

"Well?" Garrett demanded.

Stephanie clasped Dwight's hand.

"They know where Lucas is, and they believe he's alive," Dwight said, his tone as measured as if he was passing on the weather forecast. "They plan to mount a rescue mission at 0100 tomorrow. That's 1600 this afternoon, our time."

Just a few hours away. Stephanie burst into tears. Garrett wished he could do the same. *Thank You, God.*

"Is Lucas hurt?" he asked.

"They have no data on that," his father said.

Garrett wanted to punch him.

Then Stephanie wound her arms around Dwight's neck, and he clutched her so hard, she made an "oof" sound. Maybe his dad wasn't as cool as he seemed.

"So now we wait some more," Garrett said.

His father nodded.

"Will you stay?" Garrett asked Rachel.

She smiled, and his heart caught in his chest. "Of course."

He dropped a kiss on the top of her head.

"How about we go to the store? We can restock your sad bachelor pantry," Rachel said.

SHOPPING AT DUANE READE with Rachel turned out to be an education. Garrett had never met anyone so particular about what she put in her cart. His strategy was to grab whatever sounded or looked or smelled good. She read every label as if cyanide might be lurking in the ingredients list.

"We haven't got all day," he grumbled when she put a perfectly ordinary pack of peanuts back on the shelf in favor of a seemingly identical pack of peanuts.

The smile she gave him was so impish that he had to kiss her. So he did, right there in the middle of the aisle. She must have figured out by now that he wanted out of that stupid breakup.

"Hmm," she said when he pulled away. She peered at the small print on a pack of cookies, then put it into the cart. "Garrett, have you heard from Tony yet? Any news from Brightwater?"

Not the subject he wanted to discuss. "I haven't looked at my phone." He'd left it in the apartment. "Did you hear anything?"

She shook her head. "Brightwater probably haven't made up their mind yet. It's a bit soon."

"Yeah." It would always be too soon to tell her what he'd done with his pitch. He scowled at the bunch of bananas she was inspecting. "I don't care if those are black-and-blue and filled with a lethal dose of pesticide, just put them in the damn cart."

BACK AT THE APARTMENT, Rachel took orders from Stephanie as they prepared a meal. She wondered what Garrett had done in his pitch that was so extraordinary. But she didn't want to spend time second-guessing Brightwater now, not when he was so worried about his brother.

Dwight switched on the TV to see if any word of the crash or the rescue mission had made it on to CNN. "It shouldn't have," he said. "No one wants the Iranians to know we're coming, but with so many reporters over there…"

Garrett sat with him, both of them with their eyes fixed straight ahead on the screen.

"That's the closest I've seen them in fifteen years," Stephanie observed as she sautéed onion and garlic.

"You and Dwight seem closer, too," Rachel said.

Stephanie smiled. "We had dinner a few nights ago, like a date. It was lovely."

"I hope things work out for you," Rachel said.

"Dwight can seem a bit stiff to people who don't

know him." Stephanie added sliced chicken to her pan and turned up the heat. "That's his armor, his shield. But to me...I see beneath that, and I see what an effort he's making. Heroic." She looked apprehensive. "This thing with Lucas...if they don't bring him back alive... Dwight will be devastated."

"So will you," Rachel said.

The other woman nodded. "You're right. We'll get through it together. If Dwight will let me in. Could you pass me that soy sauce?"

As Rachel handed over the sauce, she hoped Dwight wasn't as big an idiot as his oldest son.

"Not all the Calder men screw up in these things." Stephanie poured the sauce from on high and immediately began turning the chicken pieces. "Garrett and Lucas aren't close on the surface, but those boys love each other fiercely."

Rachel said a silent prayer for Lucas's safe deliverance. That Garrett wouldn't lose another person he loved. And as a result be less able to trust love from those who were still in his life.

"You're good for Garrett," Stephanie said. "When I see you two together, I think he has more confidence."

Rachel felt warmth in her cheeks. She focused on topping and tailing a pile of green beans. "Garrett doesn't need more confidence."

"More confidence to be open, to give something of himself," Stephanie said. "He doesn't do that easily."

"That's for sure," Rachel muttered.

"With you," Stephanie said, "Garrett lowers his guard. If he can learn that he won't get hurt the way he's been hurt before—by his mom dying, his dad substituting control for love and me…" She paused. "Me rushing to fill a gap that I never could, which only emphasized what Garrett had lost…"

"Don't blame yourself," Rachel said. "I don't think Garrett holds a grudge. Not anymore."

Stephanie's smile was watery. "I think with you…I think he might start to trust that it can last."

It. Stephanie hadn't used the word *love,* but that's what she meant, Rachel knew.

Was Stephanie right? Could he love her back? Would Garrett know love if it clubbed him on the head with a baseball bat? Rachel wasn't so sure.

CHAPTER TWENTY-FIVE

THEY ATE DINNER in preoccupied silence, knowing the rescue mission was underway. How long it would take was anyone's guess. Dwight had said they probably wouldn't hear anything until morning but that didn't stop everyone jumping at the ring of the phone, or the honk of a horn in the street below.

"I'm exhausted. I think I'll go to bed." Stephanie stood and stretched, pushing the bulge of her stomach against her loose top.

"Good night," Garrett said. Rachel echoed it.

Dwight made an indistinct sound. He looked at his wife with such naked hunger and longing, Rachel was embarrassed. Even Garrett looked away.

Stephanie held out a hand. "Dwight, will you come with me?"

It was all Rachel could do not to laugh as Dwight just about fell over his own feet in his haste to accompany his wife.

"That looks promising," Rachel said when they'd gone. She carried a stack of plates to the kitchen and began loading the dishwasher.

"Until Dad messes up again," Garrett agreed. "Can I do something to help here?"

"Wipe the counters." She put a yellow cleaning cloth in his hand. "Your dad's not good at showing his love," she admitted. "But it's there. So long as Stephanie knows it, it doesn't matter what other people think."

"I guess." Garrett was frowning. He gave the counter one last wipe, then put the cleaning materials away. "Come sit with me," he said.

Rachel settled next to him on the sofa. He slung an arm along her shoulders, drawing her into him, then hit the remote control, so the room filled with mellow, louder than necessary jazz.

"Worried about overhearing your dad and Stephanie?" Rachel teased.

He shuddered, but didn't deny it.

They sat like that for a while. As the music washed over her, Rachel's eyes grew heavy. She stifled the first yawn, then didn't have the energy to hold back the second. It was only nine o'clock, but she'd barely slept last night. Her eyelids drifted downward.

Dimly, she heard Garrett say her name. She wanted to reply, but her whole body felt so pleasantly lethargic, she couldn't move.

Garrett's voice again, amused this time. "So much for my plan to make out." He pressed a kiss to her forehead.

Mmm, making out would have been nice. Though they should probably talk first. Rachel snuggled against him.

She awoke what felt like hours later to find the room in darkness. She was still on the sofa, lying on top of Garrett. Good grief, she could have suffocated him. As she pulled away, his arm clamped tighter around her, holding her in place.

Ah, well, if he didn't mind, why disturb him? She settled her head against his chest, listened to the steady beat of his heart.

Mmm...

"You're synchronizing your breathing to mine," he murmured in her ear.

She started, and her head crashed into his nose. He cursed.

"Sorry," she whispered, laughing.

"Sure you are." One hand caressed her shoulder, tucked her bra strap back into her blouse. "Good night, sweetheart," he murmured.

Her eyes flew open. *He called me sweetheart.* The even rhythm of his breathing told her he was sound asleep. Had he been awake when he said that?

Because I want to be his sweetheart.

Wondering whether they could get past their differences sufficiently to have a life together kept her awake even as Garrett seemed to slip deeper and deeper into slumber.

When the darkness turned to half-light, Rachel eased herself out of Garrett's arms. He muttered something in his sleep, but otherwise didn't stir.

She used the bathroom off his bedroom, then on her way back out noticed he'd dumped his briefcase on his bed.

His Brightwater pitch would be in there. The mystery pitch that he'd changed at the last minute.

Rachel hadn't checked her phone since earlier in the

evening, and now she wondered if Tony had been calling one of them to say they'd won.

She was suddenly desperate to know what his pitch looked like. One of them was going to win, and the other would be out of a job. If Garrett won, she would feel better if she agreed that his pitch was superior to hers.

It wouldn't hurt to look, now that the pitches were over. Rachel felt only the tiniest twinge of guilt as she pulled out his laptop. She'd learned that, unlike her, Garrett employed digital storyboard artists. Not for him the bulky portfolio of pencil sketches.

She opened the laptop on the bed and knelt on the floor beside it. If Garrett had a password on his laptop, she would have foundered right there. But he didn't, and within a minute she located his pitch files. Ah, there was the one she wanted, saved early this morning.

Rachel began scrolling through. Thirty seconds later, she stopped the presentation, went back to the beginning and watched again, reading it more carefully.

The campaign was a mini soap opera, to be told mainly on the internet, on sites like YouTube, but backed up with print and some outdoor. Similar to the movie *Sliding Doors,* the main character was shown living two alternate lives. In one life, she took out a student loan and went to college. In the other, she was scared of having a large debt, so she didn't go to college and instead took a low-level clerical job. There was nothing heavy-handed about it—both versions of the girl had interesting lives, highs and lows with their friends and families, but of course there was a subtle weighting in favor of college.

The noncollege girl tended to be whiny.

The college girl got the better guy.

It was brilliant. It was about Rachel.

Rachel closed the laptop.

"Snooping?" Garrett asked behind her.

Her stomach lurched. She sank down onto her heels, not ready to face him. "Yeah."

She sensed caution in his approach.

"Rach, I need to explain."

"You used me." She turned around, scrambled to her feet. "Used my family and my life. I confided in you because I thought I mattered to you. That was private. It wasn't up for grabs as pitch material."

"Everything in life is pitch material," he said. "I made sure it's not readily identifiable as your story."

"You *used* me."

His gaze dropped. "I presented the very best pitch I could, Rach. That's what it was about. You could have used your own story, but you were too scared."

Beyond the window, the sun peeped over the horizon, giving the room a faint orange glow.

"Did you know I wouldn't want you to use that material, or not?" she demanded.

A pause.

"Yes," he said.

"How do you think my parents will feel when they see that?" she asked.

"Actually," he said carefully, "they're pretty excited about it."

Rachel gaped. "They *know?*"

"Your dad was working night shift last night. I spoke to him on his cell. If Brightwater goes for this idea, there'll be a decent fee in it for your parents. They've agreed to share some family stories that the campaign can draw on over time—their official title will be storyline consultants."

Rachel reshuffled her thoughts in the light of that news. "I guess…that might not be so bad. You could pay them the fee conditional on them staying in New Jersey…"

"Rachel," he said, "your dad's going to use the money to buy his share of the hot-dog stand in Dayton."

"What?" she shrieked. "You're giving my parents money so they can move away? When you know what it means to me to have them stay?"

"It's their choice, sweetheart," he said gently.

"You jerk!" Rachel thumped him hard on the chest. It didn't seem to affect him at all, but it gave her some relief. "I came here yesterday to tell you I wasn't giving up on you. On us. That we could work through our obstacles."

"Thank you." He grabbed her hand, held it to his chest where she'd just hit him, relief breaking over his face like daylight. "Rach, you don't know how happy I am to hear—"

"I was wrong!" she snapped. "I forgot that loyalty depends on trust. You betrayed me, Garrett. I was willing to fight to the death, you and me against anything the world could throw at us. But I can't fight to the death against you. Not without dying."

Something flashed across his face. Shock…comprehension. He finally understood what she was saying. What she'd offered him. What he'd done.

"Rachel, I'm sorry." His voice was hoarse. "I didn't think. Or rather, I did, but my thoughts were all out of whack."

"No, *mine* were," she said. "I thought you had it in you to be…someone else. I was wrong."

"You were right," he insisted. "Rachel, if I could do it over… Rach, I want to be that man. The one you can trust. Give me another chance."

She shook her head.

"Sweetheart." He tried to pull her into his arms, but she was as rigid as granite, silent and dry-eyed. "You're the one who doesn't give up. Don't give up on us, Rachel."

"Check your cell phone," she said.

"What? Why?" Then he figured it out. "Let's not do this now," he said.

"I want you to check." She finger-combed her hair, using the shaving mirror on his dresser. "I haven't had any calls. At least, not from Tony."

"Later," he said.

But she wasn't about to let it drop. In the end, Garrett pulled his phone from the side pocket of his laptop bag with a sense of dread. "Four messages." He thumbed to the list of missed calls. "One from Tony."

"Listen to it." Her face was set.

He did.

"Garrett, it's Tony." His boss's voice grated on his

taut nerves. "Where the hell are you? I've just heard from Brightwater…"

Garrett listened to the end of the message. Then he deleted it.

"Well?" Rachel's voice was thin.

"I won the pitch." Crap. "I'm sorry."

"No need to be," she said briskly, even though the blood had drained from her face. "Well, I'd better go. Tony will be wanting to see me."

"Don't be dumb," he said. "It's five in the morning."

She made a dashing movement with her hand. He noticed moisture in the corner of her eyes.

"Are you going to cry?" he asked, horrified.

"Not in front of you." She smoothed down her rumpled skirt and tucked in her blouse. "Goodbye, Garrett." She headed for the door.

Garrett had to stop her. He had no idea how; he'd never wanted to keep a woman in his life before. With one exception.

"My mother…" he said. The word rang in the dawn silence.

Slowly, Rachel turned around.

He was going to have to do this. He swallowed, drew a deep breath and said the words he never had before.

"It was my fifteenth birthday. She was in the store in New London, buying milk. Just buying milk. I was in the car outside."

Rachel waited. At least she wasn't leaving.

"It was a stroke—sudden, massive. Another customer came to get me from the car. I ran inside. She was still alive, but only for a minute."

Rachel made a sound of distress.

"It was the most ordinary death. The storekeeper told me one minute she was standing at the cash register talking about the weather, and the next she was gone. Just that morning I heard I made the football team. I was waiting to announce it at dinner. She knew I was trying out, knew I was desperate to be on the team, but I never got to tell her I made it."

His voice cracked. Because that line—*I never got to tell her I made it*—summed up everything he felt about his mother's death.

"I got down with her on the floor," he said. "I tried CPR. We'd just learned it in school, and then the paramedics kept going, but they couldn't..." He ran a hand down his face. "I begged her, Rach, I begged her not to die."

CHAPTER TWENTY-SIX

BEGGING NEVER WORKS.

Garrett heard quiet sobs. Rachel was crying. For him. Hell, he had tears in his own eyes.

"I shouldn't…" He swallowed, closed his eyes. "I shouldn't have waited. I should have told her. About the team. She would have been proud."

Rachel took his hands. "She *was* proud of you, Garrett."

He was somehow both nodding and shaking his head. His mom had been proud, but he'd wanted to give her more.

Rachel moved closer, until her arms were around him. It felt like the safest place in the world. "I know she was proud of you," Rachel said, "because of what you told me about her. That whatever you chose, she supported you and wanted you to be the best you could be. She knew you wanted to play football, and she knew how hard you were working for it."

Damn, now tears were streaming down his cheeks. He couldn't talk, didn't need to talk. But it seemed he needed to wash the grief out of his head.

Eventually, he took the crumpled tissue Rachel pulled from her pocket and wiped his face.

"Thank you," he said.

She nodded. And took a step backward. Away from him. But...wasn't she staying?

"I have to go," she said.

"Rachel, no!" If she walked out now, she would never come back. He could see it in her eyes.

"Garrett." His father spoke from the doorway. He was wearing—ugh, he was wearing Stephanie's peach terry-cloth robe.

"Uh, yeah?" Garrett was aware of Rachel taking another step away from him. He wanted to grab hold of her.

"The Pentagon just called. They got Lucas out."

Joy welled inside Garrett. "Amazing. That's fantastic. When can we talk to him?"

His father grinned, and he looked ten years younger. "He's injured. They need to get him stabilized before they fly him home. They hope to ship him out in the next seventy-two hours."

For once, Garrett didn't object to his dad insisting on a more complicated way of saying "three days."

"Will he be okay?"

Dwight's face sobered. "His injuries are. Severe. But they're confident he'll recover."

"That's wonderful news," Rachel said to Dwight. "I'm so happy for you."

"Thank you, Rachel." It finally seemed to dawn on Dwight that he'd interrupted something. "Uh, I'll leave you kids to it."

"No need," Rachel said briskly. "I'm about to leave, myself. I have a million things to do today."

"Rachel," Garrett warned.

"Can you give Stephanie my best?" she asked Dwight.

"Rachel!" Garrett snapped.

She turned in the doorway. "Let it go, Garrett."

And because Garrett didn't know what else he could say, didn't know what he could give her, he didn't stop her. He couldn't argue with his own advice.

A minute later, the front door closed.

And despite his father's palpable joy and Garrett's own relief, it felt as if someone had died.

"...AND SO KBC HAS NO choice but to let you go," Tony said.

Rachel had just been fired. Tony had used the correct HR-speak—excess resources, redundancy, et cetera—but the outcome was the same. She'd lost her job.

She didn't give a damn. She'd lost way too much already today for this to matter in the least.

"As is usual in these circumstances, you will need to leave the premises immediately," Tony said.

Rachel took two minutes to tell Tony what she thought of KBC's loyalty to its staff. Five minutes to sign various forms in the HR department. Twenty minutes to pack up her personal belongings. Thirty minutes to say the most essential goodbyes.

Less than an hour after she'd walked into the KBC offices, she was standing on the sidewalk, a carton under her arm, waving down a cab.

She started to give the driver her home address, then

changed her mind. "How much to take me to Freehold, New Jersey?" she asked.

A consultation with a GPS later, she'd agreed to pay a hundred bucks plus tolls and gas. She spent the journey counting the number of white cars on the road, so she wouldn't think about Garrett and what he'd told her this morning.

The taxi pulled up outside her sister's apartment building an hour later.

"What are you doing here?" LeeAnne hugged her. "Drop that, Kylie, it's disgusting," she called to the younger twin, carrying a lump of something that might have been cat poop.

"You're really going." Rachel stated the obvious as she gazed at the sea of cartons.

LeeAnne sagged onto the sofa. "Yep. Looks like Dad's getting some money from this advertising gig."

Rachel clenched her jaw. "I'll miss you." She perched on a carton of books.

LeeAnne sighed. "Ditto. I'm sorry, Rachel, part of me wants to stay but…"

"You don't want to be away from Mom and Dad," Rachel said.

"I want to go for myself, too," LeeAnne said. "Staying has its pluses, but I'm looking forward to a new place."

"Are you nuts?" Rachel's frustration flared up.

"Of course you think that," LeeAnne said. "You'd rather die than move out of your safe life."

"Ouch!" Rachel stared at her sister. Then she slumped and huffed out a breath. "I guess I deserved that."

LeeAnne nodded. Then grinned. "Sit with me on the balcony while I let the girls tire themselves out. If we're lucky, they'll nap."

They sat in the sun, faces turned up to the warm rays, until the twins started to flag. LeeAnne got them into bed with impressive efficiency. When she came out again, she brought sandwiches and sodas.

"I hate that we'll be farther away from you," she said, handing Rachel a plate.

"It's just a short flight," Rachel said. "Besides, I might have more time on my hands." She sipped her soda. "I lost my job."

LeeAnne gasped. Rachel told her about losing the pitch.

"So because our family's going to be in an ad that was better than your ad, you lost your job?" LeeAnne said, horrified.

"Nothing to do with you guys," Rachel assured her. She took a ferocious bite of her sandwich and felt a little better. "I have a couple of other options. I spoke to a big firm, JWT, this morning. Garrett set it up for me."

"That was nice," LeeAnne said.

Yeah, it was. Rachel had tried to find some way to take offence when Hardy Campese had mentioned Garrett's involvement, but Garrett had been thinking of her and he'd done a decent thing. There was no denying the JWT safety net made her feel slightly less panicky.

Her cell phone rang. She checked the display. Garrett. She canceled the call.

"I'm sorry I pressured you," she said to LeeAnne. "Whether you go or stay is your choice. Not mine."

"Can I get that in writing?" LeeAnne said.

They started laughing and laughed until tears came to Rachel's eyes.

"Oh, Rach." LeeAnne's use of the shortened name was the last straw.

She hugged her sister hard, tears flowing freely.

"Did I ever tell you you're a great mom?" Rachel said when she'd pulled herself together. "I know wherever you end up with the twins, you'll do your very best for them. I'm going to do the college fund thing, no strings attached."

"That's wonderful. And the good news is, with this money from Brightwater, Mom and Dad might be able to make a decent go of it in Dayton. They won't be borrowing money, and they'll have a cushion for emergencies."

"That's something." Rachel picked up her purse. "Can I take your car around to Mom and Dad's? I'll see if they need any help packing boxes."

"One more thing," LeeAnne said as Rachel lowered the window of the Toyota.

Rachel braced herself. "What's that?"

"You should probably stop hiding those twenty-dollar bills around," LeeAnne said awkwardly. "And, um, I'm speaking for Mom and Dad here, too."

Rachel blushed. "No problem."

On the way, she thought about all the mistakes she'd made in her misguided belief that clinging to what she knew would make her happy. And about Garrett's mom's philosophy. Discover what you love, then do your very best.

Great advice. In fact, it gave her an idea.

Genius. If she said so herself.

She'd need a day or two to research it. She could check herself into the New York Public Library for a couple of days—she had nothing else to do.

She pulled over to the side of the road and started making some calls. It took her a few attempts to get where she wanted, but then she had a meeting set up for Tuesday morning. Today was Friday. She had three days.

CHAPTER TWENTY-SEVEN

DWIGHT STOOD STILL while Stephanie adjusted his uniform lapels. He didn't want her to stop touching him, to stop caring for him in this way, one of the dozens of little ways she showed him tenderness. One of the ways she'd found that he would accept, when he wouldn't accept mushy declarations and public affection.

"So, the plane lands at noon," she said.

"That's right."

She knew that already, but they were both anxious, both confirming all the details of Lucas's flight as if talking about it would make sure everything went smoothly. The flight would land at Andrews Air Force Base at noon. Dwight would be choppered there soon, along with other senior military personnel who wanted or needed to see the rescue mission completed.

Lucas would be taken directly to the military hospital at Andrews for further assessment and treatment.

The thought of seeing his son again was making Dwight light-headed.

Then Stephanie finished with his lapels and dropped her hands, and he realized she'd been the cause of the light-headedness. Before she could step away, he wrapped his arms around her.

"I love you, Stephanie." It didn't have the urgency or the edge of frustration that it had the times he'd said it over the past few weeks. Instead, it came out quiet and emphatic. True.

"I love you, too, Dwight."

He'd never thought those words would cut him down, bring him to his knees. But now, he had to cling to her just to stay on his feet.

She gave a kind of watery laugh against his shoulder, and he realized he was probably crushing her.

"Sorry." He loosened his grip slightly.

"Don't be." She kissed him. "I love you touching me. The last few nights have been wonderful."

Absurd that a man his age should blush at the memory of lovemaking. Stephanie's shape had meant they'd had to be quite inventive. In the small double bed in Garrett's spare bedroom—his son hadn't argued when Stephanie had suggested they all stay together until they knew Lucas was safely home—they'd both found a level of passion that surpassed anything they'd experienced before.

The hell of it was, good though their sex life had been over the years, he'd had no idea it could have been even better. Dwight had had firm ideas about the way these things were done: for the enjoyment of all concerned, but never losing control.

He'd discovered that control was overrated.

More importantly, he'd discovered some things were beyond his control.

"I built my life on structure and order," he told Stephanie now, "but that wasn't enough to prevent Michelle dying."

Her arms tightened around him in comfort. She'd always been generous to Michelle's memory. He shook his head. "So I tightened the structure, reordered the order. And all I did was be a lousy husband to you, drive Garrett away and push Lucas into joining the navy, which nearly got him killed."

"You're not a lousy husband." Amusement threaded through the words. "You've been a pain-in-the-butt husband a lot of the time, and you've caused yourself unnecessary hurt…and deprived yourself unnecessarily of your son's affection."

"I know," he said. "And now I can't think why I did it. *You're* my rock, Stephanie, not some military protocol. That stuff's important to me, but it can only go so far. Without you…" He shook his head, unable to articulate how barren the weeks without her had felt.

She didn't seem to mind his lack of words. She went up on tiptoe and kissed him deeply.

"I love you," he said, finding the words quite enjoyable now. "I want to be with you forever…and if that means trying a lot harder at being a father…well, I'm just going to have to swallow some of my rigid ideas."

"They might choke you," she murmured.

"Quite likely," he said. "But I'll do it. And I'll do better with Garrett—you might have to help me with that. Please, come back home."

"Willingly." She kissed his jawline. "I just needed you to want to change. Not for me, but for you and him."

"So, you'll come home?" he asked. "Though we can

move if you prefer. The Upper East Side would be closer to Garrett, and I know you've always wanted to live in Manhattan."

Her eyes filled with tears. "Hormones," she said. "Thank you, Dwight. I love that offer. But let's not make up our minds now. Let's wait until we've had the baby."

"You're not saying that because you're not sure if you'll stay?" he asked.

"I'm staying." She came into his arms again.

At last, reluctantly, he pulled away. "I need to leave." He checked his watch, confirming his inner clock was correct. Then he took her hands in his. "Come with me."

"Excuse me?"

"Come with me to Andrews," he said. "I want you at my side."

"But it'll be all military top brass, and you don't like the distraction."

He winced at the reminder of his own pomposity, but she was grinning.

"You're Lucas's mother," he said.

She beamed. "I had my heart set on cleaning Garrett's bathroom, but you talked me into it."

He'd parked the Hummer in a garage just around the corner; they were there in two minutes. Dwight opened Stephanie's door and she climbed in. Just as liquid gushed all over her shoes.

Dwight stared. "What's that?"

"My water broke," she said, dazed.

"It's too early," he rapped out, as if he could command the baby to stay right where it was.

"Two weeks is fine." She climbed back out of the

car, and Dwight was so shocked it took him a moment to start helping.

"I'll call Dr. Palmer and tell him, but it may be a few hours before anything starts happening," Stephanie said. A sharp spasm of pain, unlike anything she'd felt before, squeezed her lower back, and she gasped.

"Or it may not be that long," Dwight said grimly.

"Dwight, darling." Her voice was tense with the aftermath of the pain. "Go see Lucas. I'll call your cell when I know if anything's really happening here. If Dr. Palmer says I need to get to the hospital, I'll call Garrett or take a cab." She made a shooing motion. "Go. Your son needs you."

"*You* need me," Dwight said.

Another shaft of pain rocked her. He grasped her arm with a firmness that said he wasn't going to let go anytime soon. "Back in the car, Stephanie. I'm taking you to the hospital."

"But Lucas—"

"Will have more people there to welcome him than he knows what to do with. I'll get someone to give him a message that the baby's on its way, and he'll be delighted...if he's conscious."

She was about to protest again, but he silenced her with a kiss. "They can see this operation through without me. But I didn't attend the births of my other children. This baby is not coming into the world without realizing he—or she—has a daddy who's crazy about him. Or her."

Stephanie burst into tears. Then yelped as pain clenched her insides again.

White-faced, Dwight got in the car. He broke his own personal safety rule and called the doctor from his cell phone as he drove.

GARRETT PACED THE waiting room at Peregrine Hospital, as anxious as if he were the father.

When Dwight had called and asked him to come, he hadn't for one second thought of refusing. Now he almost wished he had. Who would want this kind of worry in their life? Not to mention the knowledge there were another eighteen years of worry ahead while the kid grew up. Then he acknowledged his father probably still worried about him, at the age of thirty—and recalled how frantic they'd all been about Lucas—and he groaned.

No chance of letting go. Ever.

Far better to stay out of that emotional stuff altogether.

The way Dad did.

Hell. The threat of turning out like Dwight was enough to drive a man to soppy daddyhood.

Garrett shoved his hands in his pocket and paced the room. He ended up eyeballing an antismoking poster on the wall. Those things always made him want to take up smoking.

Dwight came into the waiting room, rumpled in pale green scrubs.

"News?" Garrett asked.

Dwight wiped his forehead with a handkerchief. "All going nicely, the doctor says." Then his voice cracked. "Garrett, Stephanie's in agony!"

Garrett stared at him, equally dismayed at the thought of his stepmother in pain and his rock-solid father breaking down.

When did I start thinking of her as my stepmother?

"I—can't she—have they given her drugs?" he asked. "Can they cut her open and get it out?" He shuddered at the thought.

"I asked for an epidural but she won't let them give her the damn thing," Dwight growled.

"I thought you were stronger than that," Garrett said.

"Me, too." Dwight knuckled his eyes. "Turns out I'm a kitten."

It was so preposterous, both men burst into laughter.

Garrett felt a little better, and his father at least didn't look quite so on the verge of meltdown.

"I gather you and Stephanie are back together?" Garrett asked. No need to mention the noises coming from his guest bedroom last night.

His father blushed. This was a day of firsts.

"She took me back," he admitted. "I'll never know why, but I'll always be grateful."

Garrett nodded. "That's good news."

But Dwight wasn't done. "Things are going to change—*I'm* going to change. I don't suppose I'll get it all right, so if you see me being a cretin with this child, will you tell me?"

Garrett blinked. "You bet." Though he couldn't quite imagine having the nerve.

"I'm not saying I'll want to hear it. But I'll listen—you have my word on that."

They both knew Dwight Calder was a man of his word.

"Okay," Garrett said doubtfully.

"Same with when I'm a cretin to you," Dwight said.

Garrett gave him a skeptical look.

"Which I have been in the past. Garrett, when you asked me not to marry Stephanie…"

"That was a long time ago." Garrett didn't want to remember that day, not with his father.

"I lied to you."

Garrett's head jerked up.

"I said I was doing it for you and Lucas, but the fact is I wanted to marry Stephanie because I loved her. I lied to myself, too, but that's no excuse. I hurt you…I'm sorry. I also want to say that despite the. The rift between us." His father glared at the antismoking poster. "You've done hugely well. I'm proud of you." His own honesty didn't wait for Garrett's snort of disbelief. "I *should* be proud of you," he said, "and I intend to work on that. But in the meantime, I'm grateful for what you've done for Stephanie and the baby."

Ah, dammit, Garrett's throat was clogged, and his eyes itched.

"Nothing to say?" His father sounded anxious.

Garrett eyeballed that poster again. "I'm thinking of taking up smoking."

His father drew in a sharp breath; his face reddened. Then he expelled the air slowly. "I'm not the only one who's going to have to make some effort here, son."

Son. Garrett couldn't remember his father calling him something so corny. But it sounded okay. He sighed. "You're right." Had he ever said that to his father? "Guess I won't take up smoking, after all."

His father grinned and stuck out his hand. They shook, and to Garrett's shock, his father closed his other hand over their clasp.

A nurse stuck her head around the door. "Admiral Calder, your wife needs you right now."

Dwight jumped to attention like the lowliest rating, and strode after her, double-quick.

As he watched his dad leave Garrett felt…envious.

Yeah, envious that his dad had a wife who was crazy about him, who was better than he deserved. And he was about to have a kid who would undoubtedly be cute as a button.

I could have had that. With Rachel.

He tried to ignore the thought. But it hung in there, growing stronger. Dammit, he wanted nothing more than to have Rachel in his arms and to say things to her—crazy things—about love and permanence and kids and forever. He wanted to give her everything; he wanted to take everything she would give him and never let it go.

"Crap," he said. "I love her."

He'd imagined they would be the hardest words to say, but in fact they came out easily.

"I love her," he said again. He loved her conviction and her determination. He loved her kindness and generosity of spirit. He loved her humor. He loved that she knew what he was like and she loved him anyway…he hoped. And of course, he loved her legs.

So, he was in love with Rachel, and he'd just used

her personal history to snatch the job she cherished out from under her. And to send her beloved parents away.

She would really be feeling the love right now.

Garrett cursed. His mom would be proud of him getting the job he wanted, sure. But it wasn't "the job" she'd have cared about, it was "what he wanted."

He wanted Rachel. And he knew from the way his mother had lived and loved that she'd be prouder to know he'd learned how to give himself to a loving relationship than how to be the best chief creative officer.

She'd think he was an idiot to have taught the woman he loved how to let go.

Garrett had some work to do.

Genius that he was, inspiration came quickly. He pulled out his cell phone and dialed.

When he'd finished that call, he dialed Rachel.

She didn't pick up.

He deserved that. He borrowed Stephanie's trick, left a message saying he was at the hospital and it was urgent, that she needed to come right now. Then turned off his phone.

CHAPTER TWENTY-EIGHT

THIRTY MINUTES LATER, the door to the waiting room opened. Rachel jogged in.

The sight of her robbed Garrett of breath, made him feel as if his heart had skipped a beat. How could he have been so blind as to not realize he loved her?

She didn't exactly look loving. Her expression was anxious, but cool, her chin set at a haughty angle. If he grabbed her now and kissed her the way he wanted to, he'd likely end up with a black eye.

It'd be worth it.

Still, he should do this right.

"Hi, Rachel," he said.

"What's going on?" she demanded. "Is Stephanie okay?"

"I'm glad you came," he said humbly.

She got a suspicious look in her eye, and he laughed.

Which made her even more suspicious. "Is she having the baby?" she said.

"Oh, yeah, the baby. Yes, she is. Shouldn't be long now."

She was looking at him as if he was insane.

"I love you," he said, before he could chicken out.

The words fell into a sudden silence.

She opened her mouth, closed it again, licked her lips. Damn, he loved it when she did that.

"I love you, Rachel," he said, just for the thrill of seeing that tongue again. She didn't disappoint.

"What's this about?" she said, her voice pleasingly shaky.

"It's about the fact that sometime over the past few weeks, I've been seduced by your devious brain, your sense of humor, your bad temper…and I've fallen in love with you."

"Is this some kind of trick?" she asked. "You didn't say that the other day."

Really? She might not have left if he'd been smart enough to figure out how he felt earlier?

"I'm slow," he said. "An idiot. But, sweetheart, I've seen the light."

"If this is an elaborate way of apologizing for stealing my life story…" But she took a couple of steps toward him, so he figured he was on to something.

"I'm sorry," he said. "I've been a jerk, which I can only put down to the fact that I was fighting this thing I have about you, and sabotaging my own future."

"Tell me more about this thing," she said.

"It's driving me nuts," he said. "I can't stop thinking about you, and every time I see you I want to tear your clothes off.…"

"Which isn't actually love," she pointed out.

"It is when I want to put a ring on your finger," he growled.

She gaped.

"Hell, Rach, I know you want something permanent—that's who you are. But I want it, too, despite my best efforts to convince myself otherwise." He curled his fingers around hers and looked deep into her eyes. "I screwed up and I'm a jerk and a coward. We both know that. But I want to get past all that, and I want to be with you forever."

"You have got it bad," she said wonderingly.

"You're not giving me a lot of encouragement," he said. "It's about now that a guy likes to hear *I love you, too.*"

She raised her eyebrows.

"Or so I believe," he said. "I've never actually been here before."

"Makes sense," she agreed.

He noticed she didn't actually say the words. "Rachel..." he warned.

She had the nerve to laugh at him. "Do you really think you and I can work this out?"

"Hey," he said, "I might not have the best track record, but I can change. I'm brilliant, remember?"

"How could I forget?" she murmured. Then she burst out laughing.

"So glad me baring my heart is so amusing," he said. "Dammit, Rachel, if you won't take my words seriously, take this. I just phoned Tony and quit KBC."

She sobered instantly. "What?"

As if on cue, her cell phone rang. She pulled it out, looked at the display. "It's Tony."

"Answer it," he said. "Take the job."

"I—I can't." She stared at the phone, dazed.

"Don't let pride stop you," he urged her. "You get

to be partner and chief creative officer at KBC, all the security you want. You're wonderful—you're exactly what Brightwater needs."

"That's true," she said.

He grinned.

"I can't believe you gave up that job," she said.

"You were right," he said. "It was all about Mom. I wanted to be the best for her. But she'd be proudest of me for finding an amazing woman and making her happy."

Tears swam in Rachel's eyes. "She would," she whispered. "I know it."

"I can always find another job, but I'll never find another you. I finally found something that's irreplaceable."

She looked very pleased with herself at that.

"And you'll never find another me." He drew her closer, into his arms. "You're crazy about me, Rachel. You've got to be."

"I have no idea why I find your arrogance sexy," she said sadly.

"I can be arrogant every day for the rest of our lives," he promised.

"Thanks, but a little goes a long way." Rachel wrapped her arms around his neck, marveling that she would get to do this whenever she wanted. "Garrett, I don't want the job at KBC because I already found another job."

His hands tightened at her waist. "JWT, I bet. They'd be fools not to snap you up."

The pride in his voice made her want to laugh. "Not JWT," she said. "But thanks, anyway."

"Ogilvy & Mather?"

"Nope." She tried to contain her glee. She obviously wasn't doing a good job of it, because his eyes narrowed.

"Rachel, sweetheart, what did you do?"

"I now work for Brightwater Colleges as head of family services."

"I didn't even know they had a head of family services," he said.

"They do now," she said smugly. "I was visiting my sister and it occurred to me that Brightwater could actually do people like her some good. Kids like my nieces have a high dropout rate, either because their parents aren't college educated, or because the loans get out of control. Brightwater's hired me to develop programs that help the family support their college student in different ways, and minimize the risk of them wasting their investment."

"Incredible." He kissed her until she couldn't breathe. "That's my girl."

Her smile widened. "There's more. Brightwater wants to make a big deal out of this—they think it'll attract a lot more students. And it'll tie in perfectly with your ad campaign."

He kissed her.

"But there will be some tweaking needed, and I insist on having the best creative director in the business. So I suggest you get back on the phone to Tony and withdraw your resignation."

"You want to be my client?" he said, horrified.

"I think it's only fair after the way you behaved."

"It's a conflict of interest," he said hopefully.

"I'll risk it," she said. "I asked Brightwater to give me a year. If they're not happy with the way it's working out, I'll leave."

"Where's the security in that?" he asked.

"I won't fail, not with your brilliant ad campaign." She nuzzled his neck. "But, Garrett, the funny thing is…I'm not scared of failing, and I have you to thank for that. You made me reach beyond what I thought were my limits."

His hands cupped her derriere and he tugged her closer. "So you're looking for a way to express your gratitude? Because this building is full of beds."

She swatted his shoulder. "That's creepy. But, maybe." She shot him a wicked grin, full of promise, and he was instantly desperate for her. "First I need to say something."

He groaned.

"I *was* going to say I love you," she said with dignity, "but if you don't want to hear—mmph." Garrett's hand had clamped over her mouth.

"When I release this hand," he said dangerously, "you get to tell me you love me. Nothing else, just that. Got it?"

She nodded, eyes wide with enjoyment. He let her go.

"I love you, Garrett," she said. "I love you to the ends of the earth."

"And you'll marry me," he said.

"Purely to save you from yourself," she agreed. Then

she could say no more, as he locked her in an embrace that poured out all his love, his longing, his loyalty. All for her.

Rachel had no idea how long they stood there, holding each other up, until a cough from the doorway penetrated her consciousness.

She dragged herself away from Garrett, to face his father. Oops.

"Rachel, I see you made it," Dwight said courteously, as if she wasn't tangled and breathless and untucked. That stiff upper lip military bearing had its uses. Dwight turned to Garrett, and a smile split his face. "Come say hello to your sister."

Garrett whooped. "Sister? I was convinced it was a boy."

"Me, too, from the sonogram photo Stephanie showed me." Dwight rubbed his chin. "The nurse tells me we likely mistook the tailbone for, uh, other parts. This baby is definitely a girl."

"Well, damn," Garrett said.

"Don't talk about your sister like that," Dwight growled.

Rachel snickered.

Garrett twined his fingers through hers. "Come on, Rach. Come meet your soon-to-be sister-in-law."

They walked together to the sun-filled room where a delightfully disheveled Stephanie cradled her baby in her arms. Garrett didn't let go of Rachel once, not even through welcoming his little sister with a kiss on her tiny head.

"I'm going to need this hand back sometime," Rachel warned him. "We can't play chicken for the next fifty years."

But when he grinned at her, eyes alight with humor and love, she had a funny feeling that was exactly what they might end up doing. While she tamed her shark one day at a time.

She couldn't wait.

* * * * *

Amy Knupp lives in Wisconsin with her husband, two sons and five cats. She graduated from the University of Kansas with degrees in journalism and French and is a die-hard Jayhawk basketball fan. She's a member of Romance Writers of America, Mad City Romance Writers and Wisconsin Romance Writers. In her spare time, she enjoys reading, playing addictive computer games and coming up with better things to do than clean her house. To learn more about Amy and her stories, visit amyknupp.com.

BURNING AMBITION
Amy Knupp

Thank you, yet again, to the
most patient retired firefighter ever,
for talking me through countless fire scenarios
and answering another thousand questions
for this book.

Thank you to Denise McClain
for answering my medical questions so willingly
(and to your dad for giving me an enjoyable
glimpse of a hard-core, old-school firefighter).

Thank you to Doug McCune for educating me
on the finer points of baseball spring training.

Thanks to Tasha Hacaga, Emily Becher and
Kay Stockham for the brainstorming, the
inspiration and the motivation. And for
accommodating my sudden odd music "needs."

To my parents, thanks for being the best unpaid
promotional team a girl could have.

To my boys, thank you for putting up with a
less-than-spectacular summer when every other
phrase out of my mouth was "after my deadline!"

And as always, thanks to Justin for having an
extremely high tolerance for midnight plotting
sessions and an uncanny knack for knowing
when to slide a margarita in front of me.

CHAPTER ONE

FAITH PELIGNI FELT AS IF she was being thrown right into the fire her first day. And that was just how she liked it.

Everyone on duty at the San Amaro Island Fire Department had gathered across the street from the station at the city-owned training facility. Captain Joe Mendoza, whom Faith had known in passing since she was three feet tall and running around in her father's too-big standard issue helmet, was currently explaining the drill. It was a two-person relay that involved dragging a hundred-fifty-pound dummy, climbing the four-story tower while carrying a heavy coil of hose, then rappelling down the outside wall. Each pair would be timed, with the fastest team the winner.

There was enough trash-talk going on between some of the guys to fill the Houston city dump. Faith had been introduced to a few of them, and so far, everyone was leaving her alone. On the one hand, she was grateful for the peace, but on the other, it meant she didn't fit in. She wasn't one of the guys. Standing by herself as Cale Jackson, one of the lieutenants, demonstrated each stage of the drill, she wondered if she ever would be. Did she want to be?

Maybe. What she really wanted was their respect.

To be able to walk through the department and be confident that no one still believed she wasn't here on her own merit.

"Listen up, men. And women." Captain Mendoza sought out Faith's eyes with his coffee-black ones. "Sorry, Faith. Old habits. I'm going to pair everybody up and then we'll get started. Any questions?"

No one responded, so the captain began calling off names. Instead of worrying about who she'd be partnered with, Faith walked closer to the tower to scope it out, looking for any pitfalls, since she wasn't familiar with it.

"Peligni, you're with me," the captain said, finishing up his list.

Faith didn't glance at him, afraid she'd betray her annoyance. Was he putting her with him so he could "help" her? A charity case? She bit down on any protest and turned to face him.

"I have a reputation for winning this," Captain Mendoza said as he approached. "You think you're up for it?"

She studied him, searching for a hint of bullshitting. He was a big man, well over six feet tall and wide in the shoulders. His eyes were gentle, kind, yet he had a look about him that said you definitely didn't want to get on his bad side. His black hair was short, his face tanned. Strong. Handsome. The kind of face you wanted to trust. As far as she could tell, he was being sincere.

"I'll do the best I can," she said.

He likely thought the activities this drill involved put her at a disadvantage. The first two legs depended mostly on upper body strength, which, of course, women were lacking compared to men. However, Faith was confident that she was stronger than most people gave her credit for, thanks in large part to extra workouts every week. Even on her days off, she put in one to two hours of physical training. While it would never make her stronger than some of these guys, she could definitely hold her own.

The third leg, rappelling, was one of Faith's favorites. She loved the feeling of flying downward and bouncing off the wall. One of her brothers, Lou, had taken her skydiving once, and it had been just as fun but with less control. Lou teased her that she'd missed her calling, and had tried to get her to join him in the military.

She watched intently as the other teams took their turns, trying to pick up tips, spots where they lost time. The men watching paid attention in a general yelling and cheering way, but they'd obviously been through this drill numerous times and weren't worried about shaving off every possible second like she was. Of course, they didn't have the stakes she did. If they didn't win, it was just another day. If she didn't win, there'd be rumblings that she shouldn't have gotten the job, that a woman couldn't hack this career, and on and on. While she didn't want to let such talk get to her, she had no doubt it would. Maybe she was shallow, but she wanted her fellow firefighters' respect.

Captain Mendoza leaned in close to her and she caught a whiff of his masculine, sporty scent. "The last two stairs before the top are wobbly as hell. Watch your step up there."

She nodded, debating internally. She considered being stubborn and working things out herself. But that wouldn't serve the bigger goal of winning, would it? Though she didn't like the idea of getting help, she liked losing even less. "Any other tips?"

"You're asking for something I've never given away before," he said, watching her with those dark eyes.

"Not even to your teammates?"

"None of them has ever been smart enough to ask."

They shared a brief grin, and Faith said, "Well?"

"Avoid the handrails. They'll slow you down."

"Got it. Thanks."

"We're up next. You ready?"

"Ready as I'll ever be."

"I'll go first."

Faith nodded, and followed him to the starting line while the second-to-last pair finished up.

"Faith," the captain said, making her look up at him. "Show me what you've got."

With that, he turned around and started suiting up in full gear. Faith did the same.

"Time to beat," the official timekeeper called out as the man before them—she couldn't remember his name—crossed the finish. "Four minutes, fourteen seconds."

"Can we do that?" Faith muttered to Captain Mendoza as they continued to prep.

"Have to push it," he said. "I think we can."

She knew it was up to her to pull her weight. No sweat.

Yeah, right.

The captain finished putting his gear on, and the whistle blew for him to start. Most of the guys were loud in their support of him as he lugged the dummy over the ground, but Faith kept her cheering silent, willing him to make up for any time she might lose ascending the tower with the heavy hose.

She put her last glove on, transfixed by the sight of him. She'd guess he was around forty, based on the lines of his face, not the way he moved. He was one of the biggest men on this shift, all solid muscle, and yet his grace and speed mesmerized her. He made it look as if the hose weighed three pounds instead of thirty. When he got to the top, he quickly fastened the rappelling gear and went over the edge. Like the rest of the guys, he took the wall in four rhythmic bounces.

Faith's adrenaline kicked in as he ran toward her.

"Go for it," he said as he tagged her hand.

She took off in a sprint to the spot where he'd dragged the dummy. The thing weighed more than she did, but she was used to that. No excuses in her world. She toted it back to the starting line and then sprinted to the tower.

When she reached the coil of hose, she stumbled a bit and almost fell. Just what she needed. She caught herself at the last moment and avoided ending up on her butt, but lost a couple seconds. She heaved the hose up and took off, eyes on each step, focusing on balance, avoiding the handrails.

By the last flight of stairs, her lungs were screaming, and she wondered if the air was thinner up here, because she sure wasn't getting enough oxygen. She forged on, preparing herself for the last two wobbly steps before unloading the coil.

Now for the fun part.

She attached her rappelling equipment and, without hesitation, climbed on top of the wall and lowered herself over, her back to the group of firefighters. Instead of hitting the wall four times, she flung herself out and made it halfway down with her first release. Pushing off with her legs, she flew the rest of the way, hitting the ground hard but intact. She unfastened the rope and sprinted to the finish line, ignoring the burning in her lungs.

JOE NODDED SLOWLY to himself as he watched Faith's final approach. This woman was going to cause an uproar in the department, not only because of her looks but because she could teach several of the men plenty when it came to busting one's ass.

He didn't know if she'd make the time they needed to win, but she had nothing to be ashamed of, given the way she'd gone after it. Her rappelling was beautiful—seemingly wild, yet she'd been in control the whole descent, pulling off the time-saving move. The woman could run, too. If this was how she performed in every aspect of the job, he'd be thrilled to have her working for him.

When she raced over the finish line, he held his hand out for her to slap again and praised her effort. His eyes were on the timekeeper as he hit the stopwatch, read the results to himself and then looked up with an unreadable expression.

"Let's have it, Olin," Joe said, caring too much about the results.

"Four minutes, eleven seconds. Congratulations, Captain. You and the new girl are the champs."

"Yes!" Faith whispered her response so most of the guys couldn't hear her, as if she understood celebrating would egg on some of them. She was young—only twenty-six—but Joe could tell she had a lot of street smarts and experience dealing with animallike males from her tenure in the San Antonio Fire Department the past few years.

Her glossy, sable hair was straight and reached below her shoulders. Her eyes were the brightest blue he'd ever seen, making him think of the Gulf of Mexico on the clearest day. She'd shown up to work that morning wearing no makeup—she didn't need any to highlight her striking features.

She met Joe's eyes, her blue ones overflowing with excitement and pride at their achievement. It was impossible not to catch some of her enthusiasm, regardless of how well she tried to hide it.

He nodded at her, grinned, then looked away, seeing her father's penetrating gaze in his mind and hearing his plea, just a couple of hours ago, for Joe to take Faith under his wing.

Joe wanted to see Faith succeed, not only because her father, Fire Chief Tony Peligni, was a good man. Not just because she was the department's first woman and had to carry that burden on her shoulders. Joe wanted her to do well because he liked her and felt lucky to have her on his team.

Professionally speaking, of course.

FAITH ABSOLUTELY, positively was not going to make coffee today.

Any other day, she'd do so willingly, because she was all about sharing duties, from meal prep to cleaning the rigs. But if she brewed coffee on her first day, it could be interpreted as a statement she didn't want to make. It'd be far too easy for one of the men to see her as the coffee girl, and who knew how long it would take to outgrow that derogatory title? Didn't matter that she'd been part of the winning team in training and had gotten a couple of compliments from the others about her rappelling skills. Some of these guys were Neanderthals at heart, she suspected. Lieutenant Ed Rottinghaus, for one—the man who'd fought to prevent her from being hired. There were likely others who felt the same. All it took was one moron following her around with the coffeepot. That wasn't the way to win respect.

The bitch of it was she was dying for a cup of hot, strong caffeine. She'd missed her morning dose in her rush to get out the door, and needed it even more than she needed the lunch she'd packed.

"Hey, new girl. Nice showing at the training drill."

She turned warily to look at the man with dirty-blond hair who'd just walked in. She'd probably been introduced earlier, but all the stacked-with-muscles bodies were starting to look the same to her.

"Thank you," she said. "I'm still trying to remember names."

"Derek Severson." He held out a large hand and she shook it. "Nicest guy you'll meet in this place."

"Is that right?" She laughed. "Good to know. I'll try to remember your face if that's the case."

"Hundred percent unbiased truth. So... Awful big shoes to fill, being the chief's daughter."

At least he didn't beat around the bush or talk behind her back. "I'm not trying to fill his shoes. Just here to fight fires."

He picked up the dirty coffeepot and went to work cleaning it in the sink. Thank God. A second point in Derek's favor.

"How many scoops?" she asked, taking the bulk can of coffee grounds down from the cabinet above once he'd finished scrubbing. Helping was inherently different from making the coffee herself.

"You like it strong?" Derek asked. "Or girlie?"

She shot him a look and realized he was joking, not singling out her gender. "I like it to wake me the hell up."

He was married, she guessed. Or taken. Good-looking, if slightly shaggy, he had an easygoing, friendly manner and warm, blue eyes that put a person at ease. Impossible that a man like him would be single. Not that she was looking for someone. Not here.

"Five. Six if you want to screw with the others. They like it girlie."

Once the coffee was brewing—with six overflowing scoops—she wandered around the kitchen, snooping absently, waiting for her pick-me-up to get done. Derek poured himself some health-nut cereal and added milk from a carton that had a Don't Use My Damn Milk sign taped to it.

She unwrapped her microwave dinner, started it cooking and then went to the coffeemaker to help herself.

Two more firefighters strolled into the kitchen. One had his eyes on the coffeemaker and the other made a beeline for the refrigerator.

"Hey," the dark-haired one on the coffee hunt said to Faith.

"Penn, right?" she asked.

"That's me." He smiled at her as he took down a coffee mug that said Never Do Anything You Wouldn't Want to Explain to the Paramedics on the side. "Welcome to the department."

"Thank you."

"Ah," the second guy, a redhead, said, walking up to her at the counter. If she remembered right, his name was Nate Rottinghaus, the son of her not-so-favorite lieutenant. "You."

Faith tensed and met his eyes. "Me."

"You know, the captain would win that competition if he was paired with a three-year-old." He poured his coffee, walked to the long table that ran up the center of the room and sat down across from Derek.

"What the hell, Nate?" Derek said.

"Careful or she'll figure out what an ass you are," Penn added.

Faith moved to the end of the table to force Nate to look at her. "I like to know what I'm up against. Got anything else you want to get off your chest?"

He perused her with lazy, smug eyes, as if he was silently calculating how long she'd last in the department. She'd bet the idiot couldn't count that high.

"There are lots of jobs where your looks could help you get ahead. The fire department isn't one of them."

The microwave beeped and Faith spun around, her appetite suddenly gone.

"Ignore him," Penn said. "He's used to it."

Faith gave a forced smile. "Already done."

"I was going to track you down." Penn hoisted himself up on the counter and ripped open a protein bar. "As the new kid on the block, you've been nominated to be on the auction committee for the upcoming Burn Foundation fund-raiser."

"Nominated, huh?" She pulled out her meal and set it down to cool. "I feel honored."

"You lucked out. Not only do you get to work with me, but the auction's in a month and the bulk of the planning is already done. Easy way to get volunteer points." He took a drink of coffee. "You know, in case you need points with the higher-ups." He said it with a conspiratorial grin, taking the sting out of his words.

"I'll probably need twice as many points with my dad," she joked.

Granted, it was only her first day, but getting her colleagues to think of her as something beyond a female, beyond the chief's daughter, was going to be a constant battle. She could handle Penn's friendly jibes. Hell, she could handle Nate's asshole remarks, as well. But she couldn't wait for the day when she wasn't the newbie trying to prove herself.

CHAPTER TWO

JOE HAD COME TO DISLIKE the cheery, "sunshiny" couch in the sunroom of his mother and stepfather's house in Corpus Christi.

His mom was almost always resting there whenever he visited these days. Carmen loved the bright yellow with ivory pinstripes pattern, but the mere sight of it made Joe's shoulders tense and his mood go to hell. As if it was the couch's fault she was stuck there.

He softened when he zeroed in on her face. Even as she slept, her features weren't peaceful. Her skin creased between her eyes and her lips turned slightly downward. To see such solemnity on the face of a woman who'd lived her life full of joy was jarring.

Not wanting to bother her even though she slept more than she was awake these days, he settled into the arm-chair near her feet and picked up a golf magazine from the end table. He didn't make it through the first article before she stirred.

"Mama," he said when he saw her watching him. "How are you doing today?"

Carmen raised herself up a little, arms shaking from the effort, and leaned against the two throw pillows behind her, smiling warmly. Joe hurried to her side to help.

He shot up off the chair. "Do you need something to eat, Mama? I could use a snack myself."

"Stop doing that, Joe." Steel underlined her tone. "You know I hate it when you talk like this."

"You can hate it all you want, but you have to face the facts," she said gently. "Changing the subject every time I want to talk about the future is not only futile, but it ticks me off."

He perched on the coffee table and put his hand on her bony one. "I don't want to think about it."

She squeezed his fingers, her grip firmer than he'd expected. "Believe me, I don't want to think about it either, sometimes, but I don't have a lot of choice in the matter. It's a natural thing for a woman to want to make sure everything's in place before she goes."

"You don't know how long it will be. No need to talk like it's tomorrow."

"It could be," she said matter-of-factly, and Joe knew she was right. "If you won't find a woman who's worthy of you, my greatest wish is for you to find a place here with Jorge and his sons."

"I can't move here—"

"That's not what I mean, Joey." She gazed out the window for several weighted seconds, her eyes following the flight of a Couch's kingbird as it landed on the branch of a bush, but her thoughts were obviously elsewhere. "By place I mean…a family. I want you to feel like they're yours."

Joe leaned forward and rested his elbows on his knees, still holding her hand. He stared at the floor, debating how frank to be.

"Jorge is a good man," she continued.

"Of course he is."

"You don't like him."

Joe turned that over in his mind, shook his head. "That's not true. I didn't like him at first, but I don't dislike him now."

"But there's something holding you back."

"Not at all. I just don't fit in."

"Sure you do. You all play golf. You like sports."

"Those are interests we have in common, yes." The grand sum of shared interests, come to think of it.

"Why can't you embrace them as your family, then?"

He stood and paced. "They don't respect me. My career. To them, I'm a bumbling blue-collar guy who has no place in their overpaid lawyer world."

Concern deepened in her eyes, twisting the blade of guilt that was perpetually buried in his gut. "That's not true—"

"Maybe it'll change if I get the job as assistant chief."

"Don't be ridiculous, Joey. Jorge doesn't care what you do for a living."

"Have you ever noticed how he introduces me? And how he introduces Ryan and Troy? I'm Joe Mendoza, his stepson. End of story. They're Ryan and Troy, junior partner and partner at Smith, Vargas and Wellington. His pride and joy. Men after his own heart, men with brilliant futures."

"They're his sons, Joe."

"I know that, and I don't begrudge them the fact. It's not the lack of a blood tie I'm talking about. It's…" He shook his head, realizing he was getting worked up, which would in turn get his mother worked up, and that was the last thing she needed. "We just come from different worlds. They'll never consider firefighting as good as law."

She studied him as he forced himself to sit on the coffee table again. "Tell me why you're going for this job, Joey. Is it because you want to be assistant fire chief or because you think it will make things easier with your stepfather or, Lord forbid, make me happy?"

"I want the job," he said without hesitation. "I've had my path planned out since I was a kid. You know that. I'm going to the top eventually, just like Dad."

But she wouldn't be there to see it, possibly not when he became assistant chief and definitely not when and if he was lucky enough to climb to the top position in the department.

"I've pushed you," she said quietly, introspectively.

"You've encouraged me. There's a difference."

"A fine line," she agreed. "Have you really given this serious thought lately? You love fighting fires, Joe."

"Hell, yes, I love fighting fires. I love the fire service. I'm a good leader. The position is perfect for me—a natural next step."

"If it will make you happy. But you won't be in the action as much."

That was putting it mildly, but he merely nodded.

"You've never been the desk jockey type."

"I wouldn't call it a desk job."

She stared at him so long he squirmed. "You listen to me, Joey. I want you to think hard about this. Think until you're purple in the face. Think about what *Joe* wants. What you want your life to be like. Don't include me or the legacy of your father or anything else in the equation. Only you."

"I want to move up in the fire department."

She made a succinct sound, a cross between a hiss and a shush. "Not today. You give it some time. Don't worry about me."

As if that would happen.

He wouldn't admit it out loud, because she'd throw a fit, but he wanted like crazy to get that promotion while his mother could still appreciate it. He wanted to share that victory with her. "I won't worry about you if you won't worry about me."

She stared at him, her strong jaw set, and shook her head. "No deal."

"How about a different deal? I'm going to get that job. And I want you to be around to see it. Can you do that?"

It was a ridiculous plea, he knew, but he had to grasp on to something.

Instead of scolding him for being in denial, his mother smiled at him and nodded, as if the two of them could conspire to fool fate. With that sparkle in her eye, he could almost believe it.

"You'll make one heck of an assistant chief, Joey."

FAITH'S NERVES WOUND tighter as she and her dad approached the front door of Ruiz's Restaurante, home of the island's best fish tacos. Food was the last thing on her mind this evening, though.

She'd spotted her mom's Ford Escort in the parking

lot and thanked the powers that be when her dad didn't notice it. He'd pulled into a space about five spots down from the Escort and never bothered to look around.

Faith hurried in front of him so she would hit the host station first.

"How many?" the lanky high school kid asked as they approached.

"We're meeting someone," she muttered, and headed right past the guy, spotting her mother in a booth by the window. She didn't look back at her dad, just hoped he would blindly follow.

"Hi, honey," Nita Peligni said.

Faith smiled, bracing herself.

"What on earth—?" her mom began.

"What are you doing here?" her dad asked at the same time.

"Faith." All warmth was gone from her mother's voice.

"Dammit, Faith."

"Wait," Faith said quietly but firmly. "Dad, sit down. Please, Dad."

He studied her, as if the reason for this meeting was jotted on her forehead. Then he turned his tired eyes toward his soon-to-be-ex-wife. "Okay with you, Nita?"

"I don't know what good it's going to do, but fine. Faith, what is this about?" Nita crossed her arms, her dark hair—all natural and not a hint of gray—falling in a bob just below her ears. She wore a peach T-shirt that washed her complexion out, and the shadows under her eyes aged her. It was evident the separation wasn't agreeing with her, but far be it from Faith to point that out.

Tony slid into the booth across from Nita and Faith took a seat next to him, trapping him there.

"Well? What gives?" her dad asked her, shoulders sagging.

"I just wanted to spend some time with my parents. Together. I've been back for two months now and I'm sick of visiting you one at a time."

She was staying with her dad in the family home—which was rambling and empty with just the two of them. No wonder he'd seemed so distraught when she'd come back from San Antonio. He'd been wandering around in the echoing twenty-five hundred square foot house by himself. Her mother had moved into a sterile, colorless, two-bedroom apartment on the mainland.

"We're getting a divorce, Faith." Her mom looked at her with those unwavering dark brown eyes that could scare small children, not telling Faith anything she didn't know. Just the one fact she didn't want to accept.

"Why the rush?" Faith asked, taking a tortilla chip from the red plastic basket in the middle of the tiled table. "You have your whole life to get divorced, if it's really the right thing. What if you're making a mistake?"

"We're not making a mistake," Nita said resolutely.

Her dad was noticeably silent, crunching on chips, eyes on the table.

"Dad?"

He only shook his head. "I'm sorry, princess. I know it's hard on you kids, even though you're grown up."

"It's because of my career, isn't it?" Faith asked, desperation clawing at her to somehow find the key, keep them together, make them see reason.

"What?" her dad exclaimed with both outrage and shock. "No. Your choice to become a firefighter has nothing to do with our marriage."

"You guys have argued about it for years," Faith said, spouting the suspicion that had been gnawing at her since they'd broken the news of their separation. "Ever since I was twelve years old and told you that's what I wanted to do."

"It's something I will never understand, Faith," her mom said, repeating the same tired chorus. "It's not a job for a woman. It's not safe. I thought maybe when you broke your collarbone it might knock some sense into that head of yours, but you're back at it. Just waiting until the next injury, God forbid."

An unfamiliar uneasiness rolled through Faith's gut, but she ignored it. The collarbone had healed. The building that had collapsed on her in San Antonio should be a distant memory. "A man would've suffered the same injury I did if he'd been standing in that exact spot when the roof caved in. It had nothing to do with ovaries or breasts."

"Faith." Her dad held his palm up, as he so often had, and waited until she pressed hers to it out of habit. That it was something they'd done for as long as she could remember, a sign between her and her dad. "Your mother will always worry about you. Can't change that. You scared us when you got hurt."

"So does that mean you think I shouldn't have gone back to the career I love?"

"No," her dad said, avoiding her mother's steely gaze.

"Did you raise me to quit when bad things happen, Mom?"

This wasn't at all what Faith had planned for their evening together, but she couldn't stop the anger and disbelief from spilling out. It'd been festering for several years since her last big blowup with her mother on the topic.

"I'm not going to dignify that with an answer."

"This is my career. It's what I love doing and want to do for the next twenty or thirty years. I plan to earn several more certifications, promotions, become an officer—who knows how far I can go? But not if I run away because of a broken bone."

"I hope the next time it's not worse, Faith." Her mom's eyes shone with unshed tears that almost got to her. Almost.

Again her dad held his large, work-roughened palm out, and when Faith completed the action, it soothed her enough to take a deep breath and realize she was about to ruin this evening. She had them together at one table, creating the opportunity for them to talk about inane things—anything *but* her career—and remember what they'd had in common forty or so years ago, when they'd fallen in love.

She opened her menu and scanned it, even though she knew it by heart. "What are you guys ordering?"

"Enchiladas," they both said at the same time.

Faith hid a grin.

"Beef," her dad said.

"Seafood." Her mother glanced at her. "What sounds good to you, Faith?"

"Fish tacos, as usual." She closed her menu.

Her dad's cell phone rang and he answered, switching to his business tone and gesturing for Faith to let him out of the booth. She did, watching him walk past the host toward the front entryway.

The waiter came by to check their chip supply and take their requests. Faith went ahead and ordered for her dad, since she knew exactly what he wanted.

That turned out to be the wrong thing to do. He strode back in and grabbed the sunglasses that he'd set on the table. "I have to go. Mayor Romero called an impromptu meeting at city hall. You two have a good dinner." He leaned over and kissed the top of Faith's head before she could say anything.

"Tell the mayor he might want to rethink holding impromptu meetings over the dinner hour," her mom said coldly.

Her dad nodded, showing no emotion.

"Dad?" Faith's plan was falling apart. "Can't you stay for a little while?"

"It's important, honey, or he wouldn't phone me at dinnertime." He walked out, waving a goodbye over his shoulder.

Faith sank deeper into the booth. As she did, she caught a look on her mother's face—of disappointment. Resignation. Just for a moment.

After a few minutes of awkwardness, the two of them engaged in small talk, which was what they did best. It was safest to stay away from topics either one of them cared a lot about. Before their food arrived, Faith spotted Joe Mendoza as he walked by their table.

He turned back when he recognized them. "Faith, it's good to see you. Hello, Mrs. Peligni."

"Good to see you, too," Faith replied.

"Hi, Captain Mendoza," Nita said. "Are you here alone?"

It was impossible not to notice the way the captain's black polo shirt stretched to the limit over his shoulders. His long legs were encased in light blue jeans and he wore black cowboy boots. When he smiled, the corners of his eyes crinkled, making Faith think he must smile a lot. His dark eyes flitted over her for an extra second.

"For now. I'm meeting my great-aunt for dinner." He glanced around, presumably looking for her. "Are you ready to go at it again in the morning?" he asked Faith, referring to their shift the next day.

"Absolutely. Looking forward to it."

"Did you hear about your daughter's performance in the training drill on her first day of work?" he asked Nita.

"I did not."

"She was impressive. Part of the winning team."

"Pair me with a walking legend and it's hard to screw up," Faith said drily, trying not to bask in his compliment.

"Faith has some amazing rappelling skills," Captain Mendoza continued.

Nita's eyes widened and she nodded slowly, politely,

but she wasn't able to hide her true feelings. "That's good, I suppose."

An awkward silence fell over them. Thankfully, his great-aunt, who had to be ninety years old, came whisking up to his side.

"There's my Joey," she said, hugging him and then smiling at Faith and her mom.

Captain Mendoza introduced them all, and then the two of them made their way to the table the host had originally indicated, on the far side of the room. Faith followed him with her eyes, covertly admiring the view from behind. At the same time she was touched by the way he held on to his aunt's elbow, pulled her chair out for her and pushed her in at the table. He sat at a right angle to Faith, giving her the opportunity to appreciate his profile. He was good-looking and a gentleman, but he was probably about fifteen years older than her and, much more importantly, her supervisor.

Their waiter delivered their food, and Faith and her mother returned to their stilted, low-stakes discussion of the unseasonable weather and Faith's four brothers.

"You know, Faith," her mom said when they were almost finished eating, "you're the one who initiated this dinner. I know you're disappointed that your father walked out, but you could give me your full attention, anyway." She smiled as she spoke, but Faith frowned.

"I *am* giving you my attention." She'd heard every word her mother had said, even if she wasn't doing much of the talking.

"Could've fooled me." Her mom scooped up guacamole with a chip. "He's attractive, I'll give you that."

A flash of alarm had Faith straightening. "Who's attractive?"

"Come on. Who have you been staring at for the past twenty minutes? The captain."

"I'm not staring at him. Or if I am, it's only because he happens to be sitting directly in my line of sight. He's my officer, Mom."

"After watching how the fire department tore up your father's and my marriage all these years, I would think you'd want to find someone with a different lifestyle, Faith."

"The 'lifestyle' is something I love," Faith reminded her, picking up her glass to take a drink. "But I have no intention of dating anyone in the department."

Her mom shoveled a bit of enchilada onto her fork. "Although...you did say advancement is your goal. I imagine getting to know the captain *better* is one means to the desired end." She chuckled, amused with herself.

Faith set down her glass. Hard. "I don't believe you just said that."

"I'm kidding. It's a joke, honey."

"It may be a joke to you, but for me it's my life." She threw her napkin onto her half-finished meal. "I have enough trouble being taken seriously by the men I work with. I would think you, a female, my *mom,* for God's sake, would see the importance of dispelling clichés that weaken women."

"I'm sorry, Faith," Nita said quietly. "But the way you were staring at him, and the once-over he gave you when he was at our table—"

"There's nothing between us. There never will be. I

may be ambitious and determined to advance, but *that* is something I would never do." Faith strained to keep her volume down. "Ever."

CHAPTER THREE

"You make a lot of the guys here look bad." Evan Drake, an easy-to-like firefighter, was spotting for Faith as she did barbell squats. "I like that."

Trying not to smile, she closed her eyes and concentrated on the burn in her glutes and quads as she slowly straightened. When she nodded, Evan took the barbell from her and replaced it on the rack. Except for them, the workout room at the fire station was empty, though others had been in and out during the hour-plus Faith had been exercising.

"Spotters aren't supposed to make the lifter laugh," she said, mopping sweat from her forehead with a towel.

"Sorry. You can lift a lot, though."

"I have to. Not everyone is open-minded about women doing this job." She'd started weight lifting in high school, already accustomed to doubts from her own mother.

"You'll run into some skeptics here, if you haven't already," Evan said. "Ready for the next set?"

Faith nodded and got back into position, bracing herself for the weight.

Halfway through the set, the door opened and Captain Mendoza and Nate Rottinghaus came in. Faith was just starting to push herself up to a stand when the captain caught her eye and nodded subtly. She floundered, lost her focus and had to stop for a second to regain her composure.

Dammit. He was good-looking—especially in workout shorts that hinted at thigh muscles that didn't quit—but that was no reason to be distracted.

He was watching her, adjusting one of the weight machines, when she closed her eyes and tried to clear her thoughts so she could finish the stupid rep and not look like an idiot. Or a weak female.

"Think you're more than just a pretty face, huh?" Nate said once she was standing. He'd moved to the hand weights on the other side of her.

Instead of ramming the barbell into his head as she'd like to do, Faith didn't blink. She moved straight into the next repetition, counting to herself.

"Another comment like that will get you written up." The captain was suddenly right next to them, in Nate's face. "Faith's been working out for nearly ninety minutes. If you had a fraction of the work ethic she does, you might make something of your career."

Nate raised his chin almost imperceptibly, kept his shoulders stiff, his face expressionless. "Sorry, Captain. Didn't realize you'd taken her under your wing. Probably a good idea. It's tough when you're…new." She felt his eyes rove up and down her body, making it obvious that "new" was not what he meant.

Faith gritted her teeth and rose with the weight too quickly.

"Whoa," Evan said, steadying it.

"I'm done." She let him take the barbell from her once again, her heart thundering. Technically, she still had three more reps, but to hell with them.

What she wanted to do was storm out of the room, but she still owed herself another half hour of exercise. If she stopped now, starting again would be tough. Plus, she wasn't going to let the peanut brain scare her away.

"Thanks for spotting," she told Evan. "Let me know when I can return the favor."

"You got it."

Faith went to the other side of the room and stepped onto one of the treadmills. She'd run three miles to start her workout and normally didn't go much more than that in a day, but she had anger to burn. She turned the speed up to seven miles per hour and began hoofing.

She needed to start bringing her headphones so she could block out the world, specifically when she was in the presence of idiots. Today she had nothing to quell her nerves or distract her except the even rhythm of her feet hitting the machine. After a couple miles, it became somewhat hypnotic. Calmed her down a few levels.

At the two and a half mile mark, she noticed the captain heading for the door already. She glanced at the clock. She was six minutes short of her full workout time, but she stopped the machine anyway. Grabbing her water bottle and towel, she strode out with a wave in Evan's direction.

The captain was turning the corner toward the showers when Faith cleared the exercise room.

"Captain Mendoza."

He paused and looked back at her. She walked briskly down the hall toward him.

"We're informal around here. Everyone calls me Joe."

"I need to talk to you, Joe. In private, please."

He studied her, his eyes flickering to her lips so briefly she wondered if she imagined it. She might have liked that in another time and place...with someone who wasn't her supervisor. But here and now? Right after Nate the Flake's stupidity? Not so much.

"We can go to my office," he finally said.

As they both turned in that direction, he touched her bare waist between her sports bra and exercise shorts with his large hand. Faith flinched in surprise.

"Sorry," he said, removing his hand and increasing the space between them.

When she glanced sideways at him as they walked, he stared at the floor as if embarrassed. For some reason that was almost endearing, or would be if she wasn't already halfway to irate.

It seemed eons later when they finally got to his office, though it wasn't far from the showers. The captain let her enter first, and she stood next to the door as she closed it.

"What can I do for you?" he asked in a relaxed tone that said he had no idea how ticked off she was. He walked around his desk and faced her without sitting.

"That scene with Nate," she began.

"I'm sorry, Faith. He crossed the line—"

"He's an idiot," she interrupted. "But that's not what I wanted to talk about."

"Oh?"

She clamped her jaw for a moment to let out some of her frustration in a way that wouldn't get her in trouble. Meeting his gaze across the desk, she swallowed. "With all due respect, *please* don't do that again."

"Do what?" Joe asked, narrowing his eyes.

"Don't stick up for me. Don't jump to my rescue when a coworker acts like a pig. Just...don't. Please."

One brow flickered, hinting at his surprise. "It's my responsibility. I don't take that lightly."

"This is different."

"You think you should receive special treatment?" he challenged, crossing his arms.

"No! That's just it. I don't want any special treatment. I want you to go out of your way to *avoid* giving me special treatment." Clenching her fists, she paced in the small space, doing her best to remain calm, professional.

He stared at her, eyebrows raised.

Faith glanced at the door to reassure herself it was latched. "Can I be frank?"

"Always."

She barely registered she was picking at the cuticle of her thumb with her index finger. "In San Antonio, there were other females in the department. Even though a few of them had been there for years, we still weren't respected as equals by some of the men."

Joe nodded, acknowledging that the problem wasn't unique to San Antonio or even Texas, unfortunately.

"Here, I've got two strikes against me—my gender *and* my dad's position. I'm going to have to work three times as hard to receive half the respect. And I plan to do exactly that. It's not right, but I knew the situation coming into it."

"I have no doubt you'll succeed."

Faith shook her head resolutely. "Don't you see? If you or anyone else—officer or not—smooths things over for me, I'll never be seen as just another fire-fighter."

"We haven't worked together for long, Faith, but I'm certain you're not *just* another firefighter."

Was that to be taken as a compliment? She was momentarily surprised into silence, trying to read his intent. His face gave nothing away, so she continued. "I know the culture here. I grew up on the island. Practically grew up in the station. You may mean well, but I can't have you interfering."

Joe didn't immediately answer. He just watched her. Made her nervous. Antsy.

"I appreciate your dilemma," he said at last, in that low semidrawl of his. "But as a captain I can't allow certain things to go on in the station when I'm on duty."

"I understand that, Joe. I'm not asking you to bend any rules or allow blatant harassment or anything like that. But harmless comments from people like him… If I can ignore it, why can't you?"

"You know what your dad would say if he heard I let somebody treat you like that?"

She shuddered to think of it. "My dad doesn't have to know everything that goes on. He wouldn't want to."

"Everything, no. But I get the impression that when it comes to his daughter, he wants details."

"So you're going to tell him a bully picked on me at recess today?"

Joe shook his head. "I hadn't planned on it, no. All I'm saying is that I'm going to do what I need to do when I'm the captain on duty."

"When rules are broken, that's fine. When people are jerks, could you try to rein yourself in? Please?"

Something in his jaw ticked as he studied her again. Seconds dragged on, and at last he spoke. "I'll see what I can do. But I make no promises. Those men need to learn how to act."

"If their mothers couldn't teach them, no offense, but I doubt you can, either."

"You might be right."

"I have four older brothers. Three of them are decent human beings. The fourth, there's no hope."

"If neither the chief nor your mom could straighten him out, I might have to concede." Joe's mouth curved in a half smile but his stance remained tense. Serious. "Anything else you need?"

Faith shook her head. "Thank you, sir."

SHE'D CALLED HIM *goddamn sir*.

As Faith left his office, Joe pressed his knuckles on his desk hard enough to crack them.

He didn't mind being called sir, and received it plenty from the rest of the men. In theory, he should be fine with Faith calling him sir as well.

But he wasn't.

Because it made him feel like an old man to a young, attractive woman.

He supported having women in the station, provided they could pass all the tests, physical and otherwise. Faith could. He was okay having her here.

He'd be more okay with it if she didn't look so good, and frankly, that wasn't acceptable.

Joe grabbed his radio and headed outside to work off some serious steam. It was a pity he was on a short leash to the station because he could run all the way to the north end of the island right now...and back. Twice.

He'd left the exercise room instead of using the treadmill because watching Faith run had his mind going in all kinds of places it had no right to. Twenty minutes was not a workout, but he'd been entranced by her long, muscular legs, tanned and smooth. Her perfect breasts and slender waist, the slight curve of her hips that moved just so with every step on the treadmill.

It'd been raining all day, but Joe took no heed of the steady downpour. In fact, he welcomed it. Maybe he could drown his thoughts.

Faith had been upset by him "defending" her, but if she had any notion of the things that had gone through his mind in the past forty-five minutes...

He shook his head and picked up his already burning pace.

It wasn't just her beauty and her fit body that got to him. It was her sheer competence. Her confidence and drive. The way she didn't let naysayers get in her way. He admired her determination to earn the respect of her new colleagues.

He appreciated her desire to do it on her own. Totally understood her stance. However, as he'd told her, he couldn't promise he wouldn't interfere again. When he'd heard Nate's veiled chauvinistic comment, he'd jumped in involuntarily.

He couldn't do that again. He'd meant what he'd told her about adhering to his duties, but defending her earlier had come as naturally as scratching to a dog. There hadn't been any thought involved. His reaction had been on a basic, elemental, man-looking-after-woman level.

There was nothing to do but admit it—and only to himself. Faith Peligni was one of the sexiest, most intriguing women he'd ever met. And he was in a position where nothing could ever happen between them.

Not after her father had asked him to look out for her.

Not if he had any hope of retaining the fire chief's trust—and having a chance in hell at a promotion.

CHAPTER FOUR

FAITH HAD BEEN IGNORING the state of the Peligni family home for the two months she'd been back in town recuperating.

But when she drove up in her Subaru, frazzled and grumpy from braving the beginning of the spring break influx at the grocery store, she couldn't help noticing that the bushes, once neatly manicured, were shaggy and unkempt. The lawn, though only a square patch of grass on this side of the house, was overgrown. A broken-down charcoal grill sat to the left of the driveway.

She pulled into the garage, leaned against the headrest and closed her eyes. Her dad had always been a fanatic about the yard. Her oldest brother, Will, used to joke that their dad carried around a ruler, and when the grass hit two inches, he fired up the mower.

That was before. When their family was still intact. When her mom still lived here. Before her dad had started sinking into what Faith suspected could be depression.

She realized her hand was clutched so tightly around her keys that they were digging into her palm. Groaning in frustration, she climbed out and popped open the back.

She didn't mind grocery shopping for her and her dad. It was a lot easier than when the seven of them had been home at once and the trip would cost several hundred dollars. Their mom had always taken one child with her to the store, and the rest of the siblings had mobbed the car upon its return, helping to carry in the goods and then rummaging through them and snacking before anything could be put away.

Today, no one came out to greet her. Not that she needed assistance—there were only two paper bags stuffed with food. But the quiet, on top of the neglected state of the property, brought her down. Made her long for Peligni family chaos. Or at the very least, her old dad back. She needed to call Paul and Will tonight to fill them in on their father's state, sure, but also just to hear their voices.

As she made her way up the interior stairs to the main level of the house, she realized she was stomping her feet on each wooden step.

Where was this anger coming from?

She sympathized with her dad and had a hard time blaming him for being sad and out of sorts. Her mom had left *him*. Given up on their marriage after almost forty years, supposedly because of his dedication to his job. Nita had resented it for years, but no one in the family had ever thought it would come to her leaving.

So why, when Faith spotted her dad on the plaid sofa in the living room asleep—*again*—did she want to throw something? Wake him up with a crash?

She set the bags down on the kitchen counter and breathed slowly, summoning her patience. When she turned around, a photo on the top shelf of the baker's rack caught her eye. The whole family, taken three years ago at Christmas.

Everyone wore button-down denim shirts and everyone looked happy. Lou, who'd actually managed to get leave that coincided with the holidays that year. Paul and Will, the two oldest and brainiest Pelignis, who lived on either coast and didn't make it home often enough. Even Anthony, Faith's self-centered brother who usually had an excuse for everything, had made the relatively short trip home from Dallas. Her dad smiled widely. Her mom, too… Was it just a facade? How long had she been contemplating leaving? Faith wondered, not for the first time, whether her dad had had any inkling a separation was coming.

Her anger didn't go away, but it was no longer aimed at her father. He was the one who'd had his marriage ripped out from under him, who'd been hurt to the core. She was the only person he had to help him through it, since she hadn't been able to convince her brothers there was anything they could do to keep their parents together. It was up to her to be there for their dad—to sympathize, sure, but also to give him tough love when he needed it. Like now. He had to stop sleeping all the time.

"Dad?" She slipped her shoes off and walked quietly across the ceramic tile floor. "Dad. You have to wake up now."

He rolled over, from his side to his back. Snorted. Continued to slumber on. In the past, he'd been a super-light sleeper from years of being awakened by the alarm at the station, or so he always said.

"Dad, wake up. It's after one o'clock and I bet you haven't eaten lunch yet."

He woke with a start and sputtered, "What? What's wrong, princess?"

She sat on the edge of the sofa by his feet. "Nothing's wrong. You just need to get up and eat."

He looked around, dazed, then sat up slowly. "I could eat, I guess."

"Did you have any lunch while I was gone?" She knew the answer, but asked anyway.

Her dad checked his watch and shook his head. "Didn't realize it was so late. What are we going to eat?"

"I picked up a rotisserie chicken and some potato salad. Let's go get it ready."

Faith went into the kitchen, decorated with Southwestern style, but her dad moved more slowly. She started unpacking groceries and setting out their food on the oversize table that used to hold the whole family, trying not to think how inconceivable it would've been for her dad to forget a meal just a few months ago.

"Smells good," he said when he entered the less-than-tidy kitchen. "What can I do?"

"Grab us some drinks from the fridge."

A few minutes later, they sat at the table filling their plates.

"So how's the job going so far?" Tony asked as he served himself potato salad.

"Pretty good. Just learning how you do things here."

"Any problems?"

Nate's obnoxious face flashed in her mind and she blocked it out. He was a problem, sure, but nothing she couldn't handle on her own. Tattling wasn't her thing, anyway.

"Nope. Everything's fine. A little bit slow…"

"This isn't San Antonio, Faith. Never will be. You prepared to handle the less exciting shifts?"

"Yeah, it just takes a little getting used to. It makes it easier to fit in PT, though."

Her mind wandered to her workout yesterday. Joe's interruption. The way just the sight of him had distracted her from her routine.

"How's Joe treating you?"

She started. Had she said his name aloud? No. *Idiot.* It was a normal question. She just had a guilty conscience.…

"He's okay, I guess." She took a bite of white meat and chewed. "Actually, he hovers. I don't think he trusts me."

"I'm sure he does, princess."

She shook her head. "No matter what I'm doing, he shows up to check on me. Tries to help when I don't need it. He's not like that with anyone else."

"It's his job."

"To babysit? It's a fire station, Dad, not a day care."

A more perceptive person might suggest she protested too much, and that person would probably be right. For once, she was thankful her dad wasn't at the top of his game.

"Joe's a good guy. If you ever need anything, you can trust him. He'll look out for you."

Faith closed her eyes and set down her fork. "I don't need anyone looking out for me."

"You're new, Faith. Don't be so hardheaded. If someone wants to be nice, accept it."

She didn't respond immediately. Took a drink of cold milk instead.

"You don't get it, Dad. I can't afford to have an officer bending over backward to help me. I'm a woman in a man's job, fighting off perceptions that I'm the weak link every single second I'm on the clock." Her volume remained level, though she snapped out the words.

"Don't get upset. I know you can handle the job. There's no doubt in my mind you're as good as those men, better than a lot of them."

"How can I *not* get upset?" Now she got louder. "My own mother suggested I sleep with the captain to get ahead."

"She did *what?*"

Faith shook her head. "Never mind. She thought she was being funny. I'm just sick of having to prove myself to everyone, including my family."

"Faith." He reached across the table and held his palm out toward hers until she returned the gesture. "You don't have to prove yourself to me. Ever. But I will always worry about you." His voice was thick with emotion. Affection.

Faith couldn't help but be touched by his words. Her response got caught in her throat. It took a lot for her dad to show his feelings so openly, and once again, her irritation dissipated.

"I'll be fine."

He seemed flustered for a moment. Inhaled shakily. "If anything ever happened to you again, Faith, anything worse than last time, I don't know if I could survive it."

That did it. Tears filled her eyes. She fought them hard, refusing to let them spill over. For several seconds, she didn't dare breathe, afraid of losing it. Surreptitiously, she wiped the corners of her eyes and blinked hard until she thought she could speak.

"I'll do the best I can, Dad. But you have to let me do it my own way."

"I THINK WE'VE GOT something."

The words were nonchalant, but Joe's tone was laced with a restrained excitement Faith hadn't heard from him before.

The engine sped toward a hotel on the shore. *Something* meant a fire. A real one, not a trash fire that could be knocked out in less than ten minutes.

Adrenaline pumped through Faith's system. This was her first big fire since her injury in San Antonio.

Joe confirmed again that this one was business, and she angled herself a little in the back-facing seat to look at him as she adjusted one of her boots. He leaned forward slightly, eyes sparking with life as they skipped from Derek, who was driving, to the dark smoke a few blocks ahead of them.

He loves every bit of this, Faith thought to herself. *Like a little boy loves seeing the big rigs speed by with sirens blaring and lights flashing.* It didn't surprise her, because most people in her profession lived for the challenge of a large fire. But Joe was normally so cool and collected in the station that his tangible excitement made her smile.

As they arrived on the scene, Joe hollered orders to their crew. He jumped out of the rig and located the battalion chief in charge, while Faith, Penn and Derek worked at the truck, getting equipment ready.

The hotel was medium-size, made up of multiple structures. The involved building was six stories high. Acrid smoke filled the air and flames showed on the second and third floors.

Joe came back with more specific directions for the crew. Penn was on the nozzle, Faith with him. Without a word, they hooked up the appropriate hose to the engine and made their way to the entrance at the end of the building that Joe had indicated.

Penn glanced over his shoulder at her with a questioning look and she nodded, but her heart hammered uncharacteristically out of control. She tried to ignore it.

He headed inside and Faith, holding on to the hose, followed—until she was just inside the door.

She froze.

The scene was status quo for a seasoned firefighter. The smoke was so thick she could barely see a foot in front of her, the temperature already climbing. Her partner continued on, but Faith couldn't force her feet to move for anything.

Her chest tightened and a scream climbed in her throat. She couldn't seem to get air into her lungs, and she checked again to make sure her breathing apparatus was functioning. It was.

She glanced up and couldn't see the ceiling. Then she noticed how hard she was breathing—for no reason. *You're losing it, Faith. Get a hold of yourself.*

With effort, she slowed her respirations, closing her eyes. Gradually the need to crawl out of her skin receded, and she realized if this wasn't a heart attack, it must be some kind of anxiety thing. Whatever it was, it sucked.

The hose in her hands was yanked forward, jolting her back to the fire and the very real need to get moving. What was she doing, standing here like a probie at her first fire?

Faith reassured herself that no one had witnessed her freak-out moment. Not that anyone could see in this smoke, anyway. She hesitated again, then swore at herself and moved ahead to catch up with Penn, praying he hadn't missed her yet. If anyone found out she'd flaked, there was no hope of ever overcoming her reputation as the chief's daughter and a charity case.

HOURS LATER, Faith poured water down her bone-dry throat, surveying the fire site to estimate how much longer cleanup would take. Maybe another half hour if they were lucky.

This whole end of the resort hotel was a loss, but they'd managed to stop the fire from jumping to the other buildings. Two companies from the mainland had been called in as well, and injuries had been few and minor.

Fatigue weighed Faith down as she squatted next to the truck, leaning her back against it, finishing her drink. Ten hours was a long fight, but you never really noticed how wiped you were until afterward, when the adrenaline stopped and salvage and overhaul wound down. Once the flames were doused, the firefighters had spent time rehashing the situation as they carried out anything that could be saved, trading stories of what they'd encountered, one-upping to see who'd ended up having the best assignment. Silently questioning if they'd done the right things, made the right decisions. If there was anything they could've done better.

Faith's self-critique was easy tonight—she'd blown it. Oh, sure, she'd gotten her act together and done okay in the end. But walking into that burning building and locking up...

Unforgivable.

And the biggest problem was she wasn't sure it wouldn't happen the next time they got called to a big fire.

No one had noticed, but that didn't change a thing. *She* knew.

Derek Severson and Clay Marlow rested several feet from Faith, still talking as they rehydrated. She stood and disposed of her water bottle. She had a policy of never being the last person back from taking a break.

A few minutes later, the crews had removed as much as they could from the interior and ensured there were no remaining hot spots. Faith noticed a couple hundred feet of hose from their engine that had to be loaded. She headed over and started rolling it, though every muscle in her body was beginning to ache. She was starting to fantasize about falling into bed; it was after 2:00 a.m. and would be a short night, anyway.

She stood and was lifting the first roll of hose to take to the engine when a pain near her collarbone nearly flattened her. She sat down hard, dropped the hose on the ground, muttering swear words to herself.

When she could breathe again, she glanced around, trying to act as if nothing was wrong.

Dammit... Joe was standing near the engine and staring straight at her. If the concern on his face was any indication, he'd seen everything.

She was afraid to stand up again because it freaking hurt. Another jab of pain, on top of her exhaustion, was liable to make her cry like a girl. Instead, she busied herself with the hose, trying to make it appear as if it wasn't rolled quite right and needed to be fixed.

"Faith." Joe loomed over her in the chilly night.

"Yes, sir." She didn't look up at him, just worked intently on the nonexistent problem.

He squatted next to her. "What are you doing?"

"Fixing the hose."

"The hose is fine."

Finally she glanced up at him.

"You hurt yourself," he said in a gentle, low voice so no one could overhear. She was eternally grateful for his discretion.

"Not really," she said, giving up on the hose act.

"I saw you, Faith. Don't insult me by lying."

When she looked into those concerned dark eyes, she couldn't continue to deny it. But she could understate it.

"It was my collarbone. Just a sharp, brief pain, but

it's over now." Which was the truth. So far. "Long day,
I guess."

He watched her closely for several seconds, as if
gauging whether she was leveling with him.

"Do we need to have Scott or Rafe check you out?"
he asked, gesturing over his shoulder to the ambulance.

"No," she said quickly. "Really. It didn't hurt until
just now. I must have twisted wrong as I stood up."

He wasn't convinced, Faith could tell. So to persuade him, she had no choice but to stand and prove
she was fine.

She picked up the hoses, swallowed and braced herself. This time she rose more slowly. And yeah, the pain
was there, but not as bad. She fought through it, refusing to let it show on her face. Because, of course, he
was still staring at her.

He brushed her wrist in a touch that was probably
not professional, judging by the way it got Faith's heart
racing. Before she could scold herself for her reaction,
he spoke—again quietly, so no one could hear. "Don't
be stubborn, Faith. Let me carry one of those. You don't
want to reinjure yourself."

She didn't know if it was the mind-blurring fatigue
or the feel of his rough fingers so tender on her skin, but
she weakened. Let him take one of the rolls from her.
She walked by his side to the engine but insisted on putting them away herself. Self-consciously, she glanced
around to see if anyone had noticed that Joe had helped
her. A couple of guys were nearby, but not paying attention to them; maybe no one had seen. She should've
just carried both hoses.

"So," Joe said, still in a private voice. "I want more information on this. Did you injure yourself tonight? Run into anything? Have something fall or hit you? Did you—"

"None of the above, like I told you. You saw the first and only episode and it's gone now. Can we drop it? Please?"

"I need to report—"

"Any injuries that occur on the job. This isn't an injury and it didn't happen on this job."

"You watch that collarbone. If you have any more problems with it, I want you to see a doctor."

"Yes, sir," she said formally.

She could almost swear he flinched.

As she turned away to get back to work, a thought occurred to her. "You're not going to tell the chief, are you?" He'd flip out and go all protective-daddy on her, which was sweet in theory, but totally unnecessary. And not at all what he needed mental-healthwise, or she needed careerwise.

Joe looked off into the distance and it was all Faith could do not to beg him.

"Don't you think he would want to know?"

"He's got too much on his mind," Faith said. "He doesn't need to worry about something insignificant like this. If another building falls on me, you can mention it, I promise."

Joe didn't seem to appreciate her attempt at humor. When he said nothing, Faith grasped her thick turnout pants in her fist until her knuckles were likely white. "Equal treatment, Joe. That's all I'm asking for."

"First Nate's treatment of you and now this. I'm keeping a lot from the head of the department."

"But the head of the department wouldn't really need to know about either if I wasn't his daughter."

He exhaled and pegged her with those eyes again. "I'll keep your secret, Faith. Again. Just promise me about the doctor if you need it."

She nodded, suspecting her definition of needing it might differ from his. "Thank you."

She walked away, pretty sure that she could trust Joe's word—but not at all happy that she had to.

CHAPTER FIVE

"SURELY YOU BIGWIGS could have found someone in the firm to be your fourth?" Joe asked his stepfather, Jorge Vargas. The black-haired man wasn't quite as tall as Joe, but stood ramrod-straight, even when he was relaxed on the golf course. It was obvious the man had power and liked to use it.

The Corpus Christi Country Club golf course was already a brilliant, well-manicured green, and the air wafting over them was warm for early March. Spring break. Hell month for the San Amaro Island Fire Department. The tournament sponsored by his stepfather's and stepbrothers' prestigious law firm fell at the worst time of the year for Joe, but he'd made a point of asking for the day off. Everything had worked out, the shift at the department was covered, and here he was. For better or worse. He reminded himself repeatedly that he liked golf and didn't get on the course enough. And really, these guys weren't too bad. This was a relatively easy way to make his mom happy.

"Come on, Joe," Jorge prodded, "the Vargas men are going to take this tournament. You're one of us today. You're the best and you know it."

He didn't want to be a Vargas…but he'd happily take a quarter of their earning power.

"Joe putts like a woman." Troy, the older of his two stepbrothers and Mr. *GQ,* took out his driver at the second hole. He'd been out on the course regularly, as evidenced by his bronzed skin.

"You wish I putted like a woman," Joe said. "It's been weeks since I've played, though. Some of us have to work for a living."

"Speaking of work, did Maurice get you the info on that possible witness for the Sullivan case?" Jorge asked Troy.

"Left me a message. I'll touch base this evening and take care of it."

These three—Jorge, Troy and Ryan, the younger, lankier brother, who sported a goatee—weren't terrible company…until they started talking business. Then it was as if they turned into droning robots that didn't know when to shut up.

"You're up, man," Joe said to Troy as the group in front of them moved on, successfully ending the shop talk, at least for now.

Troy stepped up, spent forever and a half pondering the shot, then hit the ball onto the green. Looking smug, he turned around to face them. "Beat that, suckers."

"We're on the same team, dumb-ass," Ryan said. He was a pretty boy beneath the facial hair, with chiseled features and dark lashes longer than most women's.

"Same team, sure. But we could make things more interesting." Jorge dug his wallet out from his back pocket and waved a twenty. "What do you say a little wager among family? Twenty bucks a hole? Winner takes all."

"In." Ryan raised his chin, clearly thinking he had a good chance at collecting.

"Hell, yeah, I'm in," Troy said. "I could use some spending money."

Being the blue-collar guy, Joe had three measly twenties in his wallet. All the more reason to beat these paper pushers. "Might as well give me your cash now," he said, moving up to the tee, taking a practice swing.

"You're all talk, Joe," Ryan said.

"Put your money where your mouth is," Troy added.

Joe tuned out everything the morons behind him chattered about and focused. Maybe said a little prayer. He couldn't afford to lose more than a couple of holes at twenty bucks a pop. He swung and watched his ball arc through the cloudless sky, silently coaching it along. It made it to the green, barely, but he'd take it. Putting was his strong point, in spite of what Troy liked to believe.

Two strokes later, Joe collected his first sixty bucks of the afternoon.

"Can I write this off as a donation to charity?" Troy asked as he handed over his bill.

"Don't write too soon," Joe said, buoyed by his victory and letting the insult to his lower tax bracket slide right off. "I'll be taking more."

They traded taunts and insults as they walked to their carts, and Joe admitted to himself this wasn't so bad. Sunshine, golf and his artificial family. Soon they'd be the only family he had.

His mother made no secret that she wanted Joe

and his steps to form stronger bonds. The last thing he wanted her to do was worry about him, so he was making an effort. Heck, *still* making an effort, as he had been since she remarried, five years ago. He visited her and Jorge in Corpus more often, since she couldn't get out much and no longer made the trip to the island. Spent time with these three when he could be doing other things. He would never fit in, but if it gave his mother peace of mind, he'd continue to try.

"You still planning to come for your mom's birthday?" Jorge asked Joe as they climbed out of the cart at the third tee.

"Of course." That it could be her last hung heavily on his mind, and he wondered if the thought crossed Jorge's, as well.

"You got a girlfriend yet?" his stepfather continued.

"Is my mother recruiting you for the get-Joe-married campaign?" Joe took a drink from his sports bottle and closed the top.

Ryan cackled next to him. "I hope not, for Dad's sake. It'd be easier to get a twelve-year-old girl voted in as governor of Texas."

"I don't have to tell you how much your mom worries," Jorge said to Joe, and the way his tone changed when talking about her, how it softened with affection, reaffirmed his devotion to his wife. "I remind her all the damn time that you're a grown man, but you know how women are."

"As much as I'd love to put her mind at ease, I'll go out on a limb and predict I'll be showing up by myself," Joe said.

"You could always pay for a companion," Ryan suggested.

"I might be able to pay for one night, but that's eternally better than paying a lifetime for that high maintenance glamour girl you married." Joe liked what he knew of Shelly, but he couldn't pass up the opportunity to give Ryan grief.

"I reckon he got you there," Troy said, grinning.

"Reckon he did. Price you pay to sleep with a beautiful woman every night." Ryan didn't seem too upset by his lifetime sentence. "So how's the fire department?"

"Busy as a hound during flea season. On top of spring break, I'm going for a promotion. Assistant fire chief. The current guy's retiring."

"Will you be able to stay away from the manual stuff as assistant chief?" Jorge asked. "Keep your hands clean?"

Joe shook his head and grinned. His stepfather would never understand. He'd stopped trying to explain it after the first dozen or so attempts. "That's the downside. Not being able to fight fires myself."

All three men stared at him as if he'd admitted to romancing livestock.

"You all should shed your suits and ties and try it sometime," he said, gauging the progress of the team in front of them as they finished up the hole.

"I'll leave the hero-ing up to you," Ryan said. "Charred isn't really my color."

"I don't know," Troy said. "Your heart's pretty black, bro."

"Joe," his stepfather interjected. "You got anything planned in early April?"

"The usual," Joe said. "What's up?"

"The guys and I thought we'd see if you wanted to go with us to spring training."

"Astros?"

"Of course," Troy said, as if Joe was the densest man on earth.

Joe had been a Rangers fan since he was old enough to beat a plastic bat on the living room floor. Never an Astros fan. He hadn't been invited to the annual pilgrimage with the Vargas men before. Which meant one thing. "My mother put you up to asking?"

"We wouldn't listen to her if she did," Troy said.

The senior Vargas glared at his older son.

"Okay, maybe we would, but this wasn't her idea." Troy backpedaled.

"Why don't you guys watch some real baseball?" Joe asked.

"We invited you on our trip, man," Ryan said. "No need to go injuring our team."

Joe asked several questions about the trip and racked his brain for any plans he might have made. Several guys at the station would be off that week—a regular occurrence after the intensity of spring break on the island. It'd be a hassle to get away then. However, though the Astros didn't do it for him, taking a trip with Jorge and his sons would go a long way in calming his mother's worries, convincing her they'd do just fine as a family even without her. That was a gift to her he couldn't deny just because these guys were a bunch of stuffed shirts who liked the wrong team.

"Let me check my calendar and see what I can do."

CHAPTER SIX

FAITH'S EYES WERE GLAZING over as she stared at the study manual for the hazardous materials test. She hadn't procrastinated. Not entirely, anyway. She'd studied last weekend for quite a while. But now it was the eleventh hour and she was close to panicking.

She got up from the station's kitchen table and stretched her arms over her head in an attempt to get her blood flowing. She went to the counter behind her and poured herself another cup of coffee, emptying the pot. The clock on the microwave oven said 3:14 a.m. She was the only one stirring in the place, and the silence was starting to ring in her ears.

"What are you doing up?"

Joe's voice in the doorway behind her made her drop her mug, which shattered on the tile floor. Thankfully, the coffee that splashed on her was only lukewarm.

"You need to wear a bell around your neck," she said, bending to pick up the large chunks of broken pottery and trying to ignore the racing of her heart. It wasn't caused just by having the life startled out of her. Unfortunately. It had everything to do with the man who'd surprised her. She hadn't felt this kind of nervous excitement since her crush on Dylan Morrison her first year at community college.

She glanced at Joe in time to see him smile. It must be late, because she couldn't resist admiring how good-looking he was. Her tired mind was filled with the un-invited fantasy of him walking up to her and kissing her till her brain melted and her hands shook.

Oh, her hands *were* shaking. From too much caffeine, no doubt. Lack of sleep.

Faith found a dustpan and hand broom beneath the sink, and swept the little pieces. Joe mopped up the remaining liquid with paper towels.

"Test is tomorrow?" he asked, glancing toward the open book on the table.

"Technically today, I guess. I'll go take it as soon as shift is over."

They stood at the same time and her fantasy scenario of thirty seconds ago intensified. He came over to her at the counter and surveyed the coffeepot.

"Didn't save any for me, I see."

"Sorry," Faith said, putting space between them. "Didn't know you were a night owl."

"Always have been. Didn't know you were afraid of tests."

"Always have been."

Joe rinsed out the pot and refilled the filter for another twelve-cup supply. "That surprises me. You seem to know your facts."

"I'm somewhat of a perfectionist."

Joe chuckled. "And here I thought you were laid-back. Carefree."

"Maybe in a different lifetime. So what's up with coffee at three in the morning? Do you really have that much work to do or are you just afraid of the dark?"

"Never know what's under the bed."

"Want me to check if it's safe for you?" she teased. "I hear there can be some pretty ferocious dust bunnies in the corners around here."

"That's what happens when firefighters can't clean to save their lives."

"They need better leadership, clearly."

He didn't seem to see the humor in her comment.

"You take your job very seriously, don't you?" Faith asked, leaning against the counter next to him.

"About as seriously as you take yours."

She nodded at the truth in that. "Did you always want to be a firefighter?"

"Either that or a Jedi."

If she hadn't spilled her coffee by dropping it, she would've spit it out at his reply. "Jedi training didn't pan out?"

He cracked a grin and shook his head distractedly.

"How long was your dad the chief?" she asked. She vaguely remembered meeting Chief Mendoza a couple times, but she'd been so young then, maybe ten years old. At that point, the trucks and flashing lights had been much more interesting to her.

"Two years. That was before there was an assistant. It wasn't three months after he stopped fighting fires and became chief that he found out about the cancer." Joe's face hardened as he tried not to give away his feelings.

"Lungs, right?" Faith did remember, very clearly,

when his dad had died. The funeral had been gigantic, though she hadn't been allowed to attend. It'd been on the news and the front page of the newspaper. Her dad had considered Joe's father a mentor and had been struck deeply by his death.

"Yep. No doubt from everything he breathed in on the job."

"I can't imagine growing up without my dad," Faith said.

"I was twenty-five when he died."

"Oh. I guess you were grown-up." She smiled sheepishly. "Sorry."

"Yeah." His tone lightened. "Tell me I'm old."

"I'd never say that to someone who can run faster than me."

He studied her curiously. "So how is working in the same department as your dad going so far?"

"Going well," she said, refusing to get into her worries. In general, it was an honest answer. "I always dreamed of working with him. He's the reason I got into firefighting."

"You two have always seemed close. I remember that even when you were a teenager."

"Drives my mom crazy sometimes."

"That's what she gets for marrying one of the good guys," Joe said.

"I wish she remembered he's one of the good guys. Though he does make it difficult lately."

Joe turned toward her and brushed her hair behind her ear. Her breath caught, and he retracted his hand, as if realizing he wasn't supposed to touch her. "He's kind of out of sorts, isn't he?"

She looked down nervously, whether from the personal topic or the contact, she couldn't say. "That's one way to put it."

"If there was something I could do to help, I would. I like your dad. Respect him a great deal."

Faith nodded, wishing like crazy she had a clue how to help her father. "He needs something to keep him busy. The weekends with no work just about kill him. Evenings are long, too."

"Does he have any hobbies?"

"His boat," Faith answered. "But he's been on it only once since I moved back. He seems to have lost interest."

"Maybe I could persuade him to take it out. Get him to take me for a ride or something."

"You don't have to do that, Joe."

He looked into her eyes with such concern she wanted to melt. "I want to. It's not exactly a hardship having to go out on a boat."

"Feel free to try. Don't be surprised if he turns you down."

As he gazed at her, his pupils grew wider, and the awareness between them jumped way higher than it should.

"I'm...going for Jones's position," Joe said, his voice hoarser than usual, kept low so that no one could overhear their...discussion about work?

Had she missed something? Was the awareness all one-sided?

"I know." She blinked and tilted her head to the side. "Everyone knows. You and Captain Schlager."

"I really want the job." He didn't step back, didn't remove his hand from the counter right next to her body.

"You have a good chance, in my new-to-the-department opinion." Then it dawned on her what he might be getting at. "Do you think I know something? Because of my dad? Believe me, he doesn't—"

"No, Faith. Even if I thought he talked to you about it, I'd never ask you for that information."

"Okay."

Still confused, she started to move away. Joe gently caught her wrist and forced eye contact.

"I want…" He didn't finish the sentence but his eyes told her exactly what he wanted.

Okay, then. She hadn't misread the signs. "I know." She nodded nonchalantly, as if he'd just told her there were fish in the ocean.

Faith picked up the coffeepot and poured the steaming liquid into her mug. After turning away from him.

The current that had sizzled between them faded to awkwardness. Joe headed for the table and pulled out the chair next to the one she'd been sitting in earlier. "So…your test. What are you working on?"

"Really, I don't—"

"Want help. I know. As your captain, I'm ordering you to sit down and let me quiz you."

"That is so wrong, flaunting your position…." She kept her tone light.

"It's in my best interest for my people to pass tests and earn certifications. Makes me look good."

"With all due respect, I really need to change out of these coffee-soaked clothes and get some sleep." She actually hadn't planned to go to bed tonight, but lying in her bunk awake was preferable to sitting here awkwardly with him.

He looked at her hard, sizing her up as if he knew she just wanted to escape. But instead of calling her on it, he nodded once and said, "Good luck on your test, Faith."

CHAPTER SEVEN

JOE PICKED UP THE PHONE from his nightstand two nights later. "Mendoza."

"Joe, it's Derek. Slight problem." The concern in the firefighter's voice shot a dose of alarm through Joe.

He sat up in bed, rubbed his eyes and checked the digital clock. Twenty after eleven. He must've dozed off since he'd hit the sack over an hour ago. A 7:00 a.m. shift came too damn early. "What's going on?"

"I stopped by the Shack to get the nightly deposit. Chief is here."

The Shell Shack was the beach bar Derek and his wife, Macey, owned. In the past year or so, it had become a regular hangout for the department, and while Chief Peligni didn't usually join in the camaraderie, it wasn't unusual that he was there.

"He's tanked, Joe."

"Chief is?" Joe was out of bed, pulling on his jeans without conscious thought.

"You got it. Kevin says he's been here since six-thirty. Came in for a burger with Mayor Romero. Been drinking ever since."

"Can you call him a cab?"

"In his state, I don't think that's a wise solution. Cab

could take a while to get here, with all the spring breakers. I'm concerned about someone recognizing him."

"He's that messed up?" Joe couldn't fathom the man
he'd looked up to for years making a spectacle of himself. He'd never even seen the chief tipsy and couldn't
imagine how much liquor it would take to make him
falling down drunk. If he knew the chief the way he
thought he did, the man would be humiliated once he
sobered up and realized what he'd done. But hell. Lately
Chief Peligni wasn't acting like the man Joe knew.

"I'm not sure he can walk on his own," Derek said
with some hesitation. "I'd take him home myself, but
thought it'd be better for you to handle it. You're tight
with him, right?"

Joe couldn't fault Derek for not wanting to get involved in the chief's business—especially not this business. It'd be awkward enough for Joe. "I'll take care of
it. Can you stay with him until I get there?" He pulled
a wrinkled T-shirt off the floor and shook it out.

"I'll be here."

"See you in five." Joe ended the call and pulled the
shirt over his head, trying to wrap his brain around the
situation. Either he'd been sleeping harder than he'd
thought or the chief had gone off the deep end.

Without his permission, Joe's mind veered to Faith.
Did she know what her dad was up to? He doubted it.
She wasn't the type to sit back and let her father self-
destroy. After what she'd said the other night in the station kitchen, he suspected she'd take it hard if she found
out about the chief's current state. Though it wasn't
his business or his place to interfere, Joe didn't want

Faith to learn about her dad's bender. Didn't want her to be hurt.

He hightailed it the few blocks to the Shell Shack and turned into the small parking lot, taking the only available spot.

He jumped out, the brisk night breeze rustling the palms that lined the hotel lot next door. If the weather didn't make a massive turnaround in the next few days, spring break visitors to the island were going to be mighty disappointed. Maybe it would scare away a few, but likely not enough to make a difference in the havoc the month wreaked on the fire department.

When Joe cleared the doorway, he instantly spotted the chief leaning heavily on the bar. The horseshoe-shaped counter curved around such that Joe had a view of the older man's face. It was red, the skin droopy. His eyes were aimed downward but Joe could tell from here they weren't focused on anything. The chief wore a light gray polo shirt—thank God he'd changed out of his uniform beforehand—and there was a wet splotch on the front.

Derek sat on the stool next to Chief Peligni, talking to him. He glanced up at Joe and shook his head slowly.

Joe walked around the crowded bar and stopped next to them. "Evening, gentlemen."

Derek nodded in reply, looking uncomfortable as he stood up and let Joe take his place. Chief Peligni didn't react for a few seconds. Finally, he raised his gaze and squinted. "That the captain?"

"It's me," Joe affirmed. The man reeked of a distillery even from two feet away.

Glancing around, Joe took inventory of the other bar patrons, relieved that everyone was too caught up in themselves and their drinks to pay any attention to the chief.

"Can I get you anything, Captain?" Kevin asked from behind the bar.

"No, thanks."

Joe sat on the stool Derek had vacated and attempted to make small talk with the blitzed chief. To his comments about the weather and the crush of customers, Joe received unintelligible mumbles.

Okay, enough bullshitting. He needed to get Chief Peligni out of here and safely home. Wouldn't be an easy task—the older man had gained weight recently and must weigh over three hundred pounds—but Joe would do it. The chief had done a lot for him over the years. Now it was his turn to return the favor.

"What do you say we get out of here?" Joe asked, standing.

More muttering he couldn't understand.

"You need to sleep it off, Chief. Let's go before things get any worse."

It was too late, though, because at that moment, Faith's gorgeous face appeared in the doorway and she looked anything but pleased.

FAITH WAS GOING TO WRING her father's thick neck.

He'd sounded more than a little out of it when he'd called her a few minutes ago for a ride. Words slurred, train of thought easily interrupted but he'd managed to say where he was. What he hadn't mentioned was that

Joe Mendoza and Derek Severson were here as well, witnessing the show.

Her cheeks warmed and she stepped back out of the doorway to the Shell Shack to summon her game face. Glancing down at the exercise shorts and tank top she'd thrown on, she swore to herself. She hadn't counted on running into her captain. Hadn't counted on running into anyone. She'd foolishly thought when her dad asked her to pick him up that maybe he'd meet her in the parking lot.

Clearly, she hadn't fully grasped the situation. And it wasn't going to get any better while she wasted time out here trying to figure out how to save face. Wasn't going to happen.

Straightening her back, she headed inside, determined to hide her embarrassment and concern for her father. Those were family matters. Private.

Ignoring her colleague and supervisor, Faith went around to her father's side and rested her hand on his forearm. "Hey, Dad. How are you doing?"

The time it took him to react to her voice and turn his head was not a good sign. "Princessss."

Fan-freaking-tastic.

"I was just going to bring him home," Joe said quietly. "Derek called me. Did he call you, too?" He looked toward the back room, where Derek was talking to the bartender and cook.

"No," Faith said, trying to keep her frustration out of her voice. "*He* called me." She gestured to her father, who didn't seem to register the conversation going on

in front of him. "I can handle this. Thank you for trying to help."

She felt Joe staring at her as if he had something to
say, but he remained silent and she didn't look at him
again. Instead, she turned her attention back to her dad.
"How long have you been here?"

"Little bit." He took an unsteady drink from the glass
in front of him and frowned at the taste. "He's givin'
me water."

The bartender emerged from the back room as her
dad spoke, and Faith mouthed a thank-you to the man
for cutting him off.

"I'm here to help you, Faith," Joe said, still stubbornly sitting on the other side of her dad.

"We'll be fine, thanks," she replied, her jaw stiff.

Again, the captain hesitated, and she felt frustration
coming off him in waves, but that wasn't her concern.
Her dad was.

"Did you eat dinner?" she asked him, as Joe finally
walked out of the bar, turning to glance at her one last
time when he reached the doorway.

The fire chief seemed to think about that for a while,
then shrugged. "'Magine I did." He leaned hard on the
bar, as if it was the only thing holding him up.

"We need to get you home," Faith said. "What were
you thinking, Dad?"

He tried to focus on her, then turned his squinting
gaze to the bartender. And started snickering like a
teenage girl in trouble, his large shoulders shaking. "I
don' know, Faithy. You tell me."

He'd never been a hard drinker. A lot of firefighters were—their way of dealing with the things they saw on the job. They used alcohol to come down from a harrowing shift or one that ended in tragedy. But not Tony Peligni. He was hard-core and intense—and usually stone-cold sober.

Faith had been flirting with acknowledging the truth for weeks, but now there was no way to deny it. The breakup of his marriage was sending her father down a path she never thought she'd see him travel. One she couldn't bear to watch. She had to find a way to get her parents back together. They loved each other—always had. Faith was absolutely sure of it. She needed to help her mom see what she was doing to this man and get her to come to her senses.

Later.

Now Faith needed to get her dad out of the bar before someone recognized the falling-over-drunk guy as San Amaro Island's fire chief.

"How much does he owe you?" she asked the bartender, pulling her wallet out of her purse. She looked around for Derek, relieved to see he'd apparently taken off, as well.

"He's clear," the bartender said. "You going to be able to…?" He motioned toward the parking lot with his head.

Faith nodded, biting her tongue. She knew most people didn't realize she was stronger than she looked. And her dad *was* big. But she didn't do the female-in-need-of-rescuing well. Never had.

"Come on, Dad. Time to take you home."

He slowly turned and narrowed his eyes at her, as if

trying to place where he knew her from. Faith hopped down from her stool, acting much more optimistic than she felt, and offered him her hand.

"You shou' go home, Faith. Gettin' late."

She hid a sad smile, thinking how much easier it would be to have to look after only herself at this moment, instead of her sixty-year-old father.

"Let's go," she said gently. "You have to work in the morning."

Realization brightened his face for an instant and he turned to the bartender. "I'm the fire ch—"

"He knows," Faith said loudly, to cover his words, darting a look around behind them to see if anyone else had heard. "Come on, Dad. We need to go *now*." She tugged at his arm. "Stand up."

His movements were in slow motion, but he finally turned to the side and put his feet on the floor. He was so unsteady he slid right back to the stool, and Faith had to use her strength to keep him upright.

Okay, so this was going to be an undertaking.

"I'll help you, but you have to walk to the car," she told him.

She didn't give him a choice, just yanked at him, and he did his best to get to his feet. Unfortunately, his "best" wasn't quite enough. The bartender looked over in alarm as Faith braced herself with all her might against her father's weight.

"We're *fine*," she insisted through clenched teeth as her dad finally managed to establish some semblance of balance.

Coaching his every step, she supported him to the

exit, thankful there was no actual door to open. She could feel stares at their backs, but wasn't about to acknowledge them.

"I'm parked on the street," she told him. "Just a little farther." She was starting to breathe hard from the effort of keeping him upright.

Before they could even clear the side of the building, her dad shifted his weight from her to the wall and leaned hard against it. "Princess, need to rest. I'll jus' sit here for a bit."

She fought to keep him on his feet, but there was no way. He slid down the rough wall and landed on his backside on the wide sidewalk.

Tears of frustration burned Faith's eyes as he stretched out and rested his head on the pavement.

Stronger than she looked, sure, but able to lift three hundred pounds? No way. Sitting down next to him and banging her head on the wall was the most appealing option right now.

"You really have a problem allowing someone to help you, don't you?" Joe said from the darkness.

CHAPTER EIGHT

FAITH CLOSED HER EYES and leaned against the Shell Shack's exterior wall, looking defeated. Only Faith Peligni would take it personally when she failed to carry an unconscious man three times her size. And that stirred something deep inside Joe. Something that had nothing to do with sympathy.

"I thought you left," she said, annoyed with him, but fighting not to let it show. He could tell by the set of her jaw, the tight control of her voice.

"I talked to him enough before you got here to suspect something like this could happen."

"You were just waiting to come to the rescue, weren't you?" Faith looked down at her dad and shook her head. Her shoulders sagged. "I'm sorry. I guess we do need a little assistance."

"Don't worry about it. Let's just get him out of here. Come on, Chief." Joe leaned down and roused him.

The big guy muttered something and Faith avoided Joe's gaze. The urge to touch her, to try to make her feel better, rolled through him out of nowhere.

He bent over to prop up the chief, burying his mind in the task and attempting to ignore Faith. She got into position on the other side, and together they pulled him upright. Chief Peligni came to long enough to ask where the hell they were taking him and to complain about how fast they were moving.

"To my 4Runner over there," Joe told Faith, indicating the vehicle with a nod. "It's close." When they got to the passenger side, she opened the door and they awkwardly heaved him inside.

Once the door was shut, Joe locked it. He and Faith looked at each other as they caught their breath.

"Want to follow me?" she asked.

He nodded, recalling from previous visits the flight of stairs they'd have to drag the chief up once they got him home. "I'll drive you back here to get his truck once we get him settled." He searched until he spotted the chief's Suburban at the end of the row.

Faith shot a frown toward her dad and bit her lower lip before heading toward her car, parked at the curb.

Joe went around to the driver's side of his SUV. He paused before getting in and watched her walk away. Let himself admire her curves in those tiny shorts and the yellow fitted tank top. Her hair was pulled back in a ponytail. She was dressed for relaxing, not for impressing, and still his heart thundered in appreciation.

He glanced guiltily at Chief Peligni and climbed in, making a point of *not* checking out the chief's daughter again. Not that the older man had even noticed; his head was propped against the window, eyes closed. Joe reached across, drew the seat belt over him, pulled it out as far as it would go and fastened it. He could just about get drunk off the fumes coming from the passenger seat.

While Faith was careful and deliberate with just about everything she did, she apparently didn't drive the same way, speeding off like a maniac. Joe had been to the chief's house before for cookouts, so he took his time getting there. When he pulled up, her car was in the driveway and she was leaning against the wall of the garage, arms crossed. She gestured for him to drive up close to the open garage door.

After fifteen or twenty minutes, they'd managed to get the chief up the flight of stairs, into his bed, shoes off, with a glass of water and a bottle of aspirin on the nightstand. He'd been half-awake for part of it, but Joe doubted he'd remember any of this in the morning. Joe wasn't sure the man would be able to get up in the morning.

Faith drew a crocheted blanket over him, since they hadn't had a chance to pull the covers back before laying him down. When she finished, she exhaled tiredly and nodded at Joe. Together they walked down the hall toward the living room.

When they reached the last door on the right, Faith went into the room, flipping on the light. Her bedroom, he realized, as he peered in like a Peeping Tom.

"I can wait outside," he said.

"Just a sec. I need a sweatshirt, but there's something for you in the kitchen."

Curious, he stood there in the doorway, trying not to watch her every move as she searched through the drawers of an antique-looking white dresser. Instead, he took in the details of her room, still feeling somewhat like a voyeur, but unable to resist.

The room was…shockingly pink. Her bed was un-made, but there were lacy white ruffles around the bottom of the mattress and edging the pink floral pil-lowcases. The walls were painted a pale pink to match. The furniture was dainty, almost little-girllike. Clothes were scattered on the floor and he tried his damnedest to ignore the silky pink and purple underthings among the jeans and fire department shirts. He did *not* need to know what she wore beneath her uniform.

He was still staring as she approached him, pulling on an orange zip-up sweatshirt.

"Welcome to the Pepto room," she said.

Joe grinned, fighting off images of those panties….

"For my sixteenth birthday, my dad's treat was to let me have my room redecorated any way I wanted it," she explained defensively.

"I never imagined you as a pink kind of woman."

"If you wear pink, they never see the knuckle sand-wich coming."

"And you seem like such a peaceful person," he said, following her to the kitchen.

"It's the brothers. One in particular needed his ass kicked on a regular basis. Thankfully, Anthony lives in Dallas now, and doesn't make it home much. Here." She grabbed a plastic container off the counter and re-moved the lid.

"Cookies?"

"Scotcheroos. Baked them today."

He took one and bit into it. "You made these?" He couldn't keep the surprise out of his voice.

"I can do more than just put out a fire, Captain."

She grinned and helped herself to one. "Not that I bake often. These happen to be my dad's favorites. Of course, he never made it home to appreciate them." The smile disappeared instantly, as if someone had thrown a bucket of water over her head.

"His loss," Joe said, trying to keep it light.

"Take a handful. Otherwise I'll eat more than my share. I made a double batch."

He took one more, not wanting to steal the chief's treats.

"You don't like them?" Faith challenged.

"They're the best cookies I've had in a long time."

She went to a drawer and pulled out a plastic zipper bag, then shoved in as many cookies as she could fit. "If you're lying, you can give them to your dog."

"I don't have a dog," he said. "And I'm not lying. Let's go get your dad's truck."

She stuffed another bite in her mouth and nodded, turning serious again. "Thank you for helping us tonight, Joe. You were right, I don't accept help very well, but..."

"It's no problem," he said, mildly amused by her discomfort. "Middle of the night rescues are what I do. But then, you can relate."

She seemed about to say something else, but only led him down the stairs and out the door.

As they drove back to the Shell Shack, he was hyper-aware of the woman sitting just two feet away. Chief Peligni would have to give up the bottle, because this couldn't happen again. Joe realized he wasn't capable of spending time with Faith outside the station without his mind going in dangerous directions.

Thankfully, the drive was a short one. When he turned into the lot, he spotted a small object reflecting light next to the building where the chief had passed out. He pulled up behind Peligni's SUV and told Faith he was going to check it out.

A cell phone was lying on the ground about a foot from the rough wood wall, and he bent to pick it up. When he straightened, Faith was right behind him. He ran into her, unaware that she'd followed. He turned and steadied her, and she took a step back.

"Sorry," she said.

"This your dad's?" he asked, holding it out.

She took it from him and glanced at the display. "That's his." She dropped it in the pocket of her sweatshirt. "He's like an irresponsible teenager tonight."

At that instant, she looked unsure of herself. Just for a moment. Unsure and…so tired. And yet pretty and young with the moonlight illuminating her face. Her eyes darted around as she did her best to act as if nothing bothered her. He wanted to tell her it was okay to be bothered. Against his better judgment, he forced eye contact, feeling a jolt when she finally focused on him.

"What?" she asked defensively. "I look like hell, I know. I was in bed when my dad called me—"

"You don't look like hell," he said quietly, leaning closer to make the mistake of a lifetime and not giving a damn.

He palmed her cheek. Touched her lower lip with his

thumb, caressing the moist warmth of it. Felt her breath on his fingers as her lids grew heavy.

A stray lock of her dark hair fell onto her cheek, and he brushed it back.

"Joe."

It was barely more than a whisper. Definitely not a warning to back off. So he closed the space between them and gently kissed her lips, testing her. Tasting.

The contact shot heat straight through his body. For a woman who was so tough on the outside, she was soft, feminine. Her scent was light, with a hint of flowers.

She wound her hands behind his neck and pulled him closer. He should've guessed that even her kiss would be bold.

He deepened the contact, thrusting his tongue between her lips. She tasted of sugar and confidence... and damn, what a turn-on. He pulled her slender body up against his, his hands resting at the point where her waist curved into her hips. Her body was firm, fit. Strong and lean. He imagined that body unclothed....

Headlights illuminated them like a sudden spotlight on an auditorium stage, and they jumped apart. Faith ran her fingers over her lips, peering at the driver. The man, probably close to seventy years old, gave them an enthusiastic thumbs-up as he passed them.

"He doesn't know the least of it," Joe said.

Faith's low, nervous laugh was gratifying. Alluring.

"It's late," she said after a few seconds, sobering. "I need to check on my dad."

"I bet he hasn't moved an inch."

They started toward their vehicles, and Joe pressed

his hand to her lower back. His pulse was still hammering away, his body demanding more attention from this beauty, but his brain was now fighting it, letting in the message that this was a no-win situation.

Joe walked her to the driver's door of her dad's Suburban without conscious thought. She turned toward him. "You didn't have to walk me here. I'm fine." Back to Miss Independent.

He stole a glance at those lips of hers and was considering one last ill-advised taste when she broke the spell.

"I hope it goes without saying that this can't get out," she said.

"This?" he asked, surprised. "No. It's private."

"I didn't mean the kiss…but yes. That, too." Realization flitted in her eyes, and he knew the moment her regret kicked in.

"I meant my dad." Faith made sure no one was within hearing distance. "No one needs to know about tonight. It was an isolated incident. Derek won't say anything, will he?"

Shaking his head, Joe moved back a few inches and straightened, willing the haze of desire to dissipate.

She fidgeted with her keys, seeming uncharacteristically nervous, then hit the button to unlock the Suburban.

"Gotta go." She climbed in and closed the door, effectively shutting him out.

FAITH MANAGED TO ACT as if everything was fine until she pulled into the garage at home.

Everything was *not* fine. It was nowhere near fine.

What had she done?

She'd kissed her company officer. Her captain. A man who had power over her career.

It wasn't that Joe would use it against her. It was more about what others would think if they ever found out. What she thought of herself.

And how Joe would treat her now.

He already hovered, and would coddle her at a moment's notice if she'd let him. She hadn't yet figured out if it was because of her gender, her newness to the department or something else, but the last thing she wanted was for one of the other firefighters to notice Joe's protectiveness.

And kissing a man tended to arouse his protectiveness even more.

If she could've chosen the best way to lose, or never gain, her colleagues' respect, becoming involved— physically, romantically, stupidly—with one of the department captains topped the list.

CHAPTER NINE

FAITH COULD'VE USED about four more hours of sleep after the episode with her dad. Of course, lying in bed, going back and forth between beating herself up for what happened with Joe and playing their kiss over and over in her mind like some romantic airhead, didn't help.

As she walked across the apparatus floor for roll call, the buzz of energy she usually experienced at the sight of the equipment perked her up. She hoped they got an exciting gig or two today—something to keep her awake.

"Look who it is," Clay, one of the other firefighters, said as Faith headed toward the four men already waiting.

"How'd it go last night?" asked Cale, the lieutenant with short, spiky brown hair.

Faith's heart skipped two beats before she figured out they were addressing the guy behind her, Penn Griffin.

Guilty conscience much?

"Like I'd tell you bozos," Penn said. His wide grin and the sparkle in his eyes revealed more than he intended, though.

"How's it going, Faith?" Clay said. She didn't know

him well, hadn't worked many shifts with him, but his brown eyes seemed genuinely friendly.

"Pretty good. How's your baby?"

"You're thinking of Evan Drake. He's the one with the baby."

She looked at the floor, embarrassed. "Sorry."

"Give Clay a little time and he'll probably have a baby, too," Penn said. "Right now his world revolves around a couple of women."

Faith raised her brows.

"One of them is my four-year-old daughter," Clay said, smiling. "And one of these days you'll meet Andie, my wife."

"Looking forward to it."

While they waited for the captain—Faith was forever doomed to be scheduled with Joe, it seemed—she wandered over to the truck and began opening compartments. She was usually assigned to the engine instead of the truck, but just in case, she needed to be familiar with the location of each tool, every piece of equipment at this station.

She looked up automatically when Joe strode in carrying a clipboard. Their eyes met briefly, and though his lingered for an extra split second, they gave nothing away. She relaxed a little and quashed the flicker of excitement sparked by the memory of kissing him.

She joined the group as Joe began calling out assignments for the day. Once again, she was on the engine with him. Was he taunting her? Messing with her?

Just as well that he didn't make changes to the norm, she supposed. Last night shouldn't be cause for rearranging everything. She intended to go on as if nothing had happened.

"Did anybody hear if we're getting new radios yet?" Penn asked. "Mine's crapping out. Can't trust it anymore."

"You're not alone," Joe said. "Find a spare one and see if it's any better."

"I thought Chief Peligni was going to order new ones," Clay said.

Faith tensed at the mention of her dad's possible slip-up and refused to look at Joe.

"I'll speak to him about it today," Joe assured him.

"He's sick today." Faith immediately regretted speaking up. Reminding everyone she was the chief's daughter was not the brightest move. And there was no need to inform Joe that her dad hadn't made it in—he'd find out soon enough.

"He okay?" Cale asked. "I can't remember the last time the chief was sick."

"He'll be back tomorrow," Faith said quickly, cursing in her head. Might as well just blurt out that he had the mother of all hangovers. She glanced around for Derek and was glad to see he wasn't on duty today.

She felt Joe's gaze on her, questioning, wanting her to confirm that it was a case of brown bottle flu, but she made a point of ignoring him.

"Get to work," Joe said to everyone in his captain voice. "Faith, I need to speak to you."

She'd never been sent to the principal's office, but suddenly had a decent idea of what it felt like. Attempting to hide her ridiculous nervousness, she took a few steps toward Joe.

"In my office," he said, nodding in that direction. "I'll be there in a couple minutes."

Faith walked off the floor, annoyed that he'd called her out in front of everyone. Couldn't he have quietly pulled her aside as she went about her assigned chores?

Once in the office, alone, she crossed her arms and watched two of her colleagues out the window as they raised the flags for the day and picked up litter in the courtyard. Joe entered the room and closed the door with a soft click, startling Faith.

"Why the closed door?" she asked, wondering for the first time if she was in trouble of some kind.

He stopped directly in front of her, too close. His gray officer's shirt stretched over the bulk of his shoulders and muscular chest. "I didn't figure you wanted the whole department to hear our conversation about your father."

"He's fine," she said tersely.

Joe stared down at her, so close she could see the pores of his recently shaved chin. She forced her eyes to his brown-black ones, fighting the temptation to sneak a glance at the sensual lips she'd tasted last night.

"May I get through?" he asked, gesturing to the narrow path between the windowed wall and his desk.

Faith practically jumped out of his way, feeling like an idiot for the direction of her thoughts, when all he wanted to do was walk past her.

"I assume he's still sleeping off last night?" Joe

asked, pulling out his desk chair, but remaining on his feet. He leaned his fists on the clutter-free surface.

There was no sense in lying. As out of it as her dad had been last night, it'd be nothing short of amazing for him to be up and functioning before noon and they both knew it. But instead of admitting that, she didn't answer. Waited for the next, hopefully better question.

"Are you doing okay?" he asked gently, and for some reason, that made it hard for her to swallow.

"I'm fine."

Joe shook his head. "He's fine. You're fine. Everybody's fine. What am I worried about?"

"That's *my* question." She crossed her arms.

"I'm not the bad guy here, Faith."

She noticed dark shadows under his eyes and realized he had to be as exhausted as she was. All because of her family's problem.

"I'm sorry. You're right." She wasn't even convinced her dad was the bad guy. Right now wasn't the time to assign blame, though.

She sat in the chair in front of Joe's desk, shoulders slumping, suddenly overcome by fatigue and…fear. "I don't know what to do for him."

"He's a grown man. Sometimes people have to help themselves."

"That seems kind of harsh."

"Maybe. Maybe not," Joe said sternly. He walked around to the front of his desk and leaned against it, crossing his legs at the ankles. "I don't know what to tell you, Faith. But you're doing more than anyone else in your family just by being there for him. Staying with him. That's a lot."

"My brothers all have busy careers. They think I'm overreacting, but they haven't seen him. How *off* he is."

"The chief is glad to have you there."

"How do you know?" she asked, not entirely comfortable with the personal direction of the conversation. How close *were* Joe and her dad? Had they discussed her before? That didn't sit well with her.

"He doesn't hide his opinion. He's very proud of you."

Joe's words made her squirm. She rose to her feet, intent on getting the heck out of there and back to the tedium of daily chores. She found herself close enough to catch his masculine scent.

She stepped to the side, away from him. "What did you really call me in here for?"

"Faith…" Joe had been up all night trying to figure out how to broach this subject, and he still hadn't thought of a good way.

Her eyes narrowed warily.

"I'm concerned about your dad."

Her shoulders stiffened and there was a decided change in the air. No longer were they officer and firefighter standing there, or even two people who'd shared a misguided but brain-numbing kiss last night. Now there was a current of adversity…her versus him.

"He's going through hard times," she said. "But he'll be fine."

Joe ran his fingers over his chin. "I know the separation from your mom is rough, but it's starting to affect his work, Faith."

"Like I said, he'll be back tomorrow." She swallowed hard and studied the ground, looking for a moment like a little girl who'd lost her favorite teddy bear. So uncharacteristic of her.

"He's always been a model chief. Follows his own regulations to the letter. He's prompt. Exact. Thorough."

She nodded. "It's who he is."

"That's why I'm worried. He's been late recently. To meetings. To work. He's let several issues go unaddressed…."

"He's not himself some days."

"I understand that, but…"

"But what?"

Joe didn't know, exactly. "I can't continue to ignore it. He's in too important of a position. And now this…"

"So you're going to, what—tell on him? Who are you going to tell?"

"I'm not going to tell anyone. Not right now. But I am going to keep an eye on him. If Mayor Romero needs a heads-up…"

"What is this? The depression patrol? Maybe he *is* depressed, but that's a health issue. Not a professional one."

Joe exhaled loudly, exasperated. "I'm just letting you know, Faith, that while I'm not going to say a word about carrying him to his bed last night, I don't like that I seem to be repeatedly forced to keep Peligni family secrets. It puts me in one hell of an awkward position."

She stared him down, the look in her eyes combative. "We don't need your help. Consider yourself un-involved."

"I was involved the second you asked me to keep something from the chief."

Still shooting daggers at him with her eyes, she grabbed the doorknob. "I'm sorry, sir. It won't happen again."

She swung the door open so hard it bounced off the wall as she walked away.

JOE SAT DOWN HARD in the worn chair at his desk, still able to discern Faith's feminine scent in the air though she'd marched off minutes ago, once again ticked off at him.

That shouldn't bother him, but it did. He'd blown it. Whether you looked at it professionally or personally, he'd said all the wrong things, in the wrong way, when she'd just confided that she didn't know what to do about her dad.

He hadn't intended to come across as an unfeeling bastard. Wasn't trying to threaten her or the chief.

On a personal level, maybe it was a good thing that he'd lacked any kind of gentleness, but if she was just another firefighter, just one of the guys, he would've handled the situation better.

She was getting to him and that wasn't okay. Even if he didn't care what the chief thought. Even if he wasn't trying to get the assistant chief job.

It wasn't okay.

It was unprofessional and somewhat embarrassing

that the department had one woman on staff and the goddamn captain couldn't keep a rein on his thoughts.

When Faith had walked into the bar last night, he couldn't deny the buzz that had pumped through him at the sight of her. He hadn't thought twice about helping her out. At the time, he'd convinced himself it was something he'd do for any of his "men," but today, after making the mistake of ordering Faith into his office, he knew there'd been more to it than duty.

If he continued down this road, kept close tabs on Faith as the chief had requested, he risked getting in deeper. He had every intention of fighting off his desire for her, but look where that had gotten him last night. She cast a spell over him, made him stupid and lacking in judgment.

He was a lot weaker than he'd thought.

When it came to Faith Peligni and his career with the San Amaro Island Fire Department, he was screwed. Something had to give.

CHAPTER TEN

FAITH HATED HAVING TO ASK her mom for anything. Most days, she'd walk ten thousand miles to avoid it, but this was her dad. She was desperate.

She knocked on the door to the third-floor apartment. The building was box-shaped, nondescript. Everything her mother wasn't. She and her mom could disagree on anything under the sun, they could argue about the color of the sky, but the one thing Faith wouldn't debate was that her mother had good taste when it came to decorating. Cooking and dressing, too. Nita Peligni was well-versed in all things domestic. A year ago, this apartment would've chilled her mother's blood.

"Faith," her mom said, opening the door and looking surprised.

Some people would be insulted, but Faith could readily admit she hadn't visited here often—only twice before in the two months plus she'd been back in San Amaro.

"Hi, Mom." Faith held up the plastic container of scotcheroos. Her best attempt at a peace offering. "Can I come in?"

Her mother stepped back so Faith could enter. "What's with the cookies?" she asked suspiciously.

"I baked scotcheroos. Too many." That they were her dad's favorite and not her mom's remained unspoken, but hung between them.

Her mom frowned and set the container aside on the high counter that divided the living room from the kitchen, without even acting tempted. "What are you doing here?"

Faith wandered in as if it were her home, even though it didn't feel like anyone's home with its taupe walls, beige carpet and total lack of personalization. She couldn't spot anything that screamed out Nita Peligni.

"You're not planning to stay here, are you?" Faith said, falling unladylike onto the cheap, used sofa.

"What?" Her mom perched carefully on the non-matching chair. She looked out of place in this room in her casual robin's egg-blue pantsuit, her hair, as usual, perfectly in place.

"This is temporary," Faith continued, waving her arm. "To teach him a lesson."

"To teach…who? What are you talking about?"

"If you were planning to stay here, you would've bought better furniture. Added some throw pillows, some artwork. Color. Your walls are bare, Mom."

"I have upholstery covers on order, Faith. A rug. And once I get those, I'll pick out some accent pieces."

"You've been here for three months. It's not like you to live in this monotone blah."

Her mom settled back into the chair and crossed one leg over the other. "Frankly, I don't know what's like me. As a suddenly soon-to-be-divorcee at the age of fifty-eight, decorating hasn't been my top priority."

She was sincere, not just saying it to gain sympathy, and somehow, in spite of Faith's anger and her tendency to be more concerned for her dad's well-being, it was impossible to be unaffected by her mother's plight.

Her mom had left him, though, Faith reminded herself.

"If it's so bad being by yourself, why not go back?"

"Is this why you came? To browbeat me? To try to get me to move back home?"

Once again, Faith had let her emotions carry her too far, just as she had during the argument at dinner. Why she couldn't just chill out, hold herself back, when it was vital to making her point, she didn't know. Her mom had always set her off.

"I didn't come to browbeat. But…Dad needs you, Mom."

Her mother looked away and swallowed hard. Smoothed down her pants with fidgety hands. "He's never really needed me, Faith. Not like he's needed his career. And that's the fundamental problem."

"Mom—"

Nita held her hand up. "Stop. I know you want us back together, but it's not going to happen." She walked over to the sofa and sat a foot away from Faith. "It's too late for your dad and me, honey. The sooner you accept that, the better off you'll be."

"This isn't about me." Faith popped up off the sofa, uncomfortable with her mother's closeness. "Dad…" She lifted her face to stare at the ugly white ceiling through tear-blurred eyes. Pacing toward the kitchen, she swiftly wiped the moisture away. She fought to collect herself for several seconds, then finally faced her mom. "He's not handling this, Mom. At all."

For a split second, her mom's feelings showed in her eyes—concern and...love. Faith could swear to it. But then it was gone and the hardness, the hurt were back.

"What do you mean?" Nita asked.

"He's...I'm pretty sure he's depressed. Clinically. He sleeps all the time. Forgets to eat. Drinks too much." Faith was laying most of his secrets out there, but couldn't bring herself to admit how bad the other night had been. Not if she could avoid it. She wasn't even sure her dad remembered any of it. He'd walked past her this morning before she'd left, on his way in to the station after his sick day, and acted like nothing was wrong.

"I'm sorry he's having a hard time. But this isn't easy for me, either."

"So then why not try again? At this point he'd do just about anything to get you back where you belong."

Her mom shook her head slowly. Sadly. "*You* would do anything, Faith. But your father...I don't think he knows how to put me first. I've waited for thirty-eight years." Her voice wavered and she hesitated. "There comes a time when you have to face up to reality. Admit to yourself something is never going to happen."

The tears wouldn't stop filling Faith's eyes. She marched into the kitchen and grabbed a tissue to wipe them. Her mom clearly didn't realize how serious the situation was. How bad off her dad was. And short of telling her about his drunken night, Faith wasn't sure how to make her understand. The digital dots on the microwave clock blinked while she considered. Tried to convince herself to speak up. In the end, she couldn't do it. Couldn't rob her father, the person she probably loved most in the world, of his last shred of dignity. She didn't want her mom to come back out of sympathy or fear of what he might or might not do. She wanted her to come back because they still loved each other.

Faith indelicately blew her nose and threw the tissue into the wastebasket in the pantry. As she headed back out to the bland living room, someone knocked on the door. She didn't think much of it other than an inconvenience until she noticed her mom's reaction. Nita jumped up almost before the knock was over and darted a guilty glance at Faith before walking past her and opening the door.

"Hey, beautiful."

Faith couldn't see the man yet, but she'd put him in his fifties, tall and very much interested in her mom.

"Craig. Come in and meet my daughter. This is—"

"Faith," he said smoothly. Way too smoothly. "I've heard a lot about you."

She looked from him to her mom. He was indeed tall, thin, with a full head of salt-and-pepper hair. She wouldn't give him handsome, but she could see how he would catch a woman's attention. *But not her mom's.* Faith closed her eyes as the implications sank in.

Her mom had a...boyfriend? What the hell did you call it when she was fifty-eight years old and not yet divorced? Besides disgusting.

"I was just leaving," Faith said, looking around for her purse.

"Faith, don't be rude. This is Craig Eggleston. I've been wanting to introduce you."

Like hell she had. And Faith had no interest in meeting him. She didn't want to know about him, didn't want to think about him.

Were they sleeping together? God. Did people her mother's age still do that? Faith closed her eyes for a moment and pressed her lips together. Shook her head slightly. "It's nice to meet you," she said, without offering her hand. "Really, I have to go now."

She finally spotted her purse on the floor by the sofa, grabbed it and made a sincere effort to walk instead of run out the door.

Maybe Joe was right, after all. Maybe there really wasn't anything more she could do to help her dad.

No. Faith refused to accept that. To give up would be to let her dad down, and after everything he'd done for her, including putting his name on the line to get her hired, she wasn't about to do that.

CHAPTER ELEVEN

SO WHAT IF SNACKING late at night was bad? Whoever made up that rule hadn't ever taken part in a vicious fire station round of beach Frisbee. Faith had to have burned as many calories during the game as she usually did on the treadmill. Now she was famished. She couldn't get the last slice of chocolate cheesecake—sitting in the refrigerator all by its lonesome—out of her mind.

Might as well put the cheesecake out of its misery before someone else did.

Most of the guys were in the living area watching a cheesy horror movie, and the hall that led to the kitchen reeked of microwave popcorn. That didn't sway her from her sweet objective. The swear words that were uttered in the supply room did, however.

She walked beyond the kitchen and looked into the open doorway. Joe had his back toward her, hunched over a box that must have fallen off the shelf and spilled.

She hadn't been alone with him since the other day when he'd told her he was tired of being involved in Peligni family business. She didn't really want to be alone with him now, either, so she tried to back out of the room before he noticed her.

"Midnight snack run?" he asked, shoving the last rolls of bandages into the box as he stood.

Faith halted her attempted escape. "I can hear the chocolate cheesecake calling my name from my bunk. What are you doing in here?"

He replaced the box on the shelf and held up a syringe. "Come see."

Joe strode out of the room, not giving her a chance to reply. Curiosity propelled her after him. Instead of going toward the racket of male voices in the living area or heading toward the bunks, he took the hall to the wing of offices.

As they turned the corner, Faith saw light shining under his closed office door. "Working late again?" she asked.

"Not exactly."

He opened the door a few inches and cautiously peered in, then pushed it the rest of the way. He gestured for Faith to follow him in, and then closed the door behind her, reminding her of their last less-than-pleasant discussion in this room.

She glanced expectantly at his desk, but the surface was clean, with neat stacks of paper organized on one corner. Joe stepped across the room, toward the desk the lieutenants used, where a shallow cardboard box rested on the floor.

"You did not," Faith said, moving closer.

Wriggling furry bodies made stilted movements toward a large mound of gray fur. Cale had discovered the litter of kittens and the mama cat this morning in a corner of the apparatus floor, huddled in a spare turn-out coat that had fallen off one of the hooks.

"It's loud out there when the trucks start up," Joe said defensively.

"You brought them in here?" Faith was stumbling over the image of their burly, dedicated leader transporting the tiny critters to a safer haven. Where he could keep an eye on them.

"One of them isn't nursing right." He lowered himself to the chair he'd moved next to the kitten nest. "The little orange one over here," he said, pointing.

The kitten was noticeably smaller than the others, and while the rest of the litter were drinking from their mother, the orange one mewed, so quietly Faith almost couldn't hear it.

She had no experience with cats, but the troubled kitten seemed to wrap itself around her heart and take hold. "Maybe it's just not hungry now?"

Joe shook his head. "Hasn't eaten since I moved them in here. The others seem to nurse every hour or two."

"How long have they been in your office?"

He looked sheepish. "I brought them in before lunch. It was getting too hot."

She stifled a grin and knelt on the floor next to his legs and the box. He'd added a towel to cushion the cardboard, and a water dish sat beside it. "I didn't know you had such a soft heart," Faith said, not realizing until the words were out how personal they sounded.

"I try not to let it show." Joe went to his desk where a saucer of milk sat next to the carton with the Don't Touch My Damn Milk warning.

"Derek's going to miss his milk."

"I'll buy him more."

"Think the little orange one will drink it from the saucer?" Faith held her hand out slowly to the mother cat and let the sleepy animal sniff it.

Joe shook his head. "Too small. A website suggested trying this." He indicated the needleless syringe again, then filled it with milk.

"Isn't there some kind of kitten formula you should use?"

"Know any twenty-four hour pet stores where I could get some?"

"Good point." The mother cat licked Faith's fingers with her warm, rough tongue, making her smile. "I think I've been accepted."

Joe returned to the chair next to her. "The cat has good instincts."

Faith puzzled briefly over whether that was a compliment or just a statement.

"Come here, Blaze," Joe said as he cupped the tiny orange baby in his large hand.

Faith chuckled. "You named it?"

"Just this one," Joe said sternly, which amused Faith more.

He gently opened the kitten's mouth and squeezed drops of milk in. Faith watched intently and tried to determine whether any of it was swallowed.

After several minutes, they decided the kitten was getting at least a little nourishment, since the level of milk in the syringe had gone down and very little had spilled on Joe's uniform. He continued to give the sleepy animal a few drops every couple of minutes.

"Faith," he said, his tone no longer the quiet, affectionate one he used to talk to the kitten. "I'm sorry for how I came across the other day."

She ran her index finger lightly along the orange kitten's back, attempting to hide her reaction to his words. She didn't expect an apology from him. Didn't need one, really, because he'd been absolutely right. As her captain, he shouldn't be put in the middle of her family's problems. She should never have asked him to keep her collarbone pain from her dad. Derek should never have called him to go get her dad at the bar.

"There's nothing to apologize for on your end." She made her own voice businesslike. "I'm sorry you had to get involved in something you shouldn't even be aware of. Things that never should've happened in the first place."

"But they did. The scope of my job goes beyond just fighting fires to making sure all my men—*people*—do what needs to be done."

"You were thrown into the middle of our family soap opera. I wish Derek had called me instead of you."

Joe put the syringe aside when the kitten refused to take more milk, and held the rumbling fur ball in his hand, against his wide chest.

"I've worked for your father for years. He worked for mine. I'd do just about anything for him, Faith. I *am* worried about him, but I said it all wrong the other day."

She nodded. "Okay. I'd offer to shake on our peace treaty but it seems you have your hands full." She sat

"All I know is that she's seen him before and they're close enough that he knew about me, knew my name. Makes me sick to my stomach."

"I remember that feeling. Maybe the punching bag would do some good."

"Already beat the crap out of it today," Faith said. "Definitely therapeutic."

"That's my girl."

His words were extraordinarily personal, she thought. And she couldn't bring herself to hate it. In fact, the thought of being his girl warmed her to her toes.

Time to get her cheesecake and then shut herself away in her room, where she could be alone with her inappropriate thoughts of this man who had a way of endearing himself to her with his feline rescues and late night encouragement.

"I'll let you—" she raised the kitten and looked into its tiny face "—get to sleep." She set it back in the box. "And you get to work. Or babysitting or whatever it is you workaholic captain types do till all hours of the morning, squirreled away in your office."

"It's a difficult job," Joe said with mock seriousness. "I'll actually be feeding that one every two hours." He gestured to the orange kitten. "Should make the night go fast."

Faith considered offering to take a shift, but being alone with this sexy man in the middle of the night wasn't a good idea. No matter how tempting. "Good night," she said, opening the door.

"Sleep well."

The words, though innocent and innocuous, sent a shiver through her. She'd likely not sleep well, thanks to images of him nurturing a helpless little animal the size of his palm. She grinned to herself as she made her way to the kitchen.

"What's got you so happy at this hour?" Penn asked when she walked into the kitchen.

Thank God she wasn't the type to blush. "Cheesecake," she blurted out. "There's one more—"

"Too late." He held up a plate with only a few bites of said cheesecake remaining.

The dessert had been brought in by Evan's wife, Selena, and was fair game, but Faith had counted on beating the guys to it.

"I *used* to like you," she told Penn, feigning disgust.

He laughed. "You'll learn. Best to steal it and store it in your room if you really want it."

"Clearly. Oh well. This way you get to deal with the calories."

"I'll lose sleep over it," he joked as she left the kitchen.

She was disappointed she'd missed out on the sugar she'd been craving all evening, but given a choice, she'd rather witness Joe's save-a-kitten efforts any day.

CHAPTER TWELVE

MAYBE SOMEDAY she would learn to scope out a place before putting in her food order, Faith thought as she joined her friend on the patio.

"You would choose this table," she said, keeping her tone light as she took the stool beside Nadia, one of her BFFs since grade school. "You still have a talent for zeroing in on the strongest concentration of testosterone in any room, don't you?"

"Still have it?" Nadia said after sipping her strawberry margarita. "My talent is finely honed after all these years, darlin'. Most single women appreciate my skills."

"They're firefighters," Faith said of the large, boisterous diners at the next table. And of course, not just any firefighters. She was shocked to see Joe among the group that included Cale, Turner, Penn and Clay, plus Clay's family.

"Excellent," Nadia said, her eyes sparkling. "You can introduce me."

"Like you've ever needed me to introduce you to anyone."

With her long blond hair, petite body and eternal cuteness, Nadia seemed to have people flocking around her wherever she went. Men, yes, but even women instinctively liked her.

"Introduce you to whom?" Mercedes, Nadia's opposite in almost every way, climbed up on the third stool and set down a basket of chips and a Sandblaster, the Shell Shack's signature toxic drink.

"Take your pick," Nadia said, gesturing to the group. "San Amaro's bravest, ripe for the choosing."

"Some are taken," Faith said in a futile attempt to dampen Nadia's enthusiasm. And no, she was *not* referring to Joe.

"The one with the kid, I'm assuming. Too bad."

"That's Clay Marlow."

"Tell me the rest. The ones that are available."

"Some things never change," Faith said to Mercedes, who laughed and shook her head.

"Once a serial dater, always a serial dater." Mercedes casually tossed her dark, curly hair over her shoulder. "It's part of why we love her."

"True," Faith said.

"Here's to girlfriends who understand each other," Nadia said, raising her glass. Faith held her piña colada up and nodded, appreciating the sentiment.

One of the best parts of being back on San Amaro was these two. Though they didn't get to meet often enough because of their jobs and crazy schedules, it was as if they'd been together just yesterday whenever they did make plans.

"Faith, are you and your pretty friends going to ignore us all night?" Penn of the deep blue eyes, which had no doubt caught Nadia's, had angled his chair to face them.

"I don't think that's possible," Faith said, smiling. She introduced Nadia and Mercedes to everyone she knew at the firefighters' table. When she got to Joe, he wouldn't make direct eye contact. He checked out Nadia and Mercedes, nodded at them, greeted them just as Cale did, but he didn't look at Faith once.

"And I'm betting those two belong to Clay," she continued, doing her best to ignore Joe, in turn.

"This is my wife, Andie," Clay said, referring to the tall, pretty brunette with a row of earrings lining her ear. "And short stuff here is Payton."

Faith stepped down from her stool and extended her hand first to Andie and then to the little girl sitting on Clay's leg. His daughter had gorgeous shiny brown hair and eyes that matched her daddy's. "Nice to meet you," she said. "I've heard a lot about you both."

"Faith is a firefighter, too," Clay told his daughter, which made her stare up at Faith in wonder.

"I have to hang around with noisy boys a lot," Faith told her, sensing that Joe was now watching her. "Kind of like you're doing tonight."

"Boys are smelly," Payton said, making everyone laugh.

"Don't let her fool you," Andie said. "She's got all these smelly boys wrapped around her little finger."

"As they should be." Faith held up her hand for Payton to high-five her.

"Are there more girl firefighters?" Payton asked, not even blinking at the attention from all these men.

"Not here on San Amaro," Faith told her.

"There should be," Payton said, still watching Faith carefully.

"I think we've got all we can handle with one," Penn said.

Maybe Faith's guilty conscience was at work, but she could swear he glanced pointedly toward Joe.

"I bet he's scared of girls," Faith said to Payton. "What do you think?"

The little girl giggled and studied Penn, then nodded.

"Looks like my food is here," Faith said, glad for the excuse to go back to her table with her friends. "Talk to you guys later. Nice meeting you, Andie and Payton."

"They're all hot," Nadia said once she sat down again. "Not sure I can narrow it down."

"You're not dating any of them," Faith said, digging into her cheese fries.

"Which one would you pick?" Nadia continued, as if Faith hadn't shut her down.

Mercedes surreptitiously looked over the choices as she put some ceviche in her mouth. "Have to agree, difficult choice," she said quietly. "What about you, Faith? You know them beyond their pretty faces. What do you think?"

"I think I am not going out with anyone from work."

"Not interested?" Nadia looked skeptical. "You sleep with these guys every week. I think a little fire station romance could be hot."

Faith finished chewing a bite of burger before responding. "That's because you don't work there."

"I don't think everyone agrees with you," Mercedes

said. "The dark-haired one at the end—was it Joe?—keeps looking at you."

Without moving her head, Faith checked him out and, sure enough, Joe was sitting there with his arms on the table in front of him, watching her intently from behind his dark sunglasses. She glanced around quickly to see if anyone else had noticed, but her coworkers were all caught up in trying to be the funniest guy on the planet. Still, it made her nervous. Her friends had noticed. And they were watching her now, so she couldn't frown at him or give him any signal to make him realize he was being obvious.

"The captain," Nadia said, drawing out her words and smiling. "Faith's going for the big guns."

"After we eat, I'll take you over and you can get to know him yourself if you're so caught up on his position—"

"I can think of a lot of positions that would be fun with him."

Faith couldn't help laughing at her persistent, single-minded friend. It was mostly an act, she knew. Nadia was a flirt but nothing more. Which was the only reason Faith didn't feel the need to clobber her over the head with a hard object for checking out Joe so thoroughly.

"I CAN DO THAT, princess."

Faith's dad ambled out of the garage to where she was changing the lawnmower blade on the driveway.

No doubt he *could* do it, but whether he would was another story altogether.

"I got it. Almost done." She tightened the bolt that held the blade on.

"Why don't you let me mow then," he said.

"It's okay, Dad, I need the exercise." She'd still train for at least an hour, but he didn't need to know that.

She should let him do it, but she'd worked herself into enough of a lather over the six-inch-tall grass that she was determined to hack it off herself. She'd intended to finish the job before her dad even climbed out of bed. Surprisingly, it was only five to ten. Last weekend he hadn't been moving until almost noon.

He strutted up to her once she righted the mower and gripped the handle. "That's an argument you can't win. Who needs the exercise more?"

She grinned, unable to stay mad at him. "You have a cushy desk job. I need to be in top shape."

He looked down at her gruffly and she laughed.

"Go eat breakfast, Dad. I like to mow."

"I like to mow, too."

"Not to be rude, but if you like to mow so much, maybe you could do it before it hits my waist next time." She pointed toward the overgrown lawn.

He nodded soberly. "I'll do that. I hadn't noticed."

She frowned, unable to keep up the facade that everything was fine. "Dad, I talked to Mom the other day."

"How's she doing?"

"She looked tired, but seems okay."

He gazed sadly off into the distance and Faith couldn't bring herself to tell him the rest of the story as she'd intended. Couldn't mention that her mom seemed to be moving on. Before seeing the lost look on his face, she'd thought he should know about the new boyfriend. In case he ran into her mom and the smarm in public or something.

"I didn't tell her about the other night," Faith said hesitantly, hating to bring it up at all. They had yet to discuss, or even mention, his drunk fest.

He froze. Seemed to stop breathing. "You didn't?"

"I didn't think you'd want her to know."

He looked at the ground and swallowed. Avoided Faith's gaze. "I was wondering," he began in an uncharacteristically quiet voice, "how I did get home. I don't remember. Tell me I didn't drive."

"You didn't drive. You couldn't have. You don't recall calling me?"

He thought for a few seconds, then shook his head. "I'm sorry, Faith. That won't happen again."

"It better not," she said, more forcefully than she'd meant to. "Dad, Joe Mendoza had to help me get you to your room."

Tony swore and walked to the wooden bench near the front sidewalk. Sitting down heavily, he leaned his elbows on his knees and hung his head. Faith silently sat next to him.

"How did Joe get involved?" he asked.

She told him what she knew of his adventures before she'd arrived at the Shell Shack.

"I'd phoned your mother from work that afternoon," he said after another long pause. "She asked me not to call her again. Not that that's any excuse for drinking myself into oblivion."

"No," Faith said, wondering if her mom had any idea

how much power she held over this seemingly powerful man. Did she even care? "Next time you feel like that, Dad, could you call me? Before you start drinking."

"I hope to God there isn't a next time. Did anyone else see me? Recognize me?"

"Not that I know of. There wasn't anyone else from the department there that night besides Joe and Derek. Just a big crowd of tourists."

They sat without speaking for several minutes, her dad seemingly lost in his thoughts and Faith trying to appreciate the beautiful spring morning around her. Trying to figure out how to be what her dad needed right now. Whatever that was.

"I know I have to move on," he said finally. "Get over it, like she has."

Did he know about the other guy?

"Until I do that, give her some space like she asked, I'm only going to piss her off."

"I don't think you just 'get over' thirty-eight years of marriage," Faith said.

He chuckled. "When you put it like that…"

A wren landed several feet away from them and hopped across the sidewalk. It poked its tiny beak in the moist dirt of the weed-filled flower bed, hunting for lunch.

"I'm sorry you had to see me like that, princess. No daughter should ever have to deal with such a situation."

She refrained from agreeing with him aloud. "We all make mistakes. I'm sorry I had to have Joe help me. There was no other way. He said he'd keep the whole thing to himself."

Her father sighed and patted her knee. "You're a good girl, Faith. Don't know how I'd get through this without you here."

That made her think again of what Joe had said—that there wasn't much anyone could do for him except just be there. Maybe the captain had a clue what he was talking about, after all.

"I'm going to mow before it gets hotter," she said, jumping up and cutting the awkward father-daughter talk short.

He didn't say anything else as she returned to the driveway, just sat there looking so damn sad. Broken.

Not mentioning her mom's "wonder-smarm" was the right decision, Faith assured herself. She refused to be the one to crush her dad. She might not be able to get her parents back together, but she could protect him from more heartbreak.

EVERY FIREFIGHTER LOVED being on the nozzle in a big blaze.

When Joe gave Faith the assignment as they climbed off the engine a week and a half after the fire where she'd freaked out, she tried to summon her usual excitement.

As she and Nate hooked up the attack hose and lugged it toward the back of the sprawling one-story furniture store, her heart hammered. Not in a good way.

They stopped outside of the building to make final adjustments.

She couldn't lose it. Not again. Especially with Nate, her favorite naysayer, right behind her. She could work

with him even though she didn't like him, but she would
not give him more reason to doubt her abilities.

She automatically checked that her flashlight was
strapped on to her air pack, and pulled her gloves on
more securely as she fought nausea.

*No hesitation. You're not going to get hurt. Not going
to screw up. Get in there already, before someone won-
ders what the hell you're waiting for.*

She squeezed her eyes shut for a second, then forced
herself to go inside.

The fire was in the front half of the building. Working toward it was like wandering through a human-
size maze, thanks to what she assumed were furniture
displays throughout. Nausea boiled in her gut and she
felt shaky, but she kept going. Faith didn't realize she'd
made the boneheaded, unforgivable mistake of going
inside without her partner until she turned to check on
him and found herself alone. He must've let go of the
hose while adjusting his mask or something. Where
the hell was he?

The smoke was thickening, but she could still see
the door she'd come in. She could go back and get him
but the flames were advancing quickly. She needed to
knock them down. Nate would follow the hose and catch
up to her any second now.

Visibility continued to tank and the temperature kept
climbing. She'd just about reached the place she needed
to get to before opening the hose when she tripped. A
sharp corner of something jabbed into her padded coat.
The padded coat dulled the pain. She stumbled, trying
to stay on her feet, then ran into another solid object,

felt a blow to her head and found herself sprawled on her side. Disoriented. What had she hit her head on? She felt for her helmet and found it had been dislodged. She lay there for several seconds, trying to get her bearings, before she realized the flames were too close. She groped around for her helmet, the smoke black and blinding now. Having had a building collapse on her made her only too aware of how badly she needed to protect her head.

And her radio. Where was her radio? She'd had it when she'd started, she was sure.

Frantic, she slipped one glove off, hoping to find something that would help her—helmet, radio, hose. The heat was too much, though, and she was afraid she'd drop the glove as well. Swearing up a storm, she yanked her glove back on as she continued to search. Finally she located her helmet and put it back on her head.

Faith noticed she was breathing too fast, using up too much of her oxygen, about the same time she realized she couldn't find the hose. Her way out.

Her chest got that squeezed-in-a-vise feeling and she gasped for breath, even though there was nothing wrong with her supply. Sweat drenched her under her gear and it wasn't just because of the heat in the building. She crawled away from the fire a few feet, feeling for the hose on her way, unable to see a thing—whether from smoke or tears, she couldn't say.

Seconds or minutes ticked by—her sense of time was as hazy as the toxic air around her—and she stubbornly kept moving on her hands and knees, searching for the hose line. If she could just find that, she could get back to what she needed to be doing and put out the freaking fire.

There came a time—she wouldn't be able to pinpoint it later, exactly—when putting out the fire became a secondary concern and getting the hell out of Dodge took over.

Faith had known how quickly a person could become disoriented in a fire, but that didn't prepare her for the panic and terror she experienced now. All sense of direction was gone, and she could no longer see the light from the door where she'd entered. Everything looked the same—a cloud of thick, impenetrable smoke unevenly lit by flames that seemed to be everywhere. She might be five feet from where she'd originally gone down or she might be on the other side of the building. She'd tried to stay close, to avoid going more than a couple of feet in any direction as she searched. The fire was no longer on just one side of her, so she couldn't use that reference to navigate.

Why had she rushed in without Nate? If she hadn't let her panic push her, hadn't let herself wind up alone, everything would be fine. He would've seen her go down, would've made his way to her and helped her get back to the nozzle, and they would have the fire under control by now.

The fire that seemed to be everywhere. On all sides. Creeping closer.

She could die today.

The thought gripped her like a hand to her throat. She froze, unable to decide what her next move should be. Unable to even process her options, limited though they must be. The only thing that ran through her head was that those who'd doubted her—her mother, some of her colleagues—were right. She wasn't good enough for the job.

Heat at her back ripped her attention away from that pathetic line of thought, and she refused to give in to the panic that was trying to suffocate her. She crawled away from the immediate danger, feeling around on the floor for a clear path. Away from the intense heat.

When the alarm on her breathing apparatus started beeping, signaling she was about five minutes from running out of air, she frantically wondered what would get her first, lack of oxygen or a heart attack. Her chest felt as if it would explode, and the heat now seemed unbearable. Add burning to death to the list of possibilities.

Love of God, how did she get in this situation?

More importantly, how could she get out of it?

She continued feeling for a clear path, blind, alone and scared out of her mind. She kept fighting for another breath.

When she felt something yank at her leg, she nearly wept. It was a person grabbing at her—had to be. Someone had found her. Maybe she wouldn't die, after all.

CHAPTER THIRTEEN

JOE HAD RESCUED several people over the course of his career, but he'd never felt such profound relief as when he grasped an object and realized it was Faith's boot.

Relief and other things he wouldn't—couldn't—put a name to right now. He'd been searching for too long, ever since Nate had radioed that he'd found the hose, with no Faith at the end of it.

Joe had to give her air and get her out of here fast. Penn was backing up Nate now. They weren't too far away, battling the flames. Another company had been called in as well, since the fire had tripled in size and intensity, but right now, all Joe could think of was the woman on the floor in front of him.

She was beneath some kind of obstruction, likely a piece of furniture, so he had to pull her free before he could do anything. When she raised her head, he silently thanked God that she was conscious. Her alarm was sounding and she pulled off her mask. She couldn't have much oxygen left. Bending over her, Joe removed his own mask and placed it on her face long enough for her to draw several good breaths. While she filled her lungs, he cradled her in his arms and positioned them both to get the hell out.

She held the mask out to him—a good sign. He took two big inhalations and returned it to her, then eased them along, as close to the floor as he could manage. The going was slow. He'd never come across such a cluttered, confusing layout in a structure fire before.

Faith offered him the mask again. He refused, shaking his head, but either she couldn't see him or she was stubborn, because she held it out insistently. He finally paused long enough to take a fresh breath, mostly to appease her. They'd be out in less than a minute, and though his lungs were burning, he had no idea how much smoke she'd taken in before he'd found her. She needed it worse than him.

He could tell when the guys put water on the flames directly behind them, just as he neared the exit. When he got Faith outside, Rafe, one of the paramedics, rushed over to take her, but Joe carried her to a safe spot near the ambulance himself.

Joe stepped back and let Rafe and Scott get to her to check her vitals. When they got her helmet and hood off, he could see how pale she was. Her lack of protest when the guys fussed over her told him more than anything she might have said. It'd been a close call. Too damn close. He'd never lost a firefighter on his watch, and he planned to keep it that way.

The officer of the company from the mainland came over to confer with him then, and Joe forced his attention back to the fire. They'd made a big turnaround in their fight with the arrival of the second company, and it looked as if this blaze would be knocked down soon.

Then he'd be able to reassure himself he'd gotten to Faith in time, and that she'd be okay.

FAITH STEPPED OUT the back door of the beachside station at long last. The cool air on the patio was a relief after the stuffiness inside and the measuring stares most of her colleagues had tried to hide.

Darkness had fallen hours ago and the beach was mostly empty. She sat on one of the cushionless plastic chaise longues and closed her eyes, allowing the sound of the surf to isolate her with her thoughts.

It had taken a battle, quiet though it may have been, to convince Joe to let her help with the overhaul at the furniture store after the fire was out. She'd rested on her butt like an invalid for close to an hour, letting the EMTs fuss over her, appeasing her captain, soothing her raw throat.

So she'd taken in a little bit of smoke. She was a firefighter. That happened. She was lucky as hell it wasn't worse, and she knew that. But it wasn't worse.

Every muscle in her body ached, sure. She had several cuts and bruises, but everything was minor. She was fine.

Physically.

Mentally, not so much.

The sliding door whooshed open behind her and she wished she'd walked farther away, toward the water or up the shore.

Joe. He stood behind her, and she didn't turn, but she sensed him. He was one of the very few quiet men in the department; most of the guys would come out noisily and not be able to resist announcing their presence.

She could feel Joe watching her, and it made her want to jump up and run away. What did he think when he looked at her? How stupid she'd been at the fire scene? Irresponsible? That she wasn't cut out for the job?

Would he be wrong if he thought any of those things? She wasn't so sure.

A minute passed while he stood behind her, staring, not saying a word. Faith fought within herself not to acknowledge him first in this silent standoff. She willed him to turn around and go back inside—to no avail. Then decided she might go ape-shit crazy if he stood there for another excruciating minute.

"You can go—I'm fine," she finally said, cringing because of the dryness in her throat. "Feeling great."

"I know you're okay. That's not why I came out."

"Your team losing?" Faith had no idea what NBA team was his favorite, but when she'd sneaked outside, everyone had been caught up in a game on TV, acting as if the fate of the world depended on the outcome.

He entered her line of sight at last, taking the chaise next to her. And God bless him, he held out a tall bottle of ice-cold water to her. She unscrewed the lid and took a few swallows. The chilled liquid helped and hurt her throat at the same time.

"Nope," he said. "Winning."

"Then why'd you come out?"

"Heard you were alone."

She drank more water. "Nothing wrong with alone."

"Sometimes. This isn't one of them."

"Kind of thinking it is."

He stared at her hard for several seconds, making her want to squirm. "Beating yourself up?"

Damn him.

"Some." Endlessly.

"Normal."

"Sucks."

"Everyone makes mistakes," he said quietly, as if that was top secret.

"Mine could've killed me."

"That's the kind of work we're in."

She looked away, afraid her doubts would show in her eyes. Neither of them spoke for several minutes, and she was almost able to block out all thoughts and pretend everything was okay. She was starting to appreciate his company, just a little, when he ruined it.

"We can save the official stuff for later, but I'm curious…what happened, Faith?"

"I tripped," she said, knowing she couldn't avoid talking about it at some point. Might as well get it over with. "It was like a maze in there. I don't know what I ran into, but I landed on my butt. Don't think I lost consciousness, but I might as well have—I was really out of it."

She paused to take another drink.

"I've never seen an interior like that," Joe agreed.

"My radio was gone, helmet fell off. Then I realized I'd lost the hose, too."

"You weren't very far from it when I found you."

She closed her eyes. "Humiliating."

"No. Stop it, Faith."

"I don't know how long I tried to find it. I swear I was going in circles."

"Happened to me once," he said.

"What did?" She found it hard to imagine him having any difficulties in a fire, even though she knew most firefighters had stories. She'd heard plenty from the old-timers in her five years on the job.

"Lost the line once in a fire and couldn't find it to save my life, no pun intended."

"What happened?"

"I came across it eventually. But I know that feeling where you think you're not going to make it out."

Nausea welled up in her gut. She broke into a cold sweat.

"How'd you end up alone in there, Faith?" Joe's voice was low but intense. "That's not like you."

"How do you know what's like me? We've been working together for less than a month." Granted, she was with him almost every single stinking shift.

"I've seen enough to know you're a damn good firefighter. You had a respectable record in San Antonio."

Tears burned her eyes, so she closed them and rubbed her fingers over them as if she had a headache.

"That's not meant as a criticism," he said. "I'm trying to understand what happened."

"It's...I don't know." She studied the knee of his uniform pants. "The accident in San Antonio. I think it messed me up."

"The one that broke your collarbone?"

"That'd be the one." She stalled by taking another

long drink. Debating how much to say. "The fire at the Sea Breeze Hotel a couple of weeks back?"

He sat up and turned toward her, putting both feet on the ground between their chairs. "I remember it."

"You sent me in behind Penn."

He nodded and touched her forearm gently, as if urging her to continue.

"I lost it, Joe. I mean really lost it. Froze up and nearly ran back out the door as soon as we got inside." She expected him to say something, but he remained silent. "I thought I was having a heart attack for a second."

"Panic attack."

"I almost didn't make it any farther."

"But you did."

"Penn didn't notice I stopped. I had to back him up."

"It's not an unusual reaction the first time back in after an injury."

"That doesn't make it okay," she said, her voice barely more than a whisper. "It was horrible."

"But you overcame it on your own."

"Today was the first big fire since that one. I was terrified the same thing would happen. Those feelings, the panic, started as soon as the engine stopped."

She swallowed hard, the same feelings threatening to overcome her now. "I had to talk myself through it. Force myself to go inside."

"You overcompensated," Joe suggested.

"Over-somethinged. I couldn't stand the thought of someone noticing me standing there like an idiot. I didn't bother double-checking to make sure Nate was ready. Didn't even think about it. Just rushed in as soon as I could move."

"I wish you'd said something before today. That's one of the basics, Faith."

She bolted off the chaise, hands clenched, and went to the edge of the patio. "Don't you think I know that? Believe me, it's killing me."

"You could've corrected the mistake if you'd radioed out or come back to get Nate."

Yeah. She could've done lots of things a hell of a lot better. She'd been over every single option about four hundred times in her mind. She didn't need anyone telling her what she'd done wrong—she could do that herself just fine. "I'm going to the water." Maybe *into* the water. Maybe soaking her head would make her feel marginally better.

Two minutes later, after she'd sat down hard on the cushiony sand, Joe strode up beside her. She closed her eyes. Could a woman not suffer humiliation in private?

"You know I have to report it all," he said, lowering his large frame next to her on the sand.

"Of course. I can't wait till my dad hears what an idiot I am." And so much for earning anyone's respect around here.

Way to go, Faith. You deserve it.

"He knows you well enough to understand it was a fluke."

"That's just it, Joe. It wasn't a fluke. I screwed up big time because I *am* messed up. My head is wrong."

"You had a building fall on you. That can mess a person up."

"Not a firefighter." She chewed on her lip as she stared at the waves coming in. They were relatively calm right now, contrasting with a wild surf just that morning, when she and Joe had reported for their shift. Similarly, the storm inside Faith had died down and become a single nagging pulse of doubt. Fear. "Maybe my mom was right, after all," she said in a small voice.

"Right about what?" Joe asked, leaning closer. "What does your mom have to do with anything?"

"She hates that I'm a firefighter. She's always said it's not a career for women."

"I suspect you've never agreed with her about that?"

Faith shook her head.

"Then why start now?"

She pierced him with a sharp look. "Bumbling around in a fire, nearly getting myself killed. That tends to make a person doubt herself."

"Stop the doubting right now." He barked it out like a direct order.

"Sure thing. Just tell me how."

Joe locked his hands around his knees and shrugged. "Hell if I know. But I'm certain you can do it. You're smart. You told me you just passed your haz-mat certification, right?"

"That was on paper."

"Proves you know your stuff. You're a strong person, Faith."

"I don't feel strong. I feel like a fool."

He shook his head, staring out at the Gulf. Beyond. "It takes strength to stand up to a member of your family who doesn't believe in what you do."

"It's not that she doesn't believe in it. She just doesn't like it."

"Same difference."

Faith frowned. "I believe that's called stubbornness, not strength."

"Your mother has really never supported your career?"

"That's an accurate assessment. She and my dad used to argue all the time when I was a teenager and insisted I wanted to follow in his footsteps."

"I don't know what I'd be doing right now if my dad hadn't been a firefighter."

"You don't think you'd be doing this?"

Joe hesitated. "No idea. My dad was the chief, my mom is a fire buff and an original member of the Burn Foundation. I don't think I ever really considered other options."

He seemed genuinely bothered by the discovery.

"You love fighting fires," Faith said. "I can tell when we get a good call."

"I like my job."

"Sure, but this is more. You...come alive when there's a fire."

Joe nodded. "Hell, yeah. Best part of the job. Don't think you could find a firefighter who wouldn't agree with that."

She flinched. Most days, she'd be the first to agree, but lately she didn't know whether to be excited or full of dread when they got some action. "Don't you think you'll miss that if you become assistant chief?" she asked, relieved to have the spotlight off her own weaknesses.

"Might. That's the way it goes." His answer came quickly. Too quickly.

She watched him in the near darkness, wondering how much thought he'd really given to what it would be like, moving up in the department. Sure, he'd planned it his whole life. But planning as a kid with big dreams and really considering something as an adult were two different things.

Who was she to point that out to him, though?

Who was she to tell anyone how to live his or her life or do his or her job? After today she wondered if she would ever be able to do hers right again.

"We were talking about you, not me," Joe said sternly, and if Faith hadn't been so depressed she might've grinned.

"Thought we were done."

"You know I have to write you up."

That was the insult on top of the injury, as far as she was concerned. "Yep."

"There's no way around it. You could've been seriously—"

"I know, Joe." She sucked in the cool evening air, trying to calm herself. It wasn't his fault, but the way he was trying to justify it only made her feel worse. As if she'd let him down as well as herself. "I get it. I told you I don't want any special favors. Anyone else would get the same treatment."

"Correct." He glanced behind them at the station, which was lit up like a stadium on game night. He slid his hand over hers, startling Faith. "Right now, however, I'm treating you differently than I would the other firefighters."

She glanced down at their entwined fingers. Knew she should pull away, yet couldn't. Call her Ms. Hypocrite, but his hand was strong. Warm. Reassuring somehow.

"I'm going to go out on a limb here and guess that you're harder on yourself than anyone else ever could be," he said. "Speaking as your captain, we need to find a way to get you over your hesitation, because that could be deadly."

Faith nodded, her throat blocked by a lump of emotion. He wasn't telling her anything she didn't know, but his use of the word *we* made her feel as if maybe she wasn't hopeless. Maybe she could figure out how to get her mojo back.

"I'm behind you, Faith. I know you're better than what happened today."

"Is that spoken as my captain, too?"

He looked back at the water, the white tops of the waves visible in the dark. "Yes. And...as something else."

She was afraid to ask what. Her father's protégé? A friend? Something else? Something forbidden?

Yeah, definitely best not to ask.

She swallowed hard. "Thank you. I'm going to go inside now."

Before she touched him again or, God forbid, started liking him even more.

CHAPTER FOURTEEN

"GREAT DAY FOR FISHING," Joe said, leaning back in his seat in the stern of the *Hot Water,* the chief's trawler yacht. It was more a luxury boat than something meant for fishing, but it worked just fine to sit out here with a couple lines in. They were in the bay, close to where it met the Gulf of Mexico. One of the chief's preferred fishing spots. They were near enough to shore that Joe could make out some people there.

"Not too bad," Chief Peligni said, looking up at the cloudless, early evening sky through his sunglasses. "Don't get out here much anymore."

"Shame to keep this beauty tied up."

Joe had brought up the boat the other day at work, planning to get Chief Peligni out of the house, as he'd promised Faith. The chief had beat him to it, though, inviting him to an evening of fishing.

"Suppose it is. Need another beer?"

Joe nodded, and the older man stood and went into the cabin, returning a couple minutes later with two cans and a bag of cheese popcorn.

"So," the chief said, settling on one of the seats and putting his feet up. "You going to tell me what the hell happened with Faith the other day? The reality version and not some damn watered-down crap from the report."

That explained the invitation, Joe thought. Just as well. He'd been expecting to have this discussion before now. But Chief Peligni had seemed distracted, not really engaged at work.

"What do you want to know?" he asked, setting the beer aside. This could get tricky. He was sure to be straddling a fine line between what the chief needed to find out and what Faith had told Joe in confidence about her state of mind.

"How in the name of God above did she end up needing you to carry her out of a goddamn structure fire? She's better than that, Joe. What happened?"

Joe told him about the furniture store, that there had been crap everywhere, making it a bitch to get through. "She tripped. Hit her head."

"Got that from the report. Why was she alone? Did someone else screw up?"

"No. According to Faith, she thought Nate was behind her when she went in."

"Dammit. The girl knows better than that in her sleep."

Joe was in full agreement, but knowing what she'd been going through since her injury made him more sympathetic. However, he didn't dare defend her to her father without sharing that information, or the chief would be suspicious of his motives.

Granted, there was good reason for that suspicion. The dreams Joe had been having about Faith were proof enough.

He needed to do something about his attraction to her. Maybe move to North Dakota.

"She was off her game, I guess," he said vaguely. "I don't think it'll happen again."

"No. Faith's good."

Joe's cell phone buzzed in his pocket, and he took it out, surprised he had a signal out here. His stepfather, according to caller ID.

"Mendoza," he said automatically.

"Joe, I'm at the hospital," Jorge said, making Joe's gut sink. "It's your mom."

"What's going on, Jorge?" Joe stood, as if that could help him absorb the news better. His mom frequented hospitals, especially lately, but he'd never get used to it.

"Apparently she's got pneumonia in both lungs. Hitting her pretty hard."

Joe swore. That was an understatement, he knew. A head cold hit his mom hard due to her fragile health. Lupus and vasculitis weakened her system significantly. Pneumonia could... He shook his head. *Not going there.*

"You in Corpus? At Memorial?" he asked.

"Room 319."

"I'll be there. Thanks, Jorge."

"Get here safe. I'm not going to be the one to tell her you're in a car wreck."

"See you in a couple hours." Joe ended the call and swore some more.

"What's the matter?" Chief Peligni asked.

"My mom's in the hospital with pneumonia. With her other health problems, it's serious." He stared at his phone helplessly. "Possibly deadly. I need to get to her."

"She's in Corpus Christi?"

Joe nodded, pacing the deck, feeling trapped.

"Pull the lines in. I'll take you to the marina and Faith can get you up there."

"I can get myself up there, Chief." He started reeling in the lines as the chief had directed.

"You've had four beers."

"So have you."

"I've had three, and I'm not wanting to drive a hundred miles on the highway. There's no boat traffic between here and my slip." He nodded in that direction, and they were close enough that Joe could see he spoke the truth. "Besides, I got you doubled in weight."

"I'm okay," Joe said, but he knew Chief Peligni was right. "Faith has better things to do with her time."

The chief had already pulled his phone out and pressed a speed dial button for his daughter. He briefly told her what was going on, nodded repeatedly, answered her questions and ended the call.

"She'll be waiting at the marina parking lot."

"Fine." Joe was bothered by inconveniencing Faith, but frankly, he couldn't dwell on that when his mom was in grave danger. Her immune system was weak on a good day. She'd been worn down recently. After all her years of battling the autoimmune disease, he should be used to the possibility of a worst-case scenario, but he wasn't. He'd never accept that his mom wouldn't be around forever.

By the time they made it to the marina, Joe was ready to dive off the side of the boat and swim to get there faster.

He and the chief tied up the boat and he stepped ashore. "You coming?" he asked as he walked along the narrow pier to the main dock.

Chief Peligni shook his head and waved him off. Joe didn't have time to question him. It was probably best that he stayed put and let the beer lose its effect, anyway.

Faith stood against the wall of the marina store, watching him approach. As preoccupied as he was, he still couldn't help noticing how good she looked in thigh-hugging jeans that ended just below her knees, a white tank top and denim jacket. Heels made her muscled legs look even longer than usual. Her hair was held back by a thin headband, with chin-length strands left to frame her beautiful face. She looked like...one hell of a woman. A very pretty, feminine one. Her appearance revealed nothing of the very capable firefighter she was. As he walked nearer, he noted the large turquoise pendant that hung enticingly just above her cleavage.

"Took you guys forever to get back," she said, pushing herself off the wall as he approached.

"Tell me about it. Faith, I'm sorry to interrupt your night. You look like you had plans."

"Just a movie with Nadia and Mercedes. No big deal."

"Well, thank you. I appreciate it. I could've made it—"

"Joe?" she said, clicking the doors unlocked as they approached her Subaru.

"Yeah?"

"Technically, right now, you're not my officer, since we're off duty. I'm fine with driving you to Corpus. You know I respect the heck out of you, but please, just close your mouth and get in the car."

He stopped a few feet from the passenger door and stared at her.

"Your mom is waiting," she said sternly.

He mimicked her sternness, nodded and did as she said. Unfortunately, he found her sexy as hell when she got bossy.

FAITH'S HEART WENT OUT to the four men—Joe, his stepfather and two stepbrothers—as the doctor walked out of the otherwise empty waiting room on the third floor of the hospital.

No one said a word while they absorbed the prognosis: Joe's mother was severely ill, her fever climbing dangerously higher as her weakened body waited for some powerful antibiotics to knock out the bacteria. She was in intensive care and had been sleeping since Joe and Faith had arrived.

"She's stubborn," Troy said, leaning back stiffly in one of the uncomfortable, lime-green chairs. He wore neatly tailored pants and a button-down shirt, even at this late hour. "If anyone in her condition can beat this, it's Carmen."

Joe abruptly stood and walked out of the glassed-in room to the main hall. Faith craned her neck to see where he was heading, but he paced out of her line of sight.

She looked back at the three men still in the room and caught Joe's stepfather watching her.

"I'm glad you're here with him," Mr. Vargas said,

leaning forward, elbows on his knees. "He tries to be such an island, but this could really tear him up."

"I wish there was something I could do," Faith said, detesting her helplessness.

The other stepbrother, Ryan, stood and ambled to the doorway, repeatedly rubbing his fingers over his goatee. "How involved are you two?" he asked Faith.

She shook her head. "We're not." It wasn't really a lie. Kissing once didn't make them involved. Just stupid.

Ryan angled his head slightly, thoughtfully. "Must've misread things. Too bad. He needs someone like you in his life."

"He's my officer," Faith said, sounding defensive. She stood. "I'm going to go find him."

Mr. Vargas nodded, sidetracked by his own sorrow. His affection for Joe's mom was obvious. Heartwarming.

"Can I bring you guys something from the machines?" she asked. "A drink or some chips or something?"

All three shook their heads, and Troy thanked her.

She headed down the hall Joe had taken, but didn't see any sign of him. At the nurses' station, an older woman in cartoon character scrubs must have noticed her confusion.

"Looking for the big guy? Navy-blue shirt?"

Faith nodded.

"He's out on the terrace." She indicated a glass door farther down the hall.

"Thank you."

Faith went through the door, which led to an open-air

rooftop terrace. Neatly trimmed shrubs had been shaped into hearts and stars and placed at intervals around the perimeter, and a raised flower bed showed sprouts of green beginning to pop through the soil. The terrace was deserted except for Joe, who stood near the low wall that ran around the entire area. Because of the angles of the odd-shaped space, he was in partial profile to her. He leaned on the wall, looking out over who knew what, seeing nothing, she was sure.

She walked toward him, the cork soles of her wedge shoes making very little noise on the pebbled concrete. He was so lost in his thoughts he didn't appear to hear her approach. When Faith touched his forearm, he jumped.

"Hey," she said, not letting her hand drop.

He looked straight at her, a deep sadness etched into his normally stoic face. "Hey." There was no hint of the ass-kicking, confident fire captain in his voice.

"Can I get you anything? Some coffee?"

"Some grain alcohol," he said solemnly.

"I wish that would make things better somehow."

"You and me both."

"Okay if I stand out here with you?"

"Fine by me."

Faith joined him in leaning on the wall and watched the comings and goings of people below at the brightly lit entrance to the emergency department.

"You don't have to stay here. I can get back to San Amaro on my own," Joe said after several minutes.

"I don't mind."

"You go on duty in the morning. Go home. Sleep."

"So do you," she said, neither one of them admitting they didn't know what the morning would bring or if he'd be able to make it in to work at all. "I can catch a nap inside if I get tired. Right now I'm fine."

He looked down, seeming to focus on her for the first time since she'd come outside. "You won't leave, will you?"

She shook her head. "You're beginning to know me well."

"I know you're stubborn as all get-out."

"Thank you."

With a ghost of a smile, he put his arm around her and tugged her to his side. He held her there, both of them watching an ambulance pull up and unload a patient below. She figured he needed the contact, the human touch, and it felt good to be tucked into his side.

"Your steps seem like decent guys," she said after several minutes, wanting to somehow reach out to him.

"They're okay. For lawyers."

"All three of them are lawyers?" Joe didn't talk much about them. In fact, before the drive up here, she hadn't known he had any stepbrothers, and had heard him mention his stepfather only in passing.

"All three of them. Same firm. Do me a favor and don't ask them about it. They'll get to talking like a bunch of girls—no offense—and never shut up."

Smiling, she said, "No offense taken. I'm not often accused of being chatty."

"I like that about you."

"So you're not close to Troy or Ryan?"

He shook his head. "We hang out sometimes to appease my mother, but it's just for show."

"They seem genuinely concerned about you," she said, recalling the conversation after he'd walked out of the waiting room.

"No reason to be concerned. I'll be fine."

"I was once accused of overusing the word *fine* when I didn't want to get into detail."

"Yeah?" He peered down at her with a tired but almost amused expression. "Who accused you of that?"

"Some wise guy know-it-all officer type."

"As long as you don't let those officer types hear you talk like that about them you'll be fine."

She glanced up at him to gauge whether she'd offended him. It was difficult to tell. "We're not on duty right now. Technically, you're not my—"

"Not your captain. Got it."

"My captain wouldn't have his arm around me. That could get him in trouble."

A low sound in his chest was probably as close as he'd get to a laugh tonight. "Point taken."

"Are you ready to go back in? Sit with your family?"

"Surrogate family," he corrected. "It's easier to be out here."

"How come?"

He removed his arm and she couldn't help noticing the cool breeze that blew over her. Leaning on the wall again, he said, "Don't have to put on an act."

"You would with your stepbrothers?"

Joe shrugged. "Maybe."

"It seems like they care a lot about your mom."

"Jorge would do anything for her."

"Troy and Ryan must be concerned, too, or they wouldn't be here. Do they have families?"

"Ryan's married. No kids. They're here for their dad."

"They're worried about you."

Joe studied her as if he really didn't believe that. How could he not? Faith wished he saw that he was going to need those guys in the near future, especially if his mom didn't recover.

She looked at her watch. "Almost time for the next visit." The nurses were letting them in one at a time for a few minutes every other hour. "Let's go."

Straightening, he inhaled deeply, as if bolstering himself, and nodded. As they walked back inside, he put his hand on her lower back. Faith liked the feel of it more than she should, but she shoved that out of her mind. There were more pressing things to worry about.

CHAPTER FIFTEEN

JOE LEFT HIS MOM'S intensive care room when Ryan showed up for his turn. He nodded on his way out.

His mom still didn't know he was there. He'd watched her sleep for the few minutes he was allowed in, willing her to wake up for a second just so he could tell her he loved her.

The doctor had made a point of saying there was hope that the antibiotics would take hold, but he'd also made it clear they weren't seeing any signs of that yet and couldn't predict how her body would react. It would take time for the drugs to bring about any improvement. While Joe hadn't allowed his mom to speak of worst-case scenarios in the past, he was forced to face up to them tonight. Kind of like having his head rammed into a cement wall. Painful and sure to leave lasting damage.

Achy and wrung out, he walked slowly back to the small waiting room that was starting to feel like their own personal home base. Unlike the bright-as-day main hallway, where nurses and other medical personnel hurried around like busy worker bees, the room was secluded and had lights that could be dimmed. Faith had stretched out on a row of chairs and fallen asleep, her hair cascading over the side of the thin cushion.

The urge to go to her, to sit on the seat nearest her and pull her head onto his legs, run his fingers through her silky hair, overwhelmed him. Oddly, it'd be the most natural thing in the world to have her that close while she slept. But he sat near her feet, leaving an empty chair between them, because they weren't alone. Regardless of Faith's insistence that being off duty meant their difference in rank didn't matter, it did. What was more, she was the daughter of his mentor and the man who would hopefully support his bid for the position of assistant chief.

So instead of touching her, Joe reclined on his uncomfortable, too small chair, resting his head on the back and watching her surreptitiously. Finally admitting to himself that he was genuinely glad she was there.

"Joe!" Ryan appeared at the doorway of the waiting room. "Get in there, man. She's awake. Thought you'd want to talk to her before she drifts off again."

Joe rushed out, hollering thanks over his shoulder. When he got to his mom's room, her eyes were closed, and disappointment weighed him down. He stepped into the dim room, the rhythmic sound of the machines pulsing. Taking her frail hand gently in his, he sat on the edge of the chair that had been pulled up close to her side.

When she slowly turned her head toward him and her eyes fluttered open, he lowered his forehead to their entwined hands and said a silent prayer of thanks.

"Mama."

"Joey. You made it." Her voice was just a thread of sound, as if she hadn't used it for weeks.

"Of course I made it. How are you doing?"

In typical Carmen style, she nodded slowly, attempting a smile. Always keeping it positive, even when she likely felt as if she'd been dragged around by a ladder truck.

His throat swelled up and he kissed her fingers.

"Your body has to fight, Mama."

"I'll be okay. I'm not ready to leave you yet. You're not ready."

"Damn straight I'm not." If her will could keep her alive, he could rest easy. She was too worried about him and how he'd get along without her, without any true family. Unfortunately, he knew all too well it didn't necessarily work that way.

Her eyes drooped and she fought to keep them open. Her face was pale beneath the oxygen tube that ran under her nose and across her cheeks, and Joe thought how unlike his mother this woman appeared.

"Go to sleep, Mama. I love you."

He held on to her until her husband came to the door. Joe had never questioned Jorge's feelings for Carmen, but the look on the man's face as he gazed at her was so full of love and heartbreak that it finally hit Joe. When his mother passed away, this man would lose his life companion, the one he chose to spend day in and day out with.

Joe wouldn't be alone in his pain. And maybe... maybe there could be more to a stepfamily than just appeasing his mother, after all.

EVERY MINUTE OF THE NIGHT seemed to last an hour as they prayed for some change, a positive sign, even though the doctor said it was too early.

Surprisingly, Troy and Ryan were still there at 2:00 a.m. Not as surprising, so was Faith. When she'd woken up from her nap, Joe had tried again to convince her to drive back to San Amaro Island, but it had only been for show on his part. He wanted her there with him. The implications of that were something he'd have to examine later.

Faith leaned close to him, allowing him to catch her scent when he turned toward her.

"I need coffee," she said. "What can I get for you?"

He started to shake his head, but she held up a finger to stop him.

"No. You're eating something. Or drinking. Take your pick. Beer doesn't count as dinner, and even if it did, that was light-years ago."

"For being such a tomboy, you've got some serious mother hen tendencies."

"Consider me well-rounded. What do you want? Coffee?"

He nodded and twisted to take his wallet out. "A package of chips or nuts, too."

"I've got it," she said, refusing the bills he tried to hand her.

"I'll go with you," Troy said, standing and stretching. "Want anything, Ryan?"

"The biggest, most caffeinated bottle of pop you can find."

"You got it." Troy turned to Jorge, who was awkwardly sprawled in one of the chairs, snoring. The younger man shrugged and led Faith out.

Ryan stood and rolled his neck in circles. Paced

across the room. Joe's eyes were shut, but sleep eluded him in spite of how bone weary he was. He felt the chair next to him shift as Ryan sat down.

"How you holding up?" his stepbrother asked, his leg bouncing rhythmically.

"Holding up," Joe said. "Not much else I can do."

Ryan nodded and neither of them spoke for several minutes. Joe didn't have the energy to think of a coherent sentence.

"Did you know that our mom died of cancer?" Ryan asked.

"Knew she died when you guys were kids."

"Teenagers. Long, drawn-out deal."

"This must bring it all back," Joe said.

"Little bit. It's different when it's your mother."

Joe didn't respond. He appreciated the sentiment, but wasn't up for a heart-to-heart.

"All I got to say is it sucks and it's exhausting and I'm sorry as hell you're going through it, man. I'm going to track down my drink." As he stood, he clapped Joe on the back.

Several minutes later, Faith and Troy were stretched out on the floor of the waiting room, feasting on candy bars and mini doughnuts. Ryan had wandered back in as well by the time the doctor returned.

"Dad," Ryan said.

Jorge jerked awake and straightened slowly, as if his back was stiff or achy.

Joe watched the doctor for a sign of what news he might have for them, his heart thundering in his chest.

Dr. Zander sat on one of the chairs and smiled tiredly

at them. "I don't want to give you false hope. There isn't any big news. It could be days before we really know how she's going to do."

"But she's no worse?" Jorge asked.

"She's holding her own."

"If her condition was going to deteriorate, wouldn't it have already happened?" Jorge was voicing some of the thoughts that had circled repeatedly through Joe's head all night as the hours ticked by.

"It's hard to say," the doctor responded. "Let's just focus on the fact that she's hanging in there. I wish I could give you something more concrete but..."

"Understood," Troy said.

"We might be able to rustle up a place for at least one of you to sleep," Dr. Zander offered. "Like I said, it's going to be a while for solid news of any kind."

"We might take you up on that." Again, Troy acted as their spokesperson. "Thanks, Doc."

The doctor's mouth tilted into a sympathetic half grin as he nodded at them and left them alone again.

Faith came over and sat next to Joe. She didn't touch him or let on that there was anything between them more than two people who worked together, but Joe caught her concern, the understanding in her eyes.

"Are you planning to make it to work?" she asked almost apologetically.

He looked at his watch. Quarter to four. "My interview's at ten."

"For the job?" she asked, her eyes widening.

"For the job." He considered his options, feeling torn.

"Go ahead, Joe," his stepfather said. "Nothing you

can do here. You know what your mom would want if she was awake to have her say."

Joe exhaled shakily, fatigue and emotion taking their toll. "She'd tell me to get my ass to the interview and land the job."

"I'm sure you can reschedule it," Faith said. "I'll talk to my dad."

"Hell, no, you won't." Joe stood and stretched his arms over his head to get some blood flowing. "I can talk to him myself if I need to."

"If anything changes here, I'll get the company jet to pick you up," Jorge said. "You can be here in twenty minutes."

"You going to stick around?" Joe asked.

"I'm taking the day off." Jorge crossed his leg over the opposite knee. "You can spell me when your shift is over. After you get some sleep."

"I work twenty-four hours," Joe reminded him.

"I'll stop by later to give Dad a break," Troy said.

"Go to work, man. Get the promotion." Ryan stuffed the last powdered doughnut in his mouth.

"Okay." Joe was ambivalent, unable to summon any enthusiasm for his interview, but he figured that was due to lack of sleep. What drove him to agree in the end was that his mother would, indeed, be disappointed if he didn't make it to his interview because of her. Especially if she recovered enough to find out about it. There was nothing he could do, sitting here in this dingy, ugly room, and that fact was starting to drive him up the damn wall.

"You can sleep on the way," Faith said. "I have

enough caffeine in me to get through the next week."
She held up an extra large paper cup from the twenty-
four hour coffee shop on the hospital's main floor.

They said goodbye to the others, and Joe checked
for another update on his mom on their way out. No
changes whatsoever since the doctor had been in, which
was what they expected.

He and Faith rode the elevator down and walked out
to her Subaru in silence. The briskness of the night air
did nothing to wake him up, nor did the ambulance that
whisked into the emergency area down the way, sirens
off but lights flashing. That was someone else's problem. He had enough of his own.

Once they were in the car, they both sat there, not
moving or speaking. Faith leaned against her headrest
and angled her face toward him.

Joe exhaled slowly, coming down from the intense
stress of the past several hours. Not that his worries
would be over anytime soon. But just getting out of the
sterile hospital and that drab room with the puke-green
chairs made it easier to breathe.

"Thank you," he said. "I couldn't act like it in there,
but I was glad to have you with me."

"Hmm. Do I give you the company line here or the
other one?"

"What's the company line?"

"The fire chief told me to get you to your mother.
I'm sure he wouldn't approve if I had dropped you at
the front door and driven off."

"What's the other line?"

"I didn't mind any of it. Not that you needed me there, with all the Vargas men hovering."

Joe disagreed to himself about whether he'd needed her there. He thought back over the long night. "They're decent. Like you said. I don't think I really ever gave them a chance. Just assumed we were all making the best of an awkward, late-in-life blending of families."

"They kind of…acted like family."

"Yeah. They did." Joe was surprised to find that he genuinely agreed with her.

He was sure he couldn't have gotten through this night without these people. His stepbrothers, Jorge and most of all, Faith.

As he leaned his head against the window and drifted off, he was vaguely aware that that in itself was more than a small dilemma.

CHAPTER SIXTEEN

AFTER AN ENTIRE NIGHT at the hospital, the workday at the station had been anything but restful. They'd been running since eight that morning and barely stopped during the fourteen hours that followed. Faith couldn't remember when they'd had so many alarms in one shift. It'd almost compared to an average day in the San Antonio department.

She should be unconscious.

She should be curled up in her hard but sufficient bunk, sleeping like a baby.

She should *not* be lying here thinking about Joe. Drifting off every so often, but then tossing and turning, disturbed by her thoughts.

Last night she'd seen a different side from the in-charge, unflappable fire captain. She'd glimpsed a man who would do just about anything for his mother and was, understandably, scared to death of losing her. A man who wanted to be stoic and strong, but who felt things deeply.

The only opportunity she'd had all day to ask about his mother's condition had come after lunch, once he'd returned from his interview. The others had left the kitchen, and Faith and Joe had found themselves alone for all of five minutes before another alarm came in. By that point, he'd spoken to Mr. Vargas once, and not surprisingly, there'd been no significant change. And while it was good news that she was no worse, the lack of positive change was getting to Joe. Faith could tell by the raw fear in his eyes.

She whipped the sheets off and sat up in her bunk. Rubbing her hands over her eyes, she made a decision she might live to regret.

She knew Joe would be awake, in spite of their past twenty-four hours. Knew he was either in his office working or in his private bunk room. He'd told her he avoided sleeping at the station as much as he could because he hated being awakened by the alarm.

Knowing that he was up, alone, probably tormented by concern, she couldn't just sit there.

She glanced down at the clothes she slept in—yoga pants and a light blue tank with a built-in bra. Nothing she hadn't been seen in before whenever she ventured out of her room in the middle of the night. Her hair was probably a mess, but she didn't care. She wasn't going to him with the goal of turning him on.

When she opened her door, she peeked out like a fugitive in the night. There was no one stirring anywhere; most likely her colleagues were collapsed the way she should be, trying to get in more than a few minutes' nap before the alarm sounded again.

If it went off while she was talking to Joe, in his room, things could get interesting.

Yeah, she could live to regret this decision, but that wasn't enough to dissuade her. Once she was in the

hall, she couldn't make herself turn back and not find
out how Joe was doing.

She walked, acting nonchalant, past all the closed
doors, seeing no lights and hearing no signs of anyone
awake. When she got to the end of the hall, she glanced
over her shoulder before turning toward the officers'
bunks and offices, just in case.

Joe's private room was the third door on the left.
Just as she'd expected, a dim light shone underneath it.
Her heart raced and she wondered again what she was
doing. Would he be pissed that she'd crossed the line
and come to his personal quarters? Before she could
lose her nerve—or be discovered by someone—she
knocked softly.

The door opened almost immediately, but only about
a foot.

"Something wrong, Faith?" he asked.

She shook her head, about to speak, when he bent
down.

"No," he said firmly. "Get back, both of you." When
he stood, he held two kittens.

Faith tried to hide her laugh.

"Come in before the whole herd escapes," Joe said,
whisking her in and shutting the door quickly. "Cinder,
don't even think about it."

"And here I was worried you were all alone." Faith
bent down to pet the black kitten, which clawed at the
bottom of her pant leg. "I figured you'd found a home
for these guys. When did you move them in here?"

"Few days ago. Sanchez complained about having
them in the office. Wuss claims he's allergic to them."

"Where's Blaze?" she asked, scanning the cramped room for the orange kitten who'd had trouble nursing. The mama cat was snoozing in a fuzzy nest of blankets in the corner by an overfilled bookcase. A light gray baby was curled up next to her, but the rest of the litter were awake and ready to get into mischief, crawling all over the room.

"My aunt has her for now. Still needs to be fed by hand every few hours and I can't always do it when I'm on duty. I'm trying to convince her to make it permanent."

Faith knelt on the floor and held her hand out to the mother cat, speaking in a soft voice. "Hey, girlie, you're a good mama."

The cat raised her head and sniffed the offered hand, then closed her eyes again. Faith stroked her soft fur.

"Why don't you put them in one of the common areas?" she asked. "I bet some of those tough guys would fall in love."

"Maybe when they get a little bigger. Not sure I trust a couple of the Neanderthals with them."

The black kitten who'd attacked Faith's pants when she came in crawled up on her lap. Her tiny claws dug through the material into her flesh, eliciting a pained laugh.

"You need attention, obviously," Faith said, picking her up and holding her at eye level. "Are you getting the shaft from big, bad Joe?"

"She'd like you to think she is," he grumbled. He'd sat down on the low bed along the wall opposite the bookcase. The room wasn't much longer than the bed and there was only about three feet between it and the bookcase. The wall was adorned with posters of old cars. *Hot rods* was the term that came to her mind.

One of the two kittens Joe had picked up when Faith came in was now on his shoulder, nibbling at his ear. The other had decided his arm was the place to be and was drifting off to sleep, cradled like a baby. He gently put the ear-biter on the floor.

"What are you doing here, Faith?" His voice was quiet, mostly businesslike, but a hint of gentleness, of the Joe she'd spent the night in the hospital with, slipped through.

She put Cinder down beside the mother cat and moved up to the mattress next to him, since it was the only place besides the floor to sit. With one leg drawn under her, she faced him.

"Checking on you. Have you heard anything more about your mom?"

"Her temperature's still high, but that's to be expected, or so they keep telling me. In other words, no real news."

"She hasn't gotten worse, though, right?"

"Not that they've admitted to." He ran a hand over his short hair. "It's damn hard to be here, but sitting in that waiting room for another night…not sure I have it in me."

"It sucks to not be able to do something for her."

He nodded and ran his large hand over the tiny kitten's back. "Yeah, it does. Work is at least keeping my mind occupied. Or it did until everything slowed down."

"You should try sleeping."

"So should you."

"Been there, done that," she said. "How'd your interview go?"

"Not too bad, I don't think, when you take into account an all-nighter and a mother in intensive care."

At that, Faith reached out and put her hand on his thigh just above his knee. "Did you tell the committee what was going on?"

He shook his head. "Your dad referred to it once, but if I can't be at the top of my game after staying up all night, then I'm not doing my job."

"It wasn't your standard up-fighting-fires night."

He ignored her statement and she self-consciously removed her hand from his leg.

"I imagine you did well in spite of everything," Faith said. "You don't seem to let things get to you."

He turned slightly and met her gaze head-on. The kitten apparently didn't like the motion and stumbled down his leg to the safety of its mama.

"Some things I can't prevent from getting to me, it seems." His look intensified, became pointed.

Faith's pulse reacted by going triple time. "Like what?"

"I think you know." He took her hand in his, wove their fingers together. "You shouldn't come to my room in the middle of the night, Faith."

She nodded, her voice momentarily caught in her throat. "I'll go."

He nodded, too, but at the same time leaned closer and gently pulled her hand toward him. With his other palm, he cradled her chin. Caressed her lower lip with his rough thumb. His eyelids drooped heavily as he closed the space between them and touched his lips lightly to hers. His fingers wound around to the back of her neck, beneath the cascade of her hair, and the kiss became more urgent. Faith wasn't sure she could pull herself away if the alarm did go off. Some things were worth getting busted for.

Throwing what little caution she'd had to the wind, she wrapped her arms around his neck, wanting him closer still. He slid his tongue into her mouth, a sexy moan coming from his throat as they tasted each other, explored. His kiss was a reflection of the man—confident, uncompromising, yet tender. Thorough. His touch made her feel…treasured.

Without breaking the contact of their lips, he leaned her back diagonally across his narrow bed. Faith's knee came up beside him, and as Joe's body covered hers, his hardness pressed between her legs, making her body ache for him. His fingers inched up beneath her tank. She ran her hands over his muscled back. The breadth of his shoulders made her feel delicate. Decidedly feminine.

When his hand slid beneath the elastic and his warm palm covered her breast, a needy sound came from her. She arched into him.

"You're so damn sexy, Faith," he said into her ear. "Tough and hard on the surface, but soft. Beautiful."

She'd never been so turned on by a voice before. Of course the words were doing their part, too…and his hands…and lips….

Without warning, pain pricked at her thigh and she

let out a gasp. Rising up on an elbow, she realized the culprit was the little black kitten, its claws sinking into her leg.

Joe scooped up the tiny animal and held it in front of his face. "Bad cat!" A grin tugged at his lips, though, and Faith started laughing quietly.

He set it on the floor and Faith sat up, her heart still racing, blood still humming. She pulled her tank down and ran a hand through her hair as the reality of their situation sank in.

"Good thing the cat interrupted," she said. She'd been on the verge of losing her mind and her judgment.

She stood and again tried to straighten her hair.

Joe rose as well and kissed her, then pressed his forehead to hers. "Your hair is fine. You look good." His voice was gravelly. So damn alluring.

He backed her slowly up until his body held hers against the door, and once again, he sought out her lips with his. Thirty seconds ago, she'd been thinking how stupid it was to come here, and now she was succumbing to him again. Loving his touch. Wanting more.

"Joe," she managed to gasp. "I need to get out of here."

He acknowledged that with a deep, sexy sound and kissed her again.

"We're at work," she said. "What if we get an alarm?"

That seemed to penetrate his brain, and he groaned in frustration. Drawing her to him, he kissed her temple and wrapped his arms around her. "Yeah. You need to take your gorgeous self back to your room and lock the door."

"Is that an order?" Faith asked, grinning, loving the feel of his rough skin on her cheek.

He stepped back from her and straightened, looking mostly serious. "Yes. That's your captain speaking."

Faith palmed his cheek briefly. "You're kind of cute when you're all in charge. Good night, sir."

She opened the door and slipped out before any kittens could escape.

JOE LEANED HIS BACK against the door, still reeling.

Damnation. What the hell had he just done?

He closed his eyes. As his body revved down, his remorse went up proportionately.

The gray kitten, who he'd started calling Smoky, had made a nest on his pillow. He picked up the little fuzz ball, stretched out on his back and set the cat on his chest. Unbothered, it closed its eyes and was sound asleep within seconds.

"At least one of us has no worries," he said, rubbing its front paw. Contented, the cat flexed its needlelike claws.

Even with all his guilt and worry, he still wanted more of Faith. He could lie here and tell himself till he was blue in the face that he couldn't touch her again, but he knew, if given another opportunity, he'd be hard-pressed to walk away.

For the first time, he allowed himself to consider the possibility of seeing her in secret. Away from work. Just enough for them to get each other out of their systems. No one had to know. His job wouldn't suffer and his chances at the promotion wouldn't be harmed. No one would be able to accuse Faith of getting special treatment from him.

God, what was he thinking? That wouldn't be fair to Faith. She wasn't the type to sneak around and deserved so much more than that.

Which brought him back to the same agonizing dilemma. He wanted her and he couldn't goddamn have her.

Faith's scent still lingered in the air and he couldn't get her face out of his mind. Holding the cat against his chest, he sat up, replaced her on his pillow and headed to his office. If work could take his mind off his mother, then maybe it could take his mind off the vexing brunette, as well.

CHAPTER SEVENTEEN

FAITH WAS PATHETIC.

She'd fully acknowledged this when she'd casually convinced Nadia and Mercedes that this was a good spot to stake out on the beach. That it was just up from the fire station, where she could watch the trucks head out on alarms, was no coincidence. But she wasn't admitting that to anyone but herself.

She happened to know Joe was on duty today, because she'd overheard her dad on the phone yesterday. Joe had taken someone else's shift, as he frequently did, workaholic that he was. His work ethic reminded her of her father. Unless Joe had traded shifts, he was also scheduled to work with her tomorrow. She wondered if he would break down and sleep tonight, and that question brought to mind his room, his bed, his kisses....

She'd seen the engine return after a call about an hour ago, and caught a glimpse of him riding shotgun. That she was acting like a teenager with a crush disturbed her on some level, but she couldn't help it, really. She'd made a mistake the other night by going to his room, but there was nothing she could do about it now.

"What is it you're not telling us, Faith?" Mercedes sipped her margarita and set the cup back in the sand next to her lounger. "Who are you stalking at the fire station?"

Faith was lying on her front, the closest of the three to the station. She didn't look at her friends. "I'm just admiring the trucks."

"You don't lie very well," Nadia said, grinning.

To prove she wasn't staring, Faith turned on her side and took the bag of corn chips from Nadia, helping herself to a handful. "Being involved with someone at work would not be a good idea." Which, though possibly misleading, was one hundred percent true.

"If it was Mr. Right, exceptions could be made." Nadia pushed her sunglasses up over her gorgeous blond hair and squinted toward the station. "I could use a Mr. Right Firefighter with Big Beautiful Muscles myself. Maybe it's time to hang out at the Shell Shack some more."

"I've been racking my brain for you," Faith said. "None of them are bad-boy enough for your tastes."

"What? No bad boys in the fire department? I don't believe that for a minute," Nadia said.

"There are a few rebels and troublemakers, but I wouldn't really call them losers. Not your type."

"Maybe she's turning over a new leaf," Mercedes said, flipping through the latest issue of *Cosmo*. "Going for someone with a job this time."

"You two are evil," Nadia said. "So I've made a couple bad decisions. I want to know more about who you've been watching for all afternoon, Faith."

"Yeah, spill it, girl. Does it have anything to do with the all-nighter last week?"

Faith shoved a bunch of corn chip crumbs from the bottom of the bag into her mouth. As a stall? Maybe. "I told you about the captain. His mother was in intensive care. We spent the night in the waiting room."

"Is his mom okay?" Nadia asked.

"She's going to be. She finally turned a corner and they think she'll go home in another week. Nice of you to ask," Faith said drily.

"So, the captain, huh?" Mercedes said. "The one who was watching you at the bar that night?"

If she'd kissed anyone else, Faith would've fessed up to her friends in a heartbeat. But it was Joe. There was too much at stake. While Mercedes and Nadia would never outwardly accuse her of getting close to Joe for professional reasons, she couldn't stand the possibility of anyone thinking that, even in passing.

"I'm going to throw this in the trash before it blows away." Faith crumpled the empty chip bag as she got up, ignoring her friends' comments about running away from their questions.

It was almost five o'clock and this part of the beach was clearing out. Most of the hard-core spring breakers were about a mile up, close to the bigger resorts and the frequent TV coverage. The trash cans were fifty feet or so away, placed out of reach of high tide. As Faith walked toward the nearest one, a man jogging down the beach in her direction caught her eye.

She knew that gait. That large, muscled body.

Her heart raced and she quietly called herself an idiot.

He's the fire captain, she coached herself. *Not the man you've been dreaming about at night.*

"Pick up that pace," she called. "You're getting soft, Captain Mendoza."

He slowed to a walk and came over to her. "'Captain Mendoza'?" he questioned, low enough that no one else could hear, and Faith couldn't help noticing—and liking—the way his eyes roved up and down her bikini-clad body.

She smiled easily, too happy to see him. "I call you soft and you take issue with the proper use of your title and name?"

He didn't smile. "Everyone calls me Joe. If you start acting different now…"

Her grin was long gone. Something about his tone, his condescension, rubbed her wrong. "No one's around who knows any differently, Joe."

"I don't think you realize—"

"I realize perfectly. I'm sorry I said anything at all, but then ignoring the captain as he runs by might raise a red flag, too."

He wiped his forehead with the bottom of his T-shirt. "You're right. I didn't expect to see you here. Like *that*." Again, he allowed his gaze to wander downward.

"My parka is back by my beach towel," she said, pointing over her shoulder.

Joe looked where she indicated.

"Not really," Faith said. "But we could go say hello to my beautiful friends. I could set you up with one of them. Then your problem would be solved."

"I'm sorry, Faith. I'm not handling…*this* well. I've

never been in this situation before." He was obviously talking about more than just seeing her in a bikini on the beach.

"Considering I'm the first female in the department, I'm glad to hear that."

He still didn't crack a grin.

"Try to lighten up," she said, wishing she could kiss his uptightness away. "Nobody knows, and it's not going to happen again."

"What if I want it to happen again?"

Faith's breath caught and a weird lightness filled her chest.

"Wait," Joe said before she could respond. "Forget I said that."

Okay, then. Whiplash. She hardened her expression. It wouldn't do for him to know how much his admission had stirred her.

"I get it," she said firmly.

"I need to get back to the station. PT time's over."

She nodded as awkwardness fell over them. "See you at work, *Joe,*" she said obediently.

He jogged off with a vague nod.

She watched him, unable to deny her appreciation of that body and the way he moved it. She had a hard time staying annoyed for more than fifteen seconds.

No, he wasn't handling *this* well, but it was pretty much impossible for her to figure out how to navigate this thing between them, either.

His message was clear, though: there would never be a repeat of the other night.

She supported that decision. In theory.

So how to explain the tears that suddenly filled her eyes?

"FAITH, CAN I TALK TO YOU in private?" Joe asked, coming up behind her and scaring the crap out of her as she rinsed the engine off with the hose the next morning.

She turned to gauge the look on his face, but couldn't tell if she was in trouble again or if this was work related. She secured the hose back on the wall and shook her hands dry as she followed him outside.

"What's going on?" she asked.

"Have you talked to your father lately?"

A sick feeling swirled through her gut. "Not since yesterday. I stayed over at Mercedes's house last night."

"He hasn't showed up for work yet today," Joe said.

"It's almost noon." Faith frowned and tried to remember if he'd told her of any plans. "He didn't call in?"

"No one's heard from him."

She pulled the cell phone out of her pants pocket and checked for messages, but found none. Maybe he was still in bed. She pressed the speed dial for his cell phone.

"I've tried both his numbers," Joe said.

Ignoring him, she paced toward the main courtyard, listening to the empty rings on the line. When her dad's voice mail finally picked up, Faith swore and hit End. Then she dialed their home number, praying he'd answer and everything was fine. Trying to ignore the rising nausea and the weird, uneasy feeling that all was not right.

The family voice mail started playing back in her

ear. She let it finish, left her dad a message to phone her right away and ended the call. She leaned her elbows on the mural wall that curved around the courtyard, and tried to think of where her dad might be that he would ignore his phone.

Joe came up next to her. "Did you try your mom?"

She still held her phone, so she scrolled through her contacts to find her mom's new number.

"Mom, have you seen Dad today?" she asked.

"Faith, I've been wanting to talk to you. I know you were upset by Craig—"

"I'm fine, but Dad is missing. Did he call you?"

"What do you mean, he's missing?"

Gritting her teeth, Faith briefly explained what she knew.

"Faith, I have no idea." To her mom's credit, she sounded genuinely concerned. "I just saw him last night, but he didn't mention anything."

"Where'd you see him?"

"At the grocery store, across from the movie theater. Craig and I were picking up something for dinner, and your father was grabbing takeout from the Chinese counter."

"Craig was with you?" The rock in Faith's gut sank deeper.

"We'd just gone to a matinee."

Faith closed her eyes. "Mom, did he know Craig was *with* you?"

"I introduced them. He seemed fine. What else was I supposed to do, Faith? It was awkward, but we're all adults."

How about don't move out in the first place?

"Maybe he's at a doctor's appointment or something," Faith said. "But meeting your boyfriend might not have gone over as well as you'd like to think, Mom."

"I didn't plan it that way. I'll call Will and Paul and see if they've heard from him today."

Faith doubted her dad would call her brothers, even the two who checked in most often, but it was worth a try.

"Let me know. I'm at work." The alarm sounded over the intercom. "I have to go."

She and Joe headed inside to hear the details of the emergency. It was a car accident, so the engine and the ambulance would respond. Faith and Joe were assigned to the truck for the day, so they stayed put.

"Your mom saw him last night?" Joe asked as they walked off the apparatus floor, back into the station.

"She and her boyfriend." Faith couldn't help the anger that laced her words. She followed Joe into his office.

"I kind of gathered. Same guy you met?"

"Same guy. Pretty sure my dad had no idea before that." Faith sat down hard on the chair in front of Joe's desk, racking her brain. "Did you call Leo Romero?" The mayor of San Amaro was also one of her dad's good friends. Maybe he knew something.

"Wasn't sure if I should. It might be nothing. Maybe he fell asleep in a lawn chair in your backyard or something."

"It's been hours since he was supposed to be in. But you're right. Let's leave Leo out of it for now."

"Does he have any other good friends besides the mayor?"

"The police chief." Faith chuckled humorlessly. "This job is his best friend, I'm afraid."

"Why don't you run home to see what's going on?"

"Who's going to cover for me?"

"The three of us can handle things until the engine returns. Won't take you long. If we get a call, you can catch up."

She hated the idea, but concern for her dad overrode her worries about work. "It'll take me fifteen minutes, tops." Faith hurried out of Joe's office to her car.

A short time later, Faith was back at the station with no answers. There'd been no sign of her father at home, nothing unusual or out of place. His truck was missing, so he'd obviously gone somewhere of his own will. The question was where?

By eight o'clock that evening, Faith and the rest of the guys had just returned from an unexciting trash fire. Her dad still hadn't shown up at the station, and her concern had ebbed into anger, whether justified or not. Who was the parent here? Who did he think he was to disappear and worry everyone?

And what if he was in serious trouble and here she was being petty?

She started helping the guys clean up the truck and refill everything, but distraction pulled at her, made it tough to concentrate on the job. She met Joe's gaze and he walked over to her.

"Heard anything?"

"My phone's inside."

"Go check. I'll take care of this."

She hurried off to retrieve her messages, and when she heard her brother Paul's voice, her shoulders sagged in relief.

"Dad's okay, Faith. Well…yeah. He's *going* to be fine. Call me and I'll fill you in."

She clicked on her brother's speed dial number, puzzled by the somewhat ambiguous message and that he'd called instead of their mom.

"Hi, Faith."

"What's going on, Paul? Where's Dad? And Mom? Why couldn't she call me?"

"Don't you want to talk to your favorite brother?"

"Of course," she said impatiently. "Tell me. Is he okay or isn't he?" The rock was back in her stomach even though apparently her dad was alive.

"He's fine. Mom found him on the boat."

"The boat? What the hell was he doing there?"

Paul sighed, and she pictured him taking his glasses off and rubbing his forehead. "He was passed-out drunk."

It was like a bad soap opera.

"Mom had to rouse him and take him to the E.R. They're probably about done there. Faith, I'm sorry. You said he was losing it, but I had no idea…."

"Yeah, well, who would guess the model citizen would go off the deep end and turn into a binge drinker?"

"This wasn't the first time?"

"Not the first time, no. So you're sure he's going to be okay?"

"He had some mild alcohol poisoning, but they pumped some fluids through him and he's mostly coherent now, according to Mom."

Only thirteen hours after he was supposed to be at work. Faith kicked a spare helmet that had fallen on the floor.

"Mom's still with him?"

"Last I knew. She said she'd drive him home. Do I need to fly back?"

Faith blew out a frustrated breath, tempted to say yes, but... "No. I'm beginning to realize there's nothing anyone can do. He's determined to screw up his life. Who are we to try to stop him?"

"You don't mean that, Faith."

"Oh, I do," she said. "Thanks for calling, Paul. I'll go see him as soon as I'm off duty."

"Keep me posted, please."

"Yep."

She ended the call and paced back and forth in the hallway for a couple of minutes, fuming and trying not to show it. Jaw locked, she finally headed back out to the garage to help with cleanup.

"We've got it taken care of," Penn told her as she walked up. "You look like you could kill someone."

"And here I thought I'd calmed down. Thanks for covering my share of work tonight."

"You owe me one." He said it with a smile, and Faith nodded, distracted, then made a beeline for the door.

IF JOE HAD ANY QUESTION about Faith's state of mind, it disappeared the second he entered the exercise room. He admired her form as she beat the living hell out of the speed bag, hoping it wasn't his face she was imagining.

She must have gotten news about the chief.

Joe leaned against the wall near her and waited for her to take a break. She hadn't bothered to change out of her uniform into workout clothes, and sweat was starting to soak through her T-shirt.

After another couple of minutes of pummeling, she stepped back, breathing hard. Her arms had to be ready to fall off.

"Did you hear from your dad?" he asked.

Faith didn't look at him. She walked over to the hanging bag and threw a couple vicious side kicks at it.

"I heard from my brother. My dad is okay."

She kicked the bag hard enough to send it flying each time. Joe made a mental note not to piss her off. He waited for her to say more, but she was determined to destroy the bag or die trying.

"That's all?" he said between her sequence of punches and a flurry of roundhouse kicks. "You going to tell me what's going on?"

Finally, she turned and looked at him. The hair at her temples was soaked with sweat. She mopped her forehead with the bottom of her shirt, and if he wasn't so damn honorable—yeah, right—he would've enjoyed the view of her bare, flat abdomen.

"Telling you would only serve to drag you farther into the Peligni family drama."

He fought not to show how frustrating she could be. "I'm asking, Faith."

"As my captain?"

He pushed himself off the wall and closed the space between them. "No. Not as your captain." Their eyes met and held, and for a moment, he saw beyond the tough, pissed-off-woman act to the scared daddy's girl.

When she blinked, tears appeared at the corners of her eyes, evoking an unfamiliar something in Joe.

Faith sat on the bench that ran the length of the wall, her shoulders sagging. Joe settled next to her.

"I don't want to put you in an uncomfortable position, knowing stuff about my dad that maybe you shouldn't," she said after a prolonged silence.

"We can pretend I'm not an officer for a few minutes." He had no idea what he was doing, but for once he wasn't going to overthink it. He was compelled to be a sounding board for Faith, if that's what she needed.

"My dad went on another bender," she said quietly. "Drank himself into unconsciousness. My mom found him on the boat, still docked in the marina, thank God."

Joe swore under his breath and fought the urge to touch her. "Do you need to get out of here? Go see him?"

"That sounds strangely like something a captain would say."

"Probably so. Scratch that. Anything I can do, Faith?"

"There's nothing any of us can do, apparently. I've tried. I *am* going to have words with him, though."

"I wouldn't want to be in his place."

She narrowed her eyes at him. "Didn't we establish on the beach the other day that we couldn't do this kind of thing?"

"What kind of thing?" he asked, knowing full well what she was talking about.

"I'm not supposed to be chatty or casual. You're not supposed to be nice. We're not supposed to exchange more than orders and yes sirs."

"I could do without the sir," he muttered, standing up and halfheartedly punching the speed bag once. "We did. I tried. Turns out it's too late."

"Too late for what?" She eyed him suspiciously. Tiredly.

"Keeping it strictly business. There are lines I can't cross, but talking to you about something besides safety drills and hose sizes isn't one of them."

She continued to stare at him, nodding. "Do me a favor, will you?"

"What's that?"

"Give me some advance notice if you change your mind again."

"I'm not going to change my mind again. I like you, Faith. Whether that's wise or not."

She stood, her arms crossed. "Just don't let anyone know it, okay?" She smiled briefly. "I'm heading to the shower."

She walked off and left him standing there with all kinds of uninvited, unwelcome, erotic as hell images in his mind.

CHAPTER EIGHTEEN

"Good," her mom said when Faith walked in the door of the Peligni family abode after her shift ended the next morning. "You're home."

"So are you." Faith knew on some level she was being foolishly hopeful with that statement, but was momentarily thrown by her mother's appearance in the kitchen.

"No. I'm leaving for home now," Nita said pointedly. "He's threatened to go in to work, but I think he needs a day off. *Sober.*"

"She's divorcing me and still trying to run my life," Faith's dad said grumpily. He sat at the kitchen table with a steaming mug of coffee in front of him, as if everything was totally normal.

With her mom there, Faith could almost make herself believe it was.

"You won't die if you miss two days of work in a row," Nita told him. "Unless you pull a repeat of yesterday. If the alcohol didn't kill you, I would."

Just the thought of what her father had put them through had Faith's blood pressure shooting up again, and the rage she'd suppressed all night threatened to blow.

Her dad looked chagrined. He raised his hands, palms out. "I'm not going in to work and I sure as hell am not drinking anything but this coffee."

"Okay, then." Nita glanced around the kitchen—it appeared she had tidied up. "Sweet rolls will be done in a couple of minutes. I'll let Faith handle you now."

"I don't need anyone to handle me." Her dad's voice lacked conviction. Overall, he seemed subdued. He glanced at Faith with some trepidation.

"Goodbye, Mom," Faith said, having bitten her tongue since she'd arrived. She walked to the door to see her mother out.

"Go easy, Faith."

"I'll talk to you later," Faith said.

Once her mom was gone, she walked calmly— deceptively so—to the oven, removed the tray of cinnamon rolls and set them on the stove to cool. She leaned against the counter tensely, facing her father.

"What were you thinking, Dad?"

"I've heard it all from your mother, Faith. I don't need another round."

"You know what I don't need?" Her voice grew louder. "I don't need to spend the day at work wondering what the hell my dad is doing and whether he's alive. I don't need to have people asking where you are, or to try to think of a PC way to say who the hell knows."

"I'm sorry to put you in that position."

"Don't put *yourself* in that position, Dad! When did my father, my idol, the fire chief, turn into an irresponsible drunk?"

He dropped his gaze to the table and his shoulders

fell at her words. Even that pissed Faith off, because he'd never been the type to back down from a challenge or an argument and, dammit, she just wanted her dad back.

"I'm not handling anything well lately," he said.

"No, you're not. And I get that your life has been ripped out from under you, that you're hurting. I'm sorry as hell about you and Mom. If there was anything I could do to change it, I would in a heartbeat."

"I know that, princess—"

"But you need to buck up and handle that Mom is gone. Put your big-boy pants on and deal. Self-destructing is not an option."

He stood and walked to the sink, staring sadly out the window. Faith felt herself softening some.

"I know you don't understand," he said.

"I do understand. It sucks." She picked at one of the steaming cinnamon rolls, blew on it and popped the bite in her mouth. "Maybe it would do you some good to hit the punching bags at the station for a bit. Work out some of your anger at Mom."

He didn't respond immediately, just kept staring outside at the bay. He shook his head slowly. "If I could be angry at her, maybe that would work."

"If you're not pissed, I'm mad enough for both of us."

"No." Her dad turned to look at her. "You can't be mad at your mom."

"Oh yes, I can."

"It's not her fault, Faith."

The urge to shake him was overwhelming. "She quit the marriage, Dad. I can't believe I have to remind you that *she* walked out on *you*. Pretty safe to say it's her fault."

"I guess it probably looks that way from the outside."

"I'm not on the outside. I'm here in this house, living with you, watching you piss your life away. Trying to find something to help you, anything to get my dad back to the person he's always been."

He walked over to her, palmed the back of her head to tilt it forward, and kissed her forehead. "That means more to me than you'll ever know, princess." He shuffled tiredly to the table and sat in his usual place. Leaning both elbows on the surface, he ran his hands over his face. "But there are things that've gone on in our marriage that you haven't been privy to."

"I know how much you guys argue about me. My career."

"That's not it. Well, that may be a very small piece of it but it's all part of a much larger issue. *My* career."

"Not a secret, either, Dad. You've fought about that longer than you've fought about me. Mom's always hated how much time and dedication it takes."

"Yes. Rightfully so."

"It's your career. You support the family. You're the fire chief, for the love of God."

"It *is* my career. And I've chosen it repeatedly over my family."

"Sometimes there is no choice. You do what you have to do. That'd be true with other jobs as well." Faith strode over to the table and sat down hard in the chair next to him. "Why is that so difficult for her to understand?"

"She understands that. The problem…" He ran a hand through his thick graying hair and sighed. "The problem is that I've screwed it up. Pushed it. Too many times. There are instances when I had no choice but to go into work at an inconvenient time. Nights when I couldn't get around working an extra few hours. But they're few and far between."

"Like I said, you're dedicated."

"Stop defending me, Faith!" He smacked his palm on the table, his voice booming now. "Your belief in me has always meant the world to me, but this time you're wrong."

She swallowed a protest, because something in his eyes, some kind of conviction she hadn't seen there for weeks, stopped her. Made her sit there quietly and wait for him to say more.

"I could probably count on both hands the times it was justified. Staying late. Running out of here at all hours for work. I nearly missed your brother's birth. Holidays. Canceled family vacations. Hell, Faith, I was late to your high school graduation. So many of those times, I could've told the people at work no, I can't do it."

"But that's what makes you so good at your job. You make sacrifices."

He nodded sadly. "I'm afraid one of those sacrifices is my marriage, princess."

"So you're giving up?"

"You're the one who told me to move on. Something about big-boy pants."

"Quit drowning your sorrows in beer, sure, but give up?"

"I gave up weeks ago, Faith."

"Why would you do that? You love her, don't you?"

"Of course I love her." He shoved his chair back and stood again. Walked over to the counter, his back to Faith. "How long ago did you leave the house, go off to college?"

"Eight years."

He nodded, and when he turned to face her, he was biting down on his lip. "Eight years ago, when it was down to just your mother and me, she warned me. Told me that if I kept running off to work at every opportunity, this would happen."

"She threatened to leave you? That long ago?" Faith's voice rose almost to a squeak.

He nodded somberly.

"And you, what, didn't believe her?"

Her dad shrugged. It struck Faith how beaten down he looked and how that contrasted with his tall frame, his wide shoulders, his usual proud stature.

"I blew it."

"So you knew she could leave you at any time, and you still kept on working long hours? Going to fires in the middle of the night just because? Allowing the mayor to call a meeting at dinnertime?"

"It's hard to break some habits, Faith."

Something snapped inside her. She popped up from the chair and spun around. The weeks of trying to figure out what to do for him, of babying him, giving him tough love—through all of it, she'd been blind. "Cry me a damn river, Dad. You've made your bed. She gave you every opportunity and you didn't even try to keep your marriage together. As far as I'm concerned, you let the family down. Knowingly."

"Faith, I—"

"I don't want to hear it." Beyond exhausted from a near sleepless night and twenty-four hours of worry, she stormed to her bedroom and threw some clean clothes into a large duffel bag. Grabbed the dirty uniform off the floor and stuffed it into a plastic grocery sack. Made a quick stop in her bathroom to get any essentials she could fit into the duffel. Headed through the kitchen toward the back door.

"Where are you going, Faith?" Her dad hadn't moved from his spot at the counter.

"Away. I'm staying somewhere else for a while. You can go ahead and finish self-destructing. Put your job first. You obviously couldn't care less about the family or anyone in it."

Fire blazed in his eyes suddenly and he straightened. Advanced slowly, step by intense step. "I may have made mistakes, but don't you ever, *ever* say that this family doesn't matter to me. My family means more than you can ever know. And you...you've always been a daddy's girl. I love you so much, Faith...it scares the living hell out of me to have you out there fighting fires. If anything happened to you again, it would kill me. *Kill me.* I have my best captain looking out for you, for God's sake. So don't tell me I don't care about you...or your brothers or your—"

"You have your best captain *what?*" Faith clutched

the strap of the bag on her shoulder so hard her finger-nails dug into the palm of her hand. Her insides sank to the bottom of her stomach.

Her dad's eyes widened briefly, as if he realized he'd said the wrong thing. "The point is that I'd do anything for my family, but I'm only human—"

"You asked Joe to look after me? Are you paying him an extra babysitting fee, too?"

"Calm down, Faith. It's not that I don't think you can do the job—"

"That's interesting, because from here, that's exactly what it looks like." Tears burned her eyes. She sounded semihysterical. And maybe she goddamn was.

"You know better than that, princess. You're good at the job. Damn good. But bad things can happen to anyone in our world. You know that firsthand."

She shook her head, blinded by her tears. "You were the one person who was behind me all the way, Dad, and now…now you've let me down in so many ways I can't even count them."

Faith swung the screen door open and walked out of the house she'd grown up in.

CHAPTER NINETEEN

LUCKY FOR JOE, his address wasn't in the San Amaro phonebook, which meant it took Faith a while to track it down. The station was nearly empty when she arrived, since the truck and ambulance had both been called out, and that gave her plenty of opportunity to poke around and find where he lived.

By the time she reached the door of his place—a modest, narrow, two-story condo in the center of town—the tempest in her had weakened slightly. His 4Runner was in the carport beneath his unit, reassuring her she was at the right address. She knocked and waited.

When he answered, she nearly swallowed her anger.

He wore only a pair of jeans, the button undone, the worn, soft material hugging his thighs. His body was... perfect. Chest and abs sculpted as if a famous artist had chiseled the ideal male specimen. Corded biceps, wide shoulders. She managed to work her gaze upward, and realized by the drowsy look in his eyes and slightly mussed hair that he'd been sleeping.

"Faith? What's wrong?" He blinked sleepily, still distracting her from the reason she'd come here.

"Can I come in?" she asked, fully aware of how visible his front door was from the street, should anyone they knew drive by.

He opened the door wider and allowed her to enter, then closed it behind her.

"Is your dad okay?"

The mention was all it took to snap her back to her pissed off place. "So he ordered you to look out for me, huh?" She fought to keep her voice from slipping back into hysterical mode.

He closed his eyes and dropped his head. Scratched behind his ear. Studied her. "What happened?"

"He told me he asked you to watch out for me. Is that what everything is all about? The kisses, the being nice to me? You were stuck babysitting me anyway, so you might as well make the most of it?"

"Whoa. Calm down, Faith." He took her by the elbow and led her toward the big denim-blue couch in the living room.

She shook her arm away and spun to face him. "Are you going to answer me?"

"I thought we'd sit and have a civilized discussion, but I see that's out of the question. Kissing you has nothing to do with your dad."

"You must think it's amusing to have the chief's little girl in your charge. What better way to butter him up for that promotion."

Joe started laughing then. Howling so hard he threw his head back. Faith narrowed her eyes and shook with the need to conk him over the head with a heavy object.

"Really?" she said through clenched teeth. "You're laughing?"

He sobered, his dark eyes intense. Disbelieving? "Think about that for a minute, Faith. Butter up the chief by getting involved with his daughter? If you believe that, you don't know a thing about men."

"What's that supposed to mean?" She knew plenty about how stupid and proud and clueless they were.

"Cardinal unspoken rule. You don't screw the boss's daughter."

"Who said anything about screwing?"

"You know what I mean." Joe stepped closer, his eyes taking on a different mood altogether. "Besides, correct me if I'm wrong, but I'd say we were about two steps from crossing that line in my room the other night."

She couldn't correct him. He wasn't wrong. And the way his dark, smoldering eyes bored into hers right now with such heat...

"I've kissed you because I wanted to, Faith. Because there are times I can't *not* kiss you. Because something about you, about your stubborn determination, the heart you put into everything you do...those damn kissable lips..." His gaze lowered and Faith involuntarily moistened her lips. "When I kiss you, it's in spite of your father. In direct opposition to my career aspirations. It's begging for trouble. Not paving any damn road."

Her annoyance leaked out like water from a barrel with a hole in the bottom.

"I get it," she said, lowering her gaze. "That accusation was one of the dumber things I've said."

"I wasn't going to be so blunt, but yeah."

"I'm still pissed." She crossed her arms emphatically. "Just not at you."

Joe grinned and took her elbow again, leading her to the couch. He pulled her down inches away from him. "You know as well as I do that you don't need anyone watching over you."

Faith drew her knees up to her chest, hugged them to her, saying nothing. She felt Joe's eyes burning into her and avoided meeting his gaze.

"Right? Faith?"

She swallowed hard, unable to choke out an agreement.

He extended his hand and wove their fingers together. "Where's the kick-ass Faith with Texas-size confidence?"

She drew in a shaky breath. "She got crushed in a building collapse."

He squeezed her hand gently and shook his head. "She's still in there somewhere."

Before she could process what was happening, Joe slid one arm under her leg, the other behind her back, and scooped her onto his lap.

"What the…? What's that for?"

"To get your attention." He settled into the corner of the couch with her.

Faith sat stiffly, unsure how to act with Joe being so openly affectionate. His caresses up and down her thigh gradually relaxed her. Convinced her there was nothing to fight here.

"After what happened to you," he said, "it's okay to take a while to get back up to speed."

Surprised, she turned, stretching her legs out across the couch so she could see his face. "You think?"

"You don't think?"

She reached down and took off her work shoes, dropping them on the floor as she considered his question. "Maybe a little while, I guess. But you're not supposed to tell me that."

"What am I supposed to tell you?"

"Captain stuff. 'No excuses. Get over it and do the job.'"

"When have I ever given you the impression that's how I work?"

Of the three captains in the department, Joe was the most compassionate. Probably the most respected and best liked, too. He was one of those rare people who could lead without condescending. Teach without talking down.

But she didn't need to tell him that and give him a big head.

"You're the meanest. Strict, unbending. All the guys detest you."

He chuckled. "I don't care what all the guys think of me. Only the girls."

"The jury's still out. You're welcome to campaign, though."

"I'll definitely keep that in mind." He lightly grasped her forearm, becoming serious. "What it comes down to, Faith, is that you need to trust yourself. The rest of us already do."

"My dad doesn't."

"Faith." Joe stared at her until she looked at him. "Is your dad in his right mind now? Does your dad normally go out and drink himself unconscious? Does the real guy miss even a day of work?"

She shook her head reluctantly.

"He's got serious problems, but I don't need to tell you that. You know better than anyone."

"I guess so."

"Okay, then. Let it go. In his eyes, you're still his little girl."

Faith fought a grin. "Which makes it twice as twisted that I'm on your lap."

"I said in *his* eyes. There's nothing little girl about what I'm seeing." Joe's voice lowered and went sexy, making Faith's heart skip a beat.

"It's the uniform," she said, grimacing. She hadn't had a chance to change after finishing her shift this morning.

"It's more than the uniform."

He pulled her toward him and kissed her. The warm softness of his lips drew her in. He was thorough, gentle. Too damn gentle. Faith needed more.

She turned to face him fully, her knees falling on either side of his thighs, and deepened the kiss. Her tongue pushed inside his mouth greedily. She craved this man, burned for the sensations she knew he could give her. The escape.

Running her hands up his solid, sculpted chest, she kissed her inhibitions goodbye and let out a low moan of appreciation.

Joe needed no encouragement. He met her urgency, his hands on her butt, pulling her body into his hardness.

He kissed her hungrily, his tongue playing with hers,

swirling, exploring:..taking what he seemed to need. Giving exactly what she wanted.

He untucked her uniform shirt and slid his hands up her torso. The size of them dwarfed her body. Made her feel sexy. Feminine. On fire. While he took his time working his way upward, she whipped her T-shirt over her head and tossed it to the floor.

He stopped kissing her long enough to lean back and take in her lacy zebra-print bra. "Do you always wear hot little numbers like that under your uniform?"

Faith laughed. "Numbers? I don't think there's anything mathematical about it."

Joe growled, running his thumbs over the tips of her breasts, covered by the thin material. "I don't know… there's the possibility for a study of proportions. Symmetry."

"Nice intellectual touch." Her breath was uneven, shallow. "As for hot, not always. Sometimes I go with a demure yellow mesh, a simple, light pink heart motif. Depends on my mood."

"You're killing me," he said huskily into her ear. "I don't think I can work with you again. Not without trying to figure out your 'mood.'"

"It's important to know a woman's mood."

"Right now I think I've got a pretty good handle on it."

Their lips came together again. He reached behind her and unfastened her "hot little number" with one hand. Faith arched toward him, aching to feel the heat of his skin on hers.

"You're beautiful," he said, cupping both her breasts, molding them with his palms.

She rose on her knees so he could draw her into his mouth. His tongue swirled around her nipple, teased it, shot a tight ache deep inside her. Faith ran her fingers through his coarse, dark hair, cradling his head to her.

Without warning, he pushed to the edge of the couch and then to his feet, still holding on to her. Faith threw her arms and legs around him to avoid falling.

"I've got you," he said in a low voice.

"That you do."

He kissed her the entire way up the stairs, down a short hall, to his bedroom. She slid down him when he stopped in the middle of the room, and he wrapped his arms tightly around her, making her feel safe. Desired.

He walked her slowly backward until her legs hit his bed. As he strode across the room and closed the blinds on the back side of the condo, she slid onto the king-size mattress and crept up till she reached his pillows. The blankets were twisted and she could smell his scent on the sheets.

She watched him hungrily as he crossed back to her. Before joining her, he unzipped his pants and drew his jeans down his legs. Either he peeled two layers at once or he'd been commando, because now he was naked and, oh yeah, the rest of his body was just as impressive as his upper half. And then some.

Joe joined her on the bed and brushed her cheek with his knuckles. He pressed a tender kiss to her lips.

"Do you want this?" he asked, then trailed his lips along her jaw.

She wound her arms around him and ran her hands over his back, shoulders, ass. "I thought we weren't supposed to do this." She couldn't help smiling wickedly.

"Do you want to stop?"

"Does this feel like I want to stop?" she asked as she grasped the hardest part of him.

He moaned and undid her pants. Slid them down her legs and dropped them over the side of the bed. Then he took intense interest in her matching zebra bikini panties, tracing the design before peeling them off as well.

Faith playfully propped herself up on one elbow, breaking all contact and smirking. "What about you? Do you want to stop?"

In an instant, he was on top of her, covering her with his wide, solid body. "Not for a few hours, minimum."

"If you think you can last that long," she taunted.

Joe quieted her by kissing her and doing deliciously naughty things with his hands.

Faith surrendered willingly. Enthusiastically. "I love it when you get all prove-a-pointish," she murmured when he trailed his lips down to the hollow of her neck and lower.

"I may have exaggerated on the time thing. You have this way of making me lose control."

"Yeah?" She slid her knees up, opening herself to him, and rubbed her body against his. "Maybe it's your age. They say a man reaches his prime at eighteen—"

Again, he cut off her words by slipping his tongue inside her mouth, making her laugh.

"That was the wrong saying," she finally said,

breathlessly. "What I meant was with age comes expertise."

He drew his fingers downward from her breasts, inching lower, until he touched the part of her that throbbed for him. "That's not even the saying."

"Maybe not." Her breath caught. "But it feels right on about now."

When he rolled away from her, she wanted to cry, but he didn't go far. He opened the nightstand drawer and withdrew a condom. Faith held her hand out and he looked at her questioningly. She took the packet from him, ripped it open impatiently. Tried to slide it on him but her hand was shaking too much.

Joe took the condom from her and sheathed himself quickly. "Experience," he said. "With age comes experience."

She laughed and then sucked in her breath as he pressed into her, filling her, stretching her.

He was tender and patient as her body adjusted. "You okay?" he said into her ear, in barely more than a whisper.

Faith melted a little at his concern. "Very okay." She matched his rhythm, then increased their tempo, thrusting her hips up to meet him.

Their tongues mirrored their bodies with a mating dance. Her need ignited. There was nothing gentle or gradual about it—it was like having a match thrown on a propane tank. An explosion of sensation that burned, consumed her, making her cling to him for all she was worth as she climbed toward release.

Just like his kisses, his lovemaking was somehow

tender and yet urgent at the same time. He was an un-
selfish lover, as concerned about her pleasure as his
own. He made her feel more than just what he was
doing to her body, made her chest feel light, as if it was
filled with helium and he was the only thing keeping
her from floating away.

Joe said her name several times as she nearly lost
her mind, as her body began to tingle, and then she
slipped over the edge to ecstasy. He followed her, then
looked down at her with sated, drowsy eyes. He kissed
the tip of her nose, her lips, her chin and back to her
lips, where his mouth lingered. The urgency was gone
from his touch and it was all gentle adoration, making
Faith melt a little bit more. He rolled to his side, taking her with him.

She smiled, her breath shaky. "Wow."

"Yeah," Joe said into her ear, wrapping his arms
tightly around her. "Wow."

SO THAT WAS HOW IT WAS then.

There was *something* between them. Something special, beyond man parts and woman parts and biology.

Joe had been with enough women to know that sex
with Faith Peligni was nothing short of incredible. *Wow*
was an understatement.

And that was not good news.

Maybe it'd just been too long for him. He'd quit the
meaningless, short-term affairs a few years back, when
he got promoted to captain. He was usually too wrapped
up in his job or working too much overtime to expend

the energy. Maybe he needed to get back to meeting people, taking women out. To give him perspective.

Or maybe he only wanted Faith.

Well, he had her right now, and that was all he could have. He intended to enjoy every second with her in his arms.

Joe stroked her silky hair slowly, over and over, taking in her scent, light, floral...*Faith*. When her breathing deepened with the rhythm of sleep, he finally closed his eyes, smiling to himself. Though he was more content than he'd been in months—maybe years—and completely sated, he'd been determined to stay awake.

The last thing he needed was to give this beautiful woman another reason to call him "old man."

BROAD FREAKING DAYLIGHT.

Faith had left her car parked in front of Joe's house for anyone to see...in broad daylight.

She opened her eyes instantly at the realization. Checked the clock on the nightstand. Fabulous. She'd been here for over three hours. There was no acceptable way to explain that—except to say she'd been having the most amazing sex of her life, of course.

Joe's arm was slung protectively—possessively?—over her abdomen, so there was no way she could dart off without him noticing. But she had to get out of here.

Panic clawed at her, made it hard to get any air in as she imagined one of the guys at work commenting on her "career aspirations." It didn't matter that the chance of anyone she knew driving by—and knowing this was Joe's house—was slim to none. Lying there, she was convinced the whole world would be aware of her slipup. As if she'd hired a skywriter to broadcast the news.

She studied Joe to gauge how deeply he was sleeping. Even in her panic, his handsome face had an effect on her. She considered how easy it would be to slide back under his arm and wake him up with her lips all over his body. The images softened her. Weakened her—for a good ten seconds.

Faith wrapped her hand around his arm to see if he reacted. He didn't. She lifted his arm and slowly worked her way out from under him. It'd be much easier to escape quickly if she didn't have to explain to him what her rush was about. She shouldn't have to tell him, anyway. There was no question this was a mistake.

He slumbered on, breathing deeply enough that she could hear him as she gathered her underwear and pants from the floor. She put them on as she walked downstairs to the living room, picking up her T-shirt, bra and shoes there and dressing quickly. At the door, she stopped and straightened her clothes. Looked around for a mirror. The only one she could find was in the hall bathroom. She ran her fingers through her hair in an attempt to not look as if she'd just been thoroughly ravished. It didn't do much good, but her purse—with her brush and makeup inside—was in the car.

Screw it. She had to get out of here.

Before opening the door, she looked out the side window. Then the peephole. The other window at the front of the house. For what, she didn't know. She was acting like a sneaky teenager. Without a glance back, she opened the door, squinting against the blinding, late afternoon sunlight, and made her way toward the car, trying for all the world to look as if she'd just had a cup of coffee and a work meeting with her captain instead of...the truth.

An old Buick drove by as she walked down the driveway. Once she was in her car, she spotted an elderly couple strolling along the sidewalk on the opposite side of the street. Probably Joe's next-door neighbors. The kind he would chat with as he watered his flower bed—if he had one.

She started the engine and, with no idea where she was going or who she could stay with, got the hell off Blue Fin Boulevard.

CHAPTER TWENTY

"DID YOU MISS ME?" Faith asked flippantly after she shut the door to Joe's office.

He'd missed her like goddamn crazy. In his arms, in his bed, even just talking to her about things like the best way to coil a hose or how many miles on the treadmill made a good day's workout.

It had been a week since she'd crept out of his house like a criminal, and they hadn't spoken since, beyond the bare minimum necessary to work together. He'd seen her plenty in that time, but being closed in the office with her created an intimacy that had his blood pulsing with need within seconds. He gritted his teeth against memories of her in his arms and forced his focus back to the items in his hands.

"Tell me this is a misprint," he said, tossing the program for the next evening's auction to the edge of his desk nearest her. It was turned to the third page of items up for bid. Items and people.

"What?" She frowned, leaning forward.

"You. Being auctioned off."

"Oh." Her tone was suddenly less concerned. More defensive. "Yeah. It's for a good cause. I believe you've heard of the San Amaro Island Burn Foundation?"

"Don't be like that, Faith." She knew damn well his mother had been one of the founders.

"Don't think," she said, glancing behind at the closed door and lowering her voice, "that just because of... what happened, you can tell me what to do outside of this job."

"This isn't the place to discuss what happened, though it would be nice to have that conversation some-time."

Her bravado faltered. Only for a second. "There's nothing to discuss, Joe. Nothing changed, right? Still an impossible situation."

And that was the bitch of it. She was right. The big-ger question was why was he hanging on to it? Why was he letting it get to him that she treated him like ev-eryone else? That was the way he wanted it. Needed it.

"Did you really think about volunteering yourself for the auction, Faith? You work so hard to earn people's respect as a female firefighter and—"

"You think just because someone can bid on a date with me that I won't be taken seriously."

"It's a good possibility. Am I wrong?"

"Yes," she said. "You know this auction as well as I do. They do it every year. The bachelor-bachelorette bit is only a small part, but it brings in huge money. And what better way to say 'hey, look, there's a new game in town. Girls can be firefighters, too.'"

He felt the tic in his jaw as he studied her. He could just imagine all the jackasses who would jump at the chance to take out a woman like Faith. Plenty of them had money and could spend big bucks. She wasn't a piece of meat, and he hated the idea that the wrong person could win the bid for her time.

She lifted her chin and walked closer to the desk that stood between them, grinning. "You're jealous, aren't you?"

Of course, she'd hit on the truth. But hell if he was going to admit it.

"Just don't want the department to become a meat market. What if one of your coworkers bids on you?"

The way her eyes darted to the side told him she hadn't considered that possibility.

"Starting bid is a hundred dollars. No one around here can afford that."

"You'd be surprised what these boys might save their pennies for."

She straightened. "It's only a date. I'll be fine no matter who wins. My biggest worry is whether anyone will bid."

Joe laughed. "Oh, they will." As much as he wished he could prevent the whole thing, she wouldn't lack for bidders. In fact, personal issues aside, it was a genius fund-raising move. Ten firefighters up for auction, and what man wouldn't empty his bank account to get the one woman? The knockout, kick-ass woman with cool blue eyes and a killer body.

"I think you might be biased," she whispered. "But thanks for the vote of confidence. Come to think of it, maybe if no one else bids, you could save me from eternal humiliation."

"People will bid, Faith. They'll pay plenty to go out with you."

"But…" She perched on the arm of the chair, propping one foot up on the seat, and even though she wore unsexy navy-blue uniform pants, he had no trouble imagining—remembering—what that leg looked like bare. "Suppose no one does. And it's all quiet in the room. Uncomfortable. You'd throw one out there, wouldn't you?" She tilted her head just so and had a tantalizing, flirty look in her eyes.

"You know I couldn't do that." Thank God he was certain that wouldn't happen, because it would kill him not to.

"Would you want to?"

Damn, he wanted her again. Still. He walked around the desk and stopped three inches from her. "You know exactly what I want to do," he said in a quiet, husky voice.

Faith's gaze dipped to his lips, then her long lashes lifted again and she met his eyes.

"And I know how you do it, too. Very well."

His pulse was already going double time and other parts of him responded to her now, too.

A knock sounded on the door, and it opened before Joe could react. Faith whirled around guiltily as they both faced the fire chief.

CHAPTER TWENTY-ONE

"WANTED TO GET YOUR opinion of some... Oh. Hey, princess," Chief Peligni said.

Joe's heart hammered and he thanked God he hadn't actually been touching Faith—yet.

"I was just leaving," she said curtly, giving Joe the impression that she and her father were still at odds.

"Wait, Faith."

She stopped at the chief's plea. Waited for him to go on.

"Are you doing okay?"

"I'm fine, Dad."

"You can come home anytime, you know." He glanced at Joe uncomfortably, and Joe wished he was somewhere else. Anywhere else, so he didn't have to watch the chief grovel.

"I'm staying with Nadia for a while," Faith said. "But I'm looking for my own place."

"I'm sorry, Faith. I'm working on things. Making some changes."

Joe could tell the chief's words had an effect on Faith. Her posture relaxed slightly and her face softened into something less than anger. "I hope so, Dad. I need to go help Penn with lunch."

Chief Peligni watched Faith walk out, and Joe did everything in his power *not* to.

"It sucks to let down the people you care about," the chief said quietly, almost to himself.

The words made Joe break out into a sweat beneath his uniform. If sleeping with the chief's daughter wasn't letting him down...

He strode back behind his desk. Coughed uneasily. "Do you know about the auction thing? With your daughter?"

Tony Peligni, who was still looking out the door after Faith, turned around and sighed. "The bachelorette thing? Yeah. She and I *discussed* that when she decided to participate."

"I'm sorry. I had no idea she was considering it. I would have tried to convince her otherwise if I had."

"It wouldn't have done any good, Joe. Haven't you figured that out yet?"

Joe tried to hide a grin, because he had a very good grasp of Faith's stubbornness.

"Faith will do whatever she damn well pleases," the chief continued. "Oh, she'll make nice about it and act like she listens to your arguments, but then if she wants to do something, you might as well stand back and watch her do it. She doesn't worry much about what anyone else thinks once her mind is made up."

"I guess I'm surprised she doesn't see this as a negative thing." Joe should probably drop it, he knew, so that her father didn't get suspicious and wonder why he was so concerned about it. But he couldn't get over the idea of someone else taking Faith on a date. An honest-to-God, pick-her-up-at-the-door date. Something he could never do.

The chief shook his head. "She insists it will bring positive attention to the fact that there's a woman in the department. Between you and me, I think she's dreading the date part, but she's determined to make her point."

"Nothing you can do?" Joe asked.

"I intend to be there and do everything in my power to make sure no one from the department dares to so much as think about bidding on her."

"Don't want her dating one of us, huh?" Joe tried to make it sound like a joke, but he was testing the chief.

"Hell, no. You and I both know this career takes a lot out of a man. I want better for her."

Joe fought to keep his face expressionless. None of this was news to him. He'd never had a prayer of making a relationship with Faith work.

Hellfire, he didn't even want to contemplate why he'd just thought the word *relationship*. He dragged his mind back to the conversation at hand, trying to think like Faith's captain and not her lover.

"I guess you have to give her credit for believing in something so strongly," Joe said, wondering to himself if there was a cause he believed in enough to go against the opinions of the people he loved. He couldn't imagine doing something that would upset his mother. Even before she was sick. Making his mom proud had always been high on his list of motivations, for better or worse.

"Faith's a special girl," the chief said, looking hard at Joe, as if he suspected Joe might be too aware of that fact.

"Of course. She's your daughter, sir. Now, what was it you wanted to talk to me about?"

As the cleanup after the auction went on around him, Joe heard scraps of conversation that claimed the evening was a roaring success.

At the moment, he couldn't care less.

He tried to listen to the conversation he was supposedly part of, with the chief and an older couple who'd bid big bucks and won some artwork by Evan Drake's wife.

"It's beautiful stuff," Chief Peligni was saying. "Your donation will go a long way at the foundation. We're glad you could join us tonight."

The four of them shook hands and said good-night. The couple moved one way into the exiting crowd, and Joe and the chief moved the other.

The ballroom at one of the local hotels was fully decked out for the occasion, with marble columns and velvet curtains adding a touch of class. The small stage was decorated with deep red roses and other elegant floral arrangements Joe couldn't identify. Round tables with ten chairs each made the room a maze.

He was beyond ready to get the hell out of there and peel his dress uniform off. He'd had enough of this night.

"Faith looked beautiful, didn't she?" the chief said proudly as they slowly made their way toward the nearest door.

Beautiful enough that Joe had spent a good portion of the auction hard as a damn chunk of granite. "She did.

She's a pretty girl." He hoped like hell that was professional and nonchalant, because the storm that raged in him was anything but.

"My glare at the guys apparently worked. Not one of them was dumb enough to place a bid on her."

"It climbed out of a firefighter's budget pretty damn fast," Joe said through clenched teeth.

The chief smiled. "Sixty-two hundred dollars she made for the foundation. I'm going to have to check out the guy who won. Did you catch his name?"

"Yeah," Joe said as they cleared the last table. "I know his name and then some. Troy Vargas. He's my stepbrother."

The chief stopped and faced Joe. "Is he all right?"

It took everything Joe had to stand there and appear unaffected, as if he wasn't ready to bash his stepbrother's face in. "He's okay."

"What's he do?"

"He's a partner in my stepfather's law firm in Corpus."

Chief Peligni looked at him thoughtfully, then nodded once, as if that would do. "There's Nita," he said, peering out over the crowd of people. "I'm going to go say hi."

"Have a good evening, Chief."

Joe stood to one side of the crowded lobby, searching for Troy. Instead, he spotted Faith, and felt his temperature go up as if a match had been lit under his collar.

She stood about twenty feet away, surrounded by her girlfriends and mother. Her father's assessment that she looked beautiful tonight was a gross understatement.

Her gown was dark purple and sequined, with thin straps holding it up. It hugged her body, clinging to her slender waist and curving outward with her sexy hips. A side slit revealed her legs when she walked. Her hair was pulled up in a fancy 'do that made Joe's fingers itch to release it. She wore makeup, and though he was a big fan of her without it, she looked more gorgeous than he'd ever seen her. Teasing her cleavage was an antique-looking necklace with a large amethyst.

A night with Faith would be worth every penny of the sixty-two hundred bucks Troy had forked over... and more.

In his peripheral vision, Joe noticed the dark head of the man in question, tilting back in laughter. Bastard thought he was pretty slick. It figured that just as Joe was starting to see his stepbrothers as decent guys he might actually hang out with even without his mother, Troy would pull this. And of course, Joe couldn't say a word. Not here, anyway.

He turned his back on his stepbrother, not wanting to come face-to-face with him.

Matter of fact, Joe wasn't much in the mood to talk to anyone. He'd chatted with plenty of people before the auction started, and didn't feel the need to mingle anymore. He headed toward an exit, but felt a hand on his forearm. He knew who the unpainted, short finger-nails belonged to without looking at the woman's face.

"Faith."

"You're leaving already?" she asked. Her words and tone were indifferent enough, impersonal, not giving away anything of their recent history. But when he looked into her eyes, she seemed to see deep inside him, as if she could discern more than everyone else. "Are you upset?"

He took his time answering. Made a point of trying to keep every hint of anger out of his voice. "Why would I be upset?"

The knowing look she gave him made him want to punch something. Or take her into his arms and mark her as his, maybe carry her off so Troy couldn't get his hands on her.

"Gee, I don't know," she said sarcastically. "I happen to understand how brothers work, Joe."

He nodded noncommittally. "Anything else?"

"It's better than a stranger, right? We know he's okay."

The rage started its slow build up once more, like water beginning to boil. "That proves you don't understand a *thing* about how brothers work. I'll see you at the station."

Joe headed toward the long hallway that would take him to the lot he'd parked in, congratulating himself for not losing his cool in public. He couldn't make any promises about the next time he saw Troy.

CHAPTER TWENTY-TWO

"ARE YOU GOING TO TELL ME yet where we're having dinner?" Faith asked Troy, trying not to sound rude or ungrateful. He'd been secretive the entire drive, even when he'd taken the exit to Corpus Christi.

"At my stepmom's house. We're celebrating her birthday tonight. It was a couple weeks ago, but she was in the hospital. Now that she's been home a few days, we thought she'd be up for it."

Unease churned in Faith's gut as he pulled in front of a large adobe home with a grand-looking entrance. It wasn't the near estate status of the house that worried her, it was that Joe's 4Runner was parked in the driveway.

Before she could say anything, Troy was out of the silver BMW and opening her door for her.

"Troy," she said quietly, stepping onto the curb. "Joe's here."

"Uh, yeah. Look, Faith, I'll take the heat for this. I know you don't know me from Adam, but trust me, okay? He might blow up when he sees you, but it'll be all right in the end. I didn't do this to hurt him."

She studied him, wondering what the hell she'd gotten herself into. Maybe a creepy stranger winning a date with her would've been better, after all.

She saw nothing creepy in Troy's eyes, though, and nothing that hinted at anything but friendship. What she did see was the blinds in the front window of the house moving, as if someone was looking out. "If you say so," she said, wanting to get whatever scene was going to ensue over with. Get the night over with, actually.

They walked side by side up the front steps. The door opened before they got to it, and Ryan appeared with a big grin. "You are one crazy bastard," he said to his brother. "Everyone's in the kitchen."

"Nice to see you, too." Troy brushed by Ryan, leading Faith inside with his hand at the small of her back. "Kitchen's this way."

Faith braced herself for their entrance. Just as she'd expected, Joe stood there, leaning against the counter with a bottle of beer in his hand. He was laughing with the woman filling wineglasses next to him. Ryan's wife, Faith realized, when he came in and put a subtle but territorial arm around her.

When Joe saw Faith, his smile disappeared and he swallowed. "Hello, Faith," he said evenly.

Hello, awkwardness. "Hi."

Joe's jaw ticked as he completely ignored Troy.

"Faith, this is my wife, Shelly," Ryan said.

The woman turned to smile at Faith and shake her hand.

"Welcome to the Vargas-Mendoza testosterone well," Shelly said, eyeing Troy and Joe. "It's nice to meet you. And to have another female here."

"Good to meet you," Faith said, trying to ignore the thick tension in the air. "What can I do to help?"

"Have some wine," Shelly said, holding out glasses for her and for Troy. "The cook has everything under control. The salads are in the refrigerator and the hot stuff is being kept warm in the oven. Why don't we go out to the sunroom, where Carmen is? Troy, do you want to introduce Faith to your stepmother?"

The fire that flashed in Joe's eyes made Faith shudder. This was going to be ugly.

"Why don't you, Shelly?" Troy answered. "I need to talk to Joe first."

Shelly looked surprised, leading Faith to believe she didn't have a clue what, exactly, was transpiring in front of her.

"Sure. Come on, Faith. She'll be thrilled to meet you."

Faith glanced at Joe, but he wouldn't meet her gaze. Fantastic. She hadn't asked for any of this. He must know she wasn't interested in Troy. Joe's stepbrother was a nice enough guy but...he was a lawyer, for God's sake.

JOE EYED HIS STEPBROTHER as the women walked out to the sunroom.

"Easy," Troy said. "There's smoke coming out of your ears."

"Not too bright," Ryan interjected, shaking his head. "Like waving a scarf at a bull, man."

Troy glared at his brother. "What the hell are you doing in here, anyway?"

"Think I'm going to miss this?" Ryan took a swig from his beer bottle and stood back, crossing his arms. "You might need a referee."

"We don't need a referee," Joe said.

"I'm not interested in Faith," Troy stated.

"Save it. I'm not going into this with you."

"There is no 'this' to go into. I'm not an idiot, and even though we're not brothers by blood, I wouldn't home in on your woman."

Joe glanced toward the French doors to the sunroom. "She's not my woman. She works for me. Take her out if you want to."

Ryan hoisted himself up on the counter as if the NBA playoffs were starting up in the kitchen.

Troy laughed. "Yeah. I took her out tonight to the tune of a very nice donation to the Burn Foundation. You don't seem to be handling it too well."

Joe pushed himself off the counter and headed toward the formal living room at the front of the house.

"Wrong thing to say, man," he heard Ryan tell Troy as he walked off.

Joe paced to the front window and looked out at the neighborhood of impressive homes. Though it was an upper income area, there were lots of young families. Obviously not a place too many firefighters called home. A group of grade school kids ran through a sprinkler a few yards down, and two teenage boys were shooting hoops across the street. Joe heard someone enter the room behind him, but didn't bother to turn around.

"Will you hear me out?" Troy said.

"Say whatever you want to say."

"I brought Faith here for you."

Joe scoffed—he couldn't help it. "Why the hell would you do that? I told you we work together."

"Yeah, yeah, you're her senior officer," Troy said in a singsong voice. "Which translates to you refusing to take her out."

"It's not an issue."

"This is me, here. I don't give a shit if you're sleeping with one of your coworkers or underlings or whatever she is to you."

Joe turned sharply toward him. "Who said I was sleeping with her?"

"I don't know if you are, and frankly, I don't care. But that night at the hospital your feelings were obvious."

"Faith and I can't be together, Troy."

His brother laughed, and Joe tightened his fists at his sides.

"I get that," Troy said. "More than you know."

Something in his voice made Joe look at him again, more closely, beyond the remnants of the grin. He waited for him to spill the rest, whatever he was so intent on saying.

Troy lowered his voice and turned to make sure Ryan was out of earshot. "I'm seeing Betsy Wellington."

Joe stared at him blankly.

"Wellington. Of Smith, Vargas and Wellington. The daughter of the firm's president."

"Congratulations," Joe said, still unable to admit

anything about Faith. For all he knew, Troy was playing him.

"Not looking for congratulations. All I'm saying is I know it's a bitch to want someone who's off-limits. And if you're going to continue to stand there and act as if you don't care about Faith Peligni, then suit yourself. I'm not the bad guy you'd like me to be."

Joe studied him pensively. "So you're telling me you dropped more than six thousand dollars just for me to have a good time for a night?"

"I dropped six thousand dollars to support Carmen's pet charity. It just so happened I found a way to try to give you some time with Faith, no questions asked."

"I didn't know you were the selfless type," Joe said after a moment.

"Sometimes I'm not," Troy said, sticking his hand in the pocket of his dress pants and rattling his keys. "I'll admit it was fun watching you get your hackles up during the bidding."

"Asshole."

"But an asshole you owe a favor to."

"You really have no interest in her?" Joe asked, finally starting to believe that Troy's motives were just what he'd said.

"None. Hey, she's hot. Don't get me wrong. But I don't go for the type of woman who could kick my ass if I piss her off."

Joe nodded, thinking about the women he'd seen Troy with. Always a different one. Always blonde. Always the type who would cry over a broken fingernail. "Yeah, Faith could take you."

"In your dreams."

"So what do you think I'm going to do with this 'favor'? It doesn't change a damn thing for Faith and me...*if* I was interested in her. And *if* she was interested in me."

Troy shrugged. "That's your problem. I've done my part." He sat on a couch that looked as if it had never been touched before. "Tell me this. What's holding you back? Is it against policy in the department?"

"Not officially."

"Then what the hell?"

"Why do you keep your girlfriend a secret?" Joe asked.

"She works for the firm. Receptionist pool. There's a rule against it."

Joe nodded. "Have you seen the fire chief?"

"Big guy? Looks like he could kill someone with his pinkie finger?"

"That's him. He's her father."

Troy swore. "Good guy? Bad?"

"My dad was his mentor. He's acted as mine since Dad died."

"Ouch."

"Like I said, Faith and I can't be together. If she even wanted to."

"Seems like she wants to, from where I'm standing. So, what, you're worried about disappointing the chief?"

Joe chuckled without feeling any real humor. "Worried about getting a promotion. Keeping my job. Chief doesn't want his little girl with a firefighter."

"His little girl *is* a firefighter."

"He's made it clear on numerous occasions he would not be supportive."

"So you choose the job."

"I've known where I was going professionally since I was twelve. Everybody's known."

"Things change, dude."

Joe stood. "Let's go see Mom."

"And Faith. You better see plenty of Faith tonight. It cost me a pretty penny to get you two in the same room."

"You're not going to let me forget that anytime soon, are you?"

"Not damn likely."

"Hey," Joe said, pausing before they opened the door to the sunroom. "Could we not tell my mom anything? I don't want her to get her hopes up for Faith and me."

Troy frowned and shook his head. "Your call. You know, you're too much of a damn people pleaser. I reckon you ought to try worrying about what *you* want instead of what everyone else wants for you all the time."

Joe told him where he could go as he opened the door and they joined Ryan, Jorge and the women.

TROY WASN'T AS DUMB as Joe had thought.

His stepbrother had made a point of keeping his distance from Faith. Being courteous and polite but not too friendly. Not goddamn touching her.

Apparently he liked living.

They'd just sung a painful rendition of "Happy Birthday" and Shelly was cutting the cake—chocolate with white frosting, with purple and yellow pansies on top. No candles. Though his mom was feeling much better, she was still weak and her lungs weren't back to normal yet. She was such a fighter, though....

Joe's throat swelled up as he looked at her and recalled how puny she'd been in the ICU. Tonight her cheeks were pink and her spirits high.

"Biggest slice goes to the birthday girl," Faith said, coaching Shelly.

"Carmen gets this one. Two big sugary flowers."

Faith took the plate, grabbed a plastic fork and carried it to Joe's mom. She helped Carmen prop herself up again so she could eat, and then she perched on the arm of the couch, watching Carmen closely in case she needed help.

Joe tried to act nonchalant, sitting on a folding chair on the other side of the room, but he wanted nothing more than to take Faith in his arms and kiss her in gratitude. Gratitude and other stuff, as well.

She'd dressed casually tonight, in dark blue jeans so tight they looked like leggings, a Kelly-green silk tank top and killer silver heels. Her ears, wrist and neck were adorned with trendy silver jewelry that jingled when she moved. He was dying to hold her.

Troy's phone rang and he excused himself to the kitchen.

"Here's a piece with extra frosting for you, Joe," Shelly said. "You need something to sweeten you up. You're quiet tonight."

"He'll try to tell you it's a deep intellectual quiet, no

doubt," Ryan said, grabbing his own slice of cake and digging into it as if he hadn't just eaten enough slow-cooked ribs for a football team.

"No need for me to say it." Joe took a bite of cake, and once again, his eyes went to Faith. He couldn't keep them off her. He didn't know how this night was going to end, but he had to get her alone somehow.

She looked up at him then, laughing at something his mom had said, something he'd missed because he was lost in fantasies of Faith. Her gaze met his and the heat in it made his body react.

"Ryan never quite mastered the 'stay quiet to keep them wondering' philosophy," Jorge said. "We never wonder what's on his mind."

"We sometimes wonder if *anything* is on his mind," Joe said. He ducked when Ryan tossed his fork at him with a howl.

"You men are too loud—your mother needs peace," Shelly said, scraping some extra frosting off the knife and licking her finger. She carried a slice of cake to Faith and sat on the chair next to the couch with her own piece.

Joe's mom shook her head. "It's wonderful to have the noise. This place gets so quiet sometimes. I hope Faith doesn't run away scared, though."

Carmen smiled warmly at her, and not for the first time, Joe was relieved he wasn't the one who'd brought her here. His mom seemed to like Faith, and he didn't want to disappoint her when things couldn't work out between them. Better that she never know there was any kind of attraction between them. The whole family held few expectations for Troy to ever settle down, so having him bring in a woman was a whole different ball game.

Troy ambled back in then. He went over to Faith. "I'm afraid I have to take off unexpectedly," he said, mostly to her. "Got a client who's in trouble. I'm sorry to bail on you, Faith, but I'm hoping my honorable step-brother can take you home to the island for me." He shot Joe a look, and Joe instantly understood. It was a ruse. Troy's way of stepping aside.

Faith looked alarmed as she glanced from Joe to Troy.

"I'm really sorry," Troy said. "I'll owe you one."

Joe held his tongue to keep from saying *the hell he would.*

"It's okay," Faith said. "As long as Joe doesn't mind."

"I don't mind," Joe said. *At all.*

"Thanks, bro. I'd say I owe you a favor, too, but..."

"Get out of here," Joe muttered, checking his watch.

It was almost ten o'clock. Getting late for his mom. They should be able to say good-night soon without letting on that he couldn't wait to get Faith alone.

He sat back to wait—impatiently—for the moment they could leave.

CHAPTER TWENTY-THREE

"THIS WAS ONE OF the strangest nights of my life," Faith said as Joe led her down the front steps of his mom and stepfather's house after telling them good-night. The others had left a few minutes earlier, and the quiet of the evening took over. There weren't a lot of Vargases, but they were a loud bunch. They reminded Faith of her own family in a lot of ways.

"Want to make it a little stranger?" Joe took her hand in his.

The simple gesture sent a thrill through her. They hadn't touched all night. Being with him in a casual nonwork setting without letting on they were anything other than coworkers—for several hours… God, she'd longed to touch him. Her fingers had itched with the relentless urge.

They'd never held hands like this before, just walking along, side by side, hanging on to each other as if it was the most natural thing in the world. As if they didn't have to dance around their attraction. His hand was big, like the rest of him. Rough. Strong. Multitalented, she thought, pursing her lips to repress a private grin.

"What's stranger than starting the evening with one

man and ending it being ditched by him and rescued by his stepbrother?"

"Don't forget being thrown in with the crazy Mendoza-Vargas family."

"Trust me, your family's got nothing on mine when it comes to crazy."

"Troy orchestrated the whole night so we could be together, you know?"

Faith paused, touched. "Really?"

"It's why he's still breathing."

She laughed and they continued walking. "That's really sweet of him. Where are we going?"

"Not *that* sweet."

Instead of continuing to the foot of the driveway where his SUV was parked, they'd taken a brick path around the side of the house. Wide steps led downward, presumably to the backyard.

"To my secret hideaway." She could hear his smile. There was no light back here and the moon was buried by clouds, cloaking them in relative darkness under looming trees.

A secret hideaway sounded…promising.

She hadn't planned to see Joe tonight, but now that they were together, she could think of all kinds of ways she'd like the evening to end. When he took out his keys and unlocked the basement door, though, she felt slightly disappointed.

"Cars?" she asked, taking in the three-bay garage beneath the main house when he flipped on the lights.

"More than just cars," Joe said, his voice coming alive. "Classics."

She walked to the closest one. "Don't take this the wrong way, but this looks particularly unclassical."

It was a heap of junk, with dents in the back, mismatched paint on the driver's door, a broken headlight.

"You're not looking at it right," Joe said, coming up behind her. She felt his heat all along her body and, swear to God, her knees went weak.

Faith turned to look up at him, so close her head brushed against his chin. His spicy, clean, man smell teased her nose, and she longed to bury her face in his chest. "How should I look at it?"

"As potential." With his hands at her waist, he guided her past the middle bay of the garage, which was full of workbenches and tools, to the far one. "To look as sexy as this."

An old-model red car with black stripes on the hood was backed in, the rear end jacked up slightly higher than the front, the paint shiny.

"Nice," she said, walking toward it and peeking in the driver's window. "Much more classic looking."

"*Nice*. You say that like only a woman could." Joe laughed. "This represents over two years of my life."

"Wow." She started to run her hand along the side, but he caught it in his.

"Your rings could scratch the paint."

Faith tried not to laugh, because she could tell he was dead serious. "Sorry, boss."

"You did not just call me that."

"I meant car boss. Not fire boss. So are you going to tell me what this is, exactly?" Without touching it, she gestured to his pride and joy.

"It's a 1965 Super Sport Chevelle with a...you don't care about the engine, do you?" He broke off, with slightly less enthusiasm than he'd started with.

"*Care* isn't the right word. Know a thing about... no. But I'm duly impressed, anyway. You did what to this? Started with a heap like that one over there and made it pretty?"

He laughed again. "That sums it up well."

"Can I open the door?" she asked.

"Sure."

He reached in front of her for the driver's door, but an idea had blossomed in Faith's mind. She opened the door to the back.

Without waiting for his reaction, she slid in on the leather seat. The old-fashioned, wide bench seat. "Nice in here," she said, running her hand over the smooth leather. "Roomy."

Joe bent over at the door, hands braced on the roof. "It's never looked quite as nice as it does now."

"Yeah?" She leaned back across the seat, resting her elbows behind her, her feet still on the floor by his legs. "How about now?"

"I've always liked black leather, but...green silk and denim is fast becoming my favorite."

"Sometimes it's even better to touch, rather than just look."

He ducked his head inside and covered her body with his, one hand on the seat by her head and the other on the floor. "You have a naughty side to you, Faith Peligni."

"You seem to bring it out of me, Captain Mendoza." She put her arms around his neck and drew him to her.

He kissed her hard, urgently, revealing to her he'd been as frustrated all night as she had.

"Any chance of someone coming down here?" she asked when they took a breath.

Joe shook his head and nipped at her lips. "They never come down. This is my space."

"I like your space." Faith touched her finger to his moist lips, and he caught it with his mouth. The move was erotic, intimate.

"I like you *in* my space." He pressed his lower body to hers, showing her just how much he liked it as he kissed the side of her neck, just below her ear.

Faith slid her knees up to bring their bodies closer.

"As much as I'd love to have you with nothing but those do-me shoes on, you have to take them off," Joe said. "Don't want to ruin the leather."

Grinning, Faith slipped the four-inch heels off. "Or scratch the paint."

He kissed the grin away, intensely, his tongue seeking hers, tangling with it. One hand slid under her top, to her flesh. Trailed down, under the edge of her jeans. "These have to go," he said, unsnapping them. Working the zipper down.

The heat built in Faith fast, and she needed him to quell the ache. She wriggled beneath him, working her jeans off with her thumbs. His body was in the way, so she switched her efforts to his fly. He lifted, giving her access—to unzip, touch him, run her fingers along the length of him. Joe moaned and backed out of the car enough to take over removing her pants.

"It'd be faster to cut these off," he said, heat in his eyes.

"Patience. Virtue. Yada." Faith arched her hips upward and did what she could to help him.

"You turn into cliché girl when you're naked."

"You talk too much when I'm naked."

He dropped her jeans on the floor of the garage and eyed her dark purple thong. Bending over her again, he kissed her inner thigh, then worked his tongue under the thin strip of satiny material.

Joe teased her with his mouth as she ran a hand through his hair and tried to breathe. She thought she would die of wanting when he finally peeled her panties down her legs. The coolness of the leather under her barely registered.

Faith arched upward as he drew maddening circles with his tongue, inching closer to the part of her that ached most for his touch. At long freaking last, he covered her with his mouth, and she nearly shot through the ceiling, so electric was the sensation.

She pulled him upward, shaking with need. "Want you inside."

They both worked at his jeans and the boxers beneath them. When they were down on his thighs, he gave up and pressed himself between her legs.

"Faith," he breathed into her ear. "We need to use something."

Her mind was fuzzy and she struggled to think clearly. "Timing is okay."

"You're sure?"

"Very."

That was all he needed. He entered her, eliciting an unfamiliar sound from deep in her throat.

IF ANYONE HAD TOLD JOE he'd end up having sex in the backseat of his prized Chevelle, he would've laughed and said, "Like hell." Everyone he knew gave him continual crap for his meticulousness about this car. He'd never even let anyone sit inside except in the driver's seat.

He'd gotten over that the second Faith had sprawled so sexily across the black leather.

As she clung to him, arched toward him, coaxed him—as if he needed any coaxing—he lost all awareness of where they were. They could be five feet from a raging fire…God knew it was hot enough. He wouldn't notice or care. All he knew was Faith. The way her dark hair fanned over the seat. Her scent, sweaty and female, with a lingering touch of her floral perfume. The sounds she made—sexy gasps and short breaths and, damn, the things she was saying.

His need for release built, climbed so high he could taste it. He lifted her legs, angling deeper inside her, and she sank her teeth into his shoulder as she came. Joe watched her, and that was all it took for him to shatter into a million pieces.

As he slowly came out of his personal nirvana haze, he did his best to keep his weight from crushing Faith. It was nearly impossible, so he slid his arm beneath her and rolled onto his back on the small seat, holding her to his chest. They both breathed hard. The temperature in the car had to be about a hundred degrees, but he wasn't ready to bail out yet. Wanted to hold her for a while longer. Maybe a couple of weeks.

Joe brushed her hair back from her face and pulled her head closer to his for a long, quenching, soul-satisfying kiss.

For those few minutes, he was perfectly content, satisfied, at peace with everything in the world. He dared to let himself think how wild he was about this woman—only for a moment. Then he moved toward the door, telling himself it was just the combination of great sex and the backseat of the car he loved. Nothing more.

"YOU MAKE IT REALLY HARD to leave, you know that?" Faith said hours later. They were stretched out in his bed, the sheets twisted, but pulled up halfway against the middle-of-the-night chill. They'd made love twice more since driving back from Corpus.

"I'd say I'm sorry, but that would be a lie." Joe trailed his finger along the curve of her naked hip, up her side to her rib cage. "You could stay."

Her heart skipped a beat. Even though it was nearly four-thirty in the morning and the night was more than halfway over, this was big.

Scary.

If she stayed tonight, slept in Joe's arms, would she ever be satisfied to sleep without him again?

"But," Joe continued, and she expected him to cancel the offer. "Aren't you staying with your mom this week?"

"Yes." Nadia had family in town for a few days, and Faith couldn't let herself take up her friend's only guest bed. So she'd sucked up her pride to bunk with her mom temporarily. As temporarily as possible.

"Won't she wonder where you are?"

"She's well aware that I'm a big girl."

"Sure, but staying out all night? She wouldn't approve, would she?"

Faith laughed. "Of course she wouldn't approve. Does that mean I'm going to jump up and run home to her?" Faith kissed Joe slowly, tenderly, not trying to start anything. "No. I want to be here."

He studied her in the near darkness with a quiet intensity, and Faith felt it again—some new level of connection between them. A contented ease that settled in once their frantic physical hunger for each other was sated.

"That's one of the things I love about you," he said after a while.

"What is?"

"That you do what you want to do because you want to do it."

"Why else would I do something?" She touched his strong jaw, rubbed her finger back and forth, lightly, over the rough stubble.

"Troy said something to me earlier. Got me thinking."

"What'd he say?"

Joe hesitated. Rolled onto his back. "Accused me of living my life the way other people want me to. Not for myself."

"Okay. Do you?"

He looked at her pensively. "I care what others think, I guess. Maybe more than I should."

"That's pretty normal," Faith said.

"Do you care what your mom thinks?"

"That goes a lot deeper than just having her disapprove of what time I come home at night. She's disapproved loudly of my career choice for years. Before I ever got out of high school."

"But you became a firefighter, anyway."

"Wouldn't you? If you burned to do something and your mom didn't think it was a good idea?"

"I don't know."

"Come on. Really?" Faith propped herself up on her elbow.

"It's so far from what I've experienced. My family was always so deep into firefighting, there was never any question. My dad hung out at the station from the time he was in single digits. My mom, well, she jumped in with both feet when she met him."

"That's so cool. My mom married my dad in spite of his career."

"So it must've taken courage to tell her you were going to follow in his footsteps."

Faith shrugged. "Not that much. I was more interested in the chance to share it with my dad. So I'm probably not courageous at all."

Joe gave a low, sexy chuckle. "Trust me. You've got courage in spades."

They lay there in silence for a while, both of them lost in thought.

"If you couldn't be a firefighter, what would you do?" she asked.

"I don't know. I love my job."

"You know it will change a lot when you get that promotion."

"*If* I get that promotion."

"What if you don't like pushing paper, Joe?"

"I want the job."

"For yourself? Or is there something to Troy's comments?"

He didn't answer.

"What would your mom think if you decided not to go for assistant chief?"

"She'd be disappointed," he admitted. "But not for herself. Because she knows I've been aiming for chief for so many years."

Faith settled in next to him, her head on his thick chest, his arm around her. "Personally, I think you'd be good at whatever job you do for the department. But there's something I've noticed."

"What's that?"

"Whenever you talk about becoming the chief, going for assistant chief...you never use the word *dream*. Are you going for it because you want it more than anything else, or are you doing it because it's what's expected of you? What would make your mom proud? Make your stepbrothers respect you?"

Joe hugged her to him and kissed her forehead. "All of the above."

She turned to stare into his eyes.

"Really," he said.

"Okay, then. Just making sure."

He tightened his hold on her. "I care about you, Faith."

She swallowed hard. "I know. Me, too."

"Too much."

She nodded, smiling sadly. "Me, too."

"I've wanted you since the day your dad brought you into my office—"

"When I was seventeen?" she asked, with feigned shock.

"God, no. What would I want with a crazy hormonal teenage girl?" He laughed. "Since your first day at work."

"Oh, that."

"I mean all-out, can't-get-you-out-of-my-thoughts wanting. Physical."

"I kind of noticed." She tried to keep it light.

"But there's more. I don't know...."

"Shhh. We can't go there, Joe."

He nodded, seeming to understand exactly.

There was more than physical desire on her side, too, but she didn't want to think about it. Couldn't let herself. Because with every minute she spent with him, she wanted it—*him*—more and more. And knowing they were so close to almost having something, but not being able to reach out and take it, hurt a hell of a lot more than having a building collapse on you.

CHAPTER TWENTY-FOUR

As the engine roared up to the burning warehouse, Faith's nerves tangled in a tight bunch in her gut.

She should be over this by now. Over the trauma of the building coming down around her. She'd bet the other firefighters who'd been there were past it. Of course, those guys in San Antonio had probably been through ten times as many fires in that time, which gave them more opportunities to cope....

Screw that. No excuses.

She was on the verge of being the weak link, and if she didn't get over this hesitancy now, tonight, she had a lot of thinking to do about her future. You couldn't fight fires if you let your fear get the best of you.

"Faith, you're with Nate," Joe said. He pointed out their way in and told them what size hose to take. As usual, he'd come alive as they neared the site, though there wasn't any question they had "something" this time. When you were the third company called in, you knew there was a live one.

Faith busied herself in standard preparations. She turned her air cylinder on, put her mask up to her face and took a test breath to ensure it worked. Settled her

Nomex hood and helmet in place. Adjusted her air pack at her waist and donned her gloves. Breathed deeply.

Her equipment was ready.

The question was her. Was she ready?

Joe came up beside her and walked with her toward the door. Nate was about ten feet ahead of them, not paying any attention beyond a periodic glance behind him to make sure Faith was coming.

Nate paused at the entrance and checked his pocket for his radio.

Faith felt the blackness, the dread starting to seep in. Her heart pounded and bile rose in her throat. She closed her eyes, fighting it. Willing it back. Telling herself she had to stop panicking.

"Faith," Joe said, his head close enough to hers that she heard him over the chaos around them.

She met his eyes. They sparked with excitement, but she was more taken with the calm confidence in them.

"You can do this. You've done it a hundred times," he reminded her. He grasped her wrist loosely around the heavy turnout coat, a professional, supportive touch. "I trust you completely." He nodded once and gave her a long look.

Joe trusted her. He knew she could do her job. He believed in her.

As he'd told her in the past, she needed to trust herself.

He let go of her arm and moved away to talk to another officer.

Faith wasn't sure if she truly trusted herself yet, but

she decided if Joe believed in her, the least she could do was fake it.

To hell with the self-doubt.

"Let's go," she told Nate.

She followed him in with no more hesitation, giving herself a split second to savor the small victory before becoming fully engaged in the task at hand.

FAITH HAD NO IDEA how long they'd been in the building—all sense of time was nonexistent for her when she was in the middle of fighting a good fire—but she knew they were finally starting to make some progress.

She and Nate had just decided to move in order to get a better angle on the flames. Faith was ensuring the hose wasn't caught up on anything. She pulled in some extra slack, but the hose stopped before she got as much as they needed. She followed it back to free it, then held on to it as she again made her way toward Nate.

He'd just sent the message to the engine to give him water when Faith realized something wasn't right. Something was going wrong.

In half a heartbeat, she knew. Something was caving in on them. She ducked, doing what she could to protect herself, her mind screaming out in utter terror.

Excruciating seconds later, the deafening noise subsided, and it was back to just the usual roar of fire devouring a building and everything in it.

Faith opened her eyes and did a mental inventory for any pain messages from her body. There were none. Whatever had come down had missed her.

"Thank you, God," she said as she located her radio.

Tears leaked from her eyes as a hysterical relief bubbled up in her. The radio was there. Her limbs were fine. She was okay.

She crawled toward Nate, noticing he hadn't said anything. Hadn't checked on her. She'd made it only a few feet when her path was cut off by what looked to be a beam of some kind. As she stood up slowly to check if she could see Nate on the other side, something caught her eye to her left.

Shit! Nate was down.

Faith assessed the situation as quickly as she could, trying to fight off her panic at seeing him. She squeezed her eyes shut tightly against it, but instead of erasing the cold fear, she was taken back three months to when she'd been the "man down."

She shook herself and opened her eyes again. It appeared the beam or column was on top of Nate's left leg, possibly pinning him to the floor. She made her way toward his head and bent over him. He didn't acknowledge her, but at one point he moved his head slightly to the side, letting her know he was alive.

She checked the progress of the fire. It was creeping closer. She grabbed her radio and reported the situation to dispatch.

Without waiting for a response, she bent down again and tried to free Nate. She needed to get him out of there, to Scott and Paige at the ambulance, but his left leg was wedged beneath the beam.

Her brain moved on automatic then, creating a plan to get her colleague to safety. She had to fight the urge to wrestle with the beam by herself. Equally pressing was the advance of the fire.

She picked up the hose, which was lying a foot or so from Nate's feet, and opened it on the flames, waiting for help to arrive, and battling the urge to yank Nate out of danger.

Before she could make much progress with the fire, Clay and Olin got to work freeing Nate. Joe had sent in Evan to help Faith on the line.

Every so often, she glanced down to her left to check on Nate. It seemed to take them forever, but again, she had no real concept of seconds or minutes in here.

At last they managed to move the fallen beam and carry Nate out. She couldn't see whether he was conscious. Turning away and saying yet another prayer for him, Faith made her way farther in to knock out the flames in this part of the building, Evan on her heels.

"You did everything right last night, Faith," Joe said as they walked out to the parking lot just after nine the next morning. "And that's no surprise to anyone but you."

She squinted against the blazing morning sun and pulled out her discount-store shades from her bag, attempting to act nonchalant. In reality, Joe's praise had her soaring, along with the realization that she had, indeed, made the right decisions during the fire. She'd overcome the memories and the fear, and hadn't let herself or her colleagues down. Nate reportedly had a fracture in his leg, but the injury was minor compared to what it could've been.

"Thanks, Joe." She glanced behind them to assure

herself there was no one within earshot. "For...you know. The personalized rah-rah beforehand. It helped."

He shook his head. "I'm not taking any credit." They'd arrived at his SUV, and he turned toward the driver's side, while Faith kept going. "Go home and celebrate with a twenty-hour nap."

Bed for twenty hours sounded like just what the doctor ordered, but it wouldn't be her bed, and she wouldn't be alone if she had her way. Unfortunately, her way was off-limits—she and Joe had agreed they had to see each other outside work as little as possible.

"A short nap, maybe, and then Assistant Chief Jones's retirement non-party." The bar gathering was the department's way of working around his very vocal opposition to a big formal celebration.

"Might see you there," Joe said, and Faith tried not to allow herself to daydream about meeting him at the Shell Shack tonight...or leaving with him.

She climbed into her Subaru and sat there without starting the engine. She watched Joe back up and drive out of the parking lot. As he waited at the exit for a car to pass on the street, he looked in his mirror and their eyes met. He shot her a private smile, then drove away. Faith's heart raced.

She leaned back against the headrest, closed her eyes and soaked in the moment. Overcoming her hesitancy at the fire scene. Conquering her fear by forging ahead in spite of it—without being reckless. And yes, trusting her instincts in the middle of an emergency. Pour on top of those Joe's professional and personal approval, and

she was certain the only thing keeping her from floating away was her seat belt.

She laughed aloud as she started the car and drove
out of the parking lot. Instead of going to Nadia's house,
she headed to the public beach parking lot. It was still
early enough in the day that the lot was more than half-
empty. She stopped the car and got out.

Several clusters of people were scattered along the
sand, but most were gathered in front of the hotels.

Faith had changed into workout shorts, a tank and
Nike flip-flops before leaving the station. The day was
going to be hot; the humidity was already climbing and
there wasn't a single cloud in the cyan sky. The waves
reflected the color, looking brighter, more turquoise
than usual today. As she walked toward the damp sand,
she scanned the shell bits in front of her out of habit.
A large piece caught her eye and she picked it up. A
white-and-yellow snail shell, almost perfectly intact.
She slid it into her pocket and continued toward the jag-
ged foam line where the waves currently ended their
journey ashore.

Faith stretched out on her back, knees bent upward,
her toes just out of reach of the water. Her clothing
would get damp from the sand, but she didn't care.
She lay back and stared up at the breathtakingly clear
sky. Smiling.

A weight had been lifted off her shoulders just as
surely as Clay and Olin had pried the column off Nate.
She'd made it through a critical moment, one of chaos
and confusion in the heart of a fire scene, and she hadn't
let anyone down. Hadn't let herself down.

Somehow in that burning warehouse she'd found what Joe had insisted she was lacking. Trust in herself. She didn't really know if she'd had it before the beam collapsed, or if she'd faked her way through, but now she was sure—her mojo was back.

Hell, yeah, she could depend on herself in a fire. Her colleagues could depend on her, as well.

She'd always strived to work smart, and in the five years she'd been in San Antonio, she'd honed her instincts as well, so that when chaos broke out during an emergency, the two would hopefully work together— brains and instincts. She wasn't sure which she had stopped trusting when the roof had fallen on her. It didn't matter anymore.

All that mattered was that she felt better, mentally, than she had in months. And she was done hesitating before heading into a fire.

Faith noticed the waves had crept up higher when cold water hit her butt and soaked the edge of her shorts. She sat up, but didn't move out of the way. Instead, she kicked her feet in the shallow water, splashing herself even more. Laughed. Threw her head back and let the brilliant sun beat down on her, warm her. In her peripheral vision, she noticed a little boy to her left, staring at her. She grinned at him and winked.

She didn't care what people thought. And it went beyond the strangers on the beach.

Most of the guys in the department had started to respect her. Some of them would never get over her gender. Others might eventually come around, but the thing was…*it didn't matter.*

She got that now.

She'd been fighting for their approval since her first day on the job, but that would never replace trusting herself.

Her dad had had to work to convince the others on the hiring committee to take her on, sure, but Faith knew she was the best person for the job. Mired in self-doubt, she'd let herself forget it, but that was over.

Maybe she would've gotten to this point soon anyway, but there was no question in her mind that Joe had helped her along.

Joe.

He was the perfect man for her. A delicious combination of respected, don't-mess-with me fire captain and caring, patient teacher. He was looked up to and admired by just about everyone, so very good at what he did, and yet the private side of him had enough chinks to make him human…and endearing. Faith had seen the real man, vulnerabilities and all, and she loved him for who he was.

Loved?

Did she love Joe? Did she want to?

Did wanting to matter?

Because she did love him. She knew it almost instantly. Faith wanted to be with him, to know him even better. To fight his battles with him and have him at her side for hers. He understood her, really got her passion for her career and shared that passion. He was so loving toward his mother and Faith wanted to be loved by him, as well.

She knew he was concerned about what being together could do to his career, but Faith knew her dad. If they went to him and made him understand that what she and Joe shared was real, with long-term potential, he wouldn't punish Joe professionally. He wanted his daughter to be happy, didn't he?

Her objections to pursuing a real, in-the-open relationship with Joe were history. She wanted him more than she wanted to stop people from assuming the worst about her. They could think what they wanted. She knew that whatever she accomplished in her job would be due to hard work and dedication. Not because of who she was sleeping with.

She was ready to move forward with Joe and go public. The next step was convincing him his career would be just fine—he could have her *and* the job of his dreams.

CHAPTER TWENTY-FIVE

JOE HADN'T BEEN HOME an hour, hadn't even gone to bed yet, when the chief called, wanting him to come in to the station to discuss something.

Something.

The assistant chief position, he'd bet.

He felt generally upbeat, ready for the news. Knew he'd given it his best. He and Roland Schlager had different strengths, so who would get the job depended on what the committee valued most. He couldn't change who he was, he thought philosophically as he climbed back into his 4Runner.

If he wasn't the chosen one, there would be another chance someday. Chief Peligni wouldn't work forever. Schlager was a few years older than Joe, so if he got the job, there was the possibility of him retiring early. Joe didn't know anything about the third, outside candidate for assistant chief, but he could easily be closer to retirement, as well.

Joe scoffed at himself and cranked the volume of the Metallica CD in the player.

To hell with all the positive mumbo jumbo. *He wanted the goddamn job.*

He was forty years old and he'd been waiting for

the position to open up for several years. He wanted to make chief before he was a senior citizen. While he was young enough to still care so passionately about the department.

He pulled up to the curb at the back of the station and hopped out, not bothering to lock the door. It looked like everyone was across the street at the training facility; the halls were empty, quiet, as he made his way toward Chief Peligni's office.

"Thought you just left, Captain," Flo, one of the admin ladies, called out from her office.

"Figured you missed me."

"Always do." She cackled and her chair squeaked as it rolled across the thin carpet.

Chief Peligni's door was open, so Joe knocked on the jamb and went in.

"Close the door," the chief said.

Joe searched the older man's face for a clue about what he wanted to discuss. He seemed a little harried, but that was nothing out of the ordinary. It was impossible to discern anything. Joe sat on the worn vinyl chair facing the chief's desk.

"Tell me about the fire last night."

He'd called Joe in to rehash what he'd already written reports about?

"Nate okay?" Joe asked, thinking a turn for the worse would cause closer investigation of how the incident had been handled. But he'd just broken his damn leg. He was already home.

"Last I heard. He'll be out of the action for several weeks, of course."

Joe explained what had happened at the fire in as much detail as he knew. Which was the same amount he'd included in writing. He gave the chief no extra insight on Faith or what a personal victory the fire had been for her. To do so would reveal that Joe knew her better than he was supposed to.

"Faith did well, huh?" her father said, his pride showing through in his tone.

"Are you surprised?" Joe asked.

"Not in the least. She's my girl." He tapped his pen on the desk. "Saw you and her walking out this morning."

Something in his voice put Joe on alert—and the Catholic boy in him bowed under the weight of guilt.

"We were discussing her performance." *Performance?* Oh God, bad choice of words, considering that he already had to force himself not to fidget.

"She looks up to you," Chief Peligni said. "Respects you."

"I respect her. I've told you before she's got the potential to be one of the best here."

Chief nodded slowly, and Joe's possible promotion hung in the air between them.

The promotion that would suddenly become impossible if the chief were to hear about his and Faith's... involvement...from an outside source. Or worse, see them together in a compromising situation.

Joe bounced his leg repeatedly. Stared at the plaques on the wall without seeing them.

"Chief, you and I go way back," he finally said. "Our families. I'm going to level with you because I respect the hell out of you." He hoped to God this wasn't a career-killing move. "I have feelings for your daughter."

"You do." It wasn't a question. The chief's expression didn't waver, didn't show signs of surprise or even anger—at first glance. When Joe looked more closely, though, he noticed the older man's nostrils were flaring. "She's an amazing girl."

"Yes."

The office suddenly got too hot. Joe forced himself to stop with the nervous knee motion.

Chief Peligni pushed his chair back as he stood. Paced to the windowed wall. Looked out at the employee parking lot, his back to Joe.

Joe tried to figure out what to say. How to handle this. He may have just screwed himself to eternity.

The chief turned around and leaned against the sill, crossing his legs at the ankle. "I called you in here to discuss a different matter."

There was no way he would drop the subject that easily, Joe thought.

"Wanted to talk to you about the assistant chief position," Chief Peligni continued.

"Yes, sir."

"There's been a...development. As of this morning, the decision has been made to discontinue the position, effective in conjunction with Bill Jones's retirement."

Joe blinked, thinking he'd misunderstood.

"The budget has been cut again. It was decided to slice a layer off the top tier."

Joe's pulse pounded in his head and his fists tightened against the urge to let loose and damage something. "Why wasn't this decided before now?" He knew the answer before he finished asking.

"Budget time is right now," the chief said. "Funds were cut. City revenue is down. Same story everywhere."

Joe leaned forward, supporting his elbows on his knees. He ran his hands over his face as he tried to absorb what this meant to his career.

"I hate to see it myself, because I know how much work Jones does. Know how much you wanted that position, as well."

Joe couldn't speak. Just nodded dumbly.

The chief walked back behind his desk and sat slowly in his chair. "This isn't for public knowledge yet, but I've made a decision regarding my own career." He tapped his hands on the surface. "I'm retiring at the end of the calendar year."

Joe's head shot up. "Retire? You?"

The chief chuckled, but it had a nervous undertone to it. "Me. It's time." He leaned forward. "Time for me to rebuild my marriage."

Joe immediately thought of Faith and how relieved she'd be. Then he pushed her from his mind. The job had to be his main concern.

"Your absence will leave a big hole."

"About that." Chief Peligni paused dramatically. "The position will be opened up, of course."

Joe nodded. It was a no-brainer that he'd be going for it himself. Competition would be fierce, as there would be interest from all over the state and beyond.

But fire chief was his lifelong aspiration; he'd give it everything he had.

"Though the hiring committee will select my replacement, they've assured me that my recommendation will carry some weight." Chief Peligni loosely pinched his lower lip between his thumb and forefinger, studying Joe intently. "You know you've always had my support. You would even if I hadn't promised your father I'd look after you."

Hope lurched in Joe's chest. Was he understanding the chief correctly? "That's been appreciated, Chief. More than you can imagine."

"I wouldn't hesitate to recommend you for the job, Joe."

Joe nodded once, grateful and yet…wary. There was more coming, he could tell.

"But you need to make a decision," Chief Peligni said with authority. "Fire chief or my daughter."

When Faith appeared in his mind's eye, Joe shut her out. He was on the verge of making thirty-plus years of dreams come true. Of realizing his biggest goal in life.

There was no guarantee he'd get the position just because the chief was behind him, but that kind of support was beyond golden.

"You know I want the job, Chief."

"I don't question that. But you just told me you also want my daughter."

Joe cringed to hear those words come from Faith's father. He made it sound so crude.

"You're dedicated," the chief said. "Like me. You'd

do just about anything for this department. That's why I'd recommend you."

"I appreciate that." He couldn't help but notice the chief's use of "I'd" instead of "I'll."

"You're an honorable man, Joe. I want someone like you for my daughter. What I don't want for her is the fire chief. You might have a vague idea how much this job can require to do it well. But I'm living proof of what it can do to a marriage."

Joe wasn't sure what to say, so he said nothing.

"I know what you're thinking. You're thinking you could do it better. All it takes is some balance."

"No. I'm thinking all kinds of things, but that isn't one of them."

Joe had never considered his ideal job in such black-and-white terms before.

Job or woman. Job or family.

In his view of his future, the details had always been blurry. The job was clear—it was always the fire department. One day the chief. But the rest…there'd been an amorphous idea of a wife and kids floating around in his vision, but they were a consideration for later. Who knew when. And they sure as hell had never had faces.

Until now.

But he couldn't let a couple of nights of excellent sex sway him. Faith was beautiful and competent. She had her own bright future. They'd never discussed anything beyond the here and now, and that said something about her intentions—or lack of them.

"The job comes first with me," Joe told the chief. "It always has."

"I don't want you hurting my daughter. Is this going to hurt her?"

"You'd have to ask her, sir. But we're not deeply involved."

Chief Peligni nodded. "The longer it goes on, the more it will hurt her. Just talk to my wife."

"I understand."

"We're clear then?"

"We're clear."

Chief Peligni stood and held his hand out. "No guarantees what will happen, but I'm behind you one hundred percent."

"Thank you, Chief," Joe said as he rose and shook hands. "I won't let you down."

CHAPTER TWENTY-SIX

IT WAS A BAD IDEA to come here tonight, Joe thought to himself.

As a captain, he'd had to show up, but he should've toasted Assistant Chief Jones two hours ago, then cut out early.

Instead, he was still sitting here at the table in the corner of the Shell Shack patio, half listening to Ed Rottinghaus rattle on about his ex-wife, and trying not to watch Faith.

Which was next to impossible.

She sat on the concrete wall, her back to the Gulf, her blonde friend next to her and a group of firefighters around them. Some of the married ones—Derek, whose wife was working behind the bar, Evan, Olin— and a couple of single ones that Joe felt compelled to keep an eye on.

As if he had a say in who Faith could interact with. He'd made his decision earlier, surrendered the right to be involved in her life in any way.

Even if she didn't know it yet.

That was the bitch of it…he'd seen her looking his way numerous times. Caught the heat and longing in her eyes. Had to pretend he hadn't noticed.

He'd always thought she was hotter than hell in her drab SAIFD uniform after working a fire for ten hours. Tonight, she was nothing short of stunning. Her normally straight hair had a tousled-looking curl to it. She wore a spaghetti-strap black tank with rows and rows of small ruffles and sparkles that should've looked ridiculous but were sexy as hell. With black jeans that made her legs look even longer and more slender, black and silver-studded stilettos and lots of silver jewelry, she'd turned just about every head in the place at some point tonight.

And yet she met *his* eyes across the patio. Again.

FAITH HAD STOPPED DRINKING an hour ago.

She'd had only three beers, but with each one, she'd found it harder and harder to stay away from Joe. Though going public no longer worried her, she knew his feelings about it and would respect them until they had a chance to talk. Hopefully, he would see her rationale and agree to come clean with her dad.

Hyperaware of everything Joe did, Faith tried hard to pay attention to the conversation around her. Laugh when appropriate. Answer when spoken to. Damn, he was distracting.

It was nearly ten-thirty when Nate showed up, awkwardly making his way toward their group with a large cast and crutches. Everyone greeted him loudly, a little extra enthusiastically.

"Surprised to see you out and about already," Derek said, pulling up a chair for him.

A waitress came over and asked Nate for his drink order. "Shot of vodka. Make it two." When she took orders from the rest of the group and left, he said, "Sometimes you've got to self-medicate."

Everyone laughed and a few told him they were glad he was okay.

Nate leaned forward to look around Nadia's legs at Faith. "You," he said. "Thanks for not letting me lie there and die last night."

Faith hid her surprise and smiled nonchalantly, as if he hadn't been her biggest doubter in the past. "Olin and Clay deserve the credit. They did all the heavy work."

The waitress handed him his shots and distributed the rest of the drinks. Nate held up one of his glasses as a salute to Faith. "You kept your cool, got them in there and kept all of us from being barbecued. I'd fight a fire with you by my side anytime."

Faith raised her cup of water and tapped his shot glass, then they drank together.

As she drained her cup, Joe stood up across the way. Her heart inexplicably sped up, as if he might come over and talk to her group, but he didn't even look at her. He said something to the people at his table, something that looked like goodbye.

She watched him walk away. Watched for a sign, a subtle signal that he was hoping she would follow him, but saw nothing.

She waited fifteen minutes, assured herself Nadia was fine on her own, congratulated Assistant Chief Jones one more time, then followed Joe, anyway.

"It worked," Faith said without preamble when Joe opened his front door. He'd been home just long enough to grab a beer.

"What worked?"

"The playing-hard-to-get thing. I followed you home like a puppy."

"So I see." Two days ago, that would've made him a happy man. Today it was torment.

He looked behind her, checking for a car or someone who might recognize them. The street was empty of both.

He opened the door farther and let her inside. An awkward silence descended on them as his mind flipped through his options. He had to find a way to have the discussion they needed to have without touching her. Being tempted by her.

"Are you busy?" she asked nervously, looking around his living room for who-knew-what.

When she finally turned her gaze to him again, their eyes met. Held. God, he wanted to kiss her. As if reading his mind, she moved into his arms, and though he knew he should fight it, he couldn't resist one last touch.

They kissed, lightly at first, like a couple who'd been together for years and away from each other for the day. Then he was drawn in, like a hummingbird that had gotten a taste of the nectar and needed more to live.

He throbbed with need for her even though their only contact was their lips, her hands around his neck and his at the sides of her waist.

"Joe," she whispered between kisses. "Can we talk about something?"

It took him several seconds for the message to get through to his brain, for him to pull back and respond.

"Yeah. We need to talk." Before he got any more carried away. "Let's sit down." He gestured to the couch. When she sat on the end cushion, he took the chair at a right angle to it in an attempt to put space between them.

Both of them leaned forward over their knees. Faith reached out and took his hand in hers. He had to restrain the urge to draw her hand to his mouth and kiss it. He watched her thumb nervously trail back and forth over his fingers.

"I think we should tell my dad about us," she began.

Hell, that wasn't what he'd expected at all. He didn't know what he'd thought she might say, but she'd blindsided him by bringing up her father. "I thought you didn't want anyone to know."

It was a stall, he knew. He was a coward. Finding the words to tell her about his meeting with the chief was proving a challenge.

"I didn't. But that was before." She launched into an explanation of how the fire had affected her, that he'd given her the boost she'd needed to figure out how to trust herself again.

"You did that yourself, Faith."

"A little push never hurts. I was worried about what people thought. Needed to prove myself without people concluding any success I had was because of you." She smiled and his stomach knotted. This wasn't the talk they were supposed to be having.

"Faith."

She stopped short as she was about to say more, as if finally sensing they weren't on the same wavelength.

"We can't be together anymore," he said bluntly. Best to rip the bandage off quickly, for both of them.

To her credit, her expression didn't change. Showed nothing. She stared at him for several long seconds, then stood. Walked to the TV cabinet on the opposite wall. Picked up the framed photo of him and his mom and studied it. Set it down.

Her silence was killing him.

Joe got up, closed the space between them. He stood behind her.

She spun around and looked up at him. "Am I allowed to ask why?" Now the hint of vulnerability showed in her eyes.

"Chief called me in today, right after I got home from work. This isn't for public knowledge yet."

"Okay," she said slowly.

"They aren't going to refill the assistant chief position. Budget cuts."

"What?" She touched his forearm. "Joe, I'm sorry."

"Have you talked to your dad lately?"

She shook her head. "I'm not ready to yet. I know I need to…."

Damn. Joe hated to break the chief's news to her, but he didn't know how else to explain the situation.

"Maybe you should sit down."

"What's wrong, Joe? Is he okay?"

He nodded toward the couch.

"I'm not sitting down," she said. "What's going on?"

"He's fine. In fact, I think you'll consider at least

some of it good news. It's not my place to tell you this, but it's relevant to us. You and me." Joe hesitated. "He's decided to retire this year."

"My dad? He's quitting his job?"

"Retiring. To rescue his marriage, is what he said."

"He and my mom are back together?" Her head tilted in question, eyes searching. "The smarmy man is history?"

"I don't know the details. You need to talk to him about all that...."

She was thoughtful for a moment, then returned her attention to him. "So they'll have to hire a chief. And you're interested."

"Yes."

"Okay...and?"

Joe paced back to the chair and sat on the edge of it, so damn worn-out. Faith stood in front of him.

"What, Joe?"

"I admitted to your dad that I had feelings for you."

THE WEIGHT OF THAT finally made Faith sit on the couch again. "Feelings for me." One and one were not adding up to two here.

"You know that, Faith," Joe said, weaving their fingers together loosely on her knees.

"I don't know anything of the sort. You just told me we can't see each other. Stupidly, I thought things were going pretty well, and then wham! Is this supposed to make me feel better?"

"Your dad gave me an ultimatum." He said it as if that explained everything, but Faith didn't understand.

She pulled her hand away from his and rubbed her temples.

"He'll recommend me for the position," Joe said quietly. "But only if I'm not involved with you."

Faith shot off the couch, the urge to break something, anything, pounding through her. "He made you choose? Really?"

"He's afraid I'll hurt you, Faith." Joe was suddenly standing right behind her and she spun away.

"Ha. Hurt me? Yeah, I can pretty much imagine that in vivid color. Did you tell him you already were?"

Joe's eyes closed briefly. "I don't want to hurt you, now or later."

"Too late." Her damn voice wavered when she said it. "Why would he do that?" she asked, focusing on the anger at her dad to avoid letting that hurt seep in.

Joe let out a long shaky breath, making her wonder if maybe he wasn't totally okay with this.

"I'm a lot like your dad, Faith. Professionally, I take that as a compliment."

She nodded, unable to disagree.

"He's afraid I'm like him in his personal life, as well."

"Meaning?"

"Relationshipwise. Says I'm the kind of guy to put the job before a marriage."

Faith laughed at the absurdity. "We've not even come out of the closet about seeing each other and he already has us divorced? Do you know how stupid that is, Joe? How dumb it is to let him dictate what we do?"

"I told you before, I love my job, Faith," he said simply.

"That's great. How do you know you'd love being chief as much?"

He studied her. "You think I'm making a mistake, don't you? Going for these promotions?"

She stared back at those dark eyes that still stirred her. "That's not for me to say. You have to figure that out yourself, Joe. You have to figure everything out for yourself." She swallowed hard, trying to will away the emotion that was causing a lump in her throat. "All I can tell you is this. I care about you. A lot. I know we haven't known each other that long, but I haven't felt like this in—maybe ever."

"I care about you, too, Faith. Don't doubt that."

"But not enough."

"I've planned this my whole—"

"Your whole life. I know, Joe. And that's fine, if it's what you want more than anything else. If you truly want to be fire chief for your own fulfillment, more than you want to have someone to fall asleep with every night, then I'll wish you the best. If you're doing it because you're supposed to, because it's what your dad wanted, or your mom, or my dad, or anyone else…I'll be very sad for you."

His jaw and shoulders stiffened and he looked away. She had her answer. Regardless of what his reasoning was, he was going with the job.

Her chest ached as she took one last long look at him. "I hope you get the job, Joe. I hope it's worth it."

FAITH SWUNG THE DOOR OPEN so hard it crashed into the wall. If her father hadn't been awake before, he would be now. Which was her point.

"What in the name of God is your problem?" her dad said. He stood in front of the kitchen sink with a sponge and a bottle of kitchen cleaner, acting as if it was noon instead of midnight and he was used to doing house-work. It was a sight so foreign to Faith that she stared for several seconds.

Then she snapped out of it and remembered why she was there.

"As if you didn't know." She closed the door, again less than gently. "I just talked to Joe."

"Do you know what time it is, Faith?"

She glanced at the clock on the microwave. "Eleven forty-seven Peligni time. That thing's been three minutes fast for months."

"I don't appreciate you slamming in here at almost midnight like this."

"I don't appreciate you butting into my personal life."

He threw the sponge in the sink and gave her his full attention. "What did Joe tell you?"

"Everything I needed to know. You're retiring. You and Mom are getting back together. You made him choose between me and the job."

"Your mom and I are taking it slow. Working on it. I'm cooking her dinner tomorrow."

That explained the midnight cleaning expedition.

"You don't know how to cook."

"I'm grilling. Making salads."

On some level she was thrilled they were trying, but

she wasn't in the mood to give him a pep talk or con-gratulations.

"That just leaves the retirement and the ultimatum. If I can make a suggestion, you might try telling your family you're retiring from your forty-some-year career before you spread the word to others. Assuming that you're turning over a new leaf and putting family first."

He met her eyes. Nodded. "I deserved that, I sup-pose. As for Joe knowing first, it wasn't my choice. He won't tell anyone else until I make it public."

"Would've been nice to hear it from you."

"When have you been around for me to tell, Faith?" His voice climbed in volume. "I screwed up with the drink-a-thon. I understand that you're still mad. But don't go throwing around blame at me for not talking to you when you won't *let* me talk to you."

"Two topics down," she said, grabbing the sponge from the sink and the bottle of cleaner. She sprayed the counter and went after it with everything she had. "That just leaves the running-my-life one."

"Stop cleaning and let's discuss this like adults."

"This place is a pigsty. You need help."

If she didn't scrub at the stains on the counter from the past two weeks, she might end up throwing a plate or crushing a glass. Just for kicks.

"I don't want you to get hurt, Faith."

"What a coincidence. I already have been. Thanks to you."

"How involved are you two?" Her dad ran his fingers over his eyes as if this was giving him a headache. *Him*.

"Involved enough that I'm here at midnight to tell

you what I think of you trying to ruin a chance at happiness for me."

He had the gall to look pained.

"Haven't I proved that a man dedicated to that job has a tough time handling his home life?"

"Joe isn't you, Dad. He may be the best captain in the department, as dedicated as you are to the job, but that doesn't mean he'll make the same mistakes as you."

"But he might. And I can't stand the thought of anyone putting you through what I've put your mother through over the years."

"So you thought you'd rush in and save the day. Save your daughter from potential heartbreak. Or was it that you wanted him fully focused on the job? With no outside distractions?"

"Speaking as the chief, as someone who's put everything I had into that department for so long, hell yes, I do want him fully focused on the job. But more than that, I want you to find someone who will be devoted to you first, princess."

The nickname had her gritting her teeth. "I'm twenty-six years old. I can take care of myself. I've taken care of you for the past three months. And now you think you're in the position to take Joe away from me."

"Faith." He stepped closer to her, as if he was going to comfort her.

She straightened her spine and backed away.

"I didn't force Joe to give you up. I merely laid out his options." Her father's voice was calm, quiet now. "He's the one who chose the job."

Next came the twist of the blade that seemed to be slashing through her heart. Overwhelming physical pain seared through her, had her limply tossing the sponge back into the sink. She leaned on the counter, her face in her hands.

He was right, of course.

Faith had been so angry at her dad that she hadn't allowed herself to face the truth. That Joe could have said forget the job and chosen her. And he hadn't.

Didn't that just say it all?

Slowly, she nodded. Tried to pull herself together long enough to get out of there.

"I'm sorry, Faith."

"It's fine," she said, straightening. "Guess you saved me some time and future heartache."

When she finally worked up the courage to look him in the face, his pained expression—on her behalf—nearly did her in. He held out his palm, and she pressed her hand to his warm, protective one. She sucked in an uneven breath as her dad pulled her close for a hug. After a few seconds, when she was afraid she'd embarrass herself by bawling like a little girl, she drew away.

"I need to go." She forced the words out.

The compassion in his eyes belonged to the dad she'd always known and loved. Idolized. "You have a room here, princess. This is your home."

At those words, she realized nothing sounded better than the comfort of her pink bed, just down the hall from her dad.

Faith nodded. "You're right. This is where I need to be. Think I'll shower and go to bed."

After another heart-wrenching look of sympathy from him, she hurried to the hall bathroom, turned on the water and prayed he wouldn't hear her cry.

CHAPTER TWENTY-SEVEN

SPRING TRAINING BEAT the hell out of sitting at home questioning himself. Even if it *was* the Astros.

"You going to pass the bag of peanuts over here?" Troy said to Ryan, who sat on the aisle, opposite Troy.

"Told you to get your own damn nuts."

As a vendor walked up the aisle, Jorge stood and flagged him down. "Need some more nuts, please." He handed the guy cash and threw a bag of peanuts at Troy. "The two of you never change."

"Where are my nuts?" Joe asked, amused.

His stepfather attempted a stern look but ended up cracking a grin as Joe's stepbrothers chuckled. "If you don't know by now…"

"Explains a lot about why you don't have a woman," Ryan said.

"Damn well better have a woman," Troy said, taking a swig of his overpriced beer. "How's Faith?"

A crude word slipped out before Joe could stop it. "I imagine she's fine."

Troy, who was slumming in jeans and a polo for the game, groaned. "No. It's not over already."

"Afraid so."

Instead of the smart-ass remark Joe expected, Troy said, "I'm sorry, bro."

"Seemed like you two had it going on," Ryan said.

Joe nodded, watching the action on the field as if he'd never seen anything so enthralling. Unfortunately, they were only warming up a different pitcher.

"I owe you an apology," Joe said to Troy on an exhalation. "I was a prick the night you showed up with her."

Troy smiled cagily. "I could've handled it better. Might've wanted to get a rise out of you, at least a little."

"Thanks for setting it up so we could have some time together."

"Hope you made good use of the night," Troy said.

Joe couldn't allow himself to think about that. "Pitcher's looking decent."

"Astros are going to spank your Rangers this year," Jorge said.

That was all it took to get away from the subject of Faith. Relieved, Joe picked up the verbal sparring and took on all three misguided men.

He was still doing an okay job of not thinking about Faith by the middle of the sixth inning. The beer was helping, and so was the company. He'd decided last-minute to join his stepfamily on this trip, hours before they'd left, just yesterday. He'd paid a fortune for the airline ticket and had to share a hotel room with his stepfather, but he was glad he'd come.

After the scene with Faith, two nights ago, he'd needed to get the hell out of the house. Out of town. And for once, he'd decided to spend time with Jorge, Troy and Ryan because he wanted to. Not because it'd make his mom stop worrying. Not out of some pseudofamilial obligation, but because he was starting to actually like these guys. Overpaid suits that they were.

At the end of the row, Ryan let out a howl as he looked at his cell phone. The next thing Joe knew, his stepbrother was holding out a plastic shot glass.

"What's that for?" Joe asked.

"Pass it to Troy."

Joe did as he was told. Troy leaned forward to question his brother wordlessly.

Ryan handed another "glass" to Joe, one to his dad, then took out one for himself. Rustling around in an interior pocket of his windbreaker, he pulled out a silver flask.

"What the hell's going on?" Troy asked, setting his empty beer mug on the cement.

"We're celebrating." He poured a golden liquid into his own cup, then passed the flask to Jorge. It went down the line, with all of them obediently filling up.

"Tequila," Jorge said, sniffing. "This better be the good stuff. I'm too damn old to drink the cheap garbage."

"What are we celebrating, dumb-ass?" Troy nodded at the woman in the row in front of them when she turned to glare at him.

In reply, Ryan handed his phone down the line, a black-and-white photograph filling the screen. Jorge looked at it. Shrugged. Joe took it and smiled.

"What the hell?" Troy said, leaning over to see.

"Should we be congratulating you?" Joe asked.

"For what?" Troy took the phone from him.

"I'm going to be a dad," Ryan said, beaming so much he could light the stadium if the game went too long.

"Ho-ly shit," Troy said. "What is this?"

"It's the ultrasound photo," Joe told him. "With all that higher education you've got, you should know that."

Jorge slapped Ryan on the back. "I'll be damned. Didn't think either of you two bozos were going to figure out how to reproduce with a good woman."

"She is that, isn't she?" Ryan said, grinning widely.

"She went to the ultrasound without you?" Joe asked.

"I was there. Two days ago. Just took her a while to send me the photo. Had to text her to remind her, so I could show off my future stud."

"It's a boy?" Troy asked.

"According to that." He gestured to his phone. "She's nineteen weeks along. Supposed to be fairly accurate."

"Nineteen weeks and you're just telling us now?" Jorge asked.

"I wanted to tell you right away. Shelly was nervous that something would happen. She wanted to make it halfway through, but she's worried someone will notice she's getting fat."

"Not fat, son," Jorge said. "Never say fat."

"Pregnant," Ryan corrected with false sincerity.

"To another generation of Vargases." Jorge held up his liquor.

"God help us," Joe added as they all toasted.

Two more rounds emptied the flask. While Troy became louder, Joe turned oddly introspective. Though he was genuinely enjoying the day, an emptiness was starting to nag at him.

Nothing another beer wouldn't cure.

He headed up to the concession stand for one and was on his way back down to their row when the batter hit a foul ball in his direction. Not close enough to go for. Joe had left his mitt under his chair, anyway.

He watched a younger guy, probably Faith's age, grab it and high-five the guy next to him. Without deliberation, Joe headed in their direction.

Five minutes later, after making small talk and a deal, Joe returned to his seat. He tossed the ball to Ryan.

"That's for your son. From his uncle Joe."

Ryan looked confused for a moment. "Is this the ball Robertson just hit?"

"I'll even get it signed for you afterward," Joe told him.

"How'd you get it? I didn't see you catch it."

"Cost me a small fortune. But I figure he's my first nephew. He deserves it. Even if it is just an Astros ball."

Ryan looked the ball over and stuck it in the pocket of his jacket. "Thanks, man. You'll be his favorite uncle."

"The hell he will," Troy said. "He'll look just like me, be an Astros fan and grow up to be a lawyer."

"What if he wants to go the cool route and be a firefighter?" Joe said.

"Enough of the crazy talk." Ryan took out a candy bar and ripped it open. "You want another firefighter in the family, you have your own kid. Mine's going to be one of the next generation of partners at Smith, Vargas and Wellington."

"Wouldn't that be something?" Jorge said. "Bet he'll be a trial lawyer just like his grandpa."

The three law-heads engaged in a debate of what kind of law the kid would be interested in, but Joe stopped listening.

Another firefighter in the family.

Have your own kid.

Not two days ago, he'd assured himself he didn't need that. Didn't need Faith or a future that might include a family. Didn't need anything but the job.

It hit him now, like a brick to the head. He'd been dead wrong.

An image, uninvited, appeared in his mind—of Faith holding a child. Her child. Dammit, he wanted it to be *their* child. Not today. Not right away. He wanted to spend a good year in bed with Faith, practicing to make that baby first.

But he wanted to be the father of her children.

And while a boy would be cooler than hell, the picture in his imagination was of a little girl dressed in a pink dress and wearing...a kid-size fire helmet.

The crowd became noisy as someone got a hit. Belatedly, Joe stood like everyone else, but he was only half aware that there was even a game going on.

The job stood in the way...the possibility of the promotion. Fire chief.

His life's goal.

He liked his current position, he reasoned with himself. No question about that.

Would he really like being the top dog as much? He knew there was a load of bureaucracy to reckon with. Politics. City budgets. Endless paperwork and meetings.

No fires.

But he'd be running the department. Making changes that needed to be made so firefighters could do their jobs more effectively. Save more lives and buildings. He had innovative ideas.

So he would, what, move up in the department and make a difference for a few years and...then what? Retire to a garage full of cars?

Let the Mendoza family line come to an end?

Go to sleep by himself every night? Without Faith.

Joe excused himself and went back up the concrete steps, then wandered off to the right behind the stands, lost in thought. The farther he walked, the fewer people were around, which suited him fine. At the end of the line, he leaned against the wall.

His mom would understand if he didn't put his name in for chief. She'd been telling him as much for months, but he hadn't really heard her words until now. She wanted him to be happy, and in the past, he'd thought a promotion was what would do that for him.

Faith would make him happier.

He'd been miserable without her for the past two days. They hadn't been able to spend a lot of time together before, but knowing he'd put an end to any possibility of being with her, his house had vibrated with the quiet. The loneliness.

But what about his dad? The man who'd done everything in his power to pave the road for Joe, including elicit a promise from Chief Peligni to help him go far in the department. As far as Joe wanted to go.

You have to figure everything out for yourself.

Faith's words rang out so clearly in his mind she could've been standing next to him.

What did *he* want?

He wanted Faith. And he still wanted the chief's job.

And regardless of his reduced chances for the promotion when he threw away Chief Peligni's support, he was prepared to fight for them both.

CHAPTER TWENTY-EIGHT

SEVEN IN THE MORNING had been the earliest flight Joe could get out of Florida. He'd gone to the airport last night after the game, hoping like hell he could change his ticket and catch the last flight of the day, but it had been full.

He'd thought hard about renting a car and driving all night to get home, but the tequila and beer had made that a dumb idea.

As he drove up to the Peligni house, he spotted the chief in the backyard, on the side that overlooked the bay.

"Morning, Chief," he said as he walked across the small lawn.

The older man was perched on a short stool, pulling weeds out of a bed of bright yellow and red flowers. He stood, looking perplexed.

"Morning, Joe. What brings you here? Thought you were on vacation."

"I'm back. Wanted to speak to you about something."

"On a Saturday? Let's sit. I'm old. Retirement age," he joked, gesturing to a set of weathered, white lawn furniture near the water.

Joe walked with him and sat on one of the two chairs at angles to the bench.

"What's bothering you, Joe?"

Joe gazed out at the calm, shallow water. A gull swooped low and grabbed at something on the surface. Halfway across to the mainland, a pair of kayaks glided parallel to the shore.

He waited for the nerves to set in, for some kind of nagging anxiety over what he was about to do, but he was as relaxed as the turquoise bay water.

"It's about the job opportunity, sir."

Chief Peligni's head whipped toward him. "For fire chief? You change your mind?"

He crossed a leg over the opposite knee. "Did a little soul-searching on my trip."

The chief frowned. "Chief's what you've talked about for years. Since you were four feet tall and hanging out at the station after school."

Joe chuckled, thinking back to the days when he would've given anything just to get inside a fire. Some days, when they knew it was a pretty routine call, the fire crew would let him ride in the truck to the scene. "It's the coolest job on the planet. I want to be just like my dad."

"And your chances are good. So why are you here?"

"Because I want Faith in my life, as well."

"I told you where I stand on that."

"Yes." Joe rose and walked to the edge of the embankment. "I chose wrong the other day. I want Faith more than I want the promotion."

The chief appeared next to him. Nodded expectantly.

"I understand your stance, Chief," Joe said. "I intend to apply for the position with or without your backing." He looked straight into the other man's eyes. "Faith will always be most important, whether I'm a captain or the chief. And without your recommendation, I know I may still be captain for years. But I have to do what will make me happy. I have to try."

"That's a lot to take on. Faith and leading the department."

"I don't take it lightly. But I figure if I start to screw up with Faith, she'll set me straight."

"She'd have some help from me, as well." The chief's expression remained impassive.

"I get it," Joe said. "I hope Faith will give me the chance to show you both I'm up for it."

"You probably know what a stubborn woman she is."

"I'm acquainted with that part of her personality, yes."

"She's not always willing with second chances."

Joe had spent the flight home debating with himself on that very point. What if she was so hurt by the decision he'd wrongly made that she wouldn't give him the time of day?

"She gave me one, though," the chief admitted.

"A second chance?" Joe asked. "You two made up?"

The chief pointed over his shoulder. "She's inside. Probably just waking up, if you want to try your luck."

The moment of truth.

"I don't want to wake her."

Chief Peligni stared at him with mock disgust. "You

didn't cut your trip short just to sit here and shoot the shit with me. Get your ass in there."

Joe started to head inside, and then paused.

"Are you and I cool?"

The chief took his sweet time replying. "I admire your determination. As long as you understand I'll tear you apart if you hurt my girl, we're cool." His features slipped into something just short of a grin and he nodded once, almost imperceptibly. "Good luck, son."

Joe didn't miss the handle. The chief had never called him "son" before.

FAITH HAD SKIPPED her morning run for the past two days, too drained to motivate herself. But today she was determined to get over it and make up for the days she'd missed.

She'd slept in later than usual and hurriedly dressed to get outside before it was too hot.

When she opened her bedroom door to track down her MP3 player, she nearly jumped out of her skin to see Joe heading straight for her.

"Morning, sunshine," he said, smiling warmly as he looked her over.

She hadn't brushed her hair yet, hadn't showered. Thank God she had the compulsive habit of brushing her teeth first thing every morning.

Why was he smiling at her?

"Hi," she said. "Are you here to see my dad?"

"Already saw him."

The tiny glimmer of hope that he'd say he was there for her crashed and burned. "Where is he?" She craned her neck to see into the kitchen. Her dad's chair was empty.

"Outside."

"So you came inside to…?"

He'd reached the hallway. Stood two feet away from her, leaning against the wall in a very noncaptainlike way. Casual.

"Talk to you. You're better looking."

She glanced down at her purple sports bra and black running shorts. Bare feet. The tangled ends of her hair. "I need to take a shower."

"You're perfect the way you are."

That stopped her short and she looked up at him, her heart hammering. Stupid body part. She was not going to forgive him just because he buttered her up with compliments.

"Not perfect enough. Why are you really here, Joe?"

"To grovel."

She crossed her arms and leaned against the cold wall. He must've figured out how awkward work was going to be the next time they shared a shift.

"It's fine. You don't have to apologize for your feelings. I can be mature about the whole thing."

"I was an idiot, Faith," he said quietly. "I screwed up."

She stared at him, searching the depths of his eyes for his meaning. "Screwed up what?" She didn't dare to breathe.

"The biggest decision of my life. I blew it. I was stuck on what other people thought I should do, not what I want more than anything."

The hope she'd been stifling since she'd seen him in the living room took wings. Still, she needed him to spell it out. "Which is?"

"You. And the job. In that order. Without your dad's recommendation I don't know if I have a chance at the second one. And I'm waiting to hear whether I have a chance with the first."

He took her hand and pulled her to him. "I'm sorry, Faith. I know I hurt you, and that's something I never want to do again. I was so afraid of letting everybody else down that I didn't let myself think about letting *me* down. And you."

"You're stubborn," she said, unable to keep the smile off her face.

"I've been told that a time or two. I can also be persistent. So you could put me out of my misery right now and let me kiss you, or—"

"Make you grovel some more? Is that what you called it?"

"That's what I called it." He wrapped his hands around her bare waist. "I may be dense and slow, but I want you in my life. If you'll have me."

One thing kept her from jumping into his arms. "What happens if you don't get the job and realize it's because of me? What if you resent me because you're stuck at captain?"

"I won't. You made me reconsider what I want most. I want you. I want to raise our own company of little firefighters. Or doctors. Bartenders. Hell, lawyers, if that's what they choose. I want to spend my life with you. I love you, Faith."

He loved her.

She'd been determined not to forgive him, and all it took was five minutes of him saying the right things, like that he loved her. Call her easy. And over-the-moon happy.

Faith wrapped her arms around his neck and held on for all she was worth. "I love you, too, Joe."

He slid his hands down to the backs of her thighs and pulled her up off the floor. Into him. He kissed her, and his lips were like cool, lifesaving water to a woman who'd been dying of thirst. Their kiss was thorough, unhurried, as if they had the rest of their lives to love each other. Which, suddenly, they did.

Joe pulled back and gazed at her with the most tender, adoring expression in his eyes. He brushed his lips over the tip of her nose. "Do you think we can live together *and* work together?"

She smiled. "Do you think you can avoid the whole special treatment thing until we're off the clock?"

"I'll do my best," Joe said, "if you'll stop worrying about what everyone else thinks of you."

"Already done."

"Then this might work out," he said lightly, "as long as…"

Faith pulled her head back to question him. "As long as…what?"

"I seem to have acquired a couple roommates…."

Faith frowned, trying to imagine who Joe would take in and where they would sleep and, most important, how she would ever have enough privacy with this man.

"They're fuzzy, but they're small. Shouldn't take up much room. One's black, one's gray…"

Faith threw her head back, laughing. "Cinder?"

"And Smoky. I found places for the rest of the litter, but those two kittens need a home."

"If it's your home, I'm in, Mr. Soft Heart." She pressed her lips to his, thinking she would never get enough of kissing him, loving him.

"You can call me whatever reputation-ruining names you want," he said between kisses. "But you're wrong about one thing. It's no longer my home. It's ours."

"Yes, sir," she said, laughing. "That sounds perfect to me."

* * * * *

We hope you enjoyed reading this
special collection from Harlequin®.

If you liked reading these stories,
then you will love
Harlequin® Superromance® books!

You want romance plus a bigger story!
Harlequin Superromance stories are filled
with powerful relationships that deliver a
strong emotional punch and a guaranteed
happily-ever-after.

Enjoy four new **Harlequin Superromance**
stories every month!

Available wherever books and
ebooks are sold.

More Story…More Romance.

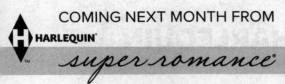

COMING NEXT MONTH FROM

HARLEQUIN®

super romance®

Available April 7, 2015

#1980 TO LOVE A COP
by Janice Kay Johnson

After what Laura Vennetti and her son have been through, she's avoided all contact with the police. Then her son brings detective Ethan Winter into their lives. Immediately Laura can see how different he is from her late husband. And the irresistible attraction she feels toward Ethan tempts her to try again.

#1981 MY WAY BACK TO YOU
by Pamela Hearon

Married too young, divorced too soon? Maggie Russell and Jeff Wells haven't seen each other in years, but as they reunite to move their son into his college dorm, they discover the attraction between them is still present—and very strong. Yet so are the reasons they shouldn't be together...

#1982 THOSE CASSABAW DAYS
The Malone Brothers
by Cindy Homberger

Emily Quinn and Matt Malone were inseparable until tragedy struck. Fifteen years later, Emily returns to Cassabaw to open a café. Matt, too, is back—quiet, sullen and angry after a stint in the marines. Emily's determined to bring out the old Matt. Dare she hope for even more?

#1983 NIGHTS UNDER
THE TENNESSEE STARS
by Joanne Rock

Erin Finley is wary of TV producer Remy Weldon. She can't deny his appeal, but Remy's Cajun charm seems to hide a dark pain—one that no amount of love could ever heal. And her biggest fear is that he'll be around only as long as the lights are on...

HARLEQUIN®

A *Romance* FOR EVERY MOOD™

Love the Harlequin book you just read?

Your opinion matters.

Review this book on your favorite book site, review site, blog or your own social media properties and share your opinion with other readers!

HARLEQUIN®

A *Romance* FOR EVERY MOOD™

JUST CAN'T GET ENOUGH?

Join our social communities
and talk to us online.

You will have access to the latest
news on upcoming titles and special
promotions, but most importantly,
you can talk to other fans about your
favorite Harlequin reads.

Harlequin.com/Community

f Facebook.com/HarlequinBooks

🐦 Twitter.com/HarlequinBooks

📌 Pinterest.com/HarlequinBooks

HARLEQUIN®

A *Romance* FOR EVERY MOOD™

**Stay up-to-date on all your
romance-reading news with the
Harlequin Shopping Guide,
featuring bestselling authors, exciting new
miniseries, books to watch and more!**

The newest issue will be delivered right to you
with our compliments! There are 4 each year.

Signing up is easy.

EMAIL

ShoppingGuide@Harlequin.ca

WRITE TO US

HARLEQUIN BOOKS
Attention: Customer Service Department
P.O. Box 9057, Buffalo, NY 14269-9057

OR PHONE

1-800-873-8635 in the United States
1-888-343-9777 in Canada

Please allow 4-6 weeks for delivery of the first issue by mail.